QUAESTOR

BOOK TWO OF THE OUTER REACHES

PETER J ALDIN

Cover Art by Sam Kennedy.

To Andre.

Thanks for your comradery,
and for helping create a universe
it's been a blast to explore.

QUAESTOR

PROLOGUE

Contact Minus 125 Hours, 6 Minutes

"YOU'RE SURE THIS IS NECESSARY?" Shill Teuku asked, tugging straight her yellow safety inspector jacket and scowling down at it.

Beside her, Jabari Mbaye cast long looks both ways along the transfer depot terminal before leaning in to elbow-nudge her. "Stop wriggling and start looking snooty. Right now, you're a low-grade, small-minded official who wields actual bureaucratic power and loves it. She also loves the *uniform*—which is a representation of her bureaucratic power."

Shill grunted something like "Erf" at him and clasped her hands behind her back, lifting her chin, practicing that snootiness.

Jabari suppressed a grin as he thought about telling her she was pretty good at it without the practice. Thinking better of it, and to hide the smile, he stole another glance along the terminal. The scale of the distribution warehouse was mind-boggling, even for someone who'd recently hiked around an ancient starship that was over five kilometers long. He and Shill were loitering on the forward edge of a pedestrian concourse that ran around the space station in a twenty-kilometer circuit. *Twenty kims*, he thought, using his original battalion's slang for the measurement. *And I reckon we walked ten of them finding this damn berth.*

The long walk had been good for him and had blown out the cobwebs from many days stuck aboard a smallish scout ship. But they should *keep* on moving, now that they'd finally reached Berth 118.

"Shall we?" he asked with a polite gesture forward.

"We better," she replied. "That ship won't steal itself."

She led the way off the concourse, between a gap in the yellow safety rails, and onto a wide gridwork gantry. When they reached the gantry's end, they paused again and stared down at the stevedore team in Berth 118's work pit twenty meters below them. Facing them from the pit's far side, a starship's bow poked through the outer hull of the warehouse. A combination of magnetic shielding and malleable-polymer seals secured the ship while holding in the station's atmosphere. The bows of five similar star-tankers were visible along the terminal, berthed at regular intervals and spaced far apart. From this position, Jabari could see directly into his tanker's cockpit windows, well enough to see it wasn't currently occupied.

It soon will be, he thought.

Taking note of the lazy pace of the workers below, he told Shill, "We're early, after all. I reckon it'll be a while before our ride's ready."

"A *long* while," she agreed. "But these poor grunfers need all the overtime they can get."

Not far above the work pit floor, two huge inlet/outlet valves protruded from the tanker, like tusks. The eight-person stevedore team's main job would be affixing hoses to them, hoses that were twice their own height. Jabari knew their business this hour was filling one of the ship's cargo tanks with drinking water and the other with liquid hydrogen, the cargo slated for a variety of businesses on the planet Vadox CX. Currently, four of the eight stevedores were prepping something at the valves—or testing them, perhaps—while the other four leaned on the nearest vertical surface and watched.

Jabari thought, *Droids could do this job. Much faster.*

But he supposed it was good these men had employment, though Shill had shown him their pay files while hacking the station's data grid. They were poorly paid for such heavy and dangerous work, especially when one considered they were out in the butt-end of a star system without habitable planets. Meanwhile, their employer made billions by mining water and hydrogen and a dozen other substances from an ice moon before processing it all for shipping to a hundred different star systems. Yes, droids could have done *most* of the jobs here—but something Jabari respected about the Imperium in this century was that it worked toward full employment within its borders.

The warehouse and the mining operations in the system were privately owned, as were most business operations this side of the now-ancient civil war. Before that conflagration, the Martianist emperors had increasingly taken direct ownership of many industries, a fact which had allowed Kaana Adjira to enlist several disenfranchised Martianist Houses to her side of the war, diluting imperial power. Ultimately, the tactic hadn't worked, but the Imperial Dynasty *had* learned something from the debacle, it seemed. Principles such as private ownership and full employment showed wisdom: a happy and busy populace was a compliant and pliable one.

Shill broke into his contemplations with a yawn. She stuffed a fist against her mouth to stifle it.

Jabari let his grin bloom this time. "Am I keeping you up?"

She soured and shoved her hands into her pockets as she glowered at a cluster of workers on the concourse behind them.

"Just exhausted from avoiding conversation with everyone here."

"Well, their preferred language *is* Imperial Common, which you and I don't speak."

"Because we're never out of stasis long enough to keep up with it. Always slagging evolves while we sleep for a few more slagging decades."

"Good news there." He sighed. "We won't see the inside of a stasis tank ever again. So, we'll have plenty of time for language learning in *this* decade."

Shill muttered something that sounded like "if we live long enough."

He let it pass, but it spread the souring of her mood to his. The idea of death raised the specter of the losses he was still coming to terms with. As was she, he knew. They'd cheated death on several occasions back on the *Iconic*. Two of their Proselyti brothers and one sister had not.

No, he thought. *No, not a 'sister.' Not Tegenwe.*

Tee had been much more than that at one point in Jabari's life. And, although he'd become grudgingly accustomed to erratic relationships that often leapfrogged each other in real time, he missed her now, missed her like... like...

There was no way to finish the thought, and it was doing him no good to dwell on such things. Finding peace was not a betrayal of the memory of the fallen. Tee would have wanted him to move forward with peace in his heart.

And she'd definitely approve of the self-appointed mission he and Shill were engaged in.

Shill had been talking, he realized. She shot him a sharp look when he didn't respond and asked, "So? Do you?"

"Do I what?"

"Think they have decent food on that tub?"

"They'll have *edible* food, which is all that matters." He tried another grin. "By the way, that should've been 'Think they have decent food on that tub, *sir*?'"

A snort from her, and a half-smile in return. "Call *you* 'sir?' Not slagging likely. You're not a soldier anymore, *Mister Mbaye*, and you're definitely not my commanding officer." It was her turn to side-bump him.

The sudden movement almost unsettled the hand-sized maintenance bot roosting on her left shoulder. She'd named the squid-like bot, with seven short tentacles and a frictionless coating on its upper casing that made it look oiled, Greasy. Apparently, it would be important in this job, an extension of Shill, herself.

Jabari studied her again out of the side of his eye, the lone surviving member from the last team he would ever command. Shill had kept her hair long since decanting, hair even blacker than Jabari's skin. And irises that weren't much lighter. By contrast, the exposed skin of her hands and face was quite pale, skin that— according to her—hadn't seen direct sunlight in several of her biological years. This was because her final few missions had all been space-based, on ships or within artificial habitats like this one. All in all, she was a handsome woman. Not a woman *he* felt any attraction to beyond the affection of two friends who'd been to hell and back together. But a woman he hoped would somehow— miraculously, perhaps—find a worthy partner, make a home...

Gods and ancestors, please make it so for her. I don't care if I make it through this mission alive but bring her *through it and on to a better life.*

Unaware of his attention, she reached up and gave Greasy a pat as the thing rebalanced itself.

He laughed. "It's not a pet, you know."

"It's a he," she responded tartly.

"What makes it a he?" he asked, wondering whether there was something about this century's droids he didn't know.

"Belonging to me makes it a he," she replied. "My bot. My choices."

"As long as *he's* on our side, I don't care if you paint him black and call him Jabari-2. Just reassure me you've retooled him. When I asked how we're going to hack into the tanker's helm, and you said 'All good,' you meant you have a male maintenance bot you've retooled to do *that* job."

Giving it another pat on the tentacle, she said, "My buddy can hack terminals and hijack servers and do all sorts of beautiful, beautiful things."

Since breaking with Alexis' crew—and fleeing the *Iconic*—Jabari had kept himself busy with research and fitness training. And he'd tried to reconnect with the meditative practices his long-dead grandfather had tried to teach him in childhood. He had to admit, the discipline of meditation had allowed him a new measure of mastery over his feelings. And Shill, too, had kept busy. He wondered, now, if their busyness had been a way of processing what they'd seen and experienced with Scipio and Kaana Adjira, as much as processing the loss of their team. There were many things, no doubt, they *should* have been discussing, including the ship and the other tech they'd been relying on.

Eyes on Greasy, he said, "You managed to completely unslave him from *Pleiades-219*'s AI?"

"I did."

"Any of the others?" Their stolen scout ship had a plethora of cephalopod and simian model minibots, some the size of Jabari's fist, like Greasy, some no bigger than his index finger.

She shook her head, making her black ponytail swing. "Was too much work to completely un-slave any more. AI's got a tight grip on 'em. This little dude will be enough, anyway."

"And how'd it go with shutting it down? The AI?" He'd let her do the piloting and realized he hadn't given any thought to the brain of the ship in weeks.

"Mm, not so good. I didn't actually try, just investigated the chances of trying and *surviving* it." She screwed up her face. "They were low."

"Oh."

"Yeah. The better the AI, the more important it considers self-preservation. We and that ship, we're traveling together like symbiotic organisms, but we are *not* on the same page. The weird bastard *enjoys* flying—as long as it gets to do something, it's happy."

"Happy, like it has feelings? I thought that wasn't—"

"No, not like that. When it moves around and gets to see new things, it's like a drinker who gets their drink or a smoker who gets their smoke."

"I think our relationship with it is too complex to continue with."

Shill made a noise of disagreement. "We can live in peace and harmony with it, as long as we make concessions."

"Cooperate with a ship." He shook his head. "Maybe we don't return to it. Plenty of ships to steal out here."

"And ship-jacking is kinda fun," she agreed. "If only these chumps would get on with their jobs..."

Down in the work pit, all eight stevedores had just started wrestling the two giant hoses into position. Even in the relatively low 0.9 G, it was hard work. The hosepipes were massive, but each of the corpiformed workers was even larger than the Corfid Otho had been.

Otho, he thought acidly. *There's one shithead the universe won't mourn.*

Casually glancing over his shoulder, Jabari felt his gut tighten. Because the eight-kilometer-wide warehouse station was a private operation, it had no imperial troops aboard, only private security, or 'rentals,' as Tegenwe used to call them. And two of those rentals were wandering along the concourse and nearing Berth 118. There was no sign of suspicion in their demeanor, just boredom. Bored security were more trouble than suspicious security, and they'd noticed him looking their way.

"Shill," he said out of the corner of his mouth. "We're going in now."

"Tanker's nowhere near loaded."

Jabari moved while talking, heading to the platform lift right of the gantry, keeping his face turned to avoid eye contact with the curious security goons. "We'll go inspect what they're doing then head over and scold the tanker captain for the poor state of his overfill probes and compression rings. Keep ourselves busy."

Shill caught up with him and asked, "Are they real things you said? Overfill probes and shit?"

"Sure," he said. "I looked them up."

"And they're what exactly?"

"No idea. The articles just said they better be in top condition when megaliters of water are flowing through an intake valve."

"You're doing all the talking then."

They'd reached the work pit's platform lift and both stepped onto it. As Jabari hit the button to take it down, he touched his finger to his forehead and nodded politely to the security goons.

They halted, visibly miffed they'd missed the opportunity to darken someone's day. But as the lift jolted into action, the pair shrugged it off and veered away in search of other hapless workers or visitors to hassle.

———

A half standard hour later, Jabari and Shill strode along the retractable catwalk that stretched from underneath the cockpit compartment and connected with Berth 118's fixed gantry. At the catwalk's end, the access hatch to the tanker's crew section lay wide open, folded against the hull.

Jabari knew from his research that tankers this size had crews of five: two humans, three droids. There wasn't much to the vessel, most of which hung outside in hard vacuum. As the ship's designation suggested, it was merely an enormous collection of cisterns with various FTL and subspace nacelles welded around and about them, plus a shallow, three-deck crew module connected flat against the prow. Both human crew—to Jabari's relief—were idling on the gantry outside the hatch, breathing space station atmo that was slightly less stale than their crew module atmo. They were passing a vaper back and forth, imbibing some kind of stimulant or relaxant into their bloodstreams.

Jabari resisted the impulse to trigger the two-way translator patch on his jacket's shoulder. They'd each had one as backup when leaving the *Maelstrom* battle station with Scipio, but everyone had used their combat suits' inbuilt models throughout the mission. The suits were gone, and the patches still worn on their undersuits had been knocked around by all the violence—to the point they could no longer rely on them to consistently translate into Common, which seemed widely spoken by the working classes.

No matter, he told himself. *Never met a professional spacer yet who didn't speak enough Imperial True to get by in their job.*

And he and Shill spoke True—the Imperium's unchanging formal language—just fine.

Better than he expected these two vaping idiots could.

"Civilian Captain Uva," Jabari said, pretending to consult his slimline datapad. "And First Officer Ziss."

The tanker captain blew chemical exhaust from her nostrils and handed the vaper to her crewmate while scrutinizing the pair who'd approached them as if they were a new species of roach. Eventually, in Imperial True, she said, "That's us. And our ship is in good condition."

Pretty well-spoken. Maybe you're not such idiots, after all.

"You know this for a fact?" he challenged her.

She said nothing, hand out, waiting for the vaper to come back. Her officer, Ziss, coughed a little, belching a mist of cinnamon-tinted air, and replied for her. "She does. The ship's perfect. Our employer keeps it that way."

The man had a frayed patch across one knee of his company work pants, and a quick glance at the inside of the folded hatch showed a couple of obvious rust spots. Jabari mentioned these facts, gaze lingering on the hatch. "Indications that 'perfect' *isn't* a company standard here."

Ziss sniffed, openly derisive. "Easy fixes, and they won't kill us. Why don't you stylus-tweakers go waste someone else's time? We're on our break."

Shill chimed in, warming to the part Jabari had encouraged her to play. "Hey, Ziss? My colleague said you're registered as the 'first officer?' Except—aren't you the *only* officer? I mean, there's the captain..." Shill held one hand at eye level, then lowered it to belly level when she added, "Then there's *you*..." She lowered it a final time, by mere centimeters. "And then there's the robots *you* boss around."

Ziss' stare grew colder. He grunted a word Jabari didn't recognize... and Shill's translator patch chose that moment to work properly, rendering the word clearly as "Bitch."

The first officer's hard expression flickered with alarm.

Oh, this should be good, Jabari thought and turned toward Shill to watch her response.

Her eyebrows rose as high as they would go, and Shill folded her arms across her chest. "You got my gender right, First Officer Ziss, but I think you're struggling with what species I am. That may well indicate you're experiencing cognitive problems, which may be caused by inhaling substances deemed illegal for starship operators. We'll have to check that. Inspector Jabari, you have blood test kits with you?"

"Two, as it happens." Jabari smiled, patting his jacket pockets.

"Uh," Ziss said, then, "Errrrr..."

Captain Uva just shook her head and looked away, turning off the vaper and sliding it into a pouch on the front of her belt.

Shill wasn't finished—intimidating these fools was a start, but the goal was to get on board their tanker. She said, "After our inspection of your inlet/outlet valves, we hold grave concerns about the state of their overfill probes and compression rings."

"What?" Ziss spluttered. "They were new two journeys ago."

"Well, I'd love to examine your bridge records on that, as well as the records of your last physical—particularly the neurological part of the test. That is, as long as we have permission to board your vessel. It's all right if we don't, except..."

Jabari completed the threat for her. "Except then there'll be a hefty fine for obstructing the authorized request of a safety inspector, which your employer will be taking out of your salaries for several years, I'd imagine."

"This is... this is..." It seemed Ziss couldn't decide what 'this' was.

His captain interrupted, as she straightened and stepped to the hatchway. "I think we can stop all this crap. Follow me, please."

"You first," Shill told Ziss, mimicking the polite gesture Jabari had given her earlier. When both crewers were inside, Shill waggled her brows at Jabari and murmured in their own language, "Looks like I *could* do the talking after all."

They followed the captain and first officer, who were dragging their feet, past a couple of closet-sized bunk rooms and then up eight narrow steel stairs to the cockpit level. Uva and Ziss entered the cockpit first, followed by Jabari, and the crew members took their seats at the helm. By the time Shill joined him, her bot, Greasy, was no longer clinging to her shoulder, since the plan was for him to get busy decommissioning the vessel's other droids.

When the captain turned her chair around to face Jabari, she was looking directly into the muzzle of the Jabari's short-burst disruptor pistol, looted from *Pleiades'* armory.

Uva spluttered something in another language that included the word *gahgagga*.

"I have bad news for you," Jabari told her. "You two are being replaced for this trip. You'll spend it locked in your crew hold where we know you have enough food, water, and sanitary supplies to survive a month. You won't be there for that long—so, actually, the news isn't all *that* bad."

The captain started to interrupt but froze with her jaw hanging open when Jabari rattled the disruptor. The safety was on—he had no intention of melting an innocent civilian—but she didn't know that.

Continuing, he said, "We estimate you'll be there eight days at most. After that time, the code lock my colleague devised will automatically open. However, it's possible someone will come looking for you a day or so earlier than that."

Speaking *Terran* True, a language 1700 years dead, Shill mumbled, "Someone'll definitely come in here early. They'll be inspecting the hells outa this ship when they realize it was our ride onto Vadox CX."

Fortunately, Jabari thought, *neither of their translator patches activated to translate that tidbit.* He shushed her anyway and asked, "How's the situation with those droids?"

She'd peeled off her yellow jacket, revealing the data cuff circling her left forearm. Checking it, she said, "Eighty per cent there. Give Greasy another minute."

Another minute. He leaned against a bulkhead and smiled at the two-person crew, keeping his weapon low and out of sight of anyone happening to enter the ship and climb those stairs. Another minute and they could lock away First Officer Ziss while Captain Uva made the necessary noises to Station Control to get them moving quickly as soon as the refill was done.

The captain spoke up again. "You realize this is a water and hydrogen tanker? We don't have gold on board. Or rare gases. Or—"

"We realize." Jabari shrugged and gave them both a big, friendly grin. "Relax. You don't need to think. You don't need to do anything except the few more simple tasks we tell you to do. The good news is you two are about to have a nice vacation in your own ship—and get paid for it while we fly it to Vadox for you. Then you'll have a story you can dine out on for years."

In Terran True again, Shill muttered, "And we're about to land a big ass water tanker outside the largest population center of a shithole planet with its own imperial garrison."

"That we are," Jabari replied and felt the buzz he'd started experiencing by pulling this off so far begin to fizzle away as more sober thoughts pressed in.

This is for you, Tee.

For you, Morten, and you, Erkan.

For every mother's daughter and son who've died under the 'Proselyti' banner.

And for the few that are left out there, enslaved to the empire...

PART ONE

MOVEMENT TO CONTACT

At the cessation of the civil war (also known as the Terranist War), most Terranist military captives were either sentenced for crimes against the Imperium or disarmed and sent home to disarmed worlds. At least to the worlds not razed as punishment.

In sharp contrast to most of their kindred-in-arms, every captured individual from the 'Elite Pure Okalasi Guard' battalions was given a choice: death or conversion.

Just over half chose death.

But those who swore fealty to empire and emperor claimed they sought to bring peace to all humankind. This became the official and public reason for their incorporation into the Imperial Army where they have served at the pleasure of every sitting emperor since, reserved for missions deemed in the best interests of advancing our borders. When not deployed, these soldiers have usually been confined to long-term stasis.

From the time of their appropriation into the Imperial Army, these converted Terranist soldiers formed a new unit: the Cohortis Proselytae *(Specialist Proselyte Battalion). As is standard for imperial soldiers, each proselyte took an Imperial True middle name. But in recognition of their willing service in repairing the damage done by Terranist hostilities, they were given dispensation to keep their birth name as their military epithet. A generous policy on behalf of the Imperium indeed.*

Not many Proselyti remain in our era, but those who do still serve at His Highness' pleasure and for the greater good of the glorious Imperium.

- Imperial Army Historical Report 272-12216-a, from the Imperator General's Office (Office of the Army and Navy) to the Imperial Senate, Year 5122

CHAPTER ONE

QUAESTOR AURELIA

Contact Minus 107 Hours, 13 Minutes

AURELIA COSSEA'S cabin speaker rumbled as a bass-baritone voice spoke through it.

"They're boarded, ma'am. Decanus Caiu is having them sign their attendance."

"Thank you, pilot," she replied and stretched in her chair with a mild groan.

She rose from behind the compartment's modest workstation and shut down her computer with a wink, brushed the wrinkles from her travel gown, and turned her head toward a wall mirror on the closet door where she could give her tousled hair a brief assessment. The gelled-up spikes and swirls she'd mussed it into earlier remained undisturbed, lending her a relaxed, professional appearance that would suit her purposes nicely now that the FTL shuttle had docked within the *Maelstrom*.

"Yes," she murmured, tilting her head this way and that. "Just so."

The added volume in her hair, she believed, made her face

appear longer, more oval-shaped, and a tad more mature than its actual years. And the red coloring she'd added accented the flecks in her orgmented eye's lens. If there was anything that her sister and mentor, Florene, had taught her, it was that appearances made as much difference as skills in moments like this. They set a certain tone and could disarm your target as effectively as a strike to the solar plexus, but without any expenditure of energy. Besides, an Imperial Quaestor didn't get a second chance to make an impression—not when one of the new arrivals would only *get* one chance to meet her.

Aurelia brushed a final wrinkle from across her breast and pulled her shoulders back.

"Just so."

The cabin recorder would be triggered the moment her two visitors arrived, capturing the Pronouncement of Guilt for Emperor Nero's later pleasure and for documenting against future legal audits or performance reviews—another good reason for looking the part today.

She plunged each hand into the opposite sleeve and settled her wrists against her belly—a relaxed pose, the very image of poise. Then Aurelia faced the cabin door and adopted a mild smile. The interstellar shuttle's boarding lock was positioned behind the cockpit. Those arriving would step into a single central passageway from which opened the shuttle's various compartments. The passage was so narrow, her escort-adjutant, Decanus Caiu, had to sidle slightly sideways whenever he moved forward or aft. She might have felt sorry for him were he not a Corfid who no doubt spied on her for the leaders of his cult. Then again, he always performed his duties with aplomb and so was perhaps equal parts asset and liability.

The shuttle was quite long, and Aurelia's cabin was toward the stern, so once Caiu had finished with the admin, it would take her visitors thirty seconds to march back to it. She checked the clock: any moment now, then. She winked again, this time at a sensor above the door, which then opened. The scuff of shoes on carpet announced her guests' arrival three seconds before the first reached her cabin. He was short, and he was skinny, and he was young, younger even than her. He'd shaved his head as bare as his chin, and his officer's uniform was impeccably pressed, fitting as if tailored for him, which with his family connections it no doubt was.

A naval lieutenant, he couldn't help but draw attention to the star-and-bar on his epaulette, as he brushed it free of imaginary dust when he came through the door.

"Quaestor, Your Honor," the young man greeted her, coming to rest three steps inside. One of his hands twitched upward in the beginning of a handshake before he saw the folded position of her arms and dropped it by his side again.

The other man had come to a stop inside the doorway and to the lieutenant's left. A sergeant, this man was middle-aged and clad in a loose-fitting gray jumpsuit with a *Cohortis Prose-lytae* patch on one breast. He, too, used the expected honorific, "Quaestor, Your Honor," and stood at attention as if she were his military superior.

"Would you mind standing to either side of my door?" she requested. "In case my crew need to come in."

"Yes, ma'am," said the NCO and took a pace forward before sidestepping.

"Er, of course," the lieutenant said belatedly and shuffled into a position on the other side of the open doorway. He clasped his hands at his waist, attempting, perhaps, to mirror Aurelia's pose.

She said, "And you may stand at ease, Sergeant."

He did so. "Thank you, ma'am."

Aurelia savored a long slow breath in and out. She so loved these first moments of meeting someone new. Getting to read them fresh—the spontaneous appraisal of their posture and micro-expressions, the way her orgmented eye picked up on skin temperature and pulse rate, the intellectual challenge of making meaning from these multiple tells.

The sergeant, she noticed, wore a professionally neutral look, the same expression she'd seen on a thousand career soldiers' faces, halfway between fake humility and outright boredom. That he was Proselyti made it interesting, as did the fact that while she and the lieutenant had spoken Imperial Common, he had relied on the breast patch's woven-in translator to make sense of what they said, their words rendered in the language he had originally spoken, a language that had been eradicated 1700 years ago. And although a version of Imperial Common was always in use, the sergeant couldn't be expected to know the latest version each time they brought him out of stasis for a few weeks or months of combat or escort duty. The man had classic, fine, Asiatic features and short-cropped black hair with hints of gray. He was somewhere in his late forties or early fifties—she might later ask to see his bio-tattoo, which was currently hidden beneath a sleeve, so she could check his actual age. Every single surrendering Proselyti had been in their late teens to late twenties at the time the war ended. Middle age meant he'd been brought from stasis *many* times to serve those eras' reigning emperors. The sergeant was a man who wasn't fazed by much. His heart rate was slow and even, as were the breaths he took through his nose. He wasn't sweating, and his skin was cool.

In contrast, the lieutenant wore a look of barely restrained panic—which warred with his obvious, strong attraction toward her. The hairstyle and the shift she wore settled nicely across her figure and were no doubt helping with the latter of his biological responses. He was young for his naval rank, and though he'd been deployed to the peripheries of the galaxy, his promotion to that rank was a sign of his distant father's favor *and* favors performed by his father for others.

With precise and formal statements, Aurelia welcomed

them both and passed on the emperor's gratitude for the duties they'd conducted out in the far-flung Perseus peripheries. She told the lieutenant his activities, in particular, had caught the eye of the emperor's staff. And just as pride registered in his eyes, she withdrew a compact laser from her left sleeve and flash-drilled a hole through the middle of his forehead.

As a small cloud of his vaporized tissue was sucked into the ceiling-fitted air handler above him, the lieutenant fell in a heap across the entranceway, narrowly missing the sergeant's closest boot. The soldier's flinch was so negligible, Aurelia almost missed it. He didn't step away but remained at ease, hands behind his back. He did stare down at the dead officer, the furrows in his brow the only thing giving away his consternation *and* the unspoken question on his mind.

"You'd like to know why?" she asked him.

The soldier straightened his spine and shifted his stare to the wall behind her. "I assume the lieutenant was guilty of something."

"Succinctly and wryly stated, Sergeant. This man committed some rather wicked acts before his father had him posted out here and covered up his crimes. Believe me when I say, there would be a half dozen young women who'd rejoice at news of his death—had they, themselves, lived to see it."

A momentary widening of the eyes. "I... see. Thank you for explaining, ma'am, but you didn't need to."

"I don't want questions and concerns to come between us, not when we'll be working together for at least a week."

His dark-irised stare shifted her way again. Once more, his wrinkling brow broadcast the question on his mind.

"When they brought you out of stasis, they indicated the lieutenant would command your mission?"

"They did, ma'am."

"They were misinformed, and so were you, since we didn't want the lieutenant getting wind of his judgment. *I'm* commanding the mission. I have the requisite documentation assigning you and your squad to my services and to this ship for the duration of the operation. The *Maelstrom* commanders are receiving that now."

He blinked once. "Yes, ma'am, very good, ma'am."

"The warrant for the Pronouncement of Guilt on the lieutenant has been outstanding for over a year. Because the *Maelstrom* is an extremely long way from any magistrate's station, it has been difficult to spare a quaestor to enact it. But since we had sudden need for a team with your, shall we say, lack of political bias, it was deemed economical for me to come here and enact this verdict while simultaneously collecting you."

He gave no reaction. No question about why the team couldn't go to her, couldn't meet her further across the Perseus Arm. Not even a deeper furrow in his brow. His stare returned to the wall as his chin lifted.

Wanting to engage him, to draw him out, she asked, "Sergeant, you were thawed yesterday?"

"By ship time, it was the day before, ma'am. And ..." He fell silent, swallowing his next words with a squirm of the shoulders.

"And what? Feel free to speak openly."

"I wanted to say we weren't 'thawed,' but decanted. Stasis doesn't freeze a person. However, I shouldn't correct you, ma'am. I apologize."

Aurelia softened her eyes. "I don't mind correction where it's warranted. I used the term *thawing* in jest, I assure you. Everyone in magistrate circles calls it freezing and such. Dark-humored fun, which I admit is in poor taste. So, if you've been *decanted* for two days, you must find yourself in good condition for the mission? You've recovered?"

"My team I have been medically cleared and are conducting light drills and exercise."

"Good. Now, your full name is Sergeant Saito Servanus

Shimada? Servanus being the Imperial True name allotted to you when you transferred allegiance."

"Yes, ma'am."

"But Saito is your *preferred* name— as a Proselyti, you have the right to use it instead of the imperial epithet."

"Yes, ma'am." He waited a beat and added, "And I do use it."

"I'm sure many Imperial officers would object, but it's fine with me. *Oh.* Pardon me a moment..."

Her escort-adjutant Caiu had appeared at the doorway— although '*filled* the doorway' would be a better description. Caiu stood a good twenty centimeters taller than Saito, with twice the bulk. This was the result, she knew, of *in utero* corpiforming, followed by years of painful mods during adolescence. All of it had purpose-built him for military life in a variety of deployments, gravities, and atmospheres. One of his treebranch arms eased past Saito who—to his credit—didn't blink and didn't appear to notice the identifying features of that arm. Caiu's sleeve had a heart-shaped sigil stitched onto it, and the hand holding out a datapad was missing its smallest finger, another sign of loyalty to the Cor Fidelis emperor-worship cult.

The Corfid said, "Here," in his husky growl.

Saito did blink, now, as he realized the pad was for him and took it.

"Mission files and briefing," Aurelia explained then focused on Caiu. The Corfid had bowed over the lieutenant's corpse. Aurelia had been so interested in the living, breathing man in the room that she'd forgotten the corpse completely. She told Caiu, "Yes, yes, remove it, but wait until we've concluded our meeting here before you send in the cleanbots. The wet patch on the carpet will be easy enough for Sgt. Saito to step over when leaving."

Without any difficulty, Caiu grabbed the body by the shirtfront and hauled it one-handed from the room. He headed forward and left a trail of leaking gore in his wake. He would leave the body with this docking area's duty officer. That paper-work had been sent to the *Maelstrom*'s commanders already.

Aurelia nodded at the pad. "You can read the files at your leisure. I'll summarize them now, so there's no great surprises, but just remember that everything you know from this point on —and everything on that pad—is confidential and not to be disclosed to anyone else aboard this station, including your people, until after we've left."

"And when is that, ma'am? The departure?"

"Is an hour long enough for you to bring your team aboard?"

"Plenty of time, ma'am."

"Sergeant, I've decided to call you Saito from now on, as long as we're alone. So, I want you to drop the 'ma'am.' Call me Quaestor in public and Aurelia in private."

"I could call you Quaestor in both situations."

"Aurelia in private," she insisted, tilting her head down a little to show she'd brook no argument. "I'd welcome such trust and informality between us."

"Very well, then, Aurelia."

"He *can* take orders. Very good. Now, about that summa-ry..." She remained standing; she'd been sitting too long this morning. And Saito didn't look uncomfortable standing at ease. She winked at the sensor above the door, sealing the compart-ment. Doubtless, she would say things she didn't want either of her two-man crew of Cor Fidelis devotees to overhear.

"Saito, since you've no doubt missed significant portions of history while in stasis, you may not know that we quaestors are judge-investigator-executioners serving at the emperor's plea-sure." She awaited a response.

The shrug was in Saito's tone. "The office has been around for nine hundred years, I believe. The last fifteen or twenty times they decanted me, quaestors were a popular subject of conversation among the Imperial Regulars and civilians I worked around."

"Have you met one of us before?"

"No."

"Nor have I met one of you: Proselyti, warriors converted at gunpoint from devotion to their Terranist Kaana to our Martianist emperors."

"Not converted at gunpoint, Quaes... *Aurelia*. We were given the choice between a noble death or living to bring order to the chaos we'd been partly responsible for creating. We chose the latter, which was also an honorable choice."

"I wasn't suggesting weakness on the part of your people. I apologize if it came across that way."

"You don't need to apologize."

"Because I'm an Imperial quaestor? We enact the law, but we're not actually the law. Not actually an embodiment of moral perfection. We make mistakes, and we should apologize when those mistakes bring offense to a civilized person like you, someone serving empire and emperor as I do. And I hope I bring no offense when I ask you—out of pure curiosity—what is it *like*?"

He blinked a couple of times. "What is what like?"

"Being seventeen hundred years old."

"Ah. Well, I'm not."

He unbuttoned then shoved back his right sleeve, the sleeve of the arm holding the datapad. Then he turned his arm to show the paler flesh along the inside. Aurelia, it turned out, got to see his bio-tat earlier than she'd hoped. It read:

cohortis proselytae: 882-Ctp

53:112:22:05

Saito's unit, the Specialist Proselyte Battalion.

His service number.

His "lived" age, the biological one: fifty-three common years, one hundred and twelve days, twenty-two hours, five minutes. The 05 flicked over to 06 as she watched it.

"Very interesting." She motioned for him to drop his arm and noticed she still held the compact laser. She returned it to its holster within her sleeve while Saito rolled down his sleeve, and then she concluded, "Well, you appear very fit for your age."

"Mid-fifties isn't old for many people throughout the Imperium," he noted.

"Mm. But for others, it is. Soldiers, for example, who've seen decades of action."

"Well, I treat my body kindly whenever I'm not in action or stasis, and the Imperial Army maintains its Proselyti with excellent care." When she waited for more, he added, "I *am* fit, yes."

"Excellent to hear. May I also say—by way of compliment and curiosity rather than patronization—you seem well-spoken for a non-commissioned officer."

Something dark passed across his features, some old offense briefly remembered. "If we ever find the time to recount life stories, perhaps I'll tell you mine."

"Intriguing. You *are* well-educated, though?"

"I *was*, for a context that existed seventeen hundred years ago."

"Good enough. It means you're literate, and, most importantly, you've learned how to learn."

He nodded, appreciating the point.

She continued, "Your *files* report you as intelligent. Given the two dolts they've saddled me with here, I'll enjoy working with someone like you."

He narrowed an eye at her, exactly as she expected him to. If his body hadn't been 'thawed' from stasis, his mood and his opinion of her were certainly beginning to thaw. Which was what she wanted.

"The High Magistrates Office provides its quaestors with all necessities including staff. I have a pilot, and I have an escort-adjutant, which is a fancy name for a bodyguard."

As if I need one, she thought sourly.

"Normally, Saito, they'd be more than sufficient to assist me as I enact Pronouncements of Guilt within friendly territory. 'Friendly' meaning places such as this roving space station where the locals won't impede my work or seek retribution for it. However, the case for which *you're* joining me is different. Quite different. I'm going to guess you've never heard of the planet Vadox CX?"

The sergeant shook his head.

"Not surprising. There are thousands of planets, and this one isn't notable. Terraformed and settled back in the 33rd century, it never really climbed out of its early status as a 'shit hole,' although it was relatively mineral rich. But terraforming was difficult. It's a very dry world, and it's situated a long way from the major trade routes of any era."

"But it *is* within current Imperium territory?"

"In a poorer area of the empire, yes, and close to wild space. It's policed and resourced by our central powers, but the High Consuls have often been grudging in their support of outer regions. This state of play has prompted the current governor to source some 'funding' of his own, most of which is diverted for his use. I mean, the man *could* have done what *none* of his predecessors did: actually govern his planet for its common citizens and migrant workers. But that's not the type of person we're dealing with; instead, he governs for the elite." She chuckled. "By that flicker of cheek muscle, I see you're thinking, 'Doesn't our emperor do the same?'"

"I wasn't thinking anything like that, ma'am."

"No? Well, others think that. There *is* a measure of inequity in our civilization, to be sure. My way of coming to terms with it is my belief that we're a meritocracy at heart. We, at least, aspire to be. And the Imperial Family and clan are designed for and committed to wholesome values and noble rulership. You follow me?"

She'd been speaking in Imperial True since judging the lieutenant. And Saito had appeared comfortable conversing in it; his translator patch certainly hadn't interpreted anything for him yet. At her question, he nodded and gestured for her to go on.

"All of the galaxy is empire, Saito, but not all of the galaxy has *submitted to* empire, to order, to the rule of common law. Three of these great *Maelstrom* battle stations conduct long and gradual sweeps of the empire's outer reaches. Any policing and defense of those sectors is always strongest *around* those military stations where imperial power is concentrated and resourced. But as each *Maelstrom* moves, the best policing and military enforcement moves with it. So even within 'imperial territory,' there are flurries of defense for areas within it before that defense becomes impractical and the marauders and vagabonds edge back in. Some systems and sectors see blitzes of military activity that achieve great gains... and then they see nothing for the following few decades. In the midst of *this*, gentlemen like our current Vadox governor see their opportunity for sedition, for separation. The temptation to elevate themselves to their own minor emperorships grows too strong to resist."

Aurelia shook herself mildly, reminding her to keep on topic, rather than drifting into political commentary.

"Vadox CX began its terraformed existence as a viable world, although it was barely populated or exploited back then. The Terranist war put an end to its early potential for relative prosperity by diverting people and trade. It floundered for several centuries, neglected and bypassed, a den of ruins where only the most desperate bandits and refugees sheltered. It took a very long time to win the sector back after your Terranists wrought havoc across the Milky Way. Again, I mean no offense by that."

"No offense taken. We did create havoc. And the Proselyti have spent seventeen centuries making amends."

"Yes, you have, haven't you? One of the reasons I need Proselyti for this mission. But I do digress. Since the Imperium moved back in, Vadox System has endured eight centuries of resettlement, then more decline, and, finally, fresh investment and growth. But it's an imperial system and supposedly governed by imperial laws and standards. Vadox CX's present governor is named Eccles Ectorius. Ectorius has been judged guilty of corruption. This, sadly, is not unusual, and, sometimes, for the empire's cohesion, it's ignored by the consuls, senate, and magistrates. Unfortunately for Governor Ectorius, he's also at the heart of a conspiracy to commit sedition and has drawn other corrupt governors and power brokers into his web. Also, and *this* is the worst of all, he's been discovered reaching out to warlords from beyond the empire for potential support."

Saito frowned. "The idiot's trying to create a breakaway bloc?"

"A coalition of the moronically suicidal, yes."

Saito grunted and nodded. "And we're to ensure that ends badly for him."

"It's time for the silly old fart to go and for a true representative of empire and the emperor to be installed. Someone who can transform a decayed world into a better representation of what the Imperium is meant to be."

And with that last thought, Aurelia saw her sister's face. She pictured Florene seated in Ectorius' chair at the next Council of Governors, and she allowed herself a small smile.

Saito said, "You mentioned this territory won't be as 'friendly' to you as most. Ectorius has amassed a degree of personal power?"

Aurelia pursed her lips a moment, thinking how to best phrase her reponse. "It's not local resistance we're concerned about, if that's what you're thinking. Emperor Nero's spies on world will ensure a bout of severe food poisoning that neutralizes the local Army Garrison. There'll be a minor infrastructure collapse on the far side of the planet which will draw away remaining healthy troopers. Relax, Sergeant: no citizens will be killed in the collapse; I've been assured of this."

Saito's gaze flicked down to the gore on the floor. "You need a team to keep any leftover heat off you while the governor meets the same fate as the lieutenant."

"Not precisely. You see, it's Ectorius' *off-world* support we're most concerned about. Though stuck with a minor appointment, Ectorius is a networker. He has a great many friends in the halls of power: the Senate, the Chamber of Magnates, even the spouses of two High Consuls. Not to mention the small number of other planetary governors we're aware are sympathetic to his conspiracy's goals. So, it simply wouldn't do to swoop in and execute him in his home or workplace. Not even to blatantly poison him. He's too 'connected' for such public acts."

"Then Governor Ectorius will vanish?"

"As he prepares for a soiree he's holding, yes. Him—and his wife if she's present."

"We go in and take them?"

"We go in. Legally, *I* take them. It's not an Army matter. You work for the High Magistrates Office until it's concluded. I have been *commanded* to facilitate this mission this way. My signed mandate is from the Magistrates, and it is co-signed by Emperor Nero, himself. These are my orders and yours: discreetness, stealth, speed, secrecy. Saito, hear this: witnesses cannot be tolerated. If hospitality or other staff see us, if any local troopers *are* present, they must not survive the encounter."

"That will... leave a mess."

"A mess is not a problem. Being seen leaving would be."

"A problem for the emperor."

It was the first time Aurelia read any kind of disapproval or reluctance in him.

She gave him a chiding look. "'For the Emperor' means 'for all of us.'"

Saito continued to look displeased at the prospect of shooting unarmed civilians, but after a moment's internal struggle, he accepted it with a grim nod. "For the empire and for order. And Ectorius? What's his fate?"

"We deliver him to Nero's examiners. Over the next few months, his worst co-conspirators will be rooted out, and they will meet with sudden, tragic accidents."

Saito shifted his feet around a little. "The reason you're seconding Proselyti is because we can't be corrupted by this governor? Or because we can't possibly be related to any Imperial Houses?"

Aurelia had a sudden flashback to her last conversation with her sister, just a week ago. Florene telling her she was mad entrusting herself to a complement of Proselyti.

To which Aurelia had replied, "Have they ever been known to mutiny? In seventeen centuries of service?" And when Florene had opened her mouth to continue her objection, Aurelia had added, "Besides, you know I'm saddled with two Cor Fideli as crew. They're well-known for sniffing out mutineers before a mutiny gets going."

Florene had grunted, ceding the point, but unhappy about it.

Aurelia had startled her sister by popping open a hidden

compartment on her mechanical arm and grinning. "Also, I do have my own protections."

"A fact I always seem to forget." Florene had laughed. "My formidable sister, the quaestor."

Here and now with Saito, she lifted her machine arm to scratch at her forehead's toughened dermis above her left eye, the machine eye. The skin orgmentation was new, as were upgrades to her musculature, lungs, and circulatory system. No mere trooper was going to get the better of Aurelia Cossea...

In answer to Saito's double-barreled question, she said, "You're correct. From our perspective, you're incorruptible. The same cannot be said of everybody. For example, the lieutenant —" it was her turn to flick her gaze toward the dark patch and streaks on the carpet "—was not only guilty of brutal crimes in his adolescence. The little shit reported for Ectorius' network."

Saito's head tilted in surprise. "A *spy*? *Here*?"

"Indeed. Reporting things that might trouble or be useful to Ectorius' chums. There's another reason you're so trustworthy: the last time any Proselyti in your team was decanted was before Ectorius' birth. He simply can't have gotten to you— even if he *had* anything to offer you."

Saito tilted his head the other way. "Sure. But you don't need *us*. Why not procure a platoon of Corfids—excuse me— Cor Fideli?"

"I call them Corfids, too," she admitted with a smirk. "And yes, we considered that. Both my pilot and my escort-adjutant are adherents to the Cor Fidelis philosophy and movement." When she caught the brief curl of his upper lip, her smile broadened. "I like them about as much as you do. Probably for different reasons. Military people dislike them because they're often sociopaths and *always* complete assholes who tend to muddle up clearcut mission objectives. *I* dislike them because of their underlying arrogance and because they bring unnecessary confusion to our society. There are no degrees when it comes to devotion or loyalty or fidelity. You either serve the emperor, or you don't. You're either devoted, or you're not. Sugar is sweet and salt is savory—no degrees, no special cases. The mere existence of Corfids casts doubts over everybody else's fidelity. Also, the bastards continually report on small and often imagined slights against the emperor by people who are just going about their business, and that makes a quaestor's job harder than it needs to be."

She shook her head sheepishly.

"I'm babbling. You unfortunately tapped into one of my pet hates. Back to the subject. I have a team of Proselyti *and* Cor Fideli. There's no way Ectorius' network could have gotten to you."

"And Proselyti have proven we're about maintaining the unity of the Imperium?"

"Correct."

He shifted again. "You're aware, Aurelia, of the latest news from this very *Maelstrom* about a mad Corfid named Scipio who took five Proselyti on some rogue mission and got them killed?"

"I'm aware. The two Corfids with me are not rogue, if that's what you're suggesting. Nor am I."

"I wasn't—"

"Check the files I've provided on the pad there, including my mandate for this mission."

"I meant that this Scipio's actions might cast doubt on all Proselyti."

"When they should cast doubt on Cor Fidelis instead. Saito, you should be assured of my trust in you. You *will* read the mandate document thoroughly. I don't want us going into this situation without having the same agenda, the same mind."

"Yes, ma'am." For the first time, he allowed himself a dry smile. "Aurelia, I mean. That's one hard habit to break. I'll check the files, and you'll have my trust. But you'll have to understand if there's some *mis*trust from my people toward your Corfids."

"That's only fair. Corfids don't trust anyone either." To build further rapport, she adopted a more relaxed pose, leaning on one hip. "You may or may not know that Scipio called a full complement of Corfid Marines out to some forsaken location before he vanished. All their searching of the area revealed zero trace, except for the wreckage and residue left by destroyed ships belonging, they think, to a criminal Qlan."

Aurelia finally allowed herself to sit and lowered herself onto her workstation's chair. "I think that will suffice as a summary, Saito. An hour until launch, you agree?"

He straightened into a posture halfway to at attention. "Yes, Quaestor."

"Excellent. See my pilot Febian for the arrangements. Once we're away, dinner will be four hours after departure. I'll join your team in the galley for it, keep things friendly and trusting. I'd like you to model the rapport we have, while keeping it appropriate."

"Yes, Quaestor."

"You're dismissed, Sergeant. And thank you."

"Very good, ma'am."

A moment later, he was gone, and the door sealed behind him.

Aurelia brought up the personal letter she'd been drafting to her sister and unclipped the screen from the workstation and laid it flat so she could apply a stylus to it. The ancient art of handwriting was an indulgence she enjoyed because it tapped into a different side of the brain from typing. It was so pleasantly physical. She completed her message of encouragement to her sister, Florene.

"Florene, that governor's seat we discussed is the one I strongly encourage you to apply for. Think of the way it will satisfy your holy desires for our empire's betterment and the boost to your influence. You mentored me well, dear sister, you opened doors for me. It's my pleasure, this time, to do it for you."

She leaned back in her chair and pictured that separatist scum Ectorius in chains in the shuttle's hold as the vessel fled the Vadox system and headed toward the imperial planet.

"Totally my pleasure," she said aloud.

CHAPTER TWO

GUNSŌ

Contact Minus 106 Hours, 18 Minutes

THE FIRETEAM WAS midway through a meal in their billet area's meal-room when Saito located them.

No, not 'fireteam,' he corrected himself, coming to rest in the egress between the meal-room and corridor. *Not for this mission. The briefing files label us 'insertion team,' so that's what I'll use.*

The compartment he faced was four meters wide and ten long, with enough space on the bench seats along its central table for the eight troopers he'd be leading to squeeze together. Other fireteams Saito had worked with over the centuries—the imperial troopers and *some* of the Proselyti ones—would have spread food all over the table by now... the table, the floor, their laps, each other's laps. Their officers and NCOs would have allowed the outlet for their juvenile impulses and natural boredom and left janitors or kitchen crews to clean up after them. Saito had made something clear during their first decantation briefing: he wouldn't tolerate that kind of grunfer shit. It pleased him to note they were keeping their discipline tight in that regard. As nonchalant as a couple of those assembled could get, as dumb as a couple others were, these people were Terranist *warriors*—all but one, at least—and they had warmed to Saito's standard of soldiery and were conducting themselves with dignity, notwithstanding the spite shown them by Imperial Regulars.

Nevertheless, after Saito had closed the door and given an ultra-short summation of the mission ahead, one trooper exploded with: "We're doing *what?*"

A brief ripple of murmurs followed the outburst, some sounding like they supported the sentiment, some just pissed off the idiot had spoken that way to their sergeant. The question had come from a very young man who'd been *trying* to grow a moustache since his awakening four days back. Wegley Tertius Mackanee was the one individual there Saito didn't think of as a 'real' soldier. He'd never met him, before the Surrender or on any mission after that, but the man's file made it obvious he'd never been a popular Imperium choice for live fire missions. Wegley had only been decanted eight times in a millennium-and-a-half, and two of those times had been for the mandatory 700-year medical checks and for routine physical therapy. Wegley was nine biological years younger than the next youngest member of the team and barely out of his teens.

The murmurs had settled down, with the rest of the team staring from Wegley to Saito.

The outburst hadn't bothered him in the least, but to give the appearance of it, Saito tapped the Quaestor's datapad against his thigh in an even rhythm and allowed some irritation to seep into his tone. "*Auxiliary* Private Wegley, you can stow that attitude inside your colon where it belongs. I saw your latest stasis lasted over two centuries, so there's a good chance it's scrambled your brain, which means I need to explain something to you that everyone else in this room understands full well. You live to *fulfil* the missions you're given, *not* to object to them."

A couple of chuckles came from the others at Wegley's expense.

Wegley, it seemed, was not deterred. "Well, I hellsdamn *do* object, Sergeant. A hell-sacking *snatch-and-flee* mission, for sack's sake? We're not assassins or kidnappers; we're infantry."

If there'd been any sympathy for Wegley's objection around the room, it evaporated with that last comment. Several rolled their eyes or squinted harshly at him. Private Mwana, opposite him, snorted. "*Most* of us are infantry."

Wegley turned his glower toward Mwana, and the big man met it squarely and smiled back mockingly. Any eyes on Wegley were definitely not friendly; his squad mates did *not* consider him one of them. Two of them called him "squeak" under their breaths. With a grunt, the young man dropped his gaze and shifted rice around his plate with his plastine spoon.

Saito knew Wegley had been a driver during the Terranist war, not a fighter. The boy had been born with no right eye and two flat feet—born into a family too poor to surgically improve those features and too proudly Terranist to seek jobs where the medical benefits would allow for corpiforming the baby. At seventeen, he'd been conscripted from his bakery apprentice-ship as logistics support for an Okalasi Elite Pure Guard unit before the empire destroyed the Kaana's flagship and Earth's moon in the same catastrophic attack. Upon Wegley's capture, he had joined in transferring his allegiance to the Imperium. The Imperium had then repaired his two feet, grown him a right eye and installed it... and retrained him for infantry work before locking him away in stasis with the rest of his Proselyti trooper brethren and sistren, most of whom he'd barely spent time with in the eon since.

The other Proselyti—seasoned, blooded soldiers—resented the Imperium treating a mere vehicle driver as their equal. And as the evolutionary purists Terranists were, they despised the lab-grown mods he'd received for his eye and feet. Obviously, he didn't have the people skills to improve that. But Saito found he had a modicum of empathy for this kid. Like Wegley, Saito hadn't begun *his* military career as a fighting man, but as a logistics officer before and during the war—until a run-in with a senior officer had seen him busted down to private one year before the Surrender. And in the conflagrations he'd been thrown into, Saito had learned to fight and found he had a knack for it.

Saito shook off the lapse into self-reflection, cleared his throat, and adopted the no bullshit, no messing around approach most dog soldiers appreciated and responded to.

"Listen to your sergeant, you mouth breathing, sweaty assed cat-sackers, and let me make this crystal clear so I don't have to put up with any more pointless brain vomit. We are *not* acting as assassins. We are *not* acting as kidnappers. We *are* being utilized for a politically sensitive mission. All of you maggots in this room—plus me and the other *non*-cat-sacker, Corporal Kirdy, there—are now an insertion team. You're acting in support of the high magistrate's official, carrying out orders from Emperor Nero XXXIV. The official has the main job of detainment; you're just there to make sure no one gets in her way. As always, your duties continue to shift the balance from lawlessness to peace and order in this galaxy. Take pride in that. Do your job properly. Refrain from hellsdamn whining." He avoided looking at Wegley while he said that, not wanting to further ostracize the young man. "And maybe this time, your performance will earn us all a sweet vacation somewhere with pleasantly high UV and sandy beaches—before we all get shoved back into a long sleep."

He waited until there were some mumbled, *Yes, Sergeant*s around the table.

"So, you *can* listen. Good to know. All right," he added, consulting his bio-tat to check the time then conducting some quick mental arithmetic. "I'm giving you thirty-six minutes to report to FTL-shuttle 21-21G in Bay 507. Couple of people repeat that back to me."

Three did—Troopers Naomi, Mwana and Temuz.

"Good. If you are one second late or if—hells forbid—Corporal Kirdy has to go looking for you, you will not enjoy your *extra* physical stamina training aboard that shuttle. Combat armor, fatigues and rations await us at the berth. Bring basic kits with you. Small arms will be provided, my mission files tell me. Temuz and Pytor, you'll go to Bay 507 and handle the loading of that materiel. Dola and Wegley, you'll bring *their* gear along with yours."

A few nods. Wegley muttered, "Yes, Sergeant."

"One last thing: we are honored to be led in this mission by an imperial quaestor, and if you don't recognize that office, read up on it. She is a young woman, young as Wegley maybe, and she is highly skilled and committed to her job. I've already seen how much of both."

"Really?" Trooper Naomi asked, interested.

"Oh, yeah," he replied without elaborating. "I don't want anyone treating her with disrespect, civilian or not. I mean it. You'll treat her as the emperor, himself, or whatever brand of deity you usually bow and scrape to. Also, in her service are a pilot and adjutant, which is like an assistant who's also a bodyguard. These two gentlemen belong to the..."

Saito tucked in one pinky finger, mimicking the sign of Cor Fidelis allegiance.

Four of his team groaned, three looked confused. Wegley said, "What's that supposed to be?"

Corporal Kirdy spoke before Saito could. "Cor Fidelis, squeak."

Still frowning and apparently unable to keep his mouth shut for long, Wegley translated it from Imperial True out loud: "The Faithful Heart. What's that?"

Kirdy kept on with the explanation. "Some of you have

been asleep for a long while or involved in actions where you missed a whole lotta different shit. Corfids—Cor Fidelis members—are soldiers who think 'emselves extra special to whoever the current emperor is. They're extra in love with him."

"And they *are* extra special to Nero XXXIV," Saito said. "So, play nice with them. Don't make small talk with them. Be polite to them. Act like they've bugged every compartment in that vessel, because apart from Quaestor Cossea's cabin, they have. Now, we've finally reached the part where I've finished talking and you all say ..."

"Yes, Sergeant," they chorused.

"Thirty-*three* minutes now."

The team bounced up chaotically from the table, and Saito stood aside to let them exit.

Three hours later, the long-hulled FTL shuttle was halfway from the *Maelstrom* to the closest safe jump point. With limited accommodations on board, the troopers had been billeted in two cabins, with Saito and his corporal sharing a third which doubled as Saito's operations office. He sat at the narrow work-station, flicking through his team's files again as he tried to anticipate performance problems and interpersonal conflicts. But all he accomplished was a fresh appreciation for how depleted the Proselyti battalion had become—they were down to the numbers of a mere platoon. With the recent loss of Lt. Jabari Mbaye and his small fireteam, Proselyti numbers had fallen to just twenty-one.

Eight of those had joined Saito for this mission.

All were Terran normal, meaning they conformed to the natural range of evolved human builds and physiognomies rather than any of the corpiformed ones prevalent throughout

Martianist-derived settlements. No elephantine ear flaps, no neck gills. No massively outsized musculature like the Corfid Caiu's. Half of Saito's team were naturally bulky based on their heredity and further developed with weight training: Privates Mwana, Dola, and Temuz, along with Corporal Kirdy. The other half remained as wiry as the racing hounds Saito's parents had bred and trained: Privates Ashima, Naomi, and Pytor, plus Auxiliary Private Wegley.

None were specialists. Among the Proselyti remnant, one specialist combat engineer and one coder remained in stasis. They'd lost another specialist coder named Shila "Shill" Teuku in the recent Optio Scipio debacle. All other specialists had fallen to the previous centuries of attrition.

It's a simple mission, he told himself. *If the rumors about quaestors are right, young Aurelia is five specialists rolled into one.*

Without notice, the cabin door whisked aside, allowing Corporal Kirdy to stomp through with a trooper in tow. Kirdy went straight to the bunks and sat on the edge of Saito's.

This left the newcomer, Private Wegley, shifting from foot to foot in the doorway. "I don't understand what I'm here for," he said.

"Makes two of us," grumbled Kirdy.

As was custom when there were no Martianist officers present, the Proselyti fell back into speaking the *lingua franca* of their era's Earth-derived colonies: Terran True.

"You're both here for a deeper briefing," Saito said and pointed to the touchpad on the bulkhead. "Close the door."

Wegley stepped in and tapped the pad, closing the door. Then he met Kirdy's stare for a moment before saying, "Why am I here for the 'deeper briefing?' I don't get it."

"No," Saito said, yawning and stretching in his chair. "You don't 'get' much. You're a lazy thinker, Wegley. Also inexperienced, socially inept, and angry at the universe. Not good soldiering material on the first or even tenth inspection. But you and I share something in common, so I'm tossing you a break."

"What in common? What break?"

"Neither of us started as infantry. Or *any* kind of fighting man. I came up through the Cala Officers Academy; you were recruited from the general populace as the Kaana's forces waged their war. You went into transport logistics; I went into armament logistics."

With a guarded look, Wegley said, "I heard you got busted down to private for striking an officer?"

"That's true."

"Was it worth it?"

The question took Saito slightly by surprise. He said, honestly, "No. And yes."

"Why yes?"

"Yes, because I learned to be a soldier. A real one. I learned I had it in me."

Wegley looked like he was resisting an eye roll. He asked, "And why no, Sergeant?"

"No, because there's *never* any point in resisting those in power above you. That's the lesson our forces learned in the war. You may *hurt* those who're in charge; you'll never *beat* them. And you only..." He hesitated, thinking of the wife who'd left him in the months before the war, the daughters he'd never seen again, women lost to the deep shadows of time. "You hurt the ones you care about."

"Doubt there's anyone he cares about," Kirdy grumped. "All I'm seein' is a selfish, whining dangle fish turd."

Wegley flashed him a filthy look, but Saito's next words snatched back his attention.

"Whether the corporal and the others like it or not, Private, you're one of the last Elite Guards and one of the last Specialist Proselyte Battalion. And the way the empire has treated you, you'll probably outlive us all."

"There's a happy thought," murmured Kirdy. "Him, the very last of us."

Wegley began staring daggers at him again.

"Well, I'm happy to see that spark in your eyes, Wegley, that fire," Saito said. "Let's see if we can find a way for you to outperform us as well as outlive us. Since our last officer was recently KIA, it falls to little old NCO me to turn you into a soldier you can be proud of."

Kirdy clapped his hands and laughed. When Saito shot him a hard stare, he swallowed and added, "Sergeant."

Saito hit the command on his workstation that generated a holo-diagram in the middle of the cabin, an exterior image of a three-story villa.

"The next step in your professional development, Private, will be you explaining the fine and gritty details of our job to the other troopers. This will force them to listen to you and force you to communicate clearly and carefully, as if their lives depend on it. Because they do."

Kirdy grunted in reluctant approval, obviously seeing where Saito was going with this. "Gunsō, here, is a smart sergeant, Squeak, and a damn nice one. This might get 'em to accept you more, you showing 'em you can remember details and explain them well."

"The living shit," Wegley swore in complaint, looking at his feet.

"You up for this, Private?" Saito asked, standing. "Because you'd better be. You're the only one among your peers who's going to hear and see this."

Wegley swallowed and raised his chin and his stare. With a little nod, he answered, "Yes, Sergeant."

"Call me Gunsō, kid. Keeps me in touch with my ethnic roots, and you can mention that to the others who've never worked with me before." Saito stepped to the holo-diagram. It reached as high as his hip, and he held one hand above the rooftop. "Our destination is a barely populated and arid world called Vadox CX. It has a longer than standard day-night cycle. At the latitude we're visiting, local daylight is 20.8 hours followed by 9.3 hours of darkness. We are slated to land late in the local morning, so there'll be plenty of daylight left for us. Local conditions are good to know, but we won't need to be concerned about light, trust me. This is an in-and-out, snatch-grab, piss-off-quick mission. With me so far?"

"Arid world. Barely populated. Arriving late morning while there's plenty of daylight, and getting the sack outa there quickly."

"Good. Now. The shuttle will park in orbit, and we'll take the attached dropskiff down to the ground. It'll be disguised as a caterer's vessel on scans, bringing in special delicacies to a party Governor Ectorius is having at his wife's luxury villa. The villa is built along the ridge line that tops the east-facing slope of a low mountain. This mountain's on the very edge of a large *range* of mountains, and it's called—wait for it—the Hill. The whole city running down that slope is called the Hill, actually."

Wegley snorted but said nothing, listening intently.

"Gets better," Saito continued. "They call the ridge line where the villa is The Summit. The richest property owners have their homes across the east face of The Summit and then west of it on a plateau with an artificial lake in the middle. The lower down the eastern face of the Hill you go, the less affluent the homes and businesses are."

He made a gesture the holo control interpreted correctly, pulling back the zoom level to reveal more of the city across that eastern slope.

He pointed. "This down here is a ring wall—though that's a dumb name when it just runs in an arc across the hillside. It marks the edge of the official city where the affluent and respectable folks live and conduct their business. You'll notice it's pretty tall, pretty thick. There's a couple of pedestrian and military entrances across it, but only one main throughway where the local highway heads out of town. Take a guess what they call this wall."

"Uh, The Wall?" Wegley asked.

"Kid's quick on the uptake," Saito told Kirdy who just rolled his eyes. To Wegley, he said, "When you run through this with the others, I'll provide you with still images of the landscape outside The Wall, but we're not actually going anywhere near it. Everything we do and see will be in the villa."

Wegley stirred. "This is for due diligence, knowing stuff about the landscape as a contingency."

Wanting to encourage the kid, Saito said, "Good words there, Wegley; you're doing well. Outside the city, the mountain drops into lumpy foothills before everything becomes a vast desert plain they call The Panlands. Only thing out there is mining and lots of it. The foothills hold ruins from earlier versions of the city and poorer people have built rough favelas around those. As I said before, the area is arid. The planet is arid. Water was scarce on this world, even after terraforming. They ship a lot of it in, but the rich along the higher parts of the Hill get natural water from mountain springs and seasonal snow melt higher back on the ranges. Which… brings us back to The Summit."

He gestured, and the zoom shot in, quickly replacing the Hill and its crowning ridge line with the villa they'd be raiding.

"Governor Ectorius' wife's villa. We'll set down on this rooftop. Because there's a small population, it was only given a garrison of eight hundred troops, and that includes infrastructure and support personnel. Governors are allowed to bolster their security with mercenaries or private security using their own purses, so we're aware there's at least a hundred more men, but they've apparently been integrated into the garrison and have to follow its procedures, which include eating. There'll only be minimal troopers on duty around the city because they all eat from the same trough… and that trough's going to give them food poisoning."

Wegley and Kirdy gasped in surprise and chorused, "The living shit!" Then Wegley ventured a sassy smile, adding, "Literally!"

Saito allowed himself a grim smile. "Exactly. Anyone fit for duty won't be up at the top end of town. Their main security concerns will be maintaining the integrity of their outer wall against the poor plebs in the favelas. There'll also be a minor terrorist incident on the far side of the planet."

"Sack me, this quaestor's gone all out on this mission," muttered Kirdy.

"Or her bosses have. Back to the governor's soiree. It's scheduled for the afternoon of the day we insert. His guests will have landed, or more likely be in orbit, but there's hours between when we arrive on site and they do. Only expecting a handful of staff plus the governor."

"Bastard's not gonna wander around without *some* kind of escort," Kirdy said.

"He'll have two or three or four, sure. We'll neutralize them."

"As in…" Wegley mimed sleeping by putting his hands together and leaning his head on them. "Or…?" He drew a finger across his throat.

"Dead," said Saito. "Anyone who's not Ectorius or his wife doesn't survive the encounter."

"Burying a few Imp Regulars is fine with me," said Kirdy with a shrug. "Bastards always call us roaches, no matter what sackin' century we wake up in."

"How do we know about this party he's having?" Wegley asked. "I mean, how does the quaestor know about it?"

"Good question, Private. The briefing files say one invited guest turned down the invitation but passed the news up-line to the emperor. Some woman who's sick of Ectorius making overtures to her."

"Overtures? What's that?"

"Trying to get her into bed."

"Oh. Right."

"She also reported him for things he said that indicate he's planning to pull his planet out of the Imperium."

"What?" Kirdy snorted.

"What a sackhead," Wegley agreed.

Saito grunted. "That was one of the big pieces of evidence in the case against him."

Kirdy rose from the bunk and came to stand over the holo. "We're landing the dropskiff on that roof?"

"Yes."

"How big is it?"

"The roof? Or the skiff?"

"Roof."

"Forty meters by fifteen."

Kirdy whistled. "That's the wife's *personal* villa?"

"Her home away from her other home that's twice the size and just three kims away. This Governor's being judged for corruption, along with the rebellion thing."

"They're all corrupt," Wegley murmured with a shrug.

The NCOs ignored him. Saito added, "Roof's rated for shuttle landings. It's how the other guests will come and go."

"Let's hope it's clear when we arrive," said Kirdy.

"That's already arranged with the fake catering company we're pretending to be. The time is booked, and the governor expects punctuality."

"He'll be getting more than punctuality," the corporal replied. He caught Wegley's eye. "All right, this is where you ask another question, squeak."

The private thought about it a second, then asked, "We

land. We run downstairs and nab this governor. Then we bounce?"

"That's a summary, sure. I've loaded the villa's schematics on the ship's data boards; you can share those with the others when you gather them in the galley for your briefing. We'll set down and secure the roof in standard fashion, and the quaestor will go in on the forward edge of our unit."

Kirdy gave him a sidelong look. "We're not clearing her path?"

"She wants to be the first to see the look in Ectorius' eyes, I guess. Two troopers will follow at her shoulder. Wegley, I'll let you decide who. The rest of us will secure the building as she arrests the governor—and the wife, if she's around."

Eyes on the holo, Wegley said, "And anyone who's not them dies."

"I'm no happier about that than you, but it's the security of the empire we're serving. Billions of people versus a half dozen at most."

Wegley still looked unhappy.

"Cough it up, Private," Saito sighed. "What's on your mind?"

"You don't wanna know," he mumbled.

"Well, *now* we do," Kirdy growled.

Wegley sighed. "It's not the civilian deaths. Sergeant, I mean Gunsō, I don't like this. Any of this. The Imperium gave me an eye and better feet. That's great. I'm happy about that. But this is the third live fire mission they've sent me on. The first two were stupid. This one is stupid. Why should I throw my life away doing dumbass assignments and risk everything for it?"

"'Cause you're told to!" Kirdy snapped at him.

Saito lifted a hand to quell Kirdy's temper. "Just when I thought you were coming aboard, Wegley, out comes that entitlement, that angry young man routine that has *not* ingratiated you to others in our battalion. Get something through your skull. Life is shit. It's been shit for 99% of the human species for

99% of our history. And you and I and Kirdy, we're at the luckier end of that spectrum. We get to live without being sexually abused or beaten or sent down tin mines."

"Yeah, but we're slaves. It's all we are."

"Well, of course we are. But we're slaves who eat, who keep their birthnames, who have healthcare and decent clothing and jobs that, at least, aren't boring. And sure, we sleep whole decades and centuries. And no, I have very little love for the latest imperial buttocks warming the throne." It was a risky thing to say in a ship with Corfids, but he hoped his next statement would balance it out. "But I had *no* love at all for Kaana Adjira. She squandered the future of all the Terranist worlds, rendered all our settlements across Sol System uninhabitable, got billions of us killed, and lowered the general standard of living across the entire galaxy. She condemned millions, across many generations, to real slavery in the wild regions outside the Imperium. We have made the best of a bad situation. It was *our* leaders and *our* Kaana who messed up the galaxy, so it's our karma to keep fixing it."

Wegley looked suitably cowed by the force of Saito's argument.

Kirdy reached across to a shelf where a bowl of grapes sat, and plucked one. Needing to put his own stamp on Saito's message, he said, "Wegley, I heard a few people over the years call our job 'hell.' But if this is hell—" he popped the grape and squished it between his molars "—it ain't as bad as I expected."

Saito took a step closer to the private and softened his tone. "You have a task I've given you. Go do it."

Wegley left without another sound.

Once the door had sealed again, Kirdy leaned toward the trasher and spat out the grape pulp. "Sackin' hells! Was that smart, Saito? Letting that idiot explain it to the others?"

"It's worth a try, and let's face it, he *doesn't* hold their lives in his hands. The job will be easy. They'll have you and me watching over them. It's one three-level house. Light resistance expected, if that. *Plus*, we're all working for a quaestor. They often come augmented—which'll be interesting to observe if she needs to kick those augments into action."

"All right, all right," Kirdy said, climbing onto his bunk. "You're the boss. As long as I get to take down a politician, I'm happy."

Knowing how rare his fellow Proselyti were becoming, Saito thought, *As long as it's as easy as I've made it sound,* I'll *be happy.*

CHAPTER THREE

CONTACT

AURELIA PREFERRED to experience atmospheric entry while seated up alongside a pilot, especially in a vehicle like her drop-skiff. In the cockpit, the inertial dampening and grav-stabilizers didn't kick in the way they did in her shuttle's cabins, comfort station, and passageway. Even this borrowed military skiff's troop compartment had the tech to get troops on the ground in the best shape for immediate action. None of that for those in the cockpit. She found the resulting turbulence and rough treatment a welcome reprieve from the cosseted lives enjoyed by affluent imperial citizens. It was a reminder that space and air travel were hazardous pursuits, with real risks and real costs. Carrying out a quaestor's duties was exactly the same: from the outside, they appeared to be accomplished routinely and without challenge, but the reality was that those duties came with clear risks... and *always* cost someone some*thing*.

Ten minutes after the initial bumps of atmospheric entry, Aurelia watched as the long and winding mountain range that split the planet's Pangaean continent grew larger ahead. The dropskiff approached it from the east, zooming across a baked desert hardpan that stretched for thousands of kilometers across that side of the continent. At first, the only signs of human presence were the plumes of smoke and dust rising from a thousand mines across the Panlands Desert, and—as her pilot slowed their approach—the specks of two long, airborne load lifters slipping sluggishly between those plumes. Then came the stain of human construction across the skirts and face of a section of mountain, Ectorius' 'Hill' city, and the favelas below it—rusty tans and sickly greens and grays against the mountain's natural deep brown. It was as if an old scab had formed across the Hill's eastern slope and dried from the bottom up.

Which is exactly what it is, Aurelia thought. *The scab that's left after failed community upon failed community have dried out and died off.*

Beside her in the narrow cockpit, Febian gibbered codes and confirmations into his ear-mounted mic, letting the planetary flight control center know this was the catering transport the Governor's staff were expecting. Aurelia heard the clearance confirmation as static-peppered chatter coming from Febian's earpiece.

They were high over the lower echelons of the cityscape where tatty ghettos covered the final knobs and bumps of the foothills before the desert gave way to the mountain. No other air traffic was visible. Via the small down-view window set into the deck beneath her feet, she watched as they approached the city's Wall—yet another feature Ectorius' preceding governors had labeled with a capital letter. The shuttle had shed enough speed that Aurelia caught sight of a gaggle of would-be migrants pressed against the stone and eternicrete footings, seeking work or asylum.

"Poor wretches," she said softly, feeling a pang of compassion and drawing a startled glare from Febian. Corfids were not known for *their* compassion. Her tone cooled as she explained, "That's not the life our merciful Emperor Nero wants for *any* of his subjects. He told me as much the last time I had an audience with him." She stressed this last part, reminding him that —although he was devoted to the emperor—her position placed her closer to the great man than a mere pilot could aspire to.

Febian focused on his task and did not respond.

They passed over the city boundary, and the shuttle banked to port across a wide thoroughfare ribboning its way down the Hill toward the Wall. Six lanes of slow-moving vehicles eased up and down it. Many of them were multi-trailered transports twice the width of the passenger cars, with entire lanes devoted to them. Aurelia knew these transports were ore-carrying road trains, automated with low-level AIs as drivers, headed in from or out to the Panlands. Those inbound would follow the highway as it passed through the mountain and under the plateau beyond, eventually reemerging in a valley two hundred kilometers west. From there, other transports would transfer the ore to refineries in the far west of the continent or off world.

"There," Febian announced in his emotionless baritone.

He gestured at his helm, and a reticle appeared on the forward window, singling out a distant building positioned just below the apex of the Hill. The villa. Its longer sides faced east and west, downslope and upslope respectively. Other homes were spaced along the hillside in line with it. Below them, a barrier of artificial pine forest—artificial because of the planet's water scarcity—kept them sequestered from less expensive properties.

The skiff's nose swung down and across, bringing the reticle and the villa to the middle of the window. "Keep the thrusters idling while we're down," she told him as she rose and eased her way to the back of the cockpit.

"Of course, Madam Quaestor."

Anticipating the debarking, Proselyti troopers had already risen from their benches and were standing in a double line along the troop cabin, each with a hand on the ceiling rail. Although many of them were tall, and some were broad and heavily muscled, her adjutant Caiu who stood at the very back was the most imposing. Her adjutant had clad himself in easy-fitting green and gray tactical clothing bearing pouches that bulged with supplies, making him look like some kind of pack animal, like the corpiformed gorillas she'd once watched working on Artemis XII. The Proselyti, by contrast, were lightly armed and armored. Their small arms consisted entirely of Glaxon Mk3 pulse rifles, adjustable for stunning or for lethal force. Aurelia didn't expect any stunning unless it was of Ectorius or his wife. None bore sidearms—an oversight, perhaps, by the *Maelstrom* commanders who'd armed this team or some form of passive-aggressive undermining of the way she'd commandeered nine of their soldiers. But Aurelia could see the handles of the knives and batons that were their backup weapons. The lightweight vests they wore over their light tan fatigues were made to 'resist' ballistic and energy fire. No matter about the lighter form of armor or the missing sidearms; Aurelia didn't seriously expect more than the most meager opposition. The Proselyti vests and belts bulged with pouches of extra rifle charge packs and the individually chosen contingency materials Saito had given them permission to carry. None had grenades; grenades were expressly forbidden by her orders.

Aurelia glanced down at her simple one-piece jumpsuit—black, and its only adornment was a narrow belt holding her sidearm. With her orgments, it was unlikely she'd need anything else, and if she did, her insertion team would provide it.

From the middle of the group, Sgt. Saito caught her eye and nodded politely. Her side of the uncarpeted patch of deck between her and the closest Proselyti would soon drop away, forming a ramp for the team to debark. Saito said nothing, and

Aurelia said nothing, for there was nothing to be said. They'd made their plan, she trusted the team knew their jobs, and most of what would transpire rested on her shoulders.

Abruptly, the deck tilted several degrees to starboard, and the shuttle lurched, as power rerouted from gravity and dampeners into the braking and landing thrusters. Then the deck righted itself before, a moment later, a double clank-and-thump announced they were down. The egress ramp unsealed with a hiss then whined and shuddered its way down, hinging on the troopers' side. Bright daylight seeped in.

Again, no words were uttered as the first four in the team surged down the ramp. Aurelia half-smiled in approval at their professionalism and confidence. These four—two males, two females—would secure the stairwell exit housing at the far end of the roof and any staff who might appear through it. The hospitality staff had arranged with Aurelia's fake catering company to have two people waiting to assist them with a quick transfer of the provisions. Now that she thought about it, the glimpse she'd caught of the rooftop hadn't shown *any* personnel waiting. They were late or arrogant enough to make the off-worlders wait.

Well, she thought as she jumped halfway down the ramp and turned to face the roof, *their lateness just bought the poor things a few more moments of existence.*

Aurelia's graceful, long-legged gait brought her out under the skiff's nose and onto the eternicrete surface of the rooftop, and she focused on the stairwell exit ahead. The remaining team members followed at her heels. The sky and the air had a sand-colored quality to them. It was cool enough up above the desert. She tasted the tang of pollution on her tongue. To her side and past the roof's eastern edge, the view stretched out over the smog haze of the city toward the distant Panlands, which were a mere smudge of yellow-tan. She had no time to utilize the zoom and resolution-enhancement abilities of her left eye; she wasn't there to sightsee. It was late morning, which put the local sun high above the pollution haze and off to one side because of their latitude. Halfway to the stairwell exit stood one service droid. Still no hospitality staff. Two troopers stopped by the droid to deactivate it; the others continued toward the structure projecting up through the roof which protected the stairs from the elements. The door remained closed, and the first alarm went off in Aurelia's gut, causing her to slow to a halt as she came alongside the droid. *Was* this a simple power play by the local servants, or was something wrong? She felt and heard the rattle and skid of the insertion team behind her battling to halt without slamming into her or each other.

Ahead, the first two troopers reached the stairwell housing, and the door burst open in front of them, causing them to drop to one knee with weapons up. Two people lunged into the sunlight, a man with deep black skin and a paler woman with black hair tied back and some kind of maintenance droid on her shoulder. The pair wore dark brown maintenance coveralls, but both had the bearing of highly exercised, well-trained people. Their shoulders were back and their legs braced, and they'd stepped out to either side of the door as if preparing to clear the rooftop.

More rattling and grunting came from the troopers by the droid and the ones behind her, more weapons snapping into position. Aurelia signaled she was about to move to avoid friendly fire from those behind, then edged that direction, out of their way, in the direction opposite the view of the cityslope.

The man who'd exited the stairwell shouted a short message, and the translator clipped to her ear lagged only a second behind as it interpreted. Belatedly, she realized he'd spoken in the Proselyti private language, Terran True.

He called out, "Sgt. Saito Shimada! Do you remember me?"

From behind her, Saito made a startled noise, not something she expected of him. He called back, "*Lieutenant? Lieu-tenant Jabari?* What in the hells?"

Jabari? The Jabari who'd vanished with Scipio's rogue mission? For a moment, Aurelia found her jaw hanging open. *Now this is curious.*

Jabari had one hand raised while the other clutched a long, rectangular shape—a device she didn't recognize—to his side, non-threateningly. One Proselyti near the droid shouted for him to drop it, but others appeared to recognize either Jabari or the woman with him and lowered their weapons.

Shifting to Imperial True, Jabari called, "We need to get into your ship and get off this rooftop, now!"

Aurelia continued slipping to the side, the alarm in her gut turning into a red-hot warning. Whatever was afoot here, she was in no way disposed toward following this stranger's orders.

Saito had recovered, and he hadn't lowered *his* weapon. Straightening, he responded to Jabari with a sharp, "Why?"

The woman with Jabari used both her empty hands to point out over the city. "*That's* why."

A deep thrumming shook Aurelia's bones even before the sound registered in her ears and a moment before the two *Charon* gunships rose into view from the cityslope side, fifty meters out with their noses and weapons nacelles angled menacingly toward the rooftop.

Troopers swore. Two broke rank and stumbled back toward the shuttle. When one of the gunships fired a missile, Aurelia was already sprinting, except she was making for the opposite edge of the roof. There came multiple shouts of "Down!" or "Drop!" and then the quaestor was vaulting over the safety wall at the roof's edge and into the empty space beyond it.

The missile impacted above her, the explosion limited enough to indicate the strike had been confined, surgical.

For a moment, Aurelia's feet speared toward the rocky ground three stories below, before she twisted in midair to face the building, and her machine arm latched onto a rough eterni-crete sill. She'd caught the edge of a window on the top floor, and her feet swung in to find purchase on the lumpy facia below it. A cool wind from across the summit snatched at her, but she held firm with her mechanical hand. She had a choice: draw her razorslinger from its side holster and shatter the window for easier access or continue dropping to the ground one windowsill and one level at a time.

Sounds flowed down along the wall from above: a five-second patter of distant weapons-fire, the violent thudding of impacts into the roof's surface, then people shouting in distress when the weapons fire ceased. Somewhere off to the rear of the building, creaking and crunching sounds announced a structural collapse of some kind. No doubt, it was the damaged skiff sinking through the damaged roof, and vibrations in her window, her sill, and her patch of wall seemed to confirm this.

This precise and deadly response to Aurelia's team's presence had come far too quickly to be a routine reaction to a security breach. Three things were obvious: her skiff was out of commission; the local garrison had been fully prepared for her arrival and waited in ambush; and the lieutenant she'd executed hadn't been Ectorius' only spy aboard the *Maelstrom*.

She ground her teeth. The Proselyti were on their own now, along with her Corfids, if any were even alive up there. None of this changed her mission. Betrayed or not, stranded alone or not, Aurelia Cossea still had a verdict to serve.

There was more clamor and chaos on the rooftop above her, but Aurelia ignored it. Below her spread a rocky garden of sorts, paving the ground between the villa and its rear security fence. Beyond that, an asphalt recreational track stretched both ways before arcing back within the artificial pine forest that crowded the rest of the hill toward its summit. Aurelia's machine eye identified a blemish in the track, a plastoid square disguised as asphalt and set into the center of the pathway. It would cap and hide an access pit down into the secret tunnels she knew had been laid within the mountain. Those tunnels would be her next destination.

Ectorius wasn't in this building, but he'd be somewhere nearby, watching the mayhem unfold, and Aurelia was more committed to judging him than ever before.

Her machine arm released its hold, letting her drop to the next window down, and then into the yard, where she broke her fall with a roll and came up running for the rear fence.

CHAPTER FOUR

ROOFTOP

HE WAS down on his forearms and thighs. Dust in his mouth and grit on his cheek.

Mere seconds had passed since one *Charon* launched its surgical rocket. Saito's face was turned away from where the gunships hovered, jaw clenched in anticipation. The missile impacted the same moment he witnessed the quaestor vault over the meter-high safety wall. She vanished, falling toward certain death, and that was the last time Saito was to think of her for a couple of minutes...

Small as the rocket and its payload had been, the nearby explosion was ear-hammering. The eternicrete shook with it. In the immediate aftermath, Saito turned his face toward the dropskiff and saw its rear end coming down hard after being lifted and knocked sideways by the blast. Even from his low angle, Saito could guess what would happen next. The skiff had been the target, and the explosion underneath it had damaged the building's roof enough that the weight of the skiff's body would compromise it further. Sure enough, the surface area around the back of the vehicle gave way. The wounded vessel began to slide down into the floor below.

He had no time to react. One of the *Charon* gunships' spitters opened up in a brief, scathing volley that blew chunks from the city-facing safety wall all around the rooftop. A fragment pinged off the right shoulder of his vest. The man in front of him—Mwana—had been intact one moment and was a shredded corpse the next. Saito awaited his own demise with a calm, fatalistic impotence.

But then the strafing stopped.

A flash came from where the gunships hovered. Through a gap in the dust and damaged edge wall, Saito could see one *Charon* reeling backward, tail down and head up like a hooked fish straining against the line. The next moment, it was gone, dropping from sight toward the city. On instinct, Saito pushed up on his forearms and craned his neck. While everyone else was on the ground—dead or hoping not to be—Jabari stood tall by the stairwell housing. He held a long plastanium object in both hands, aimed at the gunships and, apparently, pouring an invisible stream of excited particles at them.

Uncaring about his safety and still gripped by fatalistic calm, Saito pushed up onto his knees in time to see the surviving *Charon* attempt to pivot toward Jabari. Its pilot managed a brief volley of spitter rounds that sheered the top off the stairwell housing above Jabari's head, sending debris spattering across the rooftop and over its edge. Then the gunship veered away with its nose up and tail dragging until it spiraled from view. Through dulled hearing, Saito heard the early alarms raised by the first gunship's crash into the city. There was no smoke yet, but that would come if he stayed there waiting for it.

"Sack that," he grunted, pushing up onto his feet.

He threw his gaze around the rooftop, assessing the situation. Jabari had begun calling troopers into the opened-up stairwell, calling *Saito's* troopers. Kirdy and Ashima disappeared into it since they'd been closest when Jabari and his female friend appeared. The woman had vanished ahead of them.

Pytor and Temuz were also obeying Jabari's orders, but stumbling toward him, half-dazed.

Seated on his ass, Wegley was *fully* dazed and potentially wounded.

Back toward the skiff—whose ass end smoked where the missile had destroyed the drive housing—Decanus Caiu was coiled in a crouch, staring around him like a dog ready to kill the next person who came near it.

Private Dola was a bloody mess, pulverized by shrapnel or spitter rounds. Not far from her, Private Naomi sat up and stared at the ragged stump where her left arm ended just above the elbow. A freshet of blood squirted from a severed artery.

Shit!

"Caiu!" Saito shouted. When the Corfid didn't respond, Saito raised his pulse rifle and put a round into the eternicrete beside the man. Caiu turned his head. Saito pointed to Naomi. "Get a slap dressing on her! *Now!*"

Wegley started crawling Jabari's way.

Saito barked, "Private Wegley, get over here."

Saito's medical kit was spread throughout the three vest pouches closest to his belt. From one of them, he withdrew a thumb-sized injector. Wegley had paused with both knees and one hand down, the other hand raised for the next step.

Saito increased his volume. "Get *up!* Get *here!*"

Shakily, Wegley complied, swaying on his feet. He didn't seem wounded, so Saito tossed the injector to him. It hit Wegley's vest squarely, but the young man fumbled the catch and had to bend over for it. By the time he was upright again and staring at the object in his hand, Caiu had the dressing adhered over Naomi's stump. He began lifting her in his long thick arms.

Saito waved at Wegley and pointed toward them. "Injector

has battlefield nans. Get them into her triceps before you leave this rooftop." He jogged over to Jabari who consulted a palm-sized datapad he'd produced from his coverall pockets. "Lieutenant, you were reported dead."

Jabari's eyes didn't leave his screen. "Glad to hear it. Shill and two of your people are clearing the stairwell all the way to the basement."

"*Shila Teuku?*"

Jabari raised his head but ignored the question. "We need to follow them. Garrison troops are converging on this site." He pointed the tab over the side toward the downslope.

Saito glanced at the particle weapon dangling from Jabari's other hand and realized it wasn't technically a weapon—

That's a mining borer!

He shook off all the different questions knocking around his brain. *How are you here and why? How'd you know they'd ambush us? Couldn't you have warned us when we were in orbit? Why're you armed with a borer tool?*

Instead, he checked on the other three team members still on the roof and noted with satisfaction that Caiu was lumbering his way with Naomi in his arms and Wegley stumbling after.

Remembering, Saito glanced toward the upslope edge of the roof. "Damn it. The quaestor."

Jabari grunted. "Is probably not splattered on the ground, knowing the augments Shill found out she has."

Saito scanned the skies, fully expecting more *Charons*. There'd been nothing about them in the files, but surely Ectorius wouldn't spring for more. Not in a place like this. Not when he was saving his billions for when he'd need star navy vessels. Drones might be another matter...

"Shill Teuku is a data-scrier, right?" He had met her before, though he had not spoken much with her. And she, like Jabari, was presumed dead already.

"She's been called that," Jabari confirmed and put the palm pad away. "Damn good one, too."

He stepped back for Caiu to pass, then he and Saito followed Wegley into the stairwell. The chatter of weapons fire came from the flights below them. Brief. Staccato. Accompanied by a succession of shouts. One of the words was "*Clear!*"

Jabari hefted the borer with both hands, then dogged Wegley's heels, leaving Saito to periodically lean his rifle over the railing and watch for hazards and hostiles as they descended.

Picking up the conversation, the apparently resurrected lieutenant told him, "If she wasn't such a good coder and hacker, we wouldn't have found out about this ambush and beat you here." The implied message being, *we just saved your asses.*

Not one to enjoy being in debt, Saito mumbled a grudging, "Appreciate it." But there was still the question of why the lieutenant hadn't simply gotten in touch with the Army, passed a warning up through channels, and headed this off completely. And where the hell had he and Private Shila had been?

Naomi moaned loudly as Caiu leaped over the three steps to the next landing. Saito was ready to reprimand him when more shouting came from below, followed by a *krrk* of static on comms. Although they'd agreed on a comms blackout to avoid being compromised—and recorded—by locals, Kirdy must have figured all restrictions were off. It was his voice coming to life in Saito's ear.

"*Three in advance, through to basement, accessing drop pit down to underground tunnel network.*"

"Check it, but hold there," Saito told him, then cursed. "The living shit. We're fighting Regs. The Garrison sent those *Charon*s at us..."

Jabari nodded tersely at him from the steps below. "They're loyal. He pays them bonuses."

Saito wasn't sure if Jabari had heard Kirdy's voice spilling out of his earpiece, so he told him, "Your Shill's probably with my corporal accessing the mountain tunnel network."

He received a sharp look from Jabari this time. "Tell them no!"

"Oh, gods," Saito hissed, understanding registering. He tapped comms. "Kirdy, do *not* enter that pit. Hold position there. The Garrison's alerted and hostile. Someone check the ground floor for an egress path." They'd have to source a ground vehicle or beat a fighting retreat down into the warren of buildings lower on the Hill.

Only static answered his message. Someone in the local garrison had found and jammed their frequency. And they'd been fast.

"*Piss* in my *pockets!*" he swore. If they used comms again, it would be tracked.

He leaned over the railing and could make out Temuz and Pytor in the foyer below, hesitating by a door, probably the one to the basement. There'd be *another* door off that foyer, the one to the luxury house's ground floor. He hollered, "Stay on ground level! Pytor, get Kirdy out of that basement and guard the pit against hostiles from beneath. Temuz, start clearing a path through the ground level."

"And tell Shill to find us some options!" Jabari added over his shoulder.

CHAPTER FIVE

BENEATH THE SUMMIT

Contact + One Minute

THE MOST DIRECT way through the villa's rear fence was for Aurelia to pull down a support pole with her machine arm. Once she'd done that, she skipped across the collapsed sections and onto the recreation track. With a mere ten meters between her and the access cover, she realized her folly...

Figures moved between the artificial trees across the track, bunching in positions near each other. Garrison uniform colors. Ectorius' turncoats. Meaning the food poisoning gambit hadn't affected everyone—or, as far as she knew, *any*one. That was something she should have understood with the appearance of the gunships.

In too many cases, Aurelia had been unopposed, untested. Some sloppiness had crept in.

But with this extra and immediate danger, Aurelia's senses and abilities *ignited*.

Instinct made her dive and roll in the direction of the access cover. In the two seconds she was in motion, several *somethings* sailed past and over her. Probably darts or stunner pellets, she decided when a tangle net struck the paving behind her and sprang open to capture nothing but air. They wanted her alive; Ectorius planned to thwart his own abduction by abducting her.

She was up on one knee by the access plate by the time her abductors saw they'd missed. Her razorslinger had been in her left hand since she reached the fence, which kept her prosthetic arm free. The inexperienced fools wanted to bunch up, did they? Well, that gave her a more compact area to aim into. With her left hand sending a storm of tiny, accelerated razor disks their way, Aurelia's right hand punched through the veneer hiding the cover's handle. In one motion, she pulled on the handle and tore the cover from the ground. The next smattering of pellets or darts slammed into the cover as Aurelia propped it edge down on the pathway and curled her head and body behind it. She dropped onto one hip and slid into the access pit, twisting onto her belly as she went. The cover dropped over her at the last second and then *she* was dropping —six meters to the floor below. Small metal snags along the cover frame nicked and scraped holes in her bodysuit, but her orgmented skin was barely troubled by them. She compressed into a squat as she landed and found herself in a dim eternicrete corridor, flat-floored with rounded walls curving into the ceiling above her.

She had expected to meet troopers, and the group waiting below proved to be sizeable. Three stood to one side of her, maybe a dozen to the other, all of them mere meters away. The trio were focused on a narrow branch tunnel that lay to her right—one that appeared to head back underneath the villa. The *dozen* milled in two lines that faced each other. They'd been standing around, trading small talk, leaving several in such a bad position, they had to twist around to look at her— and they blocked the weapons of the others.

Holding down the handgun's trigger, she sent razor disks

carving through the trio's heads, then she turned the weapon on the others. One of the soldiers at the back got several shots off, and his kinetic rounds took out the legs of two of the forward units, toppling them toward Aurelia and clearing a path for her disks to reach the shooter and his back row pals faster. A dying front row trooper managed another wild shot, but it sailed along the corridor past her before he died. Aurelia rose from her squat with hot, sticky blood spatter on her cheek and the back of one hand and gore on her boots. Her left eye's HUD told her the razorslinger was down to its last five rounds. She dropped the mag, plucked another from her belt, and snapped it home. The counter reading changed to 40.

She spied something, stepped over to the branch tunnel, and scooped up a datapad the width of her hand that was poking out of a dead woman's thigh pouch. While jamming it into the back of her belt, Aurelia considered the long corridor that headed in the direction of the governor's mansion. Ectorius' home rose from the side of the mountain three kilometers from there and the tunnel surely passed beneath it. The floor and curving corridor wall were bare but lit from the sides every ten or so meters by glowpanels. The access hatch from the recreation path was above her, but she couldn't see any more in either direction.

Only thirty meters ahead lay the gloomy opening of another branch tunnel, which headed in the opposite direction from the one at her side. She could make it there in seconds, which would allow her a moment of shelter to reassess her safety before proceeding. As she braced to sprint, something made her glance back into the narrow shaft that led beneath the wife's villa.

Aurelia froze.

Someone moved silently in the gloom, while another person lowered themselves from an access well behind them. The one climbing down wore the boots and trousers of a Proselyti trooper. They'd moved damned fast to be down there that quick, which impressed her. The woman in front of the trooper was someone whose silhouette and clothing Aurelia didn't recognize.

"The quaestor took care of them," the stranger told the trooper in Terran True as the man dropped to the floor. The boots of another Proselyti came into view above him. The stranger took a few steps Aurelia's way, then crooked a finger at the ceiling between them. In *Imperial* True, she told Aurelia, "Above you."

Aurelia saw a miniature droid scuttling there. She didn't immediately understand what it was or what it was doing, because it wasn't military—nor did this woman appear to be. It was the maintenance bot she'd seen earlier on the woman's shoulder. The woman had also been up on the roof.

Aurelia frowned at her, and the woman said, "You're going to hate this..."

It was as if a groundcar had hit Aurelia on the right side of her body, without tossing her in the air. As if part of the universe had been snuffed out. Her left-side vision died, leaving a black nothingness. Her right arm became inert, disconnected from her brain, a dead weight suddenly dragging at the living tissue and reinforced structure of her shoulder. Aurelia faltered sideways a few steps in the direction of the governor's mansion. A commotion coming from the direction of the woman reached her ears, but she ignored it, baffled by what was happening to her. Whatever it was didn't affect her instincts or reactions when a fresh quartet of soldiers emerged from the other branch tunnel. Without conscious thought, Aurelia's legs pistoned beneath her, carrying her quickly toward them before they showed any sign of aiming their weapons.

In the first moment, Aurelia ran toward them and counted herself lucky that her biological eye was still working. In the next moment, she identified the Regulars as mere recruits and wondered why they were there. In the third moment, as they fumbled with their weapons, she decided they were young men wearing poorly strapped armor on their torsos that left their limbs and heads unprotected. But they were still a threat.

Her left hand sprayed razor disks at them, while her right flailed uselessly, slapping at the air around her.

Recruits they might be, but the soldiers took their shots when they had them—kinetic rounds, not energy ones. Aurelia felt the loss of pieces of jumpsuit, skin and hair from her scalp, and tiny chunks across her ribs and hip. The soldiers were down or falling by the time she reached them, forcing her to hurdle one, before she arrested her momentum by butting her left shoulder against the wall at the intersection and rolling around to brace her back against it. One of the men—*boys*, a part of her mind said—twitched and gasped and tried to steady his handgun. She kicked it away and ended him with a round through his forehead.

Aurelia struck her right arm with the butt of the razorslinger and felt like this *thing* attached to her wasn't real. The impact caused only distant referred vibration in the shoulder joint.

Offline! It's offline.

As was the eye, leaving part of her vision completely dark, nonexistent.

Whatever that bitch's robot had done to her, it hadn't shut down her toughened epidermis. Or her survival instincts. The nicks and bruises from their shooting would hurt later, but they were trivial. For wasteful seconds, she considered retribution against the bitch back in the other shaft, but she could hear the two Proselyti tussling with her. Let them take her down. Aurelia had a job to complete.

It occurred to her the tiny droid could be jamming her cyberbiological network. She looked for it, ready to blast it, but she couldn't see it. She decided she needed to put distance between her and it, so the limb and eye could come back online.

"Complete the job," she hissed at herself, and she thought of her sister Florene while she thumped her useless arm with the razorslinger again. "There'll be a way to fix this along the way."

She needed to change the rags hanging off her, to assess and repair the damage she'd sustained, and to find a way to get to Ectorius. An idea came to her, a possibility.

Aurelia turned into the branch tunnel the young recruits had come from and started running.

CHAPTER SIX

CHOICES

Contact + 3 Minutes

OPEN DOORS LED to Saito's left and right when he stepped into the ground floor stairwell foyer. He'd passed Caiu and Wegley one flight up. Jabari, too. Jabari had ducked into the door to the basement staircase. Saito poked his rifle out into the ground level.

Let Jabari screw around finding Shill...

The primary concern was finding a way out of this building. After that, it'd be finding a regrouping point. Once they'd achieved both, they could decide how to secure a way off Vadox CX.

Saito was staring across an open floor plan with floor-to-ceiling windows along two sides. The staircase to the roof had been fitted close to the northwest corner of the building, with an elevator beside it—one that didn't reach the rooftop, apparently. The south and east window walls overlooked a manicured lawn that sloped down toward the sprawling cityscape, with low garden beds and slabs of pretty blue and crimson stone forming a low property boundary. There was no cover in those yards, and the only cover between him and the windows was the collection of couches and chairs arranged in right-angled patterns across many square meters of floorspace. He came out, hugging the northern wall as far as the edge of the elevator housing, and double checked the blind spot where the room doglegged out of sight. Nothing there but shelf art.

Temuz had taken position at the intersection of the west and south walls, his back protected by meter-thick eternicrete, rifle aimed at the garden wall and gates that rose from the bottom of the sloping lawn area. He heard Saito, but he didn't take his eyes off the view, and he called back, "Yard clear."

Ectorius could have conceivably placed troopers on the property's rear grounds where Aurelia had dropped; but it was unlikely, given the potential for gunship destruction of the site. If there were hostiles nearby, they were in the fake pine forests downslope or well across The Summit. This was the worst kind of mission, one that left him and his people completely dependent on their senses. No drone, ship, or satellite overwatch to advise them. No back up agents monitoring enemy comms. Not even a combatdroid to send smashing through the gates or scouting around the building at high speed.

Basic tactics, then.

"Wegley, get out here."

When the young man stuck his head out, it was shaking in dismay. "These guys are gonna *hate* me. You made me tell 'em the local Garrison was outa action."

"Conditions change." Saito pointed to the joining of the home's north wall and east window wall. "That's your position now. Take it."

Grumbling, Wegley shuffled past him.

"Safe to bring her out?" Caiu called.

Saito returned to the stairwell foyer. "Not safe yet. You rated as a medic? Good. Stabilize her here. The way things are going, we'll need every arm we have. Pytor, what the hell's happening down there?" he called into the basement.

"Gunsō? Get down here!"

"Come again?"

"Troopers in the tunnel were slagged by the quaestor. And… there's more. Get down here, Gunsō, seriously."

Aurelia was in the tunnels?

"Wegley," he barked, poking his head into the living room. "Go check the other side of that front gate."

"*What!*"

"Temuz, cover him. Find out if that treeline's clear."

"Move, squeak!" Temuz shouted at Wegley, jolting the auxiliary private into action.

Saito didn't hang around to watch.

———

The basement turned out to be one-third the size of the upper floors. Shouting came from the hole in the floor where Pytor knelt, some kind of quarrel.

The trooper looked up at his approach, talking fast. "Lt. Jabari's gone down there, Gunsō. Kirdy's arguing with 'em both. Kirdy and Ashima had to restrain Shill until Jabari went down and got her calm. Kirdy said the quaestor wiped out the Regulars down there, but Shill put some kind of voodoo on *her*." He laughed, as if he'd been chewing togi leaf, which shouldn't have been available to him. "Then two Imps stuck their heads through a manhole in the roof from a parkland out back. Ashima shot one head off, and the other pulled back—but that means we got hostiles behind the villa."

The sergeant briskly shook the private by the shoulder. "*Is it clear down there?*"

"Lt. Jabari said it is."

Shit, this is a bad choice.

"Get your ass up to ground level and wait for me in the stairwell."

Pytor jogged happily up the stairs. Saito had worked with the trooper plenty of times, during the war and since. He didn't remember Pytor being this vague, this dissociated. Had the guy racked up some stasis sickness? More likely, he *had* sourced a substance he shouldn't have.

Saito stuck his head in the access hole and bared his teeth at the continuing squabbling happening just out of sight.

"Shut that shit up down there! All of you!" He didn't care if Jabari *was* a lieutenant. This was his team, his job, and the guy's arrival was a strange coincidence with things going to crap at the same time. When the arguing subsided, he said, "Tell me if we can get out that way and be damned sure about your answer."

Jabari's and Kirdy's faces both appeared beneath him, though they looked at each other more than at him. In chorus, they called up, "Clear!"

Jabari added, "Shill's disabled local AI surveillance, and she's tapping local servers to find us some fallback points."

"Ashima should be doing that," Kirdy added.

"Isn't there an open manhole in your roof?" Saito asked.

Kirdy nodded.

"Ashima watching that?"

Again, a nod.

"Then let her do that and Shill do the hacking," Saito snapped. "Where's Quaestor Cossea?"

Kirdy's face puckered in a snarl, leaving Jabari to answer.

"Ran off into the tunnels."

"Sackdammit... All right. Hold there."

Saito rocked back on his heels, thinking hard. This mission was slagged. Getting off world might mean stealing a starship from the visiting party guests—if those people had even come to Vadox, and if they were still here. He had choices. They could hit the woods out front and fight their way down the hill or across it, hoping to find a parked ship somewhere close. Or they could hope to find one by either heading out into the park Pytor had mentioned or taking the tunnels. Being in the open air, though, meant they could be attacked from 360 degrees around them plus from the air. The tunnels corralled them but simplified the threats. And so far, Jabari and Shill seemed to know their stuff...

Decision made, he launched himself off the floor and stomped over to the narrow staircase. Up on ground, Pytor's face was turned his way from the doorway there.

"Get our guys down here and into the tunnels. *Fast*."

Pytor grinned stupidly and vanished.

"Decanus Caiu?"

The big man filled the doorway above and reported, "Nanite intervention has stemmed Private Naomi's bleeding and sealed the blood vessels. She has an infusion patch, and blood pressure's improved."

"She's conscious?"

"Yes."

"Good enough. Get her down here. Wait ..." On a whim, he asked, "You have munitions?"

"Grenades. One HE, one scrambler. Plus one grapeshot mine."

None of Saito's Prosyleti had been equipped with grenades, let alone mines. They had been deemed 'inappropriate' by Aurelia and her bosses. Some dead servants were permissible, but damage a rich man's property? No way.

But trust a Corfid brute to ignore operational parameters.

He said, "Tell Pytor you're leaving the H.E. on the stairs. Last man down blows that stairway."

There was the slightest hesitation as Caiu let him know he wasn't happy being ordered about. Then, "Good idea."

That fraction of his team had their orders; now, he had to

connect with the others. Half a minute later, his boots were on the tunnel floor below. He stood in a narrow, ill-lit cul-de-sac, a kind of square side shaft. Ten steps from where he'd come down, one end was bare wall. Shill was there, busy with the data cuff she wore on her left forearm. Twenty steps the other way, the shaft met the main passageway where Kirdy and Ashima were on watch. Immediately, Saito had to shake off an impending claustrophobia, the feeling he'd just trapped himself down there. If Jabari and Shill said they had dealt with local surveillance, he'd have to trust them. It was their asses on the griddle as well as his.

"Jabari?" Saito asked Kirdy.

Kirdy nodded at the main corridor, his face flushed like a storm cloud. Saito saw a spread of bodies and gore there, plus one small maintenance bot. He joined his corporal at the junction. A corridor led in both directions, with walls that curved up and over to meet at the roof above. More than a dozen Garrison troopers had died there; no live ones were visible. Jabari was bent over near another branch corridor, searching the corpses of more dead Imperials. He still held the borer under one arm, and he didn't appear to have looted anything.

"What the sack's he looking for?"

"Said something about commlinks and unit insignia."

Saito grunted. That actually was a good idea. "How'd you get *that*?" he asked.

Kirdy had a welt across his left cheek. He took a hand from his weapon to touch the skin where it had split along the welt's ridge, then he jerked his head toward Shill. "Ask the bitch."

Without taking her eyes off her worker, she replied, "Would've done worse if *his* bitch and Jabari hadn't gotten in the way." She glanced along the shaft at Ashima. "No offense, sister."

"None taken." Ashima shrugged, without taking her focus off the tunnels.

Kirdy said, "She's angry 'cause I sacked that thing up." He pointed his stubby rifle at the small, burnt-out droid across the corridor.

Saito glanced back at the access hole he'd come down when he heard movement there. "And *why'd* you sack it up?" he asked Kirdy.

"'Cause she used it to do something to Quaestor Cossea. Knocked the lady half senseless, then *laughed* about it."

Saito could only assume that meant Aurelia had cybernetics, and Shill had disabled them. Cybernetics explained how the quaestor had survived leaping off the rooftop and getting down there so quickly. Mechanized or orgmented limbs. The new questions piling on top of the existing questions were about why Shill had attacked an imperial agent that way. Distracted by a pair of boots appearing from the access hole, he slipped beneath it to help Naomi down.

Kirdy noticed, and he swore as Naomi sagged against a wall. The woman's face was ashen, but she kept her only hand steady on the rifle Caiu had slung back over her shoulder. The sealant bandage slapped over the stump of the arm was holding well. Several red dots showed through it, but it could have been far worse than that. The job Caiu had done, and the fact Naomi was moving at all, were reasons enough to want the Corfid to stay with his team and not go chasing after the quaestor, as he suspected Caiu would.

"Any luck?" Saito asked Shill. There was no point digging into all the weird grunfershit till they were somewhere safe enough to do it.

Her response was terse. "Getting there. We'll be heading to the left from this shaft, but I'm not sure where yet. Be another minute."

"Make it half that?" he asked.

When she glanced up at him, he gave her a respectful nod,

trying to make peace. Shill accepted it with some relaxation of the tension around her eyes.

Next trooper down from the basement was Pytor. Saito instantly made him help Naomi move out into the main corridor where she could sit while Pytor and Ashima kept vigil.

He leaned out and checked the open manhole in the ceiling. "Tell me about that," he said to Kirdy.

"See that goo on the floor? Used to be the head of the idiot who poked it through. One of his buddies must've pulled the body back before it fell."

"They haven't tried anything else?"

"Nope. Might not have grenades like us."

"Yeah, city garrisons don't have much use for them. Might be waiting for combat droids, though."

At that thought, Kirdy made a face like Saito had crapped on his shoe.

Back in the side shaft, a heavy body dropped through the hole and thumped onto the eternicrete floor. Caiu.

Startled, Shill swung around. With eyes widening, she whipped out a tiny pistol. "You got *Corfids*?"

Caiu faced her but didn't draw the weapons Saito knew he was packing—a pair of thick K-70 Punch-Burner handguns.

Kirdy came around his side with *his* weapon aimed at Shill. "Drop that!"

Shill did not. "I'm not working with these slaggers."

Pytor and Naomi crouched around the corner, and Ashima was near Saito. She stared at the ruckus Shill was making. Saito clicked his fingers at her. "*Eyes on that corridor, Private!* Jabari, back here *now!*"

When Jabari joined him, he wasn't rearmed, but he was still carrying the borer. "No unit insignia among the bodies, yellow sashes only. Reservists or hired guns. Commlinks are all fried. What...?" he started to add when he caught sight of the standoff around Caiu.

Saito rested his hands on his slung rifle and eyeballed the tense knot of people. "Listen extremely closely. We've got more sacking hostiles on the ground above this tunnel, and there'll be others coming up the hill to the villa. The last of our people are about to drop into this tiny piss hole we're already in. The first Garrison Regular to add a grenade to our gathering will shred us all. I'd like to remain unshredded. So, I'm only saying this once, and you'd better listen, or it'll be me shredding you. This is my sacking team, my sacking mission, my sacking rules. Lt. Jabari and Private Shill or Shila or whatever—if you wanna be on my team, you work with us. You're not leading us. You're *not* shooting us. Decanus Caiu, *you're* on my team, right?"

"Looks that way, Sergeant."

"Right. And *you'll* follow my directions until this crisis is over—won't you, Decanus Caiu?"

The huge man simply nodded without taking his eyes off Shill.

Saito continued, "All of you have one job: work with everyone else on my team to get us off world. Can I get a 'Yes, Gunsō?'"

Kirdy and Ashima chorused the phrase; out in the corridor, Pytor did too.

Caiu said, "Of course."

Jabari said, "Agreed."

Finally, Shill returned her weapon to her coverall's pocket and grumbled something to the affirmative.

Kirdy backed off and returned to the corridor.

"Shill, you said head *left*?" Saito asked.

"Yeah."

"Caiu and Ashima, find a rally point fifty meters or so up that passage and hold it. Take Pytor and Naomi."

Ashima darted off. Caiu pushed through the small press of bodies to chase after her and finally pulled one of his enormous handguns.

"Kirdy, hold the junction where the lieutenant just was."

A pissed-off grumble came from Kirdy, but he complied immediately.

Jabari said, "Just call me Jabari, Saito, not 'the lieutenant.' I don't think I'll be drawing an imperial salary anymore."

Saito squinted at him as someone's boots emerged from the access hole. Wegley's, judging by the smaller size. He shifted to allow Wegley more space and spoke quietly to Jabari. "Sounds like you've deserted."

Jabari raised his eyebrows. "Or maybe I'm working for Cor Fidelis."

"Not the way she reacted to Caiu, you're not," Saito replied. He raised his voice and pointed toward the short corridor's end as Wegley arrived. "Take a right. Join Kirdy and watch the manhole in the roof."

Wegley swallowed and hurried away without any backtalk this time.

Saito told Jabari, "You two are a mystery I'd like to solve when we're off world in a secure vessel. Right now—and before Temuz gets down here—your sidekick better secure us a sack-damn route out of this shit mire."

"Yeah, I think I got one," said Shill.

The muffled thud of an explosion pulsed down through the access hole, interrupting her. She glanced sharply up, as did Jabari.

"Blocking the way in behind us," Saito explained. *I hope.*

Jabari nodded. "Shill?"

She led them out toward the main corridor, then angled her cuff so they could see the schematic displayed on it. "That's our level of this tunnel, and there's another level below it that we wanna stay out of. Dead ends everywhere down there. Here's us. Here's the way your grunts are heading." She shifted the map, and Saito saw a location three hundred meters along which she'd marked with a yellow circle. She added, "Lobby space for two conveyor cars."

"Conveyors? Sideways elevators?" asked Saito.

"Lateral ones, actually, but yeah. They pass through the mountain, Conveyor One at a sixty-degree down angle, Conveyor Two at seventy-five degrees. Automated, no operating personnel. Fully mechanical, no linking with anything digital. Conveyor One arrives inside the hill in a private parking garage for groundcars. There are eighteen vehicles available down there currently. Conveyor Two comes out further down at an outdoor aircar parking lot. Both conveyor cars are large enough for all of us, but they are different sizes. We could—" Her head snapped to the side as Temuz plummeted through the access hole. He came down so fast, he had to roll when he hit the floor.

"Well, this sacks royally," the brawny private muttered as he picked himself up. "There *were* Regulars in the woods out front, Gunsō. The squeak and I made twenty of 'em but might be more. They're taking it slow. Pretty sure a couple made me, too, but they didn't fire, which was weird."

"Might not have been sure who you were," Jabari said. "Ectorius doesn't exactly have the cream of the crop on Vadox."

Saito pointed left into the main corridor. "Help Ashima watch that forward area."

"Yep," Temuz said and squeezed between them.

Saito knew in which direction the governor's home lay. There was sure to be access from underneath it, but it was a distinct possibility a heavy cordon of troopers or droids guarded it above ground and below, and it was highly unlikely Ectorius was sitting up there this close to an active threat. Also, there was little chance he'd conveniently left an FTL vessel parked at home. Saito led the newcomers into the main tunnel, jogging in the direction of the conveyors and whistling for Kirdy and Wegley to follow. They'd wasted enough time...

As he moved, a new thought bugged him: where were the rest of the Regulars, the ones who should have been backing up their fallen comrades and blocking the ambushed Proselytis' escape? The partially disabled quaestor couldn't have dealt with all of them. Perhaps some *had* been struck down by the food poisoning gambit.

At his back, Shill said, "Either conveyor car is big enough to take us all in one turn. Do we want to go for groundcars or aircars?"

They were nearing the rally point taken up by the forward troopers, a parked electric buggy opposite yet another branch shaft, which he presumed ran beneath another villa on The Summit above. For the briefest of moments, Saito considered climbing into that one and risking the pine forest after all.

Sack that. We need to move away from here at speed.

"Groundcars," he told Shill.

At the same time, Jabari said, "An aircar."

Saito growled at Jabari, "My team."

"I'm trying to get your team off this planet faster."

"Splitting into multiple groundcars means not all our eggs go in one basket. An aircar exposes us: if they have skydrones or combat droids, one missile and we all die."

"Drones and droids can hit groundcars, too," Jabari replied. "An aircar gets us over the Wall faster and easier."

Saito interrupted the discussion to point at Shill and tell the troopers sheltered just ahead of him to follow her. Shill overtook the cover position at a jog, then Caiu, Temuz, and Ashima joined her.

"Pytor, you too. Naomi, rest a sec."

Pytor raced ahead and flashed Saito another grin. *Moron's drugged. Gotta be.* He always had a need for extra stimulation. That he was the only Proselyti who'd adopted a penchant for makeup spoke to that. For this mission, he'd put on black eyeliner, and he'd used henna ink to draw a black rose on one cheek. Those things were fine with Saito; drugs on-mission were not.

Behind the shelter of the buggy, Saito grabbed Jabari and turned him around. He was mindful of the fact these two interlopers had intel he didn't. They'd known about the ambush. They'd been able to remove local surveillance *and* hamstring a quaestor as if prepared for it. He demanded, "And why do we want to cross the Wall into the favelas, of all places?"

"Look, if you're thinking we grab some rich summit-dweller's FTL-yacht off their roof, forget it. Local property owners keep surface-to-orbit shuttles up there, and they've all left the area. We checked."

Saito sighed in frustration. "And they probably already slagged *our* shuttle in orbit," he growled. "Or boarded it."

"No doubt," Jabari said. "We can't use the ship Shill and I arrived in. Even if we got to where we left it, it's a gigantic piece of crap, and they'd only interdict us in orbit. Our way off world is to hide among a shadow-souk crew."

"A what?"

"Shadow-souk. What part of the dark market's called these days."

"And how—?"

"There's an old spaceport that was once privately owned then abandoned three hundred years back when rising lawless-ness forced the richer members of society to move higher up the Hill and *that* governor built the Wall to 'protect' them. Smugglers and people-traders use the port now. Ectorius' people have an uneasy relationship with the poor folk and mining companies in the favelas and Panlands. I'm not sure why your quaestor wanted him, though I can guess. He's scared spitless of the crime syndicates—his administration turns a blind eye to *them* and all those poor favela dwellers. They won't chase us out there."

As Kirdy and Wegley drew near, Saito waved Kirdy past. "Wegley, assist Naomi."

Wegley turned an offended frown toward him. "I'm not—"

"*You are!*"

Wegley let out a theatrical whine, slung his rifle, and dragged Naomi to her feet by her good arm.

Saito told Jabari, "We're here because Ectorius is building some kind of revolt from the Imperium, a breakaway. He's surely got enough forces to chase us beyond the Wall, bandits and poor folk notwithstanding."

"Then where are they?" Jabari waved a hand around the quiet tunnel. "He's poorly resourced here. We checked. He certainly has the *money* to fund a larger personal army—and navy—but he's stingy; he won't spend the currency he's hoarding."

Saito grunted. "Because he's saving it for his breakaway bid."

Jabari shook his head. "I hope, for his sake, he has powerful friends and somewhere else to base his little empire. If he bases it here—"

"The Imperial Navy will torch it from orbit. He does have powerful friends; I know that much. What else, Jabari? And make it quick."

"Half his garrison are noncompleted infantry recruits he's paid a pittance to bring here, plus reservists and conscripts from his manufacturing populations. There's also a handful of mercs whose last few battles were barfights. Despite what the asshole's planning, *right now,* he's the governor of a pisswater mining planet that was badly terraformed from the beginning. The companies out there digging up ores belong to the Chamber of Magnates—they could field a bigger army of *security* personnel than Ectorius' crop of bribed Imperial Regulars and unblooded halfwits."

Saito muttered, "I take your point." *We're facing recruits and conscripts? Unbelievable.*

"Once we're outside the main city and inside the old spaceport, we negotiate with the crime lord Lorica who occupies it. We board one of his smuggler vessels, pull a week or two's service to pay our way—or simply commandeer it—then we're clear."

"That's your intel?"

"That's my intel."

"Matches *some* of mine, but mine included nothing about what's beyond that wall besides poor people." That was an oversight on the quaestor's part—or more likely cocky self-assuredness. She hadn't expected any problems with this job.

"Shill and I spent a few stellars talking to people who'd been out there."

Saito nudged Jabari and moved them out after Wegley and Naomi while keeping an eye on the tunnel behind them. "And you came here with this intel just to save our asses and attack our quaestor, knowing you'd be stuck here with us?"

"Didn't know about the ambush until Ectorius ordered it, just an hour before you arrived." Jabari flashed a dry smile. "How about I explain everything when we're off world and on board a secure vessel?"

Saito grunted and picked up the pace. "We'll take an aircar, then, and hope we don't run into skydrones." *Never know*, he thought, *once we're airborne, I might see a better option than some dark market smuggler's hole.*

He'd just started believing they'd make it out of the tunnel unscathed when the forward troopers reached the turn off to the conveyor lobby.

And ran into heavy fire from inside.

CHAPTER SEVEN

ROJA

THE BRANCH TUNNEL had taken Aurelia deeper into the Hill, directly beneath its apex. The tunnel terminated where it connected with a broad corridor running at a right angle to it and following the direction of the mountain's ridgeline above. Aurelia remembered from the files that a left turn here would lead to a group of panic bunkers. It would also take her to a series of underground staircases and conveyors that led down the the Hill's far side to the croplands and affluent suburbs spread around the basin between the mountains and its modest lake. She wasn't convinced yet she should be fleeing to an area like that...

With her left arm holding her useless right one against her body, she came to a stop before approaching the junction. Not willing to enter the new tunnel rashly, she diverted through a doorless entry to an electrical room. Within it, a single low-wattage globe revealed the expected stateboards and switching stations. No people. A good place to take a moment.

Aurelia's breath came harder than it should have for the exertions she'd undertaken. Whatever devious blocking code that vile woman had used on her, it had been powerful and clever enough to completely overcome Aurelia's augmentations. It had also revealed how much she'd come to rely on those orgments, a weakness of character perhaps, or at least of foresight.

As she was running, she'd tried several times to access the wetware connecting her mech systems to her organic self. Nothing. No response. Now that she had some margin, she needed to attempt the relaunch routine her tech trainers had taught her when the orgments first went in. The razorslinger remained in its holster for the moment, and she allowed her right arm to dangle free. Her four left fingers pressed and held the contact patch laid subcutaneously across her manubrium bone, the firm upper part of her sternum. Voice low, she began humming the tune they'd taught her while mentally reaching for the set of phrases that went with the song.

She failed.

It wasn't that she *couldn't* remember those words. It was more that as she tried to summon them, her concentration shifted and took her desire to complete the task with it. The first time, her mind flipped to thinking about what a childish tune they'd taught her—*her*, a grown woman and servant of the empire! The second time, her thoughts flipped to worrying she would fail this job and disappoint her sister. The third time, she squeezed her eyes shut, restarted the tune, and reached hard for the first of the phrases that went with it, only to find herself caught in a memory of her trainer's bad breath on the day he'd taught it to her.

The meat of her fist struck the doorframe in frustration. It was the blocker. Somehow, the woman who'd crafted it had not only found a way to switch off her wetware and orgments, she'd found a way to depress the neural pathways associated with their integration. Who in a black sun was she? Some agent of

Ectorius'? But one who spoke *Terran* True? Whatever the case, it was an excellent thing the lead Proselyti had taken her down as it had sounded.

The Proselyti.

For a moment, Aurelia regretted leaving Saito behind. And Caiu. Continuing alone in this state might yet prove exceedingly foolish. Aurelia wanted to think she had pushed onward to maintain the speed and momentum of her work, to keep Ectorius' forces off balance. But it was really pride driving her —pride and the burning desire to see her sister elevated in status and career.

She'd begun to turn back, to return to her insertion team, but there were suddenly voices around the corner ahead. Young men, young women. Approaching. Then stationary, remaining just out of sight. Laughter, too. Brash, overly loud, a male cloaking his anxiety with bravado.

Aurelia drew the razorslinger.

I have three working limbs, two working ears, and one working eye. She'd committed to memory detailed intel on the area, and she had experience with solo infiltrations *and* escapes. Let the Proselyti be elsewhere, distracting Ectorius' forces, Aurelia Cossea was coming for the treacherous sod.

Quietly she padded closer to the corner, listened again, and ascertained that the talkers lingered only a few meters to the left of the junction. Four. Four voices exchanging banter in a dialect her ear-clip translator had no trouble deciphering: chitchat about capturing an off-worlder, about glory, about how many off-worlders each of them could take down. One male suggested making bets based on various scenarios. Soldier talk, but young and inexperienced soldier talk, a way of deferring their fear of the unknown. There might be other, quieter people present—if so, she'd have to hope they were few.

An awkward peek around the corner with her one working

eye revealed two men and two women huddled up, all freshly out of adolescence. Behind them, a male with acne listened. To the right side of the corridor, Aurelia saw an alcove with a single chair and work desk installed inside—a checkpoint or security monitoring point. Another young man in a light blue data support uniform sat inside with his back to the corridor and no weapon visible. It took her two seconds to take everything in as she prepped her razorslinger. The acne-marked man's tacky grin froze on his face when he saw Aurelia. The other four soldiers swung her way as he stammered and pointed with his finger rather than his rifle, like he should have.

By the time Aurelia cut down all five troopers in the corridor—ending their lives as cleanly as she could—the one in the alcove had turned his chair to face her. She approached him. He did not move. He was even younger than the five, a teenager, a boy. And he was weaponless. The crotch of his light blue trousers darkened, the patch spreading down the inside of his thighs. The pungent funk of urine reached Aurelia's nostrils.

At least my olfactory sense is intact...

She checked both ways along the corridor. Satisfied they were alone, she holstered the razorslinger and raised her hand. "No intention of hurting you if you work with me."

He huskily replied, "All right. Th-Thank you."

'Thank you.' A nice boy.

"What are you doing in there, fellow?"

"Uh, t-trying to fix the s-surveillance in this area."

Surveillance is down? she wondered. That hadn't been on the agenda for her office's spies.

"Then talk to me about surveillance in the area."

"Not working. At all."

"Why not?"

"Don't know." When she nodded for him to go on, he swallowed and added, "The AI was infected with something, but the language it's written in… it's totally obscure. Nothing on record compares with it."

The way this one speaks, he's an educated boy, she thought. *A useful boy.*

An intuition struck her. The kind of intuition that made her an excellent investigator, one of those sudden epiphanies that makes meaning from random strings and fragments of information. She said, "The language that code was written in was erased from records around 1700 years ago. I'd bet my other arm on it."

He frowned at the limp arm, then frowned at what she'd said. "Uh…"

"Never mind." She certainly wasn't going to explain that the coder-witch who'd killed her orgments had used a dead Terranist language to wreck the local AI. Nor would she help this kid bring that AI back online. It was a boon for her. She pulled the datapad she'd looted from a dead soldier out of her pocket. "If we go back into the electrical room down there, can you link this with local servers to research something for me?"

The young man's eyes darted across the torn-up corpses of former colleagues, his mind struggling to make sense of this abrupt horror. He was having a difficult time reconciling that carnage with the winsome way she was talking to him.

She waved the pad and dropped the warmth in her tone by several degrees. "Remember what I said about 'if you work with me?'"

Returning his focus to her, he swallowed and nodded hurriedly.

She smiled, wondering fleetingly how her decommissioned eye might be affecting her appearance, the way she came across. *Was it causing her carefully sculpted face to sag on that side? Was it weeping?* With a slight jolt, she remembered her minor wounds and the state of her bodysuit. She glanced down, saw the tears in cloth and skin, the dried and drying blood. She raised the hand with the pad in it and used the back of it to feel her scalp where earlier shots had glanced off it, and she winced as some pain stabbed through the organic inhibitors she'd been equipped with.

The face she made at him was wry. "Ten minutes ago, I was much better looking, I assure you. Now. Come with me."

She beckoned with the pad and backstepped into the other corridor. He dragged himself from the seat and followed her on shaky legs, keeping his gaze off the corpses. She kept moving back, and he kept coming. At the halfway point, he seemed to register that he'd wet himself. His hands went over his crotch, his paling face now flushing red.

"Just means you're human," she reassured him, meaning it, and led him inside the electrical room.

Inside the room, there was space for him to lean against one side and her the other. She crouched and placed the datapad on the floor. Gesturing for him to crouch also, she said, "I'm watching you. Don't signal anyone, all right?"

He swallowed and dropped to his knees so hard, she was surprised he didn't break the patellas. He stared across at her expectantly.

"Link it to the local servers," she told him.

He powered it up, then said, "Already linked."

"Good."

She thought for a moment about how those troopers in the woods behind the recreation path had grouped stupidly together, how they hadn't followed her down into the tunnel. About those already in the tunnel being so careless, unprepared for her appearance.

She commanded him, "Find information about troop composition and why I'm only fighting idiots. Present company excluded, of course."

After another loud swallow, the kid began scouring deployment orders, tracking files, and reference boards.

"You can talk *while* you work, you know." She reached over and tapped the top of his head, startling him. "You already know something. Why were your friends out there so relaxed? They didn't hear the shooting down here earlier?"

Still finding and skimming files, he said, "They... *we* just got here."

"From where?"

"Came in through the hillside entrance." He glanced over one shoulder as if he could see that entrance through all the eternicrete and rock.

"You didn't hear the shooting?"

"N-no."

"And no one reported it."

This time, he glanced up at her and indicated the datapad. "We can connect to files, but actual comms are down like the surveillance."

She nodded slowly. "Glad to hear it. Keep working and keep talking. I'm guessing your dead friends were new recruits, barely out of basic training?"

"They were. I'm... I'm different. An apprentice. I don't want to hurt you, I promise."

"Shh, dear, of course you don't. So, what's your name?"

His gaze skimmed across the damaged areas of her suit then up to the wounds across her scalp before it met hers again. "I'm Roja. No imperial name yet, m-ma'am. Not till I... er..."

"A question, Roja. Have you ever killed anyone?"

He shuddered as he answered, "No, ma'am."

"Ever fired at anyone?"

He shook his head.

That's a damned shame, Roja. I could have used that experience.

"Well," she said, "you're a noncombatant. You know what that means? Good. You're not the one I'm gunning for, and you're not in my way. Just so you know, I'm here on Emperor

Nero's behalf, and if you help me, you'll be serving him directly."

"Oh!"

"Oh, indeed. So, Roja, my dear, where are all the *well-trained* soldiers?"

"Um. Well. They're sick, ma'am. Mostly. Some died, I heard. Was bad."

"Sick? How do you know this?"

"Here." He showed her a square window on the pad that was covered in tiny type and plenty of acronyms and abbreviations to really pack the information in. "This is the command chatter between our Garrison Commander and the unit leaders."

"You can access that?"

"N-not supposed to, but I thought you'd like it."

"You thought correctly, Roja. What's it say? Just the headlines, please." She could probably read it herself, but her head was beginning to pound, and she had an ear toward the door, listening for more troopers. And it would be easier if he just told her.

"Um, let's see. The governor received warning of the action against him very late. They couldn't prevent the food poisoning which was bad enough to kill three troopers and put eight hundred and fourteen out of action. The entire kitchen staff have just been—" He swallowed again, face twitching.

"Just been what?"

"Impaled. As punishment when the spy among them wouldn't come forward. Then, apparently, he did come forward at the last minute to stop the others being executed, but the governor killed them anyway because they should have seen what the spy was doing and prevented it or reported it."

"So that you know, Governor Ectorius is guilty of the worst kind of crimes against empire and emperor, and he's paying for his protection out of pilfered funds. So. Tell me who's still standing between me and him."

"The t-troopers brought into active duty today are a combination of, um, some Regulars who avoided eating the poisoned food, and... well... they call them 'raw recruits.' Like the ones out... there. The rumor is the governor paid someone to send about a hundred to finish their basic training here. Plus, he's got a few hundred conscripted reservists that came from Vadox or were hired from off world. They all wear a yellow sash over their uniform. Half of the ones who didn't get food poisoning are on the other side of the planet..."

"You're doing well, Roja. And how about combat droids?"

"Um." He shifted windows and files around until he found the one he was looking for. "Not many. Only twenty are registered and four are out for repair. Give me a second, er, please. *Yes.* This order sent ten droids to the far side where there was some trouble earlier. A couple are guarding the Wall as relief for out-of-action troopers. I... I can't see where the other... um ..."

"It's fine, Roja. There are potentially a handful for me to face. Hopefully, I can avoid them."

"Um, ma'am, there's a receipt here for renting another four security droids from local mining magnates for city overwatch."

Sorry, Saito. You get out of these tunnels, and you've got more than kids and conscripts to fight through.

"Roja?" Pushing the burgeoning headache aside, she forced a smile. "The governor was having a party. Do you see anything about that?"

"Ah, *yes*, it was mentioned in the command chatter. I saw that it was postponed last minute, so we—they—could complete the *Charon* ambush. Was that the firefight we heard across the Hill, ma'am? At the time, we were waiting on the opposite side of the peak, you see... waiting for orders."

"That was it," she said and touched some of her damaged

flesh as if she'd sustained it on the rooftop. "You said postponed. So, they are still going ahead with the party?"

"Let me..."

He fell silent as his fingers flew over the screen and the control buttons around its edges.

"Yes!" he cried in a way that touched Aurelia's heart. The dear boy was beginning to make her mission his mission.

So sweet.

He continued, "The party is rescheduled for the Governor's rooms up in Orbital One, seventeen hours from now. A double security detail has been ordered."

A space station. "Seems our rebel politician can't let an attempt on his life stop him from rubbing cheeks with all those important people. Speaking of which, when you said they'd received the news of my mission late, was it too late to stop his party guests from arriving?"

Without consulting anything, Roja nodded an affirmative. Evidently, that was common knowledge. "Some are on world. Some are in orbit."

"What I need now, my friend, is the guest list. Please."

Half a minute later, she had it. Roja politely swung the pad around for her to read. A short while ago, she'd had an idea. Halfway down the guest list, she saw that the idea was going to work.

Well, hello, Senator Galen. You'll do very nicely.

She tapped the name and turned the pad back around. "This man. Where exactly is he right now?"

This time, the answer took two minutes. While she waited, she heard the crackle and thunder of a short firefight from deep in the tunnel network. Her Proselyti, no doubt. She wished them well, then gestured for Roja to keep working when he froze at the noise. Not long after, she had her answer in the form of a location on the device's map program.

"Please leave the map open, Roja, then open a window to

lodge an action report. But please shut down all other windows on this device."

Becoming nervous again, he did as he was told.

"Relax, please," she said. "I have four favors left to ask of you, then I'll allow you your freedom. The first task is a little grisly, but I really need it done. Come out again and help me carry a body in here."

With her headache beginning to spike harder, she helped the boy carry in the least damaged of the female soldiers, a woman roughly Aurelia's athletic size and shape. She made him peel the bloody uniform shirt and trousers off the corpse while she slashed and stripped off her own tattered bodysuit. She hoped any horror the boy felt at handling the dead body would be rewarded by the sight of naked, living female flesh close by—if Roja was oriented that way. Judging by the quick looks he stole, she ascertained he was.

She discarded her rags and dragged the uniform to her side of the room, then still in her underwear, she told him, "Favor number 2, Roja. Posing as one of the soldiers out in that corridor, please craft an action report. You know their names? Excellent. Use one. But don't send it till I say so. The report should say you fired upon 'the quaestor' while she was hiding in this electrical room and killed her. We'll attach an image of the body."

His hand hovered over the screen while he stared unabashedly at her eyes. He'd forgotten she was semi-naked.

"What is it?"

"You're a quaestor, ma'am?"

"I am."

"I-I'm honored."

"Told you I was here from the emperor. Now, get that report written."

The belt that held the razorslinger hung over some cable casing while Aurelia pulled on the new uniform. Dressing one-handed was a nuisance but not impossible. Roja composed his report with his tongue poking out of one side of his mouth. She finished buttoning the tunic at the same moment he showed her the results.

"Reads well," she told him, and he beamed at the compliment. Aurelia took the pad from him. "I'll send this in a moment. Please drag her body up against the routing board. That's right. Sit her up like she's resting there. Now drape my clothing across her. Yes, like a blanket. Do your best. That's fine. Just wipe your hands on that dry spot on my clothes. Good. Stand back, please, and perhaps avert your eyes."

She handed back the pad, drew the razorslinger from its holster, and put two rounds through the woman's head, obliterating any of the apparent differences from her own appearance. Something sparked in the electrical board and singed the hair, momentarily filling the room with a new, acrid stink. Aurelia placed her pistol on the floor.

When Roja began to gag, she slapped his chest, jolting him out of it. "Please take an image of this and shake the pad around as you do. Make it blurry."

Stomach continuing to spasm, the young man complied and attached the image to the report. The photo was as blurry as she'd hoped but displayed the right kinds of detail.

"Perfect! Don't send. Lay the pad down there for me. Now for favor number 3…" She nodded at the belt. "Strap that around my waist but wrap my right arm inside it. Against my hip. To keep it stationary. I'm already tired of it flopping around and getting in the way."

Once he'd cinched and buckled the belt, she stooped for the razorslinger and gestured for him to leave the room. He did so with a grateful expression and took huge gulps of air in the corridor outside.

She joined him and favored him with the warmest smile her aching head would allow. She nodded toward his dead colleagues. Together, they walked toward that corner. As they reached the bodies, and he stood staring down at them with his stomach heaving again, she said, "You've served the emperor well, Roja. A credit to your family and your uniform."

"Thank you, Madam Quaestor!" he gulped. He faced her as she took a couple of backward steps. "And what is the final favor?"

"The final one is don't be sad when I do this."

He barely had time to flinch before she sent an accelerated disc slicing through his brain. He flopped back on the other corpses.

Aurelia regarded him for a moment, sighing.

There was a belief that was rife throughout pockets of the empire and made popular by the Cor Fidelis cult. It claimed early Martianist emperors had found a way to manipulate and harness pan-dimensional energy and vibrations, and—in essence—had created a form of afterlife for imperial citizens. The legend went that their machinery, scattered throughout the galaxy, 'caught' the energies of departed humans, then delivered them to where the souls of emperors past presided over a higher reality. There, those emperors would judge the dead as they arrived, looking into their memories and their very characters and deeming whether they would pass into a Hell-construct or join them forever in their paradise-construct.

Aurelia didn't believe it for a second, but she could hope for some form of justice beyond death for a poor kid like this. Because ultimately, it was justice she believed in.

She told him, "Dear Roja. You were a gullible young man. If you could be turned so quickly to my side, you could easily be turned back. But you died while on the side of order, and if there is an excellent afterlife, you've earned it."

Returning to the electrical room, she holstered her weapon and crouched near the pad. One-handed, she sent the message, closed the window, and dragged the map window up from the corner to fill the screen. No more battle sounds had come from wherever the Proselyti were. She hoped they'd continued moving the enemy's attention away from her.

Aurelia stood and jogged from the electrical room with Senator Galen on her mind.

CHAPTER EIGHT

CONVEYOR

OUTSIDE THE TURNOFF to the conveyor lobby, Ashima lay lifeless, her armor vest chewed up, her torso within the vest nothing more than shredded meat. Judging by the mess Saito could see, she'd been dead before she hit the floor.

Temuz was on his back near her, just outside of cover, his torso bucking, arms akimbo, feet twitching, blood pouring from his slit throat, like a ghastly mountain spring. He probably only had seconds to live.

And Saito couldn't think about saving him. His rifle remained trained on the lobby opening as he tucked himself into the arc of the curved wall along the corridor's right.

Others had done the same—Jabari and Kirdy just forward of his own position, also along the right; Pytor ahead and over to the left. A few meters behind Pytor, Wegley had folded Naomi under the wall's curve. To his credit, the little asshole had scooted in front of her, shielding her body with his. Meanwhile, she clutched her injured arm and bared her teeth at the pain caused by all the jostling.

A brief storm of kinetic fire had blasted out of the turnoff the moment three troopers and a Corfid stepped into sight.

Saito had to assume they'd dropped their guards and come out of cover without clearing the corner properly. Temuz and Ashima had borne the brunt of the onslaught. Shill had ended up pressed against the wall on the far side of the opening, not visibly injured. Twice her size, Caiu mirrored her position on Saito's side of the gap.

The Corfid sported a slash across his right arm over the medial deltoid muscle. The green and gray sleeve showed red seeping through it. He caught Saito's eye and held up one finger. "Droid. Barrel type on castors. Twin cannons."

On the other side of the gap, Shill slipped off her cuff and angled it around the corner, clicked something, then pulled it back when a single round took a chunk from the corner near her hand. Consulting the screen, she announced, "Not advancing."

Caiu had already drawn one Punch-Burner handgun. Using the other hand, he pulled his scrambler grenade, an EM pulse weapon guaranteed to take down something as poorly shielded as a barrel droid. The problem with using it would be the team's pulse rifles and, potentially, Shill's small pistol, which Saito hadn't yet gotten a good look at. She blindly fired a couple of shots now, keeping the droid distracted. EM blasts and weapons electronics did not mix well. Back in Saito's day, frontline rifles had rig shielding against EM damage; these days, without a major war to fight, the Imperium had long since cut costs by dropping such features.

He raised his hand to pause Caiu then whistled for attention. Kirdy, Pytor, and Shill were likely the only ones close enough to have their weapons affected by the grenade, but Saito gave all of them their original Okalasi Guard Battalion's hand signal for *temporary power down*.

Shill, he noticed, didn't bother with hers, but Jabari did adjust his borer. The other Proselyti, including Naomi, stroked the appropriate control on their rifles, then Saito gave Caiu a release signal.

The scrambler went off with the palest of flashes and very little noise. Shill and Caiu took turns firing single rounds around the corner until Shill raised her arm to signal success. She beckoned the others and swung inside the lobby ahead of them. Caiu held back and found a dressing to slap over his sleeve and the wound beneath it.

Saito held back and told Kirdy to assess the safety of the conveyor that led to the aircars. He told Kirdy to bring it up, if appropriate. Saito then helped Wegley get Naomi off the floor. Pytor had also hung back, watching their backs.

"Naomi, you with us?" Saito asked when she didn't immediately get her feet under her and had to pull on Wegley's vest to make it on the second attempt.

Through gritted teeth, she said, "Always."

"How's the pain?"

She glanced toward Wegley. "When he doesn't bump me, it's a six. When he does, it's a ten."

Wegley started a whiney objection.

"Stow that crap," Saito told him, then he held him by the vest when he made to join the others. He asked Naomi, "You can walk?"

"Got both legs." She looked sick, but she also looked alert. It was against Terranist values to accept cybernetic enhancements or biological upgrading of any sort—but she would get to decide if she wanted to have some kind of replacement for the length of limb she'd lost, and he would back whichever decision she made.

Got to survive this first.

He released Wegley's vest but held the man in place with a fierce glare. "You'll care for this woman like she's your sister—because she is."

Naomi pushed carefully off the wall and stumbled along

with Wegley. Walking backward, Pytor fell in behind them. Saito overtook them and hurried into the open junction area beside the lobby turnoff. Stomach tight, he bent over Temuz. The poor bastard had either bled out or choked on blood while Caiu and Shill grappled with the droid.

"Sacking hell, Tem," he rasped. He'd played dice with the guy their last two missions. Temuz had talked of opening a tea house the moment the Imperium retired him, and Saito had promised to visit and spend an assload of stellars there.

Saito closed the man's eyes, pulled the sweat rag poking from a vest pouch, and lay it across his face, hoping he'd done enough to satisfy Islamic-Druze tradition. He plucked the Druze star from Temuz's vest—it was warped on one corner where a round had clipped it—stuffed it in a pouch of his own and shoved one of the man's spare mags in with it. Temuz's water canteen was ruined, the precious liquid spilled and diluting the pool of his blood. Saito checked the corridor again before slicing the strap holding Temuz's rifle to his body.

One look at Ashima confirmed she'd taken most of the droid fire, which had also smashed holes in the wall behind her. Her rifle was as messed up as she was. Ashima was an atheist, as he was, as were the two dead up on the villa roof. Nothing more was required except a whispered, "I'm sorry, Private."

Wegley and Naomi joined the others in the lobby. Pytor was watching Saito from the corner—wisely, he'd lost his shit-eating grin. Maybe the gravity of the situation was sinking in, now that Saito had paid respect to two more fallen comrades; maybe the drug high was wearing off.

Saito pointed to the man's feet, then hand signed, *stay till I signal.*

He closed with the rest of the group, who were milling around the conveyor doors and the droid's smoking chassis. Nobody spoke. The lobby was metal lined with two conveyor doors and scrape marks from trolleys on the floor and the frames of the doors.

"Report!" he barked.

"Both conveyors online," said Kirdy.

Shill grunted her agreement. She had her wrist turned and was busy waving the cuff device over the droid in scan mode.

Jabari had his ear to one of the lift doors. "Ours is on its way."

"How long?"

"A minute." Jabari shrugged.

Kirdy watched Shill from the side of the door opposite Jabari, his expression openly suspicious. He dabbed at the welt on his face with the back of one hand.

Saito shifted closer to the coder woman. "You *sure* surveillance is offline here?"

"Yep, and with nothing to wirelessly link into, the droid didn't report us."

Saito offered her Temuz's rifle.

Shill took note of the slashed, bloody straps, then said, "Leave it by Jabari. I just gotta..." Thought trailing off, she slipped the cuff back on her arm, pulled out a multitool, then wrestled with a sealed flap on the back of the droid.

Saito held onto Shill's rifle for the moment, one in each hand. He nodded at the new dressing over Caiu's upper arm.

"Scratched me is all," the Corfid said.

Saito nodded at the two smoldering holes in the droid's thick body. "What are you throwing?"

"Throwing?" It appeared to take Caiu a second to decipher the slang. He glanced at the gun in his hand. "Armor-piercing incendiary. Not much to burn in a droid, but it sure stopped it dead." He tapped his other Punch-Burner, which was still in its holster. "People-slammer rounds in this one. Dense polymer weave."

"And you?" he asked Shill as she wrestled with the back of

the droid. She had her small pistol stowed in a pocket somewhere. "Why's there no damage from your weapon?"

She jerked her head to the side, and he noticed a handful of light scorch marks near Kirdy's position. She said, "Disruptor pistol, demolecularizer. Eleven-charge magazines. Real nasty against living tissue."

"Then why fire it at a droid?"

"Distracting the thing for him." Though they'd just cooperated, the glance she shot Caiu was venomous.

Caiu said nothing and positioned himself before the doors just as Jabari announced, "It's here."

Caiu got down to lay prone. Jabari hefted his accelerated-particle borer well out of the way, since using it would ruin the conveyor car. Pytor and Kirdy flanked either side of the door. Saito pulled Shill away from whatever she was trying to detach, slapped the rifle into her arms, and dragged her to the left wall with Wegley and Naomi.

The conveyor door was a telescoping, foldback sort. The thing shuddered with age and squeaked and scraped aside, revealing an empty lift car. Kirdy darted inside and put a round through something in the corner of the ceiling.

"Camera's down," he reported.

"Load in," Saito ordered and followed Shill as she returned to the droid. "What in hell are you doing?"

She passed back the rifle, spent a few seconds cutting through something with her multitool plyers, then smiled as it came free in her hand. She held up a small module trailing wires. "Brain. In case I get to make another bot to replace the one your corporal slagged." She pocketed it and took back Temuz's rifle as she moved out.

Saito signaled Pytor to follow her, waited for him to pass, then took a final glance toward the bodies in the corridor before he went, too.

The car was five meters wide, six or seven deep, and its

floor was as scuffed as its doorframes. Once they'd joined the others, Shill moved to the sealed far side doors and slapped the control that sent the car shuddering down the shaft. Kirdy and Pytor took up forward positions, down on a knee. Shill moved to the side and stood the rifle against the wall to resume playing with her cuff. Naomi, Wegley, and Caiu leaned their backs against the car's left side, Jabari, its right. Most weapons were aimed toward the edge of the door that would open first.

Saito found a sheet of analgesic pills and slipped them into one of Naomi's pouches. The dressing around her stump showed some red seeping through, as was to be expected, but the nans appeared to have done their job properly. Plasma was another matter. He checked the infusion patch on her neck—empty—and gestured for Caiu to pass him another while he removed the first.

"How long's this sackin' trip?" Kirdy asked Shill.

She sniffed, not looking at him. "Six point eight kims. *Feels* slow, but there's no way of telling the speed."

"Didn't take long to come up," said Jabari.

"No way of knowing what we're walking into?" Saito asked the coder.

Shill said, "I'm filtering deployment orders, looking for that."

Saito let her be. "That was Caiu's last grenade, people. Make your shooting count. Scavenge bonus weapons as you go, so long as they don't hamper movement. Our current objective is an exfil target zone in an old spaceport lower down the Hill."

Kirdy threw him a long, surly glance, clearly less trustful of these interlopers and their intel than he was. Saito could only see that the pair were trying to save Proselyti lives, though the reason they'd gone rogue escaped him.

And then an idea occurred to him. An unpleasant one. He chewed his lip, irritated.

If this is some insane recruitment operation for that Scipio, they can shove that up their asses sideways.

From across the car, Caiu caught Jabari's eye. "Lieutenant? Correct?"

Jabari waggled his head noncommittally.

"Where is Optio-Major Scipio, Lieutenant?"

The Corfid, it seemed, was thinking along the same lines as Saito.

Jabari offered the big man a superior half-smile. "Are you even cleared to know about the Optio-Major's mission?"

"It's fairly common knowledge now."

"Well, if that's true, it goes to show how poor security is on that *Maelstrom*, doesn't it?"

"I was not stationed on your *Maelstrom*."

"It's not my..."

Something clunked above, and the car jolted. Everyone inside tensed and shifted their weapons. After a few seconds, they heard a short series of clicks then the squeals of metal on metal. Something to do with the mechanism, Saito reassured himself, not a Regular dropping on the roof, not a bot getting ready to cut through. But he kept his weapon aimed upward even as the others returned their attention to the door. How close were they to the bottom of the damned shaft anyway?

During this brief alarm, Caiu's focus hadn't left Jabari. "You two are deserters."

Saito reached into the space between the two men, although there was no sign yet of a physical altercation. Both men held their weapons—the handgun and the long particle weapon—in safe positions with muzzles angled away from each other.

Jabari asked Caiu, "You have *proof* we deserted?"

Caiu tilted his head Shill's way. "She tried to kill me, a true emperor's man. A Cor Fideli like the three missing from that mission you went on. And she did something to the quaestor." He pointed with an elbow toward Kirdy. "*He* said she did."

"Oh, I'm happy to admit that," Shill muttered, still scouring files on her data cuff.

"You what?" Caiu snapped at her.

Shill raised her head and winked at Pytor. "Man's deaf. Guess it's hard to clean your ears when you're missing this." She held up a pinky, the finger Caiu was missing.

"You..."

Caiu's weapon began rising, but Saito clamped his hand around the casing—an idiotic reflex—and he was immediately glad the muzzle had cooled since the firefight. He was also glad when Caiu's gaze snapped to him, its anger abating in surprise.

"Decanus Caiu. You gave me your word."

"I did," the big man admitted.

"So...?"

Grudgingly, he lowered the weapon and allowed Saito to remove his hand. Saito was relieved the hand still existed and wasn't scalded.

"Do I need to repeat my speech from earlier?"

"No," Jabari said before anyone else responded. "Shill won't be kicking the Corfid anymore, will she?"

Shill shrugged. "She won't. Won't be easy, but she won't."

Caiu made a noise like he'd just stepped on a turd with bare feet. "I make no promises once all loyal parties are clear of the planet."

"Dumb and dangerous thing to say, guy," Shill murmured.

"Shill!" Jabari growled.

"All right, all right."

"This is so good," Pytor cackled, his dumb grin back in place.

Kirdy's turn to growl. "Shut it, Private."

Wegley stage-whispered, "This is so sackin' *stupid!*"

As if nothing had happened, Shill announced, "Found

something interesting. Did you guys organize a massive food poisoning outbreak?"

"The quaestor did," Saito replied.

"Didn't work," Kirdy added. "This sack-up proves it."

"Actually, it pretty much did," she said and showed him the screen on her data cuff. He regarded it from a distance as if it were contaminated. Shill added, "Almost all the Regulars are down with it or dead from it, along with some of conscripts Ectorius has working here. Mostly, we're left facing raw recruits and reservists."

"Recruits?" said Wegley. "There's a Training Center in *this* pisshole?"

Shill replied, "Files indicate the governor pays someone to have a few recruits finish their training in his garrison."

Wegley snorted. "Little 'uns are lucky dey don't eat with the grownups, or dey be sick too."

Despite her pain, Naomi backhanded him across the vest with her good arm. "Like *you'd* be eating with the grownups, squeak."

"Sack you," he grumbled, his brief flare of light-heartedness snuffed out.

A downshift in speed threw them all off balance. The car filled with the shooshing sounds of arms brushing vests and the rattle of pouch fasteners tapping against rifle frames as the troopers faced front and pressed themselves into whatever cover the meager walls by the door afforded.

Shill held Temuz's rifle as she squeezed against the left wall. "That's why resistance has been so weak and random," she said, as if needing to complete her thought before the door opened. "They don't know what they're doing."

"What are we walking into, though?" Saito demanded, wishing he hadn't been so distracted that he'd neglected to ask this already.

"Open outdoor area cut into the Hill, 400 by 400 meters. One access road leading in and out."

"Cover?"

"That, I don't know," she admitted unhappily. "Vehicles, if they're there."

Saito glared at his team. "Check those sackdamn blind spots this time, people. I don't…"

The conveyor jolted to a stop. The forward door stuttered into action before retracting steadily to reveal an expanse of asphalt tarmac beneath Vadox's sandy-colored sky. Cooler air rolled into the car, carrying the far-off noises of the denser parts of the city. A lone siren sounded, some emergency vehicle responding to the *Charon* crashes, Saito presumed. For the moment, there was no other sign of life. No shouts of alarm. No incoming fire.

Shill swept out of the car first with her rifle up, headed hard left; Jabari mirrored her to the right. The instant their boots left the car, Pytor and Kirdy surged directly forward and found cover against a row of eternicrete bollards that were obviously intended to prevent vehicles rolling into the conveyor housing.

Still no shooting.

Wegley hesitated, so Caiu brushed him out of the way before stooping to drape Naomi over his shoulder. Saito punched Wegley's vest before he could complain and signaled him to follow Shill. When the young man moved, Saito chased after Jabari.

Pleasingly, the lot was mostly empty, a flat shelf carved from the hillside and floored with asphalt. There was room behind its three parked vehicles to shelter two full platoons if needed, but no Garrison troopers were there. Near the exit onto the service road stood a transparent caretaker box, also deserted. On the slope above them and beyond where the conveyor housing emerged, scrubby bushes led to what might have been the ass-side of a shopping mall for the homes further uphill.

Beyond that, the hillside continued rolling inward and over, hiding whatever expensive homes and service buildings lay between there and the woods near The Summit. Temuz and Wegley had seen troopers all the way up there; it wasn't inconceivable some had been ordered to move down their way.

Only...

The only things moving up there were the patches of fake grass swaying in the wind—a wind carrying the barest hint of warmth and burnt-dust taste from the desert far below.

No groundcars, just the three aircars to choose from. The things weren't difficult to pilot. Any idiot could fly one, as evidenced by some of the idiots who so often did, but *starting* one without the key or access code was another thing. That would be up to Shill. But which one to send her to?

Two of them could have been called skiffs. Almost the size of the vehicle his team had landed in, they were large enough to fly a family around the planet sub-orbitally and do it in luxury. Cumbersome to fly above a cityscape, though.

The other had a cabin the size of Aurelia's shuttle galley and appeared to be modeled on some kind of seashell made from reinforced glass or transparent plastoid. It had swept back airfoils with scalloped repulsor thrusters visible along the underside of the airfoil facing him. The vehicle rested atop these wings on the thruster nodules beneath them. The cabin rose above them and was accessed from apertures on top of the wings.

Hand stiff like a blade, Saito pointed at the seashell and hollered Shill's name. Wegley and Pytor had looked around at the shout, so he signaled them to shepherd her and watch the flanks. He told Caiu, "Put Naomi down."

But when he checked, Caiu had already set Naomi on her feet. The Corfid had slung her rifle over his massive shoulders and was in the process of re-strapping one of his handgun holsters to her belt. Saito rotated one-eighty—as did Jabari—

and they walked backward with their eyes sweeping the slope behind the parking lot. With every step, Saito expected the hillside to burst to life with weapons fire. It never came. For a few seconds, a second siren or alarm joined the first, way off in the city. Then both cut out, leaving faint echoes of their existence. Barely audible shouts rolled down from the built-up area up beyond the shopping mall. He pictured street searches for his people. Caiu helped Naomi along in his wake, swapping out one of her vest's spare mags for one of his, and then Saito joined the others at the shell car.

The inside of the cab was arranged like a dance club booth. A U-shaped bench seat ran around the back and sides with a small table set center-cabin. A comfortable, leather-appointed driver's seat poked from the floor up front like the pearl inside an oyster. A transparent material formed wraparound windows all around the cabin bulkheads.

Kirdy had already taken the driver's seat, and Shill crouched in the narrow space beside him. Thankfully, they weren't squabbling. Rather, they had the driver stateboard flipped up and, together, they were tampering with the electronics. In the back, Pytor and Wegley helped settle and buckle Naomi in. Jabari moved around the car to keep watch from the other side.

Saito stood on the starboard airfoil. He pointed to the seat with the most shoulder and leg room. "You next, Caiu."

The huge Corfid shook his head and dragged Naomi's rifle from his shoulders. "Perhaps we'll swap back some time in future, Private," he told her through the aperture in the canopy. He pointed to the sidearm he'd given her.

Saito said, "What are you doing?"

"Sergeant, this is where I leave you."

Saito glared at him. "I sackdamn knew you'd do this."

The Corfid was already walking backward when Saito heard the whine of the car's controls coming online. "I've only helped this far to draw attention away from Quaestor Cossea. Now, it's time for me to find and assist her."

Repulsors started up beneath Saito's boots. Warm air washed briefly up and over his back. Sighing in resignation, he said to Caiu, "You're that devoted?"

"To Emperor Nero, yes. Cossea's mission is his mission and, therefore, my mission. Escape if you must, Sergeant. Anything you do distracts the local forces. But I adjure you in Nero's name to find out what these two know." He nodded at the other side of the car where Jabari stood.

Saito ignored him. "How will you find the quaestor?"

Caiu continued to walk backward, and for the first time, cracked a smile, a grim one. "I'll follow the trail of corpses."

"We're a go!" Kirdy called from inside as Shill scrambled onto the seats.

Saito called Jabari in and piled in after him, and then the apertures sealed shut as if by sorcery. He growled at them, "Buckle in. No chances."

The aircar lifted and banked to the east. Saito's last sight of Caiu was the Corfid entering the conveyor again.

"Godsdammit," he muttered to himself. "I should have taken his grapeshot mine."

Shill said, "You know the real reason he left us, don't you?"

"Why?" asked Wegley.

"Guy was scared shitless of me," she replied with a wink.

CHAPTER NINE

HOW AURELIA MET LONZO

AURELIA WALKED the tunnel as far as it would take her in the direction opposite the Governor's Mansion. She'd seen no other short shafts she could have used to access the other villas on the summit. Sporadically, there'd been closets, electrical or piping rooms, open doors to emergency refuge rooms. Three times, branch tubes had led off to her right, away from the city on the hill, their signage indicating they led through the mountain to exits on the far side valley wall. They weren't much use to Aurelia.

Still tracing the summit's ridgeline, the corridor curved this way and that, rising and falling in places, which was perhaps a design consideration having to do with providing cover points for security people in case of an uprising or invasion.

Only, there'd been no guards. None that she'd met. *Until* she came around the final twist in the corridor that brought her in sight of its terminus.

The tunnel's end was bathed in waxy light provided by a bank of aging glowpanels set in the ceiling above. A door beckoned from the end wall. According to the datapad's map, a staircase rose behind it. But to get to the door, one first had to pass a checkpoint behind a waist-high eternicrete hedge. Two men in Regulars' uniforms with yellow sashes stood behind the hedge, and they'd closed the narrow gate set to one side of it.

Upon seeing her, their pulse rifles twitched in their arms. She was twenty meters out, well within accurate shooting range. She'd jammed the razorslinger between her belt and the back of her bloodied uniform shirt, which also bore a yellow sash. The state of the stolen uniform and the appearance of her injuries would buy her time and distract anyone she met. She raised her working arm in acquiescence, put a little stumble in her walk, and kept her right eye angled toward them as she headed in, keeping them squarely in view.

"Identify!" The younger man spat his challenge with such venom, she figured he was itching to kill someone.

It's not going to be me, she thought. *Actually, it's not going to be anyone.*

The quaver in her voice wasn't hard to manufacture, not with the pain she was feeling. "Recruit Clodia Nerian, sirs! My squad leader sent me for medical... what d'ya call it? For help. I need help!"

Both men looked at her as she staggered closer, into better light—the dried blood in her hair, on her face and uniform, the immobilized right arm—and they groaned in chorus. They dropped their weapons to their sides—they weren't slung— then the younger man leaned his up against the barrier and unlocked the gate.

"Come on, then," he called in a regional dialect Aurelia's translator had no trouble with.

They think me a local? Shame I can't speak it.

"I... I'm from Tamarina. Only speak Imperial Common, sorry, sirs." She faked a cough then wished she hadn't, as it brought back her headache with a vengeance.

The young man scowled and muttered something derogatory about people from rich planets.

The older man had uneven tufts of salt-and-pepper hair and shaving cuts across his chin and throat. He mirrored his colleague's glower. Using Imperial Common, Old Fellow told her, "Don't be callin' us 'sirs,' idiot. Look at our sleeves." He finger-flicked the markings identifying him as a private then leaned his thighs and belly against the eternicrete hedge, his rifle hanging from one hand. "What in *zri kiat* hit you, girl?"

"Yeah," said Young Fellow, switching to Common. "We heard shootin', but nobody tells us nothin'."

Aurelia's right eye was tiring; she had to squint as she hobbled closer to get a better look at the pair. They weren't local conscripts. Something about them said...

Mercs.

The rushed shaving job and pot belly on the older one. The patch on the back of the young one's hand where hastily applied makeup had sweated off or worn away to reveal a free-booter company tattoo. They were mercenaries passed off as Regulars to reassure the Senator upstairs that Ectorius had sent his best to protect him from beneath.

As it had been today, it was occasionally necessary to take down imperial soldiers or spacers who got in a quaestor's way. Aurelia had done this without guilt—but as with dear, young Roja, she often felt sad doing so. With mercs, however, she *never* felt sad.

She'd almost reached the gate through the barrier and had to force herself not to pick up the pace, to maintain the wounded, disoriented girl act till the very last second. Using the pulsing of her headache as timing for her stammer, she said, "What h-hit me, you want to know? A bloody t-team of Proselyti hit m-me, that's what. B-blew chunks of f-floor and wall into my h-head. Killed my f-friend in front of me. My poor f-friend. She f-fell onto me and dis-dis-dislocated this shoulder. *Ow*," she added as she stepped into the gap created by the gate between sections of the hedge. She leaned one hip there, keeping the razorslinger out of sight.

"*Zri*-damn, girl," the young man said, backing up a step.

Gone was his desire to shoot her—he now looked as if he thought her wounds contagious. Fine with her. Without the use of her machine arm, she didn't want him close anyway. All she needed was to have them in full sight, without the protection of the barrier to duck behind.

She asked them, "You medics?"

Young Fellow snorted. "You stupid?"

Old Fellow whipped out an arm and cuffed his partner across the chest. "Head injury, you dumb *chramiga*." He tapped his temple and spoke slowly to Aurelia. "Can't think right, yeah? Brain all messed up? We... not medics. We... soldiers."

There was at least some kindness in the older man's antics, some empathy for the injured person in front of him, which made him the one with the chance to live.

She squinted hard at the closed staircase door behind them. "Has to be medics here. In there? What's in there?"

"She's the dumb *chramiga*," said Younger Fellow to his pal. "That's a stair—"

He'd turned his head to look at the door, as had his older colleague. Aurelia saw her opportunity, and she took it, smoothly drawing her weapon from behind her and putting two rounds into the younger man's chest. She heard the double-*tak* of the discs hitting the wall beyond him with enough force to ricochet and smack into him a second time from behind. He toppled sideways, away from his pal, a surprised look on his face, but he didn't make another sound and was dead by the time he hit the floor.

Older Fellow's wide-eyed stare snapped from his colleague's leaking corpse to Aurelia's weapon, which was now pointed at his gut. He blinked and chuckled. "Can't believe I fell for that. You're the quaestor they got running around here, yeah?"

"Good deduction."

"Saw one o' you in action on Argos once. That wound on your head..." He tapped a spot above his brow, and because his rifle still dangled from his other hand, she didn't flinch at the motion. "Now I look proper, I see how tough the skin is. Gotta hurt, though."

"Not as much as one of these to the gut," she said and jiggled the gun.

"*Shla'a t'mohk.*" He chuckled. "What d'you wanna know, madam?"

"My question about the medic was serious, except I need Senator Galen's medic. She'll have an extended set of skills."

"Ah. You got orgments. She's a tech-medic, yah?"

"Precisely."

The merc took a few steps backward, carefully stood his rifle against the wall by the door, then leaned beside it, clasping his hands in front of him. It looked like he'd decided to make himself comfortable in the last moments before she inevitably shot him. She did not like mercs on principle, but this one was quickly endearing himself to her.

He said, "Your senator got two bodyguards up there, old soldiers like me from the looks. Some other *giddi* with him—giddi means a pretty woman in my homeworld tongue."

"Good to know."

"The giddi might be a doc, a medic. Looks smart, madam. Also," he went on, anticipating her next question. "One more guest's up there eating with him. A man. That one has two more guards and two droids."

"Combat or security? The droids."

"Sec-droids, both. C11-80s from the looks."

If he was telling the truth, that was very good news. She had a simple way of dealing with sec-droids. The bodyguards were another matter, hampered as she was.

Aurelia knew Senator Galen traveled pretty much everywhere with his young female tech-medic—the giddi—since Galen was mecha-orgmented, like Aurelia. His usual security escort was a pair of former Ramoran Rangers. They now served as butlers, but they were decorated veterans of the Argoni Separatist War. "Old soldiers," indeed.

The merc had more to share and happily rattled off the information. "I was up there one hour back. The old soldiers was in the living room right outside the stairs. The other two was split— one on the roof, one walking the shuttle pad out front."

"The droids?"

"One on the balcony, one top o' the stairs."

He fell silent, and she considered him for a long moment. Her pulse pounded in her head, and the vision in her good eye had started blurring occasionally.

Must keep moving.

More urgently, she had to fix herself. The droids? She could deal with them without taking a single step up the stairs. But those former Rangers? And two personal security agents with unknown skill levels? In her current state? She didn't think that would work out so well.

Besides, for all she knew, this merc was lying through his tobacco-stained teeth, and there were more than four human hostiles upstairs.

She forced a wry half-smile. "My friend, you didn't live this long being..."

"An idiot?" he finished for her.

Her grin broadened despite the thumping in her skull. "I was going to say brave. And *I* haven't survived by being a— what was it—a dumb *chramiga*?"

He returned her grin. "Want my help?"

"Explain how I can trust you, first."

"I'm asking you the same question."

"Except I'm the one with the gun and with the time pressure, so..."

He nodded. "Fair. I answer first. You can trust me 'cause I'm a hireling. 'Cause I got stuck working in this *freh'teg maakri* place where they take money outa my wage to pay for every drop o' water I drink or wash my balls with."

She laughed. "Hopefully, it's not the same water."

"Maybe you kill me, and I don't gotta pay for the water no more. But *maybe* you do justice like quaestors is s'posed to do. Maybe later, you lemme go to some better planet with bonus money in my pockets. My thinking? If you want me killing some rich *zri*'s shooters and their droids, I be happy doing it, and I take my risks." He winked at her. "*And* you a giddi, all right, even with the messed-up head."

She snorted.

He added, "Me, I never could hurt anyone pretty. One dumb thing about me."

"I think I *will* give you a chance. Your name?"

"Lonzo."

"Lonzo. As we're not quite friends yet, please keep calling me madam."

"Not friends but sounds like I work for you now, yah?"

"For the moment. And I *do* believe in justice. If you do right by me, I'll look after you. Bonus money included."

"And maybe I have a new good story to tell. To get free drinks with, you know?"

Patience and amusement wearing thin, she said, "Fine. Here's what's about to happen. I'll power down the droids from here. You'll go up the stairs with a cover story. Say a messenger came to you to report that some Proselyti bitch hacked all the surveillance and droids in the area, and her team are out front of the villas."

"There really *are* Proselyti here?" He looked amazed and

impressed, as if she'd mentioned something mythical, like an angel or alien.

"Yes, now focus."

"Sure."

"You got that cover story straight?"

"Droids and surveillance got killed by Proselyti bitch. Her buddies be out front."

"Good. Keep your rifle. You'll need it to shoot those Rangers when they're distracted. You okay with that?"

Lonzo shrugged. "Not my friends." He poked his dead comrade with the toe of his boot. "Him neither."

"These are your orders: deliver the message, move to your left away from the stairs and shoot the guards, then crouch and wait. I'll be coming up the stairs behind you, so if you betray me or turn on me, you'll die first."

A genuinely offended expression twisted his face. "I don't hurt you, pretty giddi quaestor."

"Lonzo. *Do not* shoot Senator Galen or his tech-medic."

"Sure. Senator Galen getting us off Vadox?"

"More important than that, Senator Galen is my ticket to see the governor."

CHAPTER TEN

AIRCAR

AS THE SEASHELL-SHAPED aircar eased off the parking plat-form, Saito told Kirdy, "Keep it low as you dare."

"No kidding," the corporal replied in a terse mutter. He jerked his head toward something on his console. "Local traffic control wants our destination."

Saito had placed himself on the very end of the U-shaped passenger bench and twisted himself sideways to maintain a clear view to the front and past the wing on one side. "The control's an AI?"

"Yep."

Excellent. No chitchat expected. "Jabari, Shill, you're supposed to know the way?"

Jabari leaned forward. "Corporal, first destination is City Border Crossing. We have to fly through there and above the gates for the car to be automatically tolled. After that, tell it we're headed for the Pugnum Rior mine."

"And if it asks why?" Kirdy challenged him.

"It won't."

"Sackin' hell," Kirdy muttered and stroked the words across a scribing screen. When he was done, Saito heard a pleasant tone from the dash, an acknowledgment. Kirdy checked something onscreen then banked the car right and headed out. "Gotta follow the main highway at 90 meters altitude."

When the car banked, Saito caught sight of the roadways and slow-moving vehicles. Ground traffic drove on the left on this planet, which Saito found weird.

As the car levelled out, Pytor pointed out the other side. "Look."

Two lines of smoke marked the sites of the *Charon* crashes. It looked like they'd come down in residential areas.

Kirdy pointed forward and down. He added, "Gunsō, come up here."

Saito unbuckled and duckwalked to Kirdy's side. Off to one side, a wide highway kept coming into view between buildings. The Panlands Highway—two light vehicle lanes in each direction, as well as a heavy vehicle lane beside them.

"We're told to follow that."

"So, follow it." Saito returned to his seat.

"Traffic Control's got us movin' slow, too," Kirdy continued to complain, voice rising. "Not allowed to exceed 64 sackin' kims an hour."

"Slow is good. Slow doesn't raise suspicions," Saito assured him, concerned the rising pitch in the man's voice indicated rising panic.

"Once you're through the border crossing gates," said Jabari in a glacially cool voice that was the opposite of Kirdy's, "bank to port and lift to three hundred meters altitude so we can find the target zone."

"These sackin' assholes!" Kirdy spat with a glance back at the interlopers sitting together opposite Saito.

"Corporal," Saito warned him.

Kirdy ignored him. "That bitch is crazy. Says him and her are here to rescue us."

"Corporal!"

This time, Kirdy threw his furious stare Saito's way. "Rescue us from *what*? Why'd she torch the quaestor like that? How do they know all this shit about the ambush and where to go next?"

"*Eyes on the sky, Corporal!*"

Kirdy complied and rolled his head around on his neck to keep his stress under some kind of control. "If she'd left Quaestor Cossea alone, we coulda stayed with her. We'd be *safe* with her! She'd know a way offa here."

"The quaestor's gone after Ectorius," Saito said, hoping to talk some sense into his right-hand man. If Kirdy lost his mind, Saito had no one left he trusted enough to count on. "Ectorius, you understand? That's why Caiu went after *her*. If they're not dead yet, they soon will be. You want to live, we've a better chance out here."

Most of the others' expectant stares were fixed on Saito now. Shill, Pytor, Wegley, and Jabari held their weapons angled toward the floor, their feet spread and planted for balance, as the aircar wove and swerved. Pytor's grin had receded, and his face was now blank, unreadable. Naomi's latest course of painkillers seemed to have kicked in and made her more alert. She cradled her maimed arm in her lap. Caiu's handgun rested in its holster, and her lips were pressed into a tight line. But her stare seemed more speculative, like *I'm already screwed, I wonder what's next.* Wegley appeared as angry as Kirdy, and Saito knew both men were freaking out because they were impotent, because they felt they'd been thrown in the shit and left to sink or swim. But the similarities ended there. Kirdy was angry they'd lost people, suddenly, shockingly, brutally; Wegley was just mad he might be next.

Shill remained glued to her data cuff.

And Jabari...

Jabari seemed as calm as the air on a mid-spring day in Saito's boyhood hometown. As if this was just an entertainment he was watching and wasn't invested in. As if he knew the ending and didn't care about the middle.

Saito spoke to Kirdy, but his message was for every remaining member of his original team. "We lost people on that rooftop, and we lost people in the tunnel. We could *all* be smoking corpses by now, and the only reason we're not is because these two intervened. I'm no happier about Shill attacking Quaestor Cossea than you are, mainly because of the shit it'll cause us *if* we get back. But they're on our side; they're with us. Hells, they *are* us." He lashed out and thumped the back of Kirdy's chair. "Unless you think someone *cloned* two missing Proselyti and sent them to stick their noses in our business?"

Kirdy rolled his head again and focused on keeping the car over the ribbon of highway Saito had seen snaking down the mountain toward the massive wall.

"This topic of conversation has come up too many times," Saito said in conclusion. "Until we're outbound from this system, we're all done with it."

"Yes, Gunsō," said Pytor, Naomi, and Wegley.

It seemed Kirdy was done with his bitching, so Saito brought them back to planning. For the sake of those who didn't know, he told Jabari, "Explain our target destination."

"Our destination's an old spaceport. Shill, can you provide...?"

"Sending it, now."

Kirdy's head turned as something fresh on his console caught his attention. He grunted and nodded, remaining silent.

"And how are we getting past the border control?" Wegley asked. "If questions like that are permitted."

"Operational questions are fine," Saito growled in a *stop-wasting-my-time* tone.

"We're blowing through the border control," Shill replied. "At first, I thought we'd just dodge their interdiction nets, which don't operate for vehicles leaving the city. But aircars like this have toll readers, so they're charged for flying out. There's space. Kirdy can just queue jump and ease us through the gap between the booths and the roof."

"You good with that?" Saito asked the driver.

"Looking forward to it," Kirdy mumbled.

"You sure about this intel?" Wegley persisted. When Shill flashed him some stink eye, he continued, "Hey, I'm asking an operational question. Gunsō, if the quaestor's intel was crap, how do we know this isn't?"

"Because it's based on publicly available data," Shill replied. "Details haven't changed in decades."

"Oh."

She added, "Look. We'll assess the scene first before 'blowing through.' Make sure the governor didn't change those details in the past hour or two."

No one had any objections.

It took Saito a while to realize the Wall had been visible to him when they'd been higher up near the summit. Looking out across the Hill's east face, the structure had blended in with the cityscape, its tans and grays and greens identical to the rest of it. And now that they'd descended, and residential towers from the lower steppes had risen to block the view, the Wall had become an invisible feature. Until suddenly, the highway curved sharply and broke through the last of the towers, and the structure loomed ahead, a monstrosity so large, it was impossible for Saito's monkey brain to immediately determine the dimensions. Because the traffic AI had directed Kirdy to descend to 53 meters, the Wall seemed like another mountain feature, a manmade crag or escarpment that had trapped them in the gorge below. The sight of another aircar flitting from left to right across it gave some perspective, as did the zigzag of a worker staircase climbing the side. It was someone's serious attempt at sealing off a city. Until the Terranist War—after which simple hobbies and pleasures lost their shine—Saito had enjoyed learning about human history. Walled cities had been a feature of early Homo sapiens civilizations and had evolved into border barriers to seal in countries in many places. By the outbreak of the galactic civil war, the Imperium's rule across the galaxy had made them redundant for even the poorest world. There'd been no such thing as borders. *This* wall, then, was a construction of the past 1700 years, an innovation to segregate the rich hill-dwellers from the paupers on their skirts.

The border control point appeared at first as a tiny gray smudge in the hem of the Wall and then a semicircle of gloom where the highway disappeared for a time. The traffic AI directed Kirdy to take it slow and easy as he pulled toward the wide-vehicle queue visible within the tunnel. The buildings that had framed the Panlands Highway now fell away, replaced with open areas for infrastructure and utilities—sidings for vehicles, fueling stations, telecoms towers, and generator stations.

With Kirdy feathering the controls, the aircar came in at the back of the queue of road trains. Saito felt safe enough to unbuckle and scuttle forward to kneel by his corporal. The ass of the last train in line was poking out from under the shadows in the border crossing tunnel. The heavy-vehicle lane was the outermost, and because people drove on the left, it put the two light-vehicle inspection lanes off to Saito's right. In those lanes, the queues were easier to manage and moved quicker. He saw small clusters of bikes and groundcars and hoverswoops, all advancing slightly faster than the trains. The people wanting out of the city were a mix—mining middle managers whose employers were too cheap to book tickets on an air taxi, traders with the communities that had sprung up around each mine, and families of miners making a visit. The clustering nature of the traffic indicated to Saito that whoever they were, they preferred to travel in groups, like small convoys, for protection.

And the off-world soldiers who'd caused the double gunship crash could be in any of them...

"Hold a minute." As Kirdy braked to a stop, Saito raised a monocular to one eye, closing the other and passing the viewer across what he could see of the outbound and inbound border booths. "Are there more border guards than there should be?"

Kirdy didn't need the monocular to answer. "Sure looks like it."

From behind them, Shill reported, "Standard deployment for the entire border point is one checkpoint clerk, one trooper per booth, plus three roaming troopers and one backup combatdroid."

"I count six contacts on foot and moving," Saito said. Kirdy grunted agreement.

Four of the garrison troopers inspected the first road train in line and the cars in the lighter lanes. Two more hung back toward the booths, rifles ready, keeping an eye on the area. Other figures moved at or within the booths, backlit by sunlight from the far end of the tunnel.

"Can't see droids," Kirdy said. Because the cab's canopy was transparent, they all twisted around with heads up, checking the canopy and the gantry walkways above them. Several voices agreed with Kirdy's statement.

Saito's best guess was that each road train measured 200 or 300 meters in length. And with four full trains ahead of the aircar...

We're just a kim from the gates—and freedom. Relative freedom.

A kilometer was fine in a vehicle. On foot, a kilometer's worth of hostiles *and* civs would be tough to navigate. When he glanced back, he caught Naomi's eyelids fluttering halfway between wakefulness and drug- and shock-induced sluggishness. It would be tough, all right, should they be forced down.

He dropped a hand onto Kirdy's shoulder. "These extra checks they're doing are precautionary, but the search for us on The Summit will spread down here at some point. Longer we sit here, the more we lose our—"

Kirdy hissed a curse and pointed to a text message across a console screen. It instructed him to set down inside the tunnel and await a vehicle search. "Knew this was too easy." The fingers of his left hand fast-typed a reply.

Saito read, *Setting down at toll booth.*

"Probably a good idea," he told Kirdy.

The corporal glanced at him, face grim, but calmer than it had been. "Time to buckle in again, Saito."

Saito did so, as Kirdy sidled the car over the space between the heavy and light vehicle lanes, where dividers—procrete bollards a meter tall and spaced three meters apart—kept vehicles away from each other and from changing lanes. They looked cracked and warped with age; a good knock from a grav-bike would probably snap any of them. Thank the hells there seemed to be no aircar barriers or restrictors of any sort. More affluent places inside and outside the imperium might use something like Velocity Dampening Gravity Fielding or the interdiction nets Shill had mentioned that were in place for incoming ground traffic.

Kirdy let the aircar idle half-exposed out the side of the rearmost train while he took final stock of the terrain ahead.

"If you can get close enough," Saito told him, "make a call on running for it." He glanced instinctively at Jabari for his opinion. The former officer's eyebrows just rose. Saito added, "But get ready to fly evasively."

Kirdy snorted. "As evasively as this thing'll let me, sure."

The aircar accelerated gradually and dropped altitude until it must have been flying just above the bollards between lanes. A couple of troopers glanced at them then focused again on the trucks. With no cabin lighting, Saito was hopeful the flyer's passengers were basically invisible to outsiders. He glanced aside as they passed a bus in the other lane and caught a glimpse of the men in maintenance coveralls within. None of the men returned his scrutiny. They drew closer to the gate area, and there was a break in the bollards where an aircar this size might set down. It would still leave them three or four hundred meters on foot.

There really was nothing else for it...

He told Kirdy, "Punch it!"

There followed a single second where the g-force nudged them all a little off balance, but it wasn't much. The aircar didn't have the grunt of a military vehicle, and it accelerated far more gradually than Saito liked as it climbed the dozen meters necessary to clear the barrier structures ahead. Any sight of the troopers below fell away as they rose, and no sound from outside was audible. But at this speed—

"*Push!*" Wegley barked, forgetting his place. "We're sleeping puff-squirrels like this!"

"Shitbox doesn't have the power," Kirdy snapped back. Then he gasped, "Oh, piss!"

Through the windshield, Saito made out a pair of black dots silhouetted against the arc of daylight at the far end of the tunnel.

Skydrones!

The border crossing had extra protection after all.

Or the authorities had boosted them for today. Any second now, the droids would target the rebellious aircar, and Saito's team would be shredded by a storm of cannon fire. Likely, the only thing holding them off was the fear the car contained important citizens. A scan would end that misconception.

"*Land it!*" Saito screamed.

Better to fight on the ground where the presence of civilian assets might deter the droids. He caught a flash of cannon fire —the beginning of the threatened storm—just as Kirdy braked, and the aircar plunged. He heard the patter of medium-caliber rounds skipping off the roof as he and his team fell toward the road. Impact banged Saito's teeth together and jarred the rifle he'd unslung from his grip. It bounced toward the people at the back as the car skipped a couple times, like a stone across a stream, taking out a line of bollards on its left side. Then the car clipped something more solid that whipped it around into the lighter lanes, and it slammed into the back of a groundcar. Despite the passenger restraint, Saito bounced enough to head-butt the canopy behind him. Not hard: he had some luck left. After that...

He moved. *Everyone* moved, casting off restraint straps, banging on the canopy until Kirdy got the two apertures open. No one was hit, though a couple of holes in the roof made Saito wonder how that was possible. Pytor tossed Saito his lost weapon, and the sergeant became first man out.

After sliding down the airfoil, he stagger-ran, his balance slightly off, to the damaged groundcar. It had bounced forward from the impact and had stalled diagonally across the lane with its nose pointed left and its butt pointed right. Adults hollered and groaned and cussed from within. No kids were hurt. Saito thanked his luck again. A face in a window caught sight of his rifle and recoiled from view. The shouting inside stopped as the others saw him, too. Saito took a position at the nose, with the business end of his rifle searching out the skydrones. He found one as it banked to his left toward the crossing point near the foremost road train. It had stopped firing—Collateral Avoidance Protocol, no doubt—but from his angle, Saito had no such limitation. He lined up his rifle, squeezed off a few rounds, and realized at least one had grazed the thing before it juked behind the road train's bulk. The other skydrone edged in the opposite direction, trying to find a safer down angle on his team.

Without looking back, Saito bellowed, "Jabari, cut right!

One drone that side! Pytor, other drone's coming 'round the road trains: watch our ass!"

A quarter kim of open ground lay between him and the border gate where the next cluster of vehicles had been stopped. The troopers past the crossing points had vanished and were probably sneaking around the fronts of various vehicles. Another pair peeked from between the first and second road trains, seeking a solid vantage point to nail him. Saito dissuaded them with a sustained spray of pulse rounds. One man fell; the other pulled back out of sight. There'd be more troopers on the incoming lanes' side of the tunnel, left there for contingency. Had to be at least two.

The high-pitched buzz of Jabari's particle borer came from behind Saito at the same moment the skydrone settled over the light vehicle lanes, where it appeared to have found its down angle. A puff of flame and debris, and the drone dropped like a stone.

A burst of rifle chatter came from back at the aircar. Kirdy shouted, "Hostile down!" amid more sporadic weapon fire.

A quick glance told Saito that Kirdy was firing at the gap between the second and third road trains. He noticed a good thing about the vehicles: they rode so close to the tarmac; there was no way for hostiles to crawl under them. More weapons chattered behind him, then Shill and Wegley joined him, and Naomi tumbled into him and almost knocked him out of cover. She swore an apology.

He hunkered down close to her as Wegley and Shill took turns finding targets beyond the groundcar. "Private," he told Naomi, "we'll have to fight our way out, meaning we need you firing, too."

Naomi nodded soberly, drew the monster handgun Caiu had left her, and got a workable grip on it. "Oh, I'm itching to try this, Gunsō."

A spray of ballistic rounds kicked up eternicrete chips

nearby, while another punched holes through the aircar, triggering a sustained burst of pulse fire from Kirdy and Pytor. The two were on their bellies, firing from the ground. Kirdy reported, "Shooters on our flank!"

Saito noted one kneeling and one standing trooper in the gap between trains, and they were taking turns squeezing off rounds at targets of opportunity.

Movement above the rearmost train indicated the return of the first skydrone, and drew the Proselytis' attention. The drone rose swiftly toward the tunnel roof, nose down.

Its cannons began spitting fire toward Saito's aircar.

CHAPTER ELEVEN

HOW AURELIA CAUGHT GALEN

POOR, dead Roja's map program had access to a live satellite stream from above the Summit. This allowed Aurelia to see exactly what she was climbing up into. Like the original villa she'd visited, this guesthouse's main side faced out over the downslope, providing a clear view of the city and the haze beyond it. It had two stories above ground with the kind of flat roof all Summit properties were designed with. The property had a high boundary wall and a deep front yard paved for the comings and goings of aircars and passenger shuttles.

The current satellite stream showed a tall-hulled shuttle standing atop its support fins in the yard, a double-decked hyperspace-capable beauty painted in yellow and rose pink. They were not just garish colors chosen by an owner with a flair for the opulent. Yellow and rose were a particular wealthy family's House colors. The Galen family. Typically consuls and magnates, this family's eldest son also happened to be a Senator. Senator Caecilius Galen.

The stairs Aurelia climbed bypassed the lowest bedroom-bathroom level of the house, which would have led directly into the yard, and instead took her to the upper common room and kitchen. Aurelia could already hear hollering from up above, Galen and someone else trading anxious shrieks. No doubt it was the result of her handiwork with the droids.

Back in the tunnel, Lonzo had seemed impressed when Aurelia rolled back her right sleeve and opened a tiny panel in the 'skin' of her dead prosthetic arm. Clipped inside it were two thumbnail devices. She'd taken out one and squeezed it hard for three seconds, telling him, "Those droids upstairs now have a jumble-worm burrowing through their operating systems."

"Gotta get me one o' them," he'd replied.

They passed the halfway point on the staircase as the cater-wauling from the door beyond the top grew more frantic. Lonzo had fourteen remaining stairs to take—and Aurelia nineteen—when the door flew open, and a graying man in a House Galen servant's uniform leaned through it.

Lonzo took the sudden appearance in stride—literally—as he continued climbing while shouting the cover story. "Messenger came'n updated me'n the girl there."

He swung a thumb back at Aurelia. Galen's grizzled body-guard gave her the briefest of glances, either unaware of what the troublemaking quaestor looked like *or* fooled by the wounds to her face and head. Or Ectorius hadn't informed his guests' security teams about the real cause for the morning's troubles.

Lonzo continued, "He reckons some codey-witch from the Proselyti shut down all the AI and droids round here."

"Proselyti?" the guard called down. The man had a voice like tires on gravel. "What Proselyti?"

Ah, she thought. *Ectorius, you secretive bastard.*

"Think that's what the messenger called 'em," Lonzo replied, scratching his nose with his left hand. Meanwhile, his right steadied its hold on his rifle grip. The merc even put a tiny limp into his steps as he climbed closer. The subtle touches pleased Aurelia. Her split-second choice to bring this stranger on-mission may well have been an excellent one.

The guard swore and retreated to the common room with renewed urgency, swinging the door shut in Lonzo's face and barking instructions for people to shelter by the kitchen benches. The earlier caterwauling snapped off as if a cable had been pulled. Both wealthy men upstairs would no doubt have panic alarms, and Galen would have some form of alert built into the vision orgments in his eyes or even his heart. Aurelia had another hidden compartment higher up her arm and had to tear her sleeve to get to it. There were no devices to remove this time, only a simple touchpad which was receptive to her left middle fingerprint. She pressed it, jamming their alert signals.

From above came the scrape and thump of hurried footsteps before Lonzo threw the door open. He took a moment to take stock, allowing Aurelia to close some distance, then he commenced firing his rifle from the hip. He moved out of sight and into the room, disobeying her orders, as she neared the landing. She entered warily. Two final rifle shots greeted her— Lonzo finishing his gruesome task with single shots into the fallen guards' heads. She turned her body swiftly to scan the room with her good eye, and she found two men in bejeweled House cardigans cowering in the kitchen area. Different Houses. Her scan of the room didn't make it clear whether Ectorius had accommodated *both* men in the guesthouse, or whether Caecilius Galen had invited the other across to pass the time. From the litter of dice and tiles and cash chips spread across the long slatewood dining table at the far end, she could see they'd been gambling. A woman in a teal doctor's uniform sheltered under the table. She had flawless olive skin and short, glossy, black hair. She might have been Aurelia's age, but if she'd had significant enhancements, she could be anywhere between twenty comm-years and sixty.

The common/entertaining room took up the entire level, with an open-plan kitchen at the rear. To the side of the dining table, an opening led to a staircase running both down and up. Along the front of the building, double wing doors had been folded out onto the balcony to allow in the breeze. Lonzo slunk to one of the door folds, relying on the shadows to hide him from whoever was down in full sunlight in the yard.

"One heading inside," he reported in a tight voice and rushed to the staircase entry, where he knelt with his focus on both the up and down flights.

Aurelia trained her good eye on Galen's guest...

The Imperial Palace had kept a purebred line of bulldogs since time immemorial, and this fellow reminded her of them, in face and body. He was so stout, he couldn't crouch like Galen. Instead, he cowered against an oversize refrigerator, double chins quivering. Though she knew his colors, she didn't recognize him, and the small link in her eye to the local grid was offline, making it impossible to check.

"You," she told him. "Tell your guards the droids went crazy, shooting at roaches, but they haven't hurt anyone. Tell them you need their help to carry the droids outside."

A high piping noise was the only thing that emerged from the man's mouth when he opened it.

Aurelia tutted at him, but his lack of words had provided fresh inspiration. To Galen, she said, "Actually, *you* tell them it's a medical emergency. This good fellow's having a heart attack. Might not be far from the truth."

Raising his voice to the Senate Orator levels she knew he was capable of, Galen called out her message, eyes turning to steel as he regarded her in the aftermath. His friend just hiccupped. Aurelia heard voices outside, one on the ground and one on the roof, calling to each other.

"Behave yourselves," she warned the two men and joined Lonzo at the stairs. Moving past him, she took a position with her razorslinger pointing up. He joined her and pointed his rifle down. The risers were open across the back, allowing her to see through them. A pair of boots appeared, headed down fast. When Lonzo fired first—before her target had come around the bend in the stairs to fully reveal himself—she put a disc through one of the boots. There was a sharp cry, and the owner tumbled down the stairs. Seconds later, he was dead from another disc through the heart. A quick check ascertained Lonzo's shooting remained accurate and effective.

"What are you doing? What are you *doing*?" It seemed Galen's friend had found his voice.

"I'm doing my job," she told him, returning to the entertainment room, Lonzo at her side.

Lonzo was bleeding from a cut across his cheek. She nodded at it, and he answered, "Guard got a shot at me. Musta kicked a bit of wall into my face. You didn't hear it?"

She shook her head. *I really need fixing.*

"I'll watch from out here," the merc told her with a shrug, heading toward the balcony. On his way there, he checked his wound in the glass frame of some artwork, then he turned his grin on Aurelia. "Madam! We match now."

Thinking of the abundant surface damage to her face and scalp, along with his older, grizzled appearance, she replied, "Not quite."

Galen looked more concerned than he had before. Possibly, all this killing was getting to him. Or maybe he knew why a quaestor would be there on a job. It also might have been that he'd tried accessing the links in *his* eyes...

She tapped the spot on her upper machine arm. "I have a comms and gridlink jammer powered on." The device was embedded in the arm's framework and would operate on a thirty-minute timer before needing to be triggered again. It was not linked to any of her orgments, but it *was* possible the coder bitch's magic had ruined it. However, when both men deflated a little—a little *more* in the friend's case—she figured it was working fine.

"Do they know who I am?" the overweight man, no longer looking at her, spluttered to Galen. Since the intruders hadn't immediately murdered him, he'd apparently recovered some bluster and self-importance. "*Do* they, Caecilius?"

"*She* may," Galen said, rising but keeping his hands where Aurelia could see them. He leaned his backside against the counter in the kitchen corner and flicked a hand dismissively toward the balcony. "He's her help, either a plant or freshly bribed. I expect it's me she's come to see."

Aurelia forced a chuckle. "There are politicians who serve empire and emperor, Senator. And then there are politicians like you—those who firmly believe every situation revolves around them. I'm *not* here for you. Not directly, at least."

"Who the bloody blazes *is* she?" the guest demanded, insecurity making his voice quaver again.

"I expect she'll tell you. I expect she has a *whole speech* planned for us." Galen lowered his chin, awaiting Aurelia's next move.

"The speech can wait." Aurelia aimed the razorslinger at them, setting the guest's abundant flesh jiggling and making Galen jerk back and thump his head against an above-counter cupboard. Dire as the circumstances were, the small accident was comical. Aurelia snorted. As the flesh across the senator's face darkened, she said, "Please remain there. Place your hands on your heads and keep them there until I say stop."

The guest complied. Galen hesitated as long as he dared before following suit.

She turned to the tech-medic under the table. "Currently, the person I want most to speak with is you, dear lady."

"M-me?"

Oh, please don't stammer in terror like poor Roja, she thought. "You're not in danger. I have need of your mending skills."

The woman's brow knitted a moment, then she noticed Aurelia's wounds and the strapped-up arm, and she put the clues together. "Oh. My equipment's out in the shuttle."

"Perfect! The shuttle is precisely where I want to go." *But first...* she thought. "Lonzo."

"Madam?"

"There's satellite surveillance trained on this summit. I can't risk making an appearance where face recognition will identify and target me. Would you be so kind as to delve into those bedrooms downstairs and find me a head covering. A scarf or something?"

"Cover for head, face? Sure." He started into the stairwell, but she stopped him by calling his name. "Madam?"

"Don't run off on me."

His expression turned stern. "I want to be on that shuttle, too, madam."

"Will you be able to pilot it?"

He wrinkled his face in apology.

"Never mind. Find me that head covering."

Lonzo saluted happily and bounded down the stairs.

"I can," said the tech-medic.

"You can what?"

"Pilot the shuttle. Most systems are autonomous, anyway."

"Treacherous minx!" Galen snarled at the woman.

"Sir, I can see she's a quaestor, representing His Highness." A kind of gratification appeared in her expression that told Aurelia the woman was glad her boss was in such trouble. At some point, Aurelia hoped she'd be able to find out more.

The guest had gasped so hard at the news, he'd sucked in saliva and started coughing.

Galen continued snarling. "I know what she is!"

The tech-medic explained, "Well then, sir. You also know I *have to* assist her. It's in the Physicians' Charter."

"And you're in my employ!"

The woman climbed out from under the table, looking significantly less ashen. "Madam Quaestor, I am Doctor Pieta May. I stand ready to assist."

There it was again, in her blink-fast glance toward the senator—the fleeting micro-expression that revealed the depths of this woman's contempt for her employer.

I may have lost my Proselyti today, but it seems I'm replacing them with disgruntled contractors.

"Dr. May, an unidentified agent has disabled my mechanorgments."

"Eye and arm, if I'm correct?"

"You are. Once I'm suitably disguised from satellite AI, we'll enter the shuttle, where Lonzo can watch these two while you repair me."

Hurry up, Lonzo.

"Of course, Madam Quaestor. For Emperor Nero."

"Traitor," grumbled Galen.

"Losing a staff member is the least of your concerns today, Senator." Aurelia flicked her gun toward the guest. "And to answer *your* earlier question, no I don't know who you are. Would you mind?"

"Harmonium Chebeebel." The large man raised his double chins, as if to say, *the famous Harmonium Chebeebel.* When he saw that she didn't recognize the name, he added, "Secretary to the Bursar of the Chamber of Magnates? Chief Sharetaker of Chen-Elysium Enterprises?"

She shrugged her left shoulder. "What is the Secretary to the Bursar of the Chamber of Magnates doing on Vadox CX, of all places? And why is he consorting with a suspected separatist, of all people?"

"I'm not that," Galen said in a tone that indicated he'd expected this accusation.

"He's a *what*?" Chebeebel let out another dramatic gasp— one Aurelia felt was rooted in genuine surprise—then swallowed more spit the wrong way and commenced a fresh bout of coughing. She turned her head, dismissing them both for the moment. Chebeebel's name wasn't familiar from the soiree guest list she'd read earlier. But then, the way she was feeling, there was a chance her memory wasn't as good as it should have been.

Emperor's heart, I need repair! Where in a gorzhonic hell is Lonz—

Through the growing white noise in her ears, she heard him thumping up the stairs from the ground floor.

Thank the emperor.

"I've had enough of this," Galen sneered in a sudden surge of confidence. "You storm in here, you slay my bodyguards—"

"And mine," Chebeebel coughed.

"You shut down my droids and my comms, you turn my medic against me..."

"Based on the evidence against you," she drawled, reciting the proper legal mantra, "I have full authority to hold you to account and full discretion as to the actions I take with you."

That shut him up, although his eyes flashed with rage.

Lonzo bustled through the doorway, waving a floppy rectangle of cloth as if it were a flag. "Pillow cover. Couldn't find nothin' better. Can cut holes in it." His glance over his shoulder toward the staircase said, *And there could be hostiles coming in here at any moment.*

"It's fine," she replied and gestured toward Dr. May and then to her immobile arm. "Doctor, your help making a mask would be appreciated. Lonzo, get them downstairs and ready to walk across the yard."

He tossed the cloth to May before grinning malevolently at Galen and Chebeebel. "Up, you *vrendeel chramigas*! I's working for His Highness today, so for once, you rich pricks does what *I* says."

CHAPTER TWELVE

THE LIVING SHIT

THE SKYDRONE WAS BALANCED PRECARIOUSLY on top of the road train's rear trailer, one wing leaning over the edge. What Saito could see of it was buckled and smoking. Similarly, the aircar had collapsed through the center, crackling and sparking, after the brief storm of skydrone rounds had torn it down the middle and sent those sheltering nearby scurrying and rolling for cover.

In the wake of those chaotic few seconds, Jabari alone stood tall, bearing the borer that had felled the drone and turning it now against the enemy positions. Saito wondered if the man had no fear standing up like that, no regard for his own safety. He'd known him off and on since the capitulation, and he'd overheard enlisted troopers chatter about him. Jabari was known as a relaxed officer and a circumspect and thoughtful tactician, nothing like this reckless individual.

What happened to him on the Corfid mission?

Saito barked for attention before making hand signals and pointing to the layer of border check booths. Remaining here any longer would be suicidal as it would allow for reinforcements and the allocation of more droids. Saito chose instead to use shock, awe, and momentum. His hand signals directed his team into a fire-and-maneuver tactic—leapfrogging positions in small clusters of two or three troopers, with weapons primed, as they rushed to new positions in five- or six-second sprints. With his team numbering seven, that made for three clusters. One could watch the rear flanks and the second the way ahead. Those two clusters could provide suppressive fire while the third pair or trio rushed to and past the forward position and took up a new station ahead. The roles would shift as the clusters moved.

In this way, the survivors stormed along the lighter vehicle lane, which was now devoid of vehicles and cover this side of the booths and their lowered barrier booms.

By the time he rushed the booth in their lane, Saito had counted three more garrison troopers down, two deceased, one of whom had dropped from sight, screaming for his mother, long past being a threat. A trooper risking occasional potshots from inside the booth met his end via a sustained volley that Saito sent through the booth's walls until the man spilled onto the ground outside it.

The driver of a low-chassis car had crashed into the barrier gate beside the booth in panic and had been smart enough to flee the scene. It didn't exactly offer great cover. When Saito reached it, he kept low and slipped around it to the right while Shill went left. This placed them a meter or so beyond the barrier, technically outside the main city.

Weapons hammered from team members behind them, and the particle borer burred once. Shill opened up on whatever resistance still lingered in the heavy vehicles check booth on her side, leaving Saito to focus on the remaining troopers in the incoming traffic lanes. Vehicles had stopped outside the check booths on that side, and a few had rearended others. Saito saw three bodies felled in the mayhem—one civ, two troopers. He also saw one resilient booth-trooper kneeling by her station. Saito held his trigger down, only to find his charge pack depleted after just two rounds. He swapped it out and discarded the old one.

The resilient booth-trooper scampered for safety along the favela-side highway verge beyond the tunnel. She climbed up onto it, perhaps in the hope the scraggly-looking fake trees installed at intervals would make better cover, perhaps from a belief that the higher ground would be to her advantage. It was a mistake. She would have been better served to throw herself on the tarmac and keep her head down as the Proselyti moved on. Instead, she exposed her back to Saito as she climbed. Saito sighted on her then resisted firing as he spied shapes detaching from the shadows up where the road shoulder met the tunnel's support structures and signage. He'd seen enough in his years to know who they were and how things would end for the booth-trooper who appeared not to have noticed them. The fleeing trooper's mistake proved to be even dumber since she should have known this area. The shapes surging down the slope resolved into humans, a dozen of them, wrapped in rags and armed with clubs and makeshift blades. Mercy dictated Saito spend a round or two taking the woman down; wisdom and experience dictated he conserve ammunition.

Saito turned away and checked on the rest of his team as they drew near. It was time for him to lead them into the area where the booth-trooper would shortly meet her end. From that direction, there came a terrified shout, followed by a weapon's discharge, and then a series of agonized screams that were quickly cut off.

Another sacking reason I need ammo, he thought, bleakly, although he'd be better off sparing as many favela-dwellers as possible if he wanted their sympathy.

"My side clear!" he called to Shill.

"My side clear!" she returned. "Clear ahead!"

"Confirmed!"

The tunnel's hostile troopers appeared to have been dealt with. One kept shrieking in agony down among the road trains. The rest were either deceased or they'd run. As the other clusters of his team came in hot, he turned his decision-making to the next leapfrog point. With no resistance visible ahead, he and Shill could take off and let another subgroup rest by the car and watch their asses. But he had choices...

If they vectored left out of the tunnel, the next significant cover—from where he could survey the way ahead *and* provide supportive fire for his followers—would be either of the two support footings at the very end of the tunnel. These eternicrete and steel structures were up on the verge the booth-trooper had died on. Security fencing had been erected across that area, but between the uppermost footing and the point where the siding met the tunnel roof, it was bent. That must be where the shadow huggers had crept in and, perhaps, where his team would need to creep out. Alternatively, the leapfrogging clusters could keep to the roadway and hope to identify a solid escape route once they were in full daylight with a better view of the terrain. If they took the second route, they could use the sparse, staggered lines of traffic coming into the city— where he could see civilian faces staring out of vehicle windows. He could commandeer another vehicle...

Just act! he rebuked himself.

"On me," he told Shill as he broke cover for a forty-meter sprint. He kneeled on the road by a stalled light vehicle, and to her credit, she joined him only a second later.

"See that?" she asked, gesturing with her rifle muzzle along the roadway.

He did. A length of empty highway stretched almost a kilometer downslope, by his reckoning, sided by cleared rocky patches. Beyond that, the first row of piecemeal favela constructions rose on both sides. Five-meter-high steel mesh fencing had been erected along the rocky sidings to ensure the security of this stretch of highway, and an energy shield shimmered across the highway between the ends of the fences. Local vehicles were probably equipped with some kind of passcode or phasing system that allowed them to pass through the shield; it was likely intended to keep the lowland's poor from encroaching on the highway and rushing the border booths. But people had begun climbing the fences along both sides. Thirty or forty souls, all adults. Saito could make out their tatty clothing, like the pinned-together outfits he'd once seen on the residents of Tellandan City on Hamuz. The Hamuzites hadn't been in favor of imperial uniforms hanging around their streets, and judging by the swift and eager punishment the shadow huggers had dealt to the booth-trooper, Saito imagined these people would be no friendlier.

As Pytor and Jabari hustled past him toward a new forward position in the middle of the road, Saito glanced up at the verge and, for a moment, watched the shadow people tearing equipment and clothing off the dead woman's corpse. They must have sneaked in through the gap in the fencing in ones and twos, keeping their numbers low to avoid notice and waiting for some opportunity. The people climbing the fences further down had sensed an opportunity, too.

"They're going to catch us on their way through," he told Shill.

She must have been following the same line of thought because she merely nodded and pointed at the security gap. "That way?"

"No, no!" a voice piped up from somewhere to their right. "This-a way, this-a way!"

It was the first time Saito had noticed the access hole set in the road five steps to his right. Its steel cover had become so dirty and tire stained, it blended in with the tarmac, but two lads had raised it from below. Each of the lads propped the cover open with one arm while their other arm anchored them in place below street level.

"Hallo, sirs, hallo!" called the second of the boys.

Shill responded with a "Slag off, kids! Get down!"

But Saito's gaze lingered on them, calculating.

"Us showing this way for youse," the first boy shouted, his voice the pitch and quality of the annoying tin flute Saito's parents had made him learn to play.

He was still deciding which way to go when another shout demanded his attention, this one from Kirdy who was coming up behind them.

"Incoming!"

Saito swiveled in place and did not like what he saw through the gaps in the booths and barriers. Bounding along on four legs, a new droid, a robot Caiu's size, raced along the sides of the road trains. Saito had seen one before.

Pursuit droid!

Governor Ectorius hadn't been as miserly as they'd hoped. These things were high-end, top shelf. A class and make that had been in operation for several centuries now. It came into better focus as it neared the line of booths and readied to leap over a barrier. It was vaguely dog-shaped, and the domes of personal shield generators sat where ears would be on an animal's head, looking for all the world like bright red buboes. An olfactory sensor intake took the place of a dog's mouth, while a single band of receptors across the face formed its visual input. There were—Saito knew—audio pickups where a dog's sternum would usually sit.

He'd hesitated too long. Jabari gave the order before he could, just as the thing leaped over the barrier. Without a hack code or serious explosives, Jabari commanded the team to do the one thing that would slow the droid down.

"Pour fire!"

Four people—Kirdy, Naomi, Wegley, and Saito—dropped

to one knee and hammered the thing with energy pulses. Relying on the strength of its personal shield, the dog-droid might have shrugged off a scattering of pulse rifle bolts, but when Jabari added the boosted firepower of the particle borer, it skidded to a halt, folded its legs beneath it, and flattened itself to shrink its surface area, then it put all available power into its shield bubble.

Still on one knee, Saito glanced up the verge at the gap in the security fencing past the gaggle of shadow huggers. There'd be more of those people outside the fencing, many more than the dozen on the hill. He glanced toward the raised utility cover shaking on top of the kids' skinny arms.

"Pleasing, sir. Pleasing. Come-a this ways. Us helps, us helps."

"The living shit," Saito sighed.

CHAPTER THIRTEEN

REPAIRING THE GIRL

AURELIA DIRECTED Lonzo to secure her prisoners in a small reading lounge in the aft of the shuttle's lower deck. He was to keep watch over them lest they trigger some kind of alert her device didn't cover. After, she waited in the cockpit while Dr. May fetched her things.

The control helm had been left on standby, but it was the type that required layers of security procedures for access. If she'd had use of her arm and her eye...

"No matter. I will, shortly." She spun the pilot chair to face the hatch and sank into it.

The cockpit was situated on the lower of the two decks, and the designers had positioned it just to the left of the passenger ramp, as if the vessel were a commercial aircraft. This made security a simple thing for Aurelia—facing through the door and along the passageway, she had a clear line of sight that would easily forestall any attempt to flee the ship before launch.

May returned wearing a diagnostic glove with a nanite-ink display built in the back. She carried a flip case neatly outfitted with mysterious instruments and materials. Aurelia motioned for her to get out her palm-sized datapad and hand it over. Gridlink was partially active for the ship, so the quaestor began accessing certain local government and news media files while May commenced tinkering with Aurelia's cybernetics. Aurelia ascertained that the governor had headed up to Orbital One— Vadox's primary space station—for a series of 'crisis meetings' ahead of the rescheduled soiree. She then laid the pad down and watched May work.

The tech-medic spent fifteen minutes accessing systems and running diagnostics, even popping out Aurelia's right eye at one point, along with clipping tiny components from her flip case together to create specific modules for replacement. The eye sat in the case, awaiting repair, and when May sprayed a lubricant inside the vacant socket, Aurelia felt the cool of the ship's air handlers against her flesh.

After fifteen minutes, May apologized. "I'll have to duck back to my cabin for components for the arm. Whatever command code went through your wet-wiring and operating systems caused a brutal power surge that burned out the grip motors for the hand." After hesitating a moment, she added, "You said a *Proselyti* did this to you?"

"I'm assuming that's what she was, yes."

"Huh. I always thought they were some kind of legend, an embellishment on a less colorful truth from the Terranist war era."

"Doctor, any other time, I'd enjoy chatting about history with you, but..."

"Yes, of course. My apologies." May rose and hurried out.

The repairs took the better part of another hour, with Aurelia feeling each passing minute scraping at her patience. The physical sensations of May's tinkering bothered her not one bit. The delay did. As the tech-medic labored, muttering to herself in a technical language Aurelia could only vaguely follow, the quaestor distracted herself by pondering the issue of Chebeebel...

When enacting any normal judgment, it would be dicey to kill a magnate or Chamber official who wasn't completely and clearly implicated. Even terminating their higher placed employees without just cause would be a risk. Any direct underlings of Ectorius' who got in her way were legally considered 'acceptable marginal casualties'—even Senator Galen because of the growing mountain of evidence implicating him.

Chebeebel, however, was a legal complication.

She couldn't simply judge him. Vadox CX had no link to the galactic Grid—which was shaky or non-existent in many periphery star systems—so she had no way of sifting through data about the man. She couldn't allow him to run free once the shuttle arrived at Orbital One. At the same time, legally, she had to assume Chebeebel was a law-abiding citizen. 'Disappearing' him would not merely be unethical and unlawful, it would be complicated to cover up; a distraction.

I could lock him out of the house in the tunnels below. Leave him to navigate them, hope he runs into the Proselyti who might accidentally kill him. That would at least delay his contact with anyone in authority.

Alternatively, she could poison the fellow, make it look like cardiac arrest. Unethical, sure, but he didn't seem to be the kind of person the universe would miss. As far as poisonings went, the required toxin and injector had been installed in her prosthetic's pinky finger, but her fellow quaestors had reported that poisoning usually proved pointless against the hyper-wealthy. Most had spillover shunts installed in their circulatory systems, with removal filter-collectors-pumps fitted to syphon off any excess drugs they might be partial to *and* to guard against poisonings. To create a cardiac arrest, she *could* potentially bypass those shunt systems and administer an overdose of party drugs if Galen had any aboard. It would be the first time she'd used that technique, but she'd read about it. However, it relied on too many things, including the time and freedom to carry it out without interference from the others aboard. It was also off-mission, a sidetrack.

A breakthrough idea for dealing with Chebeebel came to her just as the pounding and buzzing in her head began to fade.

"Oh, that's *good*," she told May who was busy refitting her eye. "Drugs?"

The tech-medic shook her head. "The inflammation around your wet-wiring is subsiding. Improved blood and ferrofluid flow are improving your pain management and higher brain function."

Higher brain function, she thought, as May continued working. *Hence the breakthrough idea...*

The doctor had left an obvious tissue weld along the inside of her arm, something that might take a week or more to heal given the lack of proper surgical nanites, but it seemed as if May was finished tinkering. Her face remained close to Aurelia's, and she fussed over the insertion and rebooting of the eye. *Some* of Aurelia's headache persisted—the result, she figured, of bullets glancing off her skull and cheekbone and the need for the bruising to subside. But the discomfort caused by the attack on her orgments was completely gone. The next major milestone of relief—and hope—came when May sat back, and Aurelia felt the cybernetic eye move inside its socket. A moment more, then a gray static fuzz replaced the black deadness she'd experienced on that side of her face.

"*Ah*," she said, "this is..."

The relief was short-lived. As images became clearer, Aurelia almost vomited when the eye zoomed close enough to May's face to pick out her individual pores, then retreated to normal, before zooming back in and staying there. Aurelia swore lavishly and squeezed her natural eye shut to try to gain control over the orgment. To no avail. The zoom remained stuck, forcing her to keep her left eye closed. The HUD was also offline.

She told May as much. The tech-medic consulted the diagnostic on her device, paired it with the eye, and attempted a fix. Then she laid down the device and turned an apologetic expression toward Aurelia.

"If I had proper facilities..." she started. "Perhaps if we go to the orbital clinic?"

"Slap a patch over it," Aurelia snapped, squeezing that eye shut and opening the other. "I have no more time for dallying."

She would just have to work without it. But the arm...

The limb still lay immobile in her lap where May had laid it.

"This is functional?" she asked.

"Oh," said May, a little more brightly. "Just allow me to ..." She typed some commands then pressed a point on the inside of the elbow.

Aurelia's arm twitched. Then, no longer a dead weight off her shoulder, it came alive with a gleeful jolt. As if the limb were alive, sentient, and joyful of its own accord, it jerked up and almost smacked her face with the wrist before she got control. There were no pins and needles as one might expect from a biological limb that had been 'asleep.' She scratched her nose with her index finger, then she stretched to the side and extended then withdrew the toxin injector in her pinky. She clenched and unclenched her fist, then she gripped the chair arm and crushed the plasti-steel frame as if it were a paper bag.

She continued wiggling her fingers in front of her face and crowed, "Excellent! Dr. May, you've worked wonders."

May leaned in and applied a sticky dressing over the malfunctioning eye. "I'm so sorry about *this*," she sighed. "The damage must be worse than I could detect."

"No matter. I can work without it for the time being."

May had an antiseptic wipe ready. She lifted it toward Aurelia's damaged face and froze when Aurelia caught her hand. The tech-medic said, "Madam Quaestor, your epidermis might be modded, but it can still become infected from these wounds."

"I won't be here long enough for infection."

"I really should clean your wounds and apply the proper dressings."

"There'll be time for that when I leave this system. For now, the final thing I need from you is a non-drowsy analgesic I can take with me. The skin modding you mentioned does help with the pain, but I can't afford to have it return in force and become a distraction."

"Of course, Madam Quaestor." May tossed the wipe onto a corner of the floor for a maintenance bot to clean up later and began fishing in the medications compartment of her case.

"This will be enough," Aurelia added, flexing her right hand, then arm. "Quite sufficient."

She rose, feeling an unaccustomed stiffness in her legs and back and neck. Her change in position forced May to scuttle backward in a duckwalk, dragging her case with her. The tech-medic rose in the doorway, closed the snaps on her case, and regarded Aurelia expectantly.

"Actually, Doctor, I'll also need a shot of something to overcome fatigue and general muscle stiffness."

Never needed that before. Not as invulnerable as I thought. Well, I'm not 18, anymore.

"Of course, madam. Would you like to follow me to my cabin while I source that? Or...?"

"I'll meet you back on this deck. I have an urgent matter to discuss with Master Chebeebel before we fly."

CHAPTER FOURTEEN

BY LAMPLIGHT AND FLASHLIGHT

THE BOYS' names were Eggo and Glark. They were probably pre-pubescent, though they might have been older. Their stunted growth, faces, and skin tone hinted at malnourishment. The kids had wrapped themselves in layers of rags so thick, they were either meant to provide protection from the hard-edged environment *or* make them look heftier than they were. If it was for the latter reason, Saito thought it didn't work—the tiny heads and thin faces made the bulky clothing look comical.

Once the team joined them in the underground tube, and the access lid was firmly secured above their heads, the lads indicated another hole, this one leading further down into the earth. The tube they stood in appeared relatively short in both directions. In the light of his rifle-mounted flashlight, Saito could make out a roof collapse in one direction beneath the favelas. In the other direction, beneath where the border booths sat, the way had been sealed with procrete or eterni-crete. Seeing the crumbled lines of ancient cabling and piping, he assumed the tunnel had once been used for city communications in an era when the affluent sector extended further down the Hill.

One boy—the lad with marginally darker skin and marginally curlier hair who'd called himself Glark—dropped through the second hole and out of sight. Naomi, standing closest to the hole, clamped her hand on Eggo's shoulder rags to prevent him from following his buddy.

She snarled, "Where in sack're you runts takin' us?"

"Yeah," Wegley said, matching her tone and coming over to tower above the boy. "What she asked."

Saito dragged Wegley out of his way and gently pried Naomi's fist free, but he held the boy in place with an *I've-no-time-for-any-grunfershit* glare. He spoke slowly and clearly in Imperial True. "We need to get to the old spaceport. It's in that direction, that way. If you take us to it, we will pay you well."

In the shifting, uneven light from various vest lamps and weapon lights, the boy's saucer-like eyes glittered back at him. They revealed nothing of the thoughts inside the juvenile's head.

"Spaceport," Saito said. "You understand?"

Shill was suddenly at his shoulder. She molded her hands into a flat bowl shape and added, "Looks like this. Ships come in and out."

From beneath the access hole, his eyes on the lid they'd replaced overhead, Jabari interjected, "Lorica owns it. That's the local crime boss," he added for Saito's benefit.

"You know Lorica, right, Eggo?" asked Shill.

The boy's response was telling and revealed how accurate Jabari's and Shill's intel was.

The boy nodded. "Youse helps Lorica, Lorica helps youse."

All right. Solid intel, then.

"*Spaceport* youse saying it?" Eggo continued, his calculating gaze flitting between Shill's and Saito's. "I knows Lorica's place *very* good, good. Us takes youse for it, in it, at it. Pleasing, sirs.

Pleasing. You pays-a us, us helping, us liking youse. Youse fighting the *governor*?"

"Yes, we fight the governor," Saito replied.

"Us friendings youse. Us not likes governor. Bad, bad man, bad, bad troopers."

"We're different troopers."

Eggo nodded, taking in Saito's uniform, then Shill's coveralls, and, finally, Naomi's bandaged stump. "Good, good."

Further along the tube, Pytor coughed as he examined something on the side and stirred up dust.

Beneath the manhole, Kirdy and Jabari still had their rifles trained on the access cover. The corporal muttered, "Come on, come on, come on..." It wasn't clear whether he wanted Saito to hurry or was longing for another shot at the pursuit droid.

"Well, we're not staying here," Saito said.

Naomi's expression demonstrated her reluctance to climb through another hole in the ground. Saito ordered Pytor, the largest of his remaining troopers, to help Naomi descend. Wegley took point. The youngest trooper climbed down, only interrupting his complaints to report that it was a 'real long' ladderwell they were heading into, and the rungs looked 'real sacking old.'

"Then be real sacking careful," Saito growled down at him. The complaints and swearing continued as the young man descended. More mildly, Saito told Pytor and Naomi, "You two take your time."

"But also go fast, right, Gunsō?" Naomi asked.

His smile was as brief as the tired wink she'd given him. "Absolutely."

He watched as Kirdy entered next, then Pytor slipped into the hole just ahead of Naomi. She crouched and readied to navigate the hole one-handed, with her lips pressed together and jaw set. In his heart, Saito took a moment to marvel at the difference between the whining Wegley and this stoic, good-humored woman. Then he returned his attention to Eggo, while Shill danced from foot to foot, clearly eager to follow the others out of the tight space. Jabari remained the only person who seemed totally unfazed.

To Eggo, Saito said, "The next tunnel down, which way does it go?"

Shill came in close and gestured in the direction of the spaceport. "It goes this way?"

The boy painted an imaginary line in the air between them, confirming the direction. "Glark, Eggo, us good for youse. Very good for youse. *Friends* youse saying it? Us friends?"

"*Friends* is the word." Saito nodded and, for the first time in his life, felt an impulse to tousle a kid's hair, an impulse he immediately rejected as stupidity and stress. Once Naomi vanished through the hole, he directed the boy to follow her.

While Shill readied for her turn at the edge of the ladder-well, Saito sidled up to Jabari. If the dog-droid was up there, it wasn't attempting ingress. That might simply mean it was marking the spot for a fresh Garrison squad to drop in grenades.

The former lieutenant's expression was blank, as unread-able as Eggo's. Saito murmured to him, "If you're thinking I've just made us all easier to kill by coming down here, I might just agree with you."

Jabari shook his head. His voice was equally quiet to keep the conversation from carrying into the ladderwell. "This was the only place we could sensibly go. I *was* thinking how few of us there are left, and that I wish we'd intercepted you in orbit, neutralized the quaestor and Corfids there, and gotten *all* of you away."

Saito found bleak humor in that idea. "If you'd attacked up *there*, you'd be fighting all of us, not just Cossea and her Corfids."

"I suppose that's true," Jabari said, the tiniest note of

sadness creeping into his tone and expression. "And I'm glad you trusted us. I'm only sorry about how many we've lost already." Vigorously, he shook his head, like a dog dislodging water, to focus himself. "Gunsō, I await your next order."

"Very well. Follow me down the ladderwell, Former Lieutenant."

The ladder wasn't as unreliable as Wegley had suggested—but neither was it a joy to use. The way down was *quite a way* down. By the time Saito's boots hit the gritty floor of the new subterranean walkway, he estimated he'd descended one hundred meters. He stepped along, so Jabari, who was bringing up the rear, had space. Like the tube above, the new tunnel was lit only by vest and weapon lamps, their beams crisscrossing in the moist air. And the air *was* moist, he realized, clammy. He'd become so used to the dry atmosphere on Vadox, wet air felt *wrong*. Lichen-begrimed stone lined the squarish subway in both directions. Three meters to his left, Naomi squatted with one of her boots pressed into a centimeter-deep slick of liquid.

"Broken pipes," Kirdy reported, approaching from his right. It looked like he'd been reconnoitering up that way. He gestured at a series of damp patches up the wall behind Naomi's position, then back along the tunnel. "Pipes are in the walls. Stones've come away from some further up. This is a pretty robust design, but the pipes look real old."

Nothing lasts forever, Saito thought, morbidly. *Not robust pipes. And definitely not former Terranists who skip decades and centuries by sleeping in stasis...*

At his back, Shill said, "I'd say they were used to deliver potable water to the old city's lower ring before they pulled back up the Hill. Now, it's just a trickle."

"A wonder there's not some poor slag-wad in here mopping it up," Naomi muttered.

The new situation would have been a perfect opportunity for Wegley to cut loose with whining or sarcasm. To his credit, however, their youngest trooper had gone scouting down the lefthand stretch of tunnel with the Glark kid in tow. Down that way, the passageway appeared to descend further; as Saito watched, Wegley and the kid trod out of sight. The glow from Wegley's lamps became the only sign they were down there.

Pytor lingered halfway to Wegley's position. Saito signaled him to stay there since that was the direction they'd be taking.

He clicked his fingers at Shill and nodded at her cuff. "Your map files mention this route?"

She made a regretful face. "They *mention* water, telecommunications, and sewage lines, but they don't mark them."

"Just as well these brats didn't bring us into the sewage area," Kirdy grumbled, eying Eggo.

Saito drew a lungful of fusty air and asked the boy, "Glark knows the way?"

Eggo nodded.

"Then let's follow him and Wegley," he told the others.

It wasn't just the pipes. Further exploration showed a minor reservoir had long ago burst and evaporated in the stuffy heat. Dampness clung to every surface, softening the floor beneath their boots, infusing the air with musty odors, and causing their uniforms to cling to them.

It took twenty minutes of picking their way through slicks of oily water and patches of slime before the passageway ended in a deep chamber that had once been a pumping station for water *and* sewage. The mezzanine level, ten meters up, appeared devoted to relaying and monitoring power and telecommunications. In places, the roof had been propped up, reinforced with scaffolds of rotted timber and alloy. By the time Saito, the third man back, entered the room, Wegley and Pytor had withdrawn to the walls on either side of the emergence point. In the middle, the pumping equipment was little more than a ruin. A small crowd of favela dwellers had gathered there. Scrunched up on their knees in pools of filthy water where runoff collected, they dipped plastoid receptacles into them to fill larger containers sitting on the floor beside lanterns. The lamps burned an oily fuel mix that gave off sickly, black smoke. It drifted lazily up to the eternicrete ceiling high above. The crowd froze under the scrutiny of the Proselyti rifle lights. They were dirty, emaciated, and pitiable. Their faces held the blank expressions of animals sizing up a meal or deciding whether to flee. A single voice rose from their midst, calling out a phrase Saito's translator rendered as, "Garrison pigs, Garrison pigs. This is not your place." Several people spat to the side.

"Wonderful," he muttered.

He saw movement in the gloom up on the sagging mesh mezzanine. Two meager lanterns burned up that way. In their light, four or five children were working, but the nature of their work was impossible to make out. They kept to the inner edges of the mesh floor where it was presumably more secure—or where they could grab handholds on the walls if their section gave way.

"What are they doing?" he asked Eggo.

"Theys getting the, uh, *soongdoh.*"

Saito's translator rendered the word as *wedding music*, but it must've mixed up languages. "The what?"

"The... food... plant. Growing in the..." He whisked his fingers through a patch of moisture on the wall beside them. "The waters."

"The humidity? They're harvesting slime mold?"

Kirdy had taken back the monoscope earlier, and he held it up to his left eye, checking out the mezzanine. "Not slime, Gunsō. Something growing in it. Some kinda prickly crap."

Saito shook off his curiosity. He'd seen all sorts of habits and traditions and survival strategies around this arm of the galaxy, and he'd seen many forms of poverty. This wasn't so weird. Eggo had his fingers inside some furry moss where the wall met the floor. He plucked something dark and multilegged out, huffed in pleasure, and popped it in his mouth. In the silence, Saito clearly heard the crunch.

"All right, I've had enough of this room. Eggo, tell your friends we're just passing through. Tell them," he said more slowly, mindful of the language barrier and lack of translator, "we go and won't hurt them. Tell them, don't hurt us."

"So," the boy said, nodding. "Yes, yes."

He stepped out from the pack of troopers. Some kind of signal passed between him and the tallest of the women, who'd risen to her feet and walked out of the wet. She replied in a flurry of hand signals, with a single slurry word added to them. Behind her, others rose, and Saito saw long knives and a model carbine he'd last seen used by Damalastan separatists a thousand chronological years ago.

Eggo turned, wearing the sleazy smile of the practiced salesman. "Lady says youse give-a things to she. Youse give-a... uh...?" He didn't have the word, so he darted up to Kirdy and patted the vest pocket with the first aid symbol on it. The corporal shoved him roughly away.

"They want medicine?" Saito asked.

"Just shoot 'em," Wegley grumbled.

Kirdy demanded, "You wanna scratch a dozen unarmed, scrawny-assed civs, squeak? That the kinda man you are?"

"Slag you, Corp," Wegley said, turning his face away.

Saito hushed them both. "All right, Eggo. You say to the lady we'll give some things." He pointed at the man with the carbine. "He puts the gun on the floor first." He mimed it. "Gun on the floor until we are gone."

"Yes, yes," the boy said, "I says it to she."

He told her something, and the leader lady accepted it with a flicker of irritated resignation. She motioned her people to put away their blades and barked another indistinct word at the carbine wielder. He laid down his weapon with a snarl then stalked off to the periphery to sulk.

Saito directed Kirdy and Pytor to give Glark and Eggo a single field dressing each, plus an ampoule of caffeine-yohimbine solution and another of antibiotics. From his own pouches, he removed two of his five antiseptic swabs and passed them to Eggo. For a second, he considered adding the two energy bars he'd packed, but they reminded him it was past time his team ate something. And drank something. The team's energy bars were all they had for food, unless they wanted to eat bugs or that *soongdoh* crap. And only Caiu, Dola, and Temuz had carried water canteens. Dola's was up on the villa roof, Temuz's shot up, Caiu's taken with him.

"That's all," he told Eggo.

The boy ran them across to the woman.

Then Glark pointed to one of three exits from the chamber. Saito ordered everyone to eat one of their energy bars and told the kids he'd give them more medicine when they arrived safely at the spaceport. He made Kirdy, Eggo, and Shill take point, with Pytor and Glark nestled in behind them. He and Jabari followed, and Wegley helped Naomi and brought up the rear. Within seconds of the front trio entering the new passageway, Kirdy and Shill could be heard trading bickering and insults.

Jabari and Saito shook their heads.

Jabari said, "She doesn't like people destroying her tech."

"He doesn't understand why she took down our quaestor and put us all under threat of mutiny charges. Neither do I."

"If I can convince you to come with *us*, you can forget about Imperial Army tribunals and so forth, and they'd drop the mutiny charges, anyway, in favor of desertion charges." He flashed a tired grin.

"Hilarious. And where would we be going? If we came with you?"

"We have some options."

"So, from this, I can confirm Optio-Major Scipio wasn't the only one who went rogue."

"From an Imperial Army viewpoint, I guess that's true."

"What other viewpoint is there, Jabari? For us, I mean."

"There's a Terranist one."

"No such thing anymore."

"As long as we live, there is."

Saito gave him a long look. "Something happened to you out there. Something extreme."

"You could say that."

"But you have our backs."

"We're here to get you off Vadox alive and to present some choices to you."

"I like the first part."

"If you'd come with Scipio and seen what we saw, you'd be in total sync with me, Saito."

"So mysterious," Saito grunted, deciding it was time to change the subject. He nodded at Jabari's coverall pockets. "You have food?"

"Shill and I had a big breakfast."

"I wish we'd brought clean water."

"You weren't expecting a protracted mission. Neither were we, to be honest." Jabari patted Saito's shoulder in comradely fashion. "There'll be food and water at the spaceport. Smugglers normally have the good stuff."

"Which is what we're angling to become? Smugglers?"

"For as long as it takes to get off world."

"The living shit," he sighed. "How'd this mission go so sideways?"

"All started back when we surrendered to the Imperium and switched fealty to its emperors."

When Saito looked at him sharply, Jabari shrugged and gestured politely for him to pass first through a narrow entry to a new stretch of tunnel.

The beams from various lamps and flashlights bobbed about, casting shadows that ducked and swayed and morphed and zigzagged like nervous boxers skirting each other. The bickering ahead had fallen silent. For the next few minutes, the operators kept to their own counsel and own thoughts.

From behind them, Wegley broke the silence. "Lieutenant Jabari?"

"Yes, Private?"

"How in a sack skimmer's armpit are you so calm during all this shit? Don't you care about dying?"

It's a good question, Saito thought as he watched Jabari throw an answer over his shoulder.

"Simple, Private. We were already dead. Or as good as. Shill and I faced it together. Made our peace. Then death passed us by. Gave us an extension, you might say. So, the breaths I've taken since are gifts, bonuses. And whatever breaths I'm to take in the future are the same." He paused to let the two in back catch up a little. "By the way, let's make a deal, Private Wegley. You don't call me Lieutenant, and I don't call you 'squeak' like I've heard the others do."

Not that he's ever called him that, thought Saito. *He's treated the little snot with the same respect as the rest of us.*

"Deal," Wegley responded quickly, as Naomi laughed.

"I'm still calling him 'squeak,'" she said. "Even if it means he stops helping me, which you're really bad at, by the way, squeak. I don't need your slaggin' arm around my shoulder when it's my arm that's missing, not my leg."

Wegley had already separated from her before she finished speaking, cursing her. "Gunsō told me to help. What am I meant to—"

"What I really need you to do is *open this sackin' protein bar for me.*"

"Well, how was I s'posed to—"

"What? You couldn't see me struggling with it one-handed?"

"I was too slagging busy getting my own open one-handed."

"Because you had your other hand around me, where it wasn't slagging needed."

And on it went. The squabbling had shifted from the front pair to the rear pair. No point micro-managing it, Saito figured. So long as they focused when it was necessary, any kind of conversation might be what they needed to keep the exhaustion at bay, to keep their energy up, to bleed off their anxieties.

Sidestepping an old brown rat carcass, Saito split the wrapper around the top of his protein bar. He tore off the top third and held it toward Jabari. The man didn't take it. "Gotta fuel up," Saito said, "big breakfast or not."

After a half beat's pause, Jabari took it with a nod of thanks.

The passage was wide enough to easily walk two abreast. The two men did so, chewing the tasteless military issue 'food.' Saito used the back of one hand to wipe a fresh sheen of sweat from his brow.

"Godsdamned warm down here."

Jabari nodded. "One thing the Hill had going for it: the air up above the desert was cool. You know, where I lived when I was a boy, the dawns were the only time of day…" He paused a moment then exhaled softly. "I sounded like an old man talking."

"You *are* an old man. We're all old. A couple more stints in stasis, a couple more decantings, and we'll have been around for two millennia."

Jabari's next snort was even softer. "Even so, I think I've been decanted more than most."

Saito glanced at Jabari's dark, springy hair and his profile. The guy looked about his age in biological years, maybe older. He stuffed the stub of the protein bar into his mouth and dropped the wrapper, then swung his rifle to his back, unbuttoned his right sleeve, and dragged it back to reveal his bio-tat. He held it up in his vest's lamplight, revealing his biological age.

Jabari passed the borer cannon back to Wegley, teased his own sleeve, and leaned into the sergeant's light since he didn't have any of his own.

"Forty-nine," Saito read.

"You have just a few years on me, Sergeant Saito."

"I'm your senior in maturity; you're mine in rank."

Jabari let the sleeve go and retrieved the borer. "I told you, I'm—"

"Not a lieutenant anymore. Yeah, yeah, I copy." It was risky continuing this conversation in full hearing of the two behind them—and Pytor could probably hear them up ahead—but Saito's curiosity had been held at bay long enough. "You really deserted?"

Jabari chewed on his answer a while, then said, "Some of our story I'm not sure you'll believe. But the bottom line is that Corfid bastard led us into Hell. Real Hell. He got good people killed for nothing—just as your quaestor did today."

Unsure why it rankled him, Saito's face heated up, and he blurted, "Not her fault."

Jabari went on without acknowledging the interruption. "Also, Shill and I saw something… something we can't unsee. Everyone else who went on that mission died because of it, except for us. And like I said, I'm not sure you'd believe it. But we cheated death. There has to be a purpose in that. There *is* a purpose. It's why we're here."

"Rescuing us."

Jabari nodded. "From Ectorius' ambush—and more." He half-twisted a moment, considering the two behind and squinting into their lamps. "I know you two."

"Well, I don't know you," said Wegley. "Sir."

"I've served with you, sir," Naomi said. "The time they unfroze five hundred of us, right?"

"The D'jiit Offensive, yes. *And* you were also in the over-watch squad for the Qlan Zufondi takedown."

"Yes, sir. You led the fireteam down in the town. Sack..." She winced from a jolt of pain in her arm, then steadied. "I was way up on the hill, nothing to do with your guys, and you remember me there? You've a good memory, sir."

Jabari winked at Saito. "Not so old, then. If the memory's still sharp."

A pause. Saito knew exactly what would end it and placed a bet with himself that Wegley wouldn't last the minute.

And he was right.

"Sir. How about me? Where'd you see me?"

"You, Private? I saw you in your stasis tank and in your records, the last time I was given freedom to check them. You're one of the last, Wegley. One of the chosen to carry our name and—if possible—even our genes forward."

The message was similar to the one Saito had given the young man back in his cabin on the quaestor's shuttle. *One of the last.* The Proselyti would *all* vanish one day, no matter how many times they went into stasis. The thought of how quickly those remaining numbers had been depleted in the last few weeks, in just two missions, was gut-wrenching. He calculated mission elapsed time by checking his bio-tat. He, himself, had lost four Proselyti in less than two hours! It felt like they'd been on Vadox for *days*!

"I'll do us proud, sir," Wegley said behind him, replying to Jabari.

It sounded like he was finding his courage, his heart, and it had taken over an hour and a half in hell to do it. Saito had no doubt Lt. Jabari Mbaye's stoic example had helped. Another man might have experienced jealousy that Jabari had inspired Wegley when his own efforts hadn't. Saito felt nothing of the sort. Undoubtedly, there'd been dozens of leaders of various types who'd tried to harden the kid, to polish his character. Jabari was the latest, and if that was what it took to make a man of Wegley, so be it. Saito just hoped the kid would live to see a full lifetime.

Naomi had said nothing to disparage Wegley's last remark, and the group fell silent. That suited Saito...

The passage seemed to be following a contour line around the slope, staying mostly level without climbing or descending noticeably. For the next half hour, they followed it, picking their way carefully through three places where there'd been collapses, and the locals had shored up tight accessways through them. Finally, light bloomed ahead, obvious enough for the forward troopers to turn off their lamps. Saito followed suit and told the two at his back to do the same. Pytor and Glark were visible ahead as silhouettes against a garish glow. Pytor had stopped and was holding the boy in place. Past him, Kirdy hissed something. Pytor dropped into a crouch and passed the message back in a stage whisper.

"Gunsō, they need you."

Saito left the others where they were and hustled past Pytor and Glark. He found his footing unsteady as the floor became increasingly littered with pieces of stone and eternicrete. Ahead, Kirdy, Shill, and Eggo had ducked down and were framed against a ragged rectangle of bright midday sky. As Saito drew near, he saw steel beams chocking up the walls and roof, keeping them in place. The leading trio was staring down at something—and he could hear what sounded like crowd noise outside, along with the moaning of the wind across the tunnel mouth. He duckwalked the final few meters. Shill drew Eggo aside to make room for him at the front. Saito peered out.

At some point in the past, there'd been a landslide or an explosion. Whatever it was had taken a two-hundred-meter-wide swathe of hillside with it, a section that had included the next stretch of the passageway. He stared directly down into a bowl-shaped gouge in the slope—just rock and dirt with a reservoir of trash in its belly. To the right was a sea of four-, five-, and six-story hovels, along with other ruined buildings that appeared to have been repurposed, judging by the fragments of cloth and awnings stretched across some of them. To the left was the upslope toward the affluent parts of the Hill. And the Wall.

Where the earth had come away just below the Wall, a plat-form had been built, perhaps as part of some engineering effort toward reinforcement that prevented the wall from crumbling. Across the platform, a crowd of hundreds had gathered. Because his vantage point was sixty or so meters below it, Saito could only see those milling at the edges, but the sounds were those of a multitude—shouting, wailing, and some chanting. The crowd seemed to bleed from either side as people came and went along the base of the wall where narrower ledges were visible from below.

"What in hells are they doing?" he murmured.

"What youse saying is in here?" Eggo asked him.

He frowned at the boy as he watched him tap both sides of his chest with his index fingers. "*What*?"

"What are making this...?" The lad exaggerated an inhale and exhale, then tapped his ribs again. "What are making me do-a this? What youse saying it?"

"Lungs?" Shill asked him. "You mean your lungs? Where the air goes in and out?"

"Air going in *lungs*? Yes?" He pointed up to the crowd.

"Theys families. Theys' loving peoples who got-a the, uh, black lungs."

"Black lungs?" Saito, Kirdy, and Shill all said in perfect unison.

"The guards walkings on the wall, they helpings one peoples once a day, one family."

"They help one family? Help *how*?" Saito asked him. If the guards were observing the crowd, they'd be in perfect position to spy a group of fugitive off-world troopers sneaking out of a broken tunnel directly below them...

"They saying it a 'lottery.' You saying same word? Pay-a five stellars for one ticket. This day, they say, 'This ticket winning. You-family bring your black lungs person up to door, us medic helping youse."

"Goddamn slaggers," Shill muttered. "A lottery."

Kirdy added in the same tone, "Dark-hearted dog sackers."

"And and and," the boy added, face alight with enjoyment over the reaction his report was provoking. "Theys guards soming times put the foods and... med-i-cines... out the window and laughing when-a the families fightings for the foods and med-i-cines."

"Yeah," Shill said, catching Kirdy's eye. "Dog sackers, all right."

"Poor folks shouldn't be entertainment," the corporal muttered. The distaste etching itself into his features might have been more about how he was agreeing with Shill than about the treatment of the favela dwellers.

"What is black lungs?" Saito asked Eggo. "What makes black lungs?"

"The dirt. In the mines." The boy pointed to the right in the direction of the Panlands. He slapped his chest. "Sick. Sick." He coughed to emphasize it.

"Ah," Saito said. "That's the way of it here, is it?"

"Rich get richer," Shill murmured. "The poor just get sicker."

Her gaze tracked a surveillance drone that whizzed over the crowd and came to rest at the crowd's backs off the end of the platform. Yet another 'observer' the team had to dodge getting out of there.

Saito craned his neck and whistled the rest of the team forward. Then he asked Shill, "Where's that spaceport from here?"

She pointed. "See that orangey brown past those buildings?"

For a few seconds, Saito couldn't focus on anything in that direction other than the first layers of poorly constructed housing towers and the rickety walkways slung between them. Then a background resolved between them—a distant smudge in the same butterscotch shades as the legendary soil of Mars. Making out more detail was impossible with all the other crap in the way and the fact it was kilometers distant. To move out directly toward it would involve a mad downhill dash across the landslide area before plunging into the unknown dangers of the favelas themselves.

"And how in the mythical hells are we going to get there without anyone seeing us?"

Without Garrison troopers or favela dwellers murdering us...

In the interval, Glark had crept up to join them. He patted Saito's shoulder and grinned madly, saying, "Us helping youse get-a out, sirs. But youse paying us now."

Saito had known in the back of his mind it would come to something like this. They didn't have much choice, so he narrowed his eyes at both boys and said, "Tell me what you have in mind."

PART TWO

ADAPTIVE STRATEGIES

"More than a millennium has passed since the defeat of the Terranists. Anyone who could claim to be purely 'Earth-descended' is long gone, due to centuries of successful genetic integration since the War.

"After a thousand years of peace, the writers of this book believe it is time to call a star a star and an empire an empire. Our Imperium is not the Martianist *Imperium. We all know from whom we descend. The blood of ancient Martian colonists flows in all of us to varying degrees.*

"We are the Imperium; the Imperium is us.

"And to those who maintain rebel factions outside our frontiers, we say this: once and for centuries, the empire encompassed the entire galaxy. One day, it will again..."

The Layperson's Guide to the Glories of the Imperium, First Edition, Year 4690

CHAPTER FIFTEEN

WAITING FOR EGGO

"GUNSŌ, how long're we sitting here waiting?"

The question came from Wegley. The others would—like Saito—be wondering if he'd made the right choice, paying the boys in trivial knickknacks and first aid items before letting them scamper free, not to mention making everyone wait here. Unlike Wegley, they were too experienced and disciplined to let those thoughts spill out.

"*Gunsō?*"

"Shut it, squeak!" Kirdy snapped. The corporal was squatting in the middle of the group, which had arranged itself into two lines facing each other across the narrow tunnel. One line of three, one line of four.

Saito and Jabari sat on their asses up front. The floor and walls were bone dry, entirely free of the earlier moisture and the associated slime and moss. Although the breeze was warm near the bottom of the Hill, Saito was glad for it as it asserted itself through the passageway's exposed mouth. The wind had shifted direction in the past ten minutes and now blew directly at them, drying the sweat from their exposed skin and helping lower their body temperatures. They'd still require water, although the need wasn't urgent yet. Perched on the ruined section of hillside, Saito sensed the ambient temperature outside the Wall and along the lower reaches of the Hill was at least ten degrees higher than it had been at the summit. If they needed to exert themselves for a prolonged period and move downhill where the air grew hotter, the potential for dehydration would only increase.

For millennia, the Imperial Army had issued combat suits that recycled the body's sweat and urine. The suits wicked it, filtered it, then provisioned it back to the wearer via a sipping tube in the collar. They'd not been issued *those* suits, of course. A simple snatch-grab-run mission didn't anticipate long hours spent in near-desert conditions. And there was still the distinct possibility some pissed-off *Maelstrom* commander had passive-aggressively undermined the quaestor who'd danced in and borrowed their prized Proselyti.

"Gunsō, if that pursuit droid comes up behind us..."

"Wegley," Saito said levelly, "I believe the corporal gave you an order."

After a loud sigh, the young private fell quiet. The outburst hadn't really been an outburst, but it was an indication Wegley hadn't had a miraculous change of character, hadn't grown fully into his soldier role after all. Across from him, Naomi stretched out a leg and tapped his boot with hers. "Pursuit droid *can't* come up behind us. Too bulky to get in that first manhole. No hands to open the cover."

"Oh." Wegley nodded in relief. "Right."

"Nah," she chuckled and kicked him harder, more playfully. "It'll come in the front and take out Gunsō first."

"You slagging grunfer," he muttered, but he was smiling.

She chuckled again, drew her knees up to her vest, and hugged them with her arm.

Pytor's feet were tapping arrhythmically, Saito noticed, shifting around the dust. The trooper's legs were swinging side to side, his eyes squeezed shut and his chin lowered to the top of his vest.

Withdrawal? Saito wondered. *Or simple antsiness?*

He checked the narrow shadows outside and cleared his throat. "It's about midday in these parts. We have ten hours of daylight left. Those boys don't return, we can wait and descend into the favelas under cover of dark." He waited for someone to object or interject. Nobody did. So, he added an objection himself. "Except delaying that long will allow the Garrison to recover from their gut bug and regroup, or the pursuit droid might have time to locate us."

Several people groaned, but it was half-hearted.

Wegley cleared his throat and said, "Gunsō, I'm only offering a suggestion here. But we could go back to that room where the civs were getting water and stuff. None of them have been coming out this way, so that means one of the other exits leads into the favelas."

Jabari said, "Private, there might be a dozen reasons why they haven't followed us: wariness; a lack of progress with their daily tasks; this not being the way to *their* part of the favelas. It's good you considered backtracking, but underground and without local guides, we'd risk getting lost in a potential maze." He flicked a hand toward the open air outside. "From here, at least we have a clear line of sight to our objective."

"Agreed," Saito sighed. He leaned toward the lip of the tunnel and used Kirdy's monocular to look at the Wall and confirm details he'd marked before: the two visible ledges with sally ports further along where at least one guard loitered; the series of embrasures at varying heights and distances where plenty of weapons and weapons wielders might easily focus on the ground between the Wall and the closest favela housing towers.

Shaking his head, he marveled, "Those sackheads."

"Who?" asked Kirdy.

"Those guards up there have time to make sport of a crowd of lottery applicants down on that platform even though they're shorthanded from illnesses."

"And still have a team of hostile intruders wandering their city," Shill said by way of agreement.

Jabari's shrug was evident in his tone. "It wouldn't be the first time we've come across a *that's-someone-else's-job* attitude among soldiers. That kind of thinking has been a steady feature of human behavior across all epochs…"

Saito nodded at the intelligent analysis, but he was still taken aback by the soldiers' stupidity. He put the monocular inside a vest pouch and faced the team, drawing their attention. "If the upper part of the city is rich enough to man and maintain a wall like this, they're rich enough to equip them with solid night vision *and* adequate sensor tech. Daytime, nighttime —it won't make much difference to them when we exit this hole. Before he ran off, Eggo told me the guards often drag out the medical lottery till the middle of the afternoon. There'll be a commotion when they announce it—or a commotion if they do the other thing he said they do."

Shill nodded. "Chucking out goodies to the paupers and watching 'em fight over them."

"If the lads aren't back, no matter which distraction comes first, it's our time to go." He made a knife blade out of his hand and stabbed it down toward the favelas. "Two groups, three in one, four in the other. We straight-line it down to the nearest structure. First team who makes it watches both ways till the other joins them. From there, we'll again be in Shill's hands in terms of directions."

From the corner of his eye, he saw Jabari nod with approval.

It irritated him that it made him feel good.

CHAPTER SIXTEEN

HOW DO WE SOLVE A PROBLEM LIKE CHEBEEBEL?

"COME IN, MASTER CHEBEEBEL, COME IN."

The pilot's seat had been swiveled to face the cockpit doorway, allowing Aurelia a direct view along the length of corridor on the lower deck. It was Dr. May who'd summoned Galen's guest out of the cabin. Having fetched Chebeebel, the tech-medic departed for her cabin on the upper deck where she was to await another summons to come pilot the craft.

Chebeebel ventured no closer than the doorway, since the cockpit lacked standing room or extra seating. For several reasons, Aurelia felt the arrangement suited the situation, with her seated comfortably and him standing uncomfortably before her. He regarded her sullenly and remained gratifyingly silent.

"Let's get down to business, shall we?" she asked.

A micro expression rippled across the man's face, one that stated, *I wish you would!* But a new light had entered his eyes at her use of the word "business." It was a word he liked, and apparently, it gave him hope.

Flourishing her now-functioning right arm, she said, "I have a recorder embedded here, and it's recording this conversation as a legally admissible verification of the information exchanged between us and of the offer I'm about to make."

At her next pause, Chebeebel couldn't help himself. He leaned one hand against the doorframe and pretended to be indifferent. "Offer, you say? Since I'm your *prisoner*—" presumably the emphasis was for the benefit of the record "—I suppose I must listen."

Aurelia lowered the arm to her lap. "The recording bears my official code so no one can claim it's been faked. If our conversation concludes in a way that aids my assignment here, I'll transfer a copy to your files before we part company. I assume you have...?" She touched her temple.

Chebeebel hesitated for a moment then touched the folds of thick flesh at the side of his neck. "I had it put here," he said, meaning one of the implanted personal storage drives that had become fashionable.

"Wonderful. Now. You informed me upon our meeting that you're currently the Secretary to the Bursar of the Chamber of Magnates?"

"That's correct. And the Chief Sharetaker of Chen-Elysium Enterprises."

"That sharetaker role doesn't interest me; it's based on how you spend your money. The secretarial role does; it's how you make your money... and your prestige." When he had no response, she pressed on, baiting her hook. "How would you like to improve your position in our empire, advance your career? In other words, would a promotion of sorts be of interest?"

The bait was enticing, she could tell. His nostrils flared as if he could smell it, while his eyes darted around the room as if following a hook being jerked through the water. "Go on," he said.

"*Secretary to the Bursar* is a role that's at least two steps away from any meaningful power and influence. It's like saying you're a servant of a servant."

The hand against the doorframe slipped off as the insinuation rocked him. He drew himself up, mustered his dignity, and said, "I wield *great* influence, I'll have you know! 'Servant of a servant,' indeed! If I *am* a servant, then I serve in one of the greatest halls of power that exists in this entire galaxy!"

There was more of his blustering. A full minute more. She let him tire himself, then pressed on, dangling the baited hook nearer.

"But you wouldn't turn down a role in which you could *directly* influence imperial policy? A role in which you'd enjoy a biannual face-to-face audience with His Highness Emperor Nero himself? Where you'd be seen on gridcasts across this entire galaxy, demonstrating your flare for economic management and strategy? Would you?"

"I... uh... the emperor, himself? Ah... hm." His hand went back to the doorframe as his outrage dissolved. With his double chins lifted, he gestured with his other hand that she should continue.

Straightening her back, she said, "Master Chebeebel, I'm in a position to offer you a seat on the Imperial Treasury Policy Committee for Taxation, Appropriations, and Spending."

The position—the seat—was Florene's. Her sister had already told Aurelia she'd be stepping down from it once Ectorius' removal was complete. Aurelia had Emperor Nero's assurance he'd appoint Florene as Ectorius' replacement if that's what she wanted; in turn, Aurelia was completely confident her sister would back her recommendation for this Chebeebel fellow as *her* replacement on the committee. It was established tradition for committee members to appoint the next person to hold their seat when they vacated it. And there could be no complaint that Florene had made a poor appointment. The man might appear to be a buffoon, but a position such as he already held was one that depended upon merit, ability, and performance. The kind of knowledge, skills, and contacts he'd demonstrated would make him a competent member of the committee.

At the mere mention of the position, Chebeebel's face flushed red, and his jaw fell open. His eyes widened, narrowed, then widened. Aurelia had him. The hook was in. She just had to *land* the great fish—and guarantee he'd stay on the boat rather than wriggling or thrashing his way off it again. If *that* happened, there'd be no choice other than killing him. This great fish could not be allowed his freedom.

"I'll attach two notes to this audio file for your eyes only, dear sir, one explaining how all of this will transpire, another introducing you to the current seat holder who'll vacate it ahead of your appointment. I assure you, the offer and the opportunity are real. All you need to do to secure them is one simple thing."

"What, ah, what is it I need to do? To, ah, secure this opportunity?"

"Leave this star system immediately and make no mention of your contact with me to anyone at any time. Ever. Raise no alarm today. Do not alert Governor Ectorius or anyone connected with him. Have no further conversation with anyone, even Senator Galen. I'm spelling this out so there can be no misunderstandings."

Expression sober, but eyes alight over the boon he'd been handed, Chebeebel didn't seem to care one iota about Galen or Ectorius. He told her, "Your mission, your presence here, my experiences with you—I'm happy to never mention any of it again, honored Madam Quaestor. I promise you."

"I promise you." The man's like a child at Year's End, bargaining to get the gift they want.

"You're sure? Because you're entering into a legal contract, one that will be your ruin if you break it."

"Oh, my stars, no, I won't break it! You can be assured of that. I have a shuttle in orbit. I'll leave immediately. I'll pass on a message about work matters requiring my presence to excuse myself from the soiree."

"Oh, the soiree? You were invited to that? It's still slated to go ahead?"

"On Orbital One." He checked the time on the helm over her shoulder. "Pre-party commences in around an hour."

This confirmed what the files had stated. Ectorius would be staying up there. All she had to do was get to him.

I was forced into a change of plans, she thought, rehearsing her report to her supervising magistrate. *Ectorius nestled himself away behind multiple lines of defense after sidelining my insertion team, thereby removing my ability to simply abduct or disappear him. I made the decision that the next best thing would be to have his staff find him dead in his Orbital stateroom of an apparent cardiac arrest.* Reflexively, she extended and withdrew the injector in her pinky, wondering how she might circumvent his poison buffers.

The man in the doorway cleared his throat, reminding her he was there. "Er, shall I...?" He gestured behind him.

"If we have a deal, by all means, retire to a comfortable compartment on the top deck while we head for orbit."

"We most certainly do have a deal, Madam Quaestor. If you'd be so kind as to...?" He tapped the spot on his neck.

Aurelia mentally actioned the command string that ended the recording, saying, "When we're closing on Orbital One, I'll end my comms jamming and transmit the files to you."

"Marvelous. And may I say this has been a most fortuitous meeting, and I'm glad to have met you, and His Highness will be glad of my appointment to his committee." The man couldn't have been friendlier—now that she'd changed his life for the better.

"It's worked out rather well," she agreed. "Please send down Dr. May from the top deck."

"Indeed, I shall," he announced, all helpfulness and smiles. He turned to go.

"Master Chebeebel, one more thing?"

He turned back. "Yes?"

"You'll be giving my trooper Lonzo a ride directly to the residence of the current seat holder on the committee."

"Oh. Very well."

"And when you meet that seat holder, please give her my love."

Aurelia and Lonzo watched as May went about removing or disabling Senator Galen's various implanted alerts and comms modules. It took her all of nine minutes. Galen fumed and glared at her the entire time, but May never once made eye contact with him.

When she was done, she reported, "He has a *defensive toxin delivery system* built into the fingernails of his left hand. I've disabled that, too."

"Dear lady," Aurelia replied, "you'll receive special mention in my report to the Magistrates and emperor."

May flushed, and Aurelia beamed at her before sending her forward to fly them to Orbital One with a message for its traffic control that the senator and his staff wanted to do some shopping before the big party.

When she was gone, Galen curled his lip at Aurelia. "Manipulative bitch."

"You're just miffed you won't be able to scratch me and make me curl up and die."

"Sure am. I see May repaired *your* arm."

"A terrific tech-medic. Your House always did employ the best."

"Not terrific enough to fix your eye," he sneered, flicking his fingers at her eyepatch.

"Let's put that one down to an enemy of the state I met earlier."

He scoffed, "'Enemy of the state!' Delusions. Shadows. Fantasies. That's the basis for the High Magistrates' existence and power. In all probability, you disabled your cybernetics to garner sympathy from the simpleminded—Dr. May and this sewer rat." He nodded toward Lonzo.

"Sure, I did." She gestured to the firearm damage across her face and head. "I also grazed myself with a dozen ballistic rounds from a distance of three to eight meters away."

The faintest of vibrations ran through the deck—the shuttle's thrusters starting up.

Undeterred, Galen continued ranting from his seat. "You've detained me—a duly elected senator, born of a High House!—without due cause or evidence of malfeasance. You've murdered or stolen my staff. Presumably, you've murdered my *friend*. Are there no limits to the insanity of your office and its agents? What will you do for your next barbarous trick? Vent me out my own airlock near Orbital One?"

"Actually," she said, "that's one of the options I've been considering."

"I'm unsurprised." He folded his arms and leaned back.

The fingers of his left hand flexed and tapped over his right bicep, as if he was imagining scratching her with his nails. She saw they were a tad long and chided herself for not noticing upon first meeting him. Then again, she hadn't really been in a fit state.

"We'll discuss the other options once Lonzo has departed, and I'm poised to visit Ectorius."

He regarded her with outright detestation from behind hooded eyes.

At her choice of words, Lonzo stirred and came to stand beside her.

"Pardon me, Madam, but *what*? Whadda you mean, when I depart?"

"You perhaps imagined you'd be fleeing *with* me once my job was done? Dear Lonzo, that won't be the case, largely because I can't guarantee I'll be alive once my job is done. Also, because the senator and Dr. May are the only assistance I'll require moving forward."

"What?" Lonzo repeated.

Galen merely snorted and turned his head away, no doubt imagining several uses she might have for him.

"Madam..." Lonzo started.

"I'll leave you to guard Senator Galen for a short period while I change outfits and complete a handwritten note of introduction that you'll present to my sister, Florene Cossea. She'll receive you based on my handwriting and certain coded phrases I'll place within the message. She'll reimburse you for your efforts in assisting me, *and* she'll ensure the High Magistrates Office rewards you a further thousand stellars for your service to justice today."

"Service to justice," Galen muttered.

Ignoring him, she met Lonzo's stunned stare. "From there, you'll have your freedom, Lonzo. Freedom from your employment contract here on Vadox CX, from any charges Chebeebel or the Galen family might try to press against you—they can't do that by the way—and from *any* legal obligations to Governor Ectorius or his garrison. Your life will be your own, and you'll have money in your pocket to start over."

Lonzo rubbed the back of his head and switched his focus to Galen as he thought everything through. "I'd'a just done this for the fun, Madam. Honest. Making him and the other rich shit-pie suffer. Ain't many people what gets to enjoy this *fleh'ten maakri* life. That's coz the rich ones make life bad for the poor ones. I mean, the emperor's all right, Madam, and his Imperial Family. I believe *they* tries the best for us poors. But if us poors wants to make money and get any pleasures, we gots to find jobs like merc jobs or sales jobs or something like them that makes you do bad things for your money. So, I likes making rich shit-pies hurt a little. And if that's 'service to justice,' then fair enough. And if this is all you needs, Madam, fair enough too. But if you wants me to hang about the space station and make more rich ones hurt some, I'll do it. Even if it kills me, I'll do it. And I'll do it for you. You's been better to me in two hours than all the other rich ones I met in all my fifty-seven years."

"My, what a magnificent speech," Galen scoffed. "Profound. Deeply moving."

Still ignoring him, she moved across and placed a hand on Lonzo's arm to give it a friendly squeeze. "I think you'll hurt these 'shit-pies' best by going and living a happy life from here on out. To spite them. Just promise me one thing?"

"Anything, Madam."

"Live lawfully the rest of your life. Live justly, kindly, and generously toward those with less fortune."

He nodded solemnly. "If that's your orders, then that's what I'll do."

Another squeeze and she released his arm. "I have clothes to find and a letter to pen. After that—" her attention swung Galen's way "—we'll be docking at Orbital One, and this shit-pie and I will have *our* next steps to discuss."

CHAPTER SEVENTEEN

CLOAKING STRATEGY

THE TWO BOYS returned before another exit strategy became necessary. Saito noticed them coming before Jabari did. The lads were laboring uphill, dragging a makeshift sled behind them across the dirt and shale. What the wall guards made of them, if they were even looking, was anyone's guess. Certainly, nobody up there challenged the kids. Perhaps they were used to the scavengers coming and going from this hole in the mountain; perhaps anything beyond the base of the wall didn't concern them. In any case, Eggo and Glark arrived at the tunnel mouth without harassment and gratefully accepted help to drag the sled the final meter or so into cover. They'd raised the hoods attached to the backs of their ragamuffin shirts, ostensibly against the early afternoon ultraviolet rays, but Saito knew it was to assist with the ruse the team was about to engage in.

He and Jabari unloaded the sled's cargo of oversized cloaks and tossed them to the others. As they shook them out, they appeared to be of similar design—woven from thin material, many years old, open at the front, with string fasteners in place of a belt and sun cowls stitched behind their necks. They smelled musty from old sweat and spices. No one complained, not even Wegley. Saito figured they'd smelled a lot worse today.

"Us giving *all* the things youse givings us," Glark told Saito.

Saito puzzled over the meaning of his words for five seconds before he got it. "Cost you everything I paid you, huh? Don't worry, we'll still pay you again at the other end. Lorica will too, I imagine."

"Turns out Gunsō knew what he was doing, huh?" Naomi asked Wegley with heavy sarcasm. When the young man didn't immediately reply, she added, "Help me get this on, squeak. It's another thing I need your help with."

The cloaks didn't fit everyone equally. Shill, Naomi, and Wegley were comfortably concealed by theirs, although the troopers' vests and hidden rifles added some bulk. Saito, Jabari, Kirdy, and Pytor would have to hold the fronts of their cloaks closed across their vests and equipment pouches. Those with rifles hung them from one shoulder before putting their cloaks on, keeping the weapons flat against the right sides of their bodies. It might work if they remained facing away from the Wall as they descended; it wouldn't work inside the favela.

"We're Lorica's people," Jabari told the local boys. "All right?"

When they frowned at him, Saito used their form of pidgin Imperial True. "Us working for Lorica. Understand? When people down there stopping us, you saying them: Lorica us boss. Not Garrison; Lorica people."

The boys shrugged in unison. Eggo replied, "Good. We saying it. Good good."

Jabari had moved back to where he'd left the accelerator borer. "I'm not getting *this* under my cloak."

Shill suggested, "We could lay it on the sled."

He shook his head. "If we don't cover it sufficiently, any AI-cameras along that Wall will mark it as stolen mining equipment."

"Airborne drones, too," she agreed unhappily.

Kirdy scratched his scalp. "Use the rope from the sled, then? Cut some cloth from everyone's cloak and wrap it?"

"Not bad, Corporal." Saito nodded. "Make it happen." He signaled for Naomi to come forward and checked her eyes. They seemed alert. He asked her, "You can do this?"

"I'll go with the rear group, keep it slow and steady."

"Good. Jabari, if I carry your borer, you all right to stick with her?"

"Sure, Gunsō."

"Naomi, give Jabari your sidearm till you're in the favela. Take Glark. Wegley, you're with Jabari, too."

"Fine," the young man said without enthusiasm.

Saito rolled his shoulders, swung his arms, and stretched his back to the left and the right, limbering up after the long period of inactivity. When everyone was set, he led the first group down the slope in a careful jog that turned out to be *half*-jog, half-slide where the earth and shale were loose. Same as with the boys coming up, his group met no opposition going down. Lower down and closer to the chaos of the favela construction, Saito lost sight of the spaceport's swash of color. When they reached the shade between the two closest housing towers, they leaned against the walls, with their fingers on the triggers of their weapons. Saito and Pytor watched the second team coming down after them; Shill and Kirdy faced the alley that led into the favela's heart.

Up slope on the platform, the shouts and wails and chants continued, mixing in Saito's ears with the sounds of the town-scape he'd entered. The shouts and arguments of people mashed close together. The clanks and clatters and thuds of urban life. The screams of delight and the screams of outrage or angst he associated with heavily populated townships throughout all human civilizations and throughout history. *Homo sapiens* was a damned noisy species, and they'd spread that noise throughout a galaxy that had otherwise been silent. They'd taken Earth's flora and fauna and adapted them to every other lifeless rock ball they'd moved onto and into, then had the audacity to complain about the noises and messes made by the animals kept inside their cities. Give Saito a hike into isolated wilderness over a densely populated city any day. Give him poor, dead Temuz's dream of a quiet tearoom on a windswept mountainside where the only patrons were contemplatives, recluses, and introverted hikers. *Homo sapiens* were entitled to their lives, and Saito was committed to the peace that governed those lives, but he didn't like cities, no matter what form they took.

"Gunsō?" Pytor asked beside him, breaking into his thoughts.

Saito blinked himself back to the here and now. "Yeah?"

"All right if I gob a stim?"

Gob a ...?

Oh, right.

"Go for it. Just one, though."

"Yeah."

It took Pytor three seconds to get the ampoule of caffeine-yohimbine out of his aid pouch; he must have had it ready. The plasticoid capsules were meant to be loaded into the small injector each trooper carried; Pytor simply popped one in his mouth and started chewing it.

As long as it keeps him alert, Saito figured.

Jabari, Naomi, Wegley, and Glark descended the last twenty meters. Once their feet hit more solid ground, they picked up so much pace, that Saito had to catch Naomi in his arms to prevent her careening past. He swung her around like a dance partner until he could safely dump her on her ass against a windswept pile of soil. Wegley had to arrest himself against the wall of a building. Less panicked perhaps, Jabari and Glark skidded the final meter into the shade on hips and boots.

"So far, so good," Jabari said, moving down the alley to find a new point position.

The 'alleys' Saito had seen from above were really nothing more than space between buildings, paved with slabs or chunks of rock, eternicrete, concrete, and other materials, pressed down to create a rough-hewn hardiness. Jabari knelt at the first intersection where two channels of empty space collided; Kirdy moved forward to join him without being asked. Saito jerked his head at Pytor, and he broke position to go with them, Glark trailing behind.

To Shill and Eggo, Saito said, "Which one of you is guiding us?"

"This adorable child is," Shill said, ruffling the boy's hair.

Eggo pulled back from her touch, irritated. "I knowing. I taking youse."

Shill flashed the kid the working map on her data cuff. "And *I'm* making sure it's in the right direction."

Down the alley ahead of them, Pytor spat out the depleted ampoule.

The dry wind swirled and eddied among the favela's haphazard lanes and structures. It had swept up from the Panlands, picking up heat from the sunbaked earth and then from brick and stone, adobe and eternicrete.

The favela looked and felt like it had been hobbled together in the aftermath of a devastating war, but Saito knew it had been this way for centuries, a marriage of human desperation and human resourcefulness. It teemed with life, mostly human, though there was evidence of humanity's constant companions: flies, ants, roaches, and rats. No doubt, there'd be fleas and lice, too. He hoped to see *no* evidence of those.

In some places, Saito's nose wrinkled at the reek of raw

sewage or a drying puddle of some local's piss. In other places, his stomach tightened in hunger when he caught a whiff of exotic spices or frying onions. Staircases and gantries weaved and coiled about the overhead spaces, some of them defying gravity—or at least, defying sound engineering practices.

The team maintained the best diamond formation they could along a route whose paths broadened and narrowed without rhyme or reason. Naomi and Shill were in the center of the diamond, Jabari and Pytor in front, Wegley in the rear, and Kirdy on the left flank, with Saito on the right. Glark was all over the place and occasionally disappeared completely before popping out from some fissure or rubble heap to join them again. Eggo remained at Jabari's side. Jabari kept his borer wrapped up and was otherwise weaponless as far as Saito knew. Heads down and cowls up, they maintained their pace. Suspicion followed them, but the boys headed off inquiries and deflected abuse with sass and charm.

Fifteen minutes in, Saito turned a corner and found half his team blocked by a quintet of local lads who'd bottlenecked a thin lane with rocks and steel rods.

Eggo and Glark puffed out their chests and shook their fists and shouted at the youths. "Lorica *h'nagang*, Lorica *h'nagang. Fenni chleng, fenni chleng!*" Meanwhile heads poked from windows and rooftops above, spectating.

"Gods, I hope 'Lorica *h'nagang*' means Lorica's best friends," Shill muttered near Saito. The sergeant just grunted back, his focus on the body language of the five youths barring their way.

"Lorica *h'nagang! Fenni chleng!*" Eggo insisted in a yell that was close to a shriek.

Whatever the message meant, either the boy's tone or the frequent mention of the smuggler boss' name seemed to do the trick. The youths stepped aside, expressions stuck somewhere between resentment and envy. Saito's team began slipping through the gap in the crap piles one by one, keeping their body language liquid and confident.

When Saito reached Glark—who stood with one of the youths—the boy told him, "You giving." His small, brown hand lashed out and flicked Saito's vest beneath his cloak. Saito batted it away. "Giving something," the boy insisted.

Without comment and holding the stare of the closest youth, Saito reached into a pouch. His fingers found another antiseptic swab. He pulled the packet out and dropped it at the young man's bare feet. A smuggler gang's muscleman wouldn't be happy about handing over his hard-earned goods, he figured, so it was better to show a small amount of disrespect and displeasure as he did so. As expected, the youth didn't look down at it, let alone reach for it. He maintained his macho poise until the intruders moved out of his small patch.

Two minutes later, Saito took his turn easing over a rough edge where the pathway abruptly dropped five meters, then he descended a ladder that shook with his weight. All the while, he was trying to shake the gnawing intuition in his gut. The youths owned very little in life other than their patch and their pride. His team had sauntered through their patch at the cost of a packaged swab, and they hadn't pandered at all to the youths' pride. Some folks would let that go. They'd take the hit and spin the story to say they'd stared the intruding assholes down or embellish the tale so it looked like they'd taken an entire pallet of swabs as payment. Some folks. Smart folks. Older and wiser folks. The guardians of that patch of alleyway had neither been old nor wise—he hadn't seen a touch of smarts in those surly eyes.

"The living shit," he whispered as his boots touched ground again, and he watched Shill come down after him. He had a bad feeling those youths wouldn't let this go. They'd do something risky and stupid against these representatives of Lorica, something intended to entirely screw up Saito's day.

It happened barely fifteen minutes later.

The team emerged from another shadowy lane at the top of a kind of combined plaza and park. The surface was broken and jagged, and it sloped steeply down and ended in a berm of dirt and debris that rose nine or ten meters at the bottom. Perhaps the gradient and the unreliable surface marked it as a poor site for construction; perhaps the locals, at some point in the past, had simply decided they needed an open area to meet and mingle. Saito called a momentary halt at the top of the plaza and surveyed the area as it stretched a good three hundred meters downslope ahead of them. He took in the mishmash of improvised play equipment utilized by the children and teenagers interspersed among the informal market stalls where people haggled over foods and consumer items he didn't recognize. To the left and right of the plaza, a sea of tents and lean-tos marked a return to living space. The trading stalls closest to those flanks looked as if they'd simply spilled out from among the lean-tos.

"What are the chances of water here?" Naomi asked.

"*Bottled* water," Shill added. "If they have some, Gunsō, Jabari and I have stellars. No need to barter using first aid equipment."

"If they have some," he repeated and whistled for Eggo to come back. The kid obeyed reluctantly, eager to keep moving, if the way he was dancing from foot to foot was anything to go by. Saito mimed drinking. "Water. You saying *water* in your language?"

He had used the Imperial True noun's basic form in his question—*aqua.*

"*Aqua*, yes," the boy confirmed then appeared to repeat the word in a variety of other languages as he mimed drinking. "*Wasa. Vessee. Wa'ha. Nŭe. Su-su.*"

"*Aqua* will be fine, but in bottles," Saito told him. Once again, he performed a simple mime, pretending to hold something round while twisting off a lid.

Eggo led them to the middle of the plaza. A bubble of quiet followed them as members of the crowd grew silent at their approach and picked up their conversations after the final pair of troopers passed. Saito heard Glark use Lorica's name once, and then the word was passed around the crowd as people noticed the group of strangers who all sported high-quality weapons inside their robes. The stall Eggo halted by was a frame of sticks with a thin red and blue striped cloth stretched over it for shade. A middle-aged man missing his left hand sat on a box surrounded by wares—mismatched sandals, dusty eyewear, and a half dozen bottles of different sizes containing various beverages. Eggo gestured to the bottles with a flourish then glanced toward the bottom end of the plaza, clearly in a hurry to move on.

Saito took a long look at the stallholder. Everyone he'd seen outside the Hill had been a brown-skinned mélange of ethnicities, which was common across the Martianist worlds. Some blue and gray eyes could be found among the darker sets of irises, but there was little variation beyond that. The favela dwellers had the same kind of hair, similarly same shaped faces, and so on, but this man was black. A deep, almost calming midnight black. Like Jabari.

Saito asked him, "You're an off-worlder? You speak True?"

The man obviously spoke enough of it to understand the question, but he shook his head. "Not good. Speaking Vulgari, Tenosh, *et* Blairharic."

"Vulgari is fine," said Saito with relief. Vulgari was Imperial Common, and whatever the era, his translator patch was set for it. He set the patch to interpret both ways via a small, imbedded speaker, then asked, "What's in the bottles?"

The man tapped them in turn. "Water. Spacers' Ale. Lemon

drink. Vitamin juice." Then, before Saito could say any more, he waved his wrist stump at Naomi. "How did you lose yours, sister?"

"I kicked the Governor's ass, and he bit off my arm."

Kirdy *ssst*-ed at her to shut her up. Surely news of the skirmish in the tunnel had long ago reached everyone here, along with the noise from the exchange of fire with the *Charons* and, perhaps, the news that there were off-world soldiers in town.

However, to maintain the Lorica story, Saito told the vendor, "Let's just say the customs officials don't always cooperate willingly with Lorica."

At the mention of the crime lord's name, the comradely grin eroded from the vendor's face. He became all business. "If you have cash chits, the prices are: water, 15 stel; Spacers' Ale, 35 stel; lemon drink, 25; vitamin juice—"

"Forget the 'juice;' I don't think that's actual juice. And your prices are high." He didn't know for sure, but it made sense they would be.

"Prices for tourists." The grin flashed again but faded quickly, and his voice dropped as he added, "For Lorica's people, any bottle for 10 stels."

"Which is totally profit if you stole these," Saito said, then realized with a hand like that, the fellow probably hadn't. He'd paid someone else for them. "All right. How many of these are new? Unopened? Fresh? And don't lie to me."

The man's stump touched his chest in a way that said, *Me? Lie? Never!* "The lemon drink and water. Got them from a friend who supplies one of the mines."

That made five of the bottles. Saito lifted one water and one lemon, checked their seals, and stirred the contents within.

Sack, but I'm thirsty.

The others had to be equally so. Having lost blood, Naomi would be far closer to dehydration than the rest of them, even with the infusion packs from earlier. The five bottles varied in size but looked to contain around 2.5 liters total. Not much to split seven ways but better than nothing.

Jabari was a little way off, scanning their surroundings, so Saito summoned Shill first.

Dropping into *Terran* True, he asked her, "You have 100stel on you?"

"A hundred? Some of these bottles look—"

"We're not taking all of them." His gesture took in the five he wanted. "Just these."

"Slagging expensive!"

And this guy's a vet of some kind. I'm sure of it. And damned poor.

"You thirsty?" he asked her.

She nodded, pouting, knowing what he'd say.

"Then pay the man."

Upon seeing how much money was coming his way, the vendor beamed his gratitude via his huge, gap-toothed grin.

Once they'd made the transaction, Saito drew his team into an area as wide as he could and glared at the locals to get more privacy. They all kept their cowls pulled forward against the chance of some form of airborne surveillance. One bottle of lemon drink was half a liter. Saito twisted off its lid, sniffed it, then handed it to Naomi.

"All yours. You need more than this, but it'll replace some of the fluids you lost."

She accepted it with her eyes averted, knowing she needed it, but embarrassed she'd be drinking more than the others.

"Two liters for the rest of us. Not you boys, though," he told Eggo and Glark whose eyes were fixed on the lemon drink. They slunk to the periphery of the space the team had created and restarted their *eager-to-get-moving* dance.

"It's all right?" he asked Naomi after she'd taken a long gulp. She wiped her lips, nodded, and resumed drinking. Saito had the rest of them take swigs from the other bottles and pass them around until all were drained. The empties were returned to the vendor who nodded his thanks.

At Saito's shoulder, Pytor eyed the ale bottles and muttered, "Do anything for two fingers of vodka right now."

"You and me, both," said Wegley.

"Shut up, squeak," Pytor replied.

Saito was in the process of mentally rearranging the diamond when a shout came from the top of the plaza. A line of men incoming were incoming, wending their way between the play equipment and market stalls. Saito's reflexive fast count was fifteen. Fifteen potential hostiles. Clad in favela clothing, they weren't Garrison. They did carry weapons across their chests, though none of them were pointed Saito's way. Yet.

"What the sack now?" asked Kirdy.

The rest of his team noticed, as did the locals who started packing up their businesses, or simply headed off with whatever they held most valuable. The team spread out, matching the oncoming line's positions as best they could, while Saito stayed where he was.

Pytor lingered near him. "Weapons out, Gunsō?"

"Fingers on triggers," Saito replied, activating comms. He was grateful comms were working now. The whole team had heard the order, judging by the series of grunts that replied to it. "Don't draw yet."

In the middle of the approaching group strode a man who was taller than the others. He kept on the most direct path toward Saito. He had an escort by his side, a stumpy-limbed man who scampered to stay in step. Saito kept the tall man in his peripheral vision while he quickly checked for Eggo. The boy had gone, vanished under a table or behind play equipment. His buddy, Glark, was making haste toward a rough-and-ready climbing apparatus for cover. Their quick flight didn't bode well.

"Red Belts," the one-armed drink vendor told him as he

gathered his most valuable stock against his chest. "Militia in this part of the favelas. Speak nicely to them." And with that, he was off in a hobbling jog toward the nearest tents.

"Just great," Saito said, remembering the five youths whose blockade they'd blown through. "This is payback, I'm betting."

"What?" asked Pytor.

"Just be ready."

"Yeah." Pytor spat to the side and stepped after it.

Saito took a few strides forward, putting air between him and his closest teammates, and raised his left hand in a peaceful greeting. *Red Belts,* he thought. Sure enough, the ones he could see wore swashes of red cloth around their waists. These "belts" were of no use—they weren't robust enough to hang machetes or handguns from—they were just a simple uniform marking the assholes as homegrown, self-appointed authorities.

Wishing Glark and Eggo had been smart enough to source red sashes for his team, he triple-tapped a comms control on his collar, activating his vest speakers, and he cranked the volume. He then addressed the leader who'd halted forty paces uphill from his position. "Hello, friend! We're on our way back to Lorica. Passing through. You'll get no trouble from us."

The militia leader took this in with his head cocked, then raised his voice to reply in Imperial True, but he mangled his syntax as badly as Eggo did. "Youse no troubles? Pah! Youse *did* making troubles with some-a boys up theres, hurting some-a boys."

"We hurting nobody!" Kirdy barked back from his position ten meters to Saito's left. The corporal edged closer to a market table he could flip on its edge for cover... which probably wouldn't be enough.

Saito gave the hand signal for *silence,* though no one would be looking his way if they were doing their jobs properly. This conversation needed one speaker; it needed to be simple and clear. To the leader, he called, "We gave *medicine* to those boys. You know 'medicine?' We helped those boys."

Arms resting on the ancient carbine hanging from his shoulders, the tall man straightened and peered down his nose at Saito, while his short-limbed offsider studied Pytor, then Kirdy, then Pytor again. The other members of the tall man's militia were out of Saito's view, hidden behind play equipment or the awnings over stalls. It didn't take a tactical genius to know this conversation was probably a pointless effort toward peacemaking. These bastards were hungry for action, thirsty for blood.

The tall man replied, "You from *Lorica*? Whyma youse walking here, eh? Lorica having cars. Lorica having flyers." He stretched out one of his long arms to make a lateral gesture from left to right, indicating the market and the plaza. "Here my place. No Lorica place. *My* place."

And there it is, Saito thought, with an internal sigh. As if today hadn't gone badly enough already, this minor league slaghead wanted to pick a fight.

"Car crashed," he replied in a last-ditch attempt to calm things down. "Lorica pay you for us walking here."

He performed a quick head check and noted the position of his team. All of them were near some kind of cover, apart from Pytor who, no doubt, planned to drop to the floor as Saito did when the first shots rang out. The only one who was nowhere to be seen was Jabari, but there were plenty of lumps and clumps the way he'd been headed...

Saito's few steps forward had brought him level with a bump in the eternicrete. Tectonic activity—or some underground landslide or slippage—had buckled and cracked the surface to create a triangle of solid material high enough to drop behind.

Someone among the right flank of the militiamen took a shot.

Pytor yelped and hopped in place a few times before dropping. Saito bobbed behind the uplift of eternicrete as more carbines and rifles—all gunpowder models from the sound of them—opened up from Red Belt positions.

Pulse rifles replied. Children and adults screamed and hollered along the peripheries, cheering for one side or the other, perhaps terrorized or outraged as the shooting strayed their way. Saito wrestled off his cloak and grasped his weapon. After a flurry of slugs kicked fragments from the top edge of his cover, the shooter's focus appeared to shift. Saito scrambled to his right, set his weapon in a notch in the eternicrete, and sprayed rounds across the approximated positions of his closest enemies. His aim had been a calculated guess meant to intimidate and force them to stay behind their cover, but a lucky shot caught one asshole running between locations and spun him off his feet and out of sight among the market stalls. From near that position came a cry of grief and shock that told Saito he'd just killed somebody's brother or lover. He pumped a few rounds toward the location of the cry then rolled back the other way milliseconds before a group of bullets punched into the eternicrete where he'd just been.

"Damn it," he muttered. "Just my luck they're good."

He started to call Pytor to check on his status. The words froze in his throat. Pytor's ass and legs were the only parts of him visible; he lay face down in the jumbled mess he'd caused by falling through the one-armed vendor's makeshift sunshade. His legs weren't moving. A sizeable puddle of blood had spread under them. The way Pytor had yelped and hopped indicated he'd been hit in his leg or hip. If he'd bled out—or was close to it—the round had probably hit the femoral artery. Saito's impulse to scurry over and check him was snuffed when bullets stitched a line between him and his trooper's unmoving boots.

With no other choice, Saito snapped his attention back to the firefight.

The next few minutes passed in organized chaos. Saito caught a whiff of cordite on the mountain breeze and wondered where they'd gotten such ancient designs for their weapons and how they made or sourced the ammunition. Then he wondered why his mind was turning to such irrelevant details in the middle of an active threat. He managed another head-shot and hoped the guy was the one who'd nailed Pytor.

Jabari, wherever he was, had finally taken the wrapping off his mining drill. Every thirty or forty seconds, he ran its beam in a tight, tidy zigzag across Red Belt positions. Twice, screams of agony and outrage followed his action. The agonized shrieks continued, while the outraged ones dissolved into renewed gunfire. Dust and smoke clouded the air across the Red Belts' line in the wake of Jabari's attacks and hampered vision for both sides, but the regular exchange of fire continued.

One of Saito's female units yelled, "Out!" Either Shill or Naomi, he couldn't tell from the voice. It was time he started thinking about everyone withdrawing to the rubble wall at the bottom of the plaza. Everyone except Pytor, probably.

Then something unexpected happened.

Something Saito *should* have expected if he'd thought it through.

During the past minute, a rising wave of screaming and hollering had started coming from higher up in the favela in the direction his team had come from. It was audible between lulls in the shooting and screaming down below. Some part of Saito's brain had noticed it but had filed it away as irrelevant given their immediate crisis, until he saw two Red Belts stand behind their cover and turn toward something. He lifted his rifle toward them, but before he could squeeze off a shot, the pair were ripped apart by high-energy pulse fire from somewhere upslope.

"What in...?" he started, then he saw it. "Oh, *no*."

Three seconds after the men's demise, the cause of the tumult in the favela appeared where they'd been standing.

A dog-shaped droid placed its front legs up on the steel crates they'd used as cover.

The pursuit droid.

CHAPTER EIGHTEEN

ZIGGURAT IN SPACE

ORBITAL ONE OCCUPIED a point in space three hundred and thirty kilometers above Vadox CX's equator. The space station, obviously some designer's showpiece, was shaped like a squashed pyramid, a ziggurat with ten levels. Its lowest level, the hangar deck, measured almost four kilometers square. Owned and operated by Shadow Gate Mining & Astrospacial Incorporated—a corporation of which Ectorius owned a 14% stake—the orbital was Vadox CX's *only* space station. A trade and transfer hub, it served passing interstellar ships wanting to resupply without a surface landing, along with Vadox's mining operations and that of two nearby star systems that were even less developed than the Vadox System.

Orbital One's hangar only allowed entry to smallish freight and passenger vehicles. Anything taller or broader than Galen's shuttle needed to find its own orbital parking spot before transferring goods and people via the smaller vessels.

While Aurelia stood behind May in the cramped compartment, the tech-medic/pilot used Galen's identity codes to register the vessel with Orbital One's AI and gain permission to dock at a berth that was well inside the lower deck. Working with the shuttle's onboard navigation intelligence, May nudged the vessel through the designated hull aperture and into an entry passage. There, she lined it up with the blue lane markers before the station's automated systems took over and, using a tractor beam, moved the shuttle onto a massive trolley that carried it deeper and slotted it across Berths 12-23 and -24.

A secure transfer fixture mushroomed from the berth deck and sealed like a bubble around the shuttle's exit hatch then expanded upward, forming a tube that connected with the ceiling high above. Once the hatch was opened, disembarking passengers would be conveyed up the tube by a combination of zonal low gravity and air currents until they reached the transit lounge above, where a new floor would slide in beneath them and allow a gentle touchdown. It was an arrangement Aurelia had used three or four hundred times before. But before she used it this time, before May opened the exit hatch...

"Now comes the first of the tricky parts," she told May who shuffled to the cockpit door to make way for her at the helm.

Aurelia settled into the seat and pondered why it *seemed* as if May held her in high esteem, *seemed* as if she was enthralled by the presence of an imperial quaestor and the opportunity for direct service. As with Lonzo and Roja, Aurelia had to trust this woman and be prepared to improvise in case of betrayal. There was always the possibility Dr. Pieta May's loyalties lay with Galen or that she'd have a change of heart. This last thought caused Aurelia's fingers to pause above the keypads and touchscreens, and she threw a glance over her shoulder. But the woman still stood in the doorway, vibrant with an excitement that lit her eyes and flushed her cheeks.

Aurelia relaxed a notch and returned to business. She accessed the station's files using untraceable imperial subroutines that were built into much of the coding used throughout the empire. For safety reasons, all space stations logged the arrivals and departures of visitors, staff, and property holders.

Among the names of other highly placed imperial officer holders was Ectorius'. She located the level on which the governor leased rooms and discovered further confirmation of his presence. While almost all vessels were directed into the hangar deck, the orbital had been reinforced with landing pads for small, personal ships on the outer hull of some levels. Ectorius' office and money ensured he had one right above the outermost of his rented rooms, and his private ship—a FTL yacht two-thirds the size of Galen's shuttle—was docked there. Other windows opened to reveal excited personal comms chitchat about the soiree's new location up in the governor's private orbital rooms. The logs showed very few Garrison troopers present, which was not surprising given the day's events and how secure the governor likely felt away from the action below. The schematics showed Aurelia the relative positions of her shuttle berth and the entry doors to Ectorius' domain a couple of levels up.

"This may be simpler than I anticipated," she told May. She swung around to face her, and May straightened, almost like a soldier awaiting orders. "Although Trooper Lonzo is about to depart us, I still have need of your services. I hope that's acceptable."

"Of course, Madam Quaestor!"

"Lovely. In the transit lounge, I'll log in using the identity-fabrication transmitter in my arm." As she spoke, she mentally began feeding it information, creating enough of an ID to pass the checkpoints. "You and Lonzo will pass fine as yourselves. However, because the station will be rife with facial and iris analyzers, I'll need to masquerade as your patient, with my face bandaged and tinted glasses protecting my other eye. For the next short while, I'll be Jamala Karassano, a civilian injured by those dreadful intruder gunmen. I sustained ocular damage, which you're currently treating. All right, so far?"

May nodded and grinned like a schoolgirl up to mischief.

"Good." Aurelia brushed away the crinkles in a fresh outfit pilfered from Galen's rooms. Since Galen was a slim individual, roughly her height, it hadn't been difficult to find a shirt and trousers that fit well enough. She'd quickly donned them as the shuttle rose through the atmosphere, but she'd had to put the deceased trooper recruit's boots on since Galen's feet were larger. "I'm an eyewitness who's been called up here for debriefing. The clerks and officers we'll need to talk our way past won't need to know who our debriefing is with. If anyone gives you trouble, you can take them aside and whisper, 'We just came up in Senator Galen's personal shuttle. The woman is the senator's second cousin, and he'd like her treated expeditiously.' Then you can add that he's been known to cause financial problems in far-flung sites like this which have caused mass employee firings."

"And after that," May said when Aurelia paused for breath, "we use the senator's invitation to get into the party area?"

Aurelia smiled but shook her head. "If only it were that easy. I don't think they'll buy a wealthy guest looking like this..." She indicated the facial wounds, the eyepatch, and Galen's casual clothes. "And I didn't see any formal gowns in his cabin."

"You wouldn't," May replied, face twisting slightly with distaste as she added, "He isn't traveling with his wife—or either of his mistresses."

"Delightful." Aurelia stood, stretched, winced at some persistent nagging pains, then patted May's arm. "Go freshen up, Doctor. We'll meet at the exit hatch in five minutes."

"You want my ticket, yes?" Galen asked when she entered the compartment.

The room was a tight 2.5-by-3-meter rectangle with a bank

of three chairs fitted to the aft bulkhead and wall slits behind them for emergency crash webbing to emerge. The forward wall had four entertainment screens. Directly in front of her, two dirty glasses sat on an open drink cabinet. Presumably they belonged to Galen and Chebeebel, which was a testimony to Lonzo's discipline, unless the mercenary had simply taken his liquor straight from the bottle. There were several bottles—ornate glass flagons in various shapes and configurations—to choose from. Lonzo leaned against one of the entertainment screens, and Galen slumped on one of the seats.

The senator continued, "Or is it my security pass you'd like to steal?"

"Neither," she told him and took a step to the side of the doorway. "Lonzo, it's time to leave. With all the knocks to the head today, I forgot to explain you'll be leaving with Chebeebel. He's your ride to my sister's."

Lonzo pushed away from the wall. "You been more'n kind to me, ma'am."

She offered her hand. He took it with a solemn nod, then after a final sideways sneer at Galen, he took his leave.

"Oh, the company you keep, dear girl," said Galen.

"Don't call me 'girl.'"

"What is it you want from me?"

She sealed the door and faced him, while tapping a ship's datapad against her left thigh. "I require additional evidence from you. We have evidence *on* you, you know we do. So, let's make this simple, shall we?" She showed him the pad. "A note is open onscreen. You'll record a thirty-second witness statement against Ectorius, sign it with your voiceprint and House authorization, and then I'll lock you in here until my work is concluded."

"And you'll soften my punishment."

She waggled the pad in her left hand. "Those details are also in the note and part of the statement you're making."

Galen eased himself to his feet and, reading Aurelia's wariness in her posture, made no sudden moves. "Very well. I am, after all, a dealer, a negotiator, a pragmatist."

"I do admire a pragmatist," she said as he started toward the offered datapad.

What happened next occurred so blindingly fast, it was only later that her short-term memory could break it down into its component actions.

Without warning, Galen lunged sideways toward the drink counter. Aurelia darted after him, and some reflex caused her machine arm to fully extend the toxin injector. Faster than she anticipated, he swung to face her and swept a bottle around to intercept her hand. A random blip against the otherwise blackness of her machine eye HUD showed that the needle had been bent and blocked. She lurched back to dodge an upward swing of the bottle and felt the breeze as it passed her chin. Then she brought her right hand up to latch onto the hand that held the bottle and propped it up and away while she jabbed the datapad repeatedly into Galen's midriff, drawing grunts from the man as she forced him against the counter. The bottle fell from his hand, and his other crawled across her shirt, grappling for a hold. She drew away, releasing his arm, and smashed her prosthetic elbow into his cheek, then drew further back and punched him hard enough with her fist to cave in his face. He crumpled to the floor.

The opposite wall halted her backward stumble and gave her something to lean against to catch her bearings. Seconds ago, the compartment had been clean and tidy. A bottle and datapad lay on the carpet, and blood trickled down the senator's face onto his clothing. The face was a wreck, a horror.

"*Shit.*" The word came from the doorway where May now stood, looking at the dead or dying Galen through wide eyes.

Aurelia began to replay the events of the past twenty seconds in her mind, and she shook her head in wonder. "I have a feeling he found a way to get some of his orgments back online without you, Doctor."

She considered the collapsed topography of the senator's face then lifted the hand that had caused the damage.

"It's nice to know mine's working again. I was thinking about the needle earlier. Must be the reason it came out without me summoning it." She tried to straighten the injector against the drink counter but couldn't retract it; the warping was too pronounced to fix. It left more than half the needle exposed. "I'm going to need some decent pliers to cut this off at the skin, and then we need to finish our work before someone comes looking for Caecilius Galen."

CHAPTER NINETEEN

KILL-DOG

AS THE DOG-SHAPED kill-bot paused with its forelegs up on the steel crates and its head-mounted sensors raised in the air, a woman sheltering under a table near its position made the worst decision of her life. She dashed for the tents closest to the side of the plaza. The droid's targeting system registered the movement as a threat and turned a brief storm of blaster fire on her. What was left splashed and sprayed across the ground— and in an ironic twist, her remains almost reached the closest tent, her intended destination.

The living shit, Saito thought as heat rushed up his neck and into his cheeks. Targeting an unarmed civilian attempting to remove herself from a combat zone—in his book, that was murder. Completely unnecessary. Another black mark on the record of Ectorius' Garrison and local procedures.

"Pour fire!" he shouted. He propped his weapon on the eternicrete mound and fired repeatedly into the droid's barrel 'chest.'

In a repeat of the earlier scene, the droid leaped over the crates then folded down in full view, fortifying its shields and riding out the fresh storm of rifle fire. Jabari's particle beam was invisible, but Saito assumed it had joined the fight, since the droid's shields remained colored whenever troopers dropped charge packs and magazines before reloading. A few Red Belts were seen fleeing the scene, headed back up into the lanes of the favela.

Cowards!

When it was Saito's turn to swap mags, he yelped in fright as someone nudged his arm. He only just prevented himself from slamming an elbow into Eggo's face as the boy crouched by his side.

"Where in *sack* did *you* come from?!"

Voice tight, hurrying his words, Eggo said, "I helping. Theys sending kill-dogs before. Two times before. Us knowing what killing it. Shields stopping the—" He made the sound of an energy weapon and then a ballistic one. He continued, "It not stopping the slow somethings."

Saito squinted at him and tried to decipher the muddled sentences. Then the kid's meaning clicked. This droid used a basic form of shield tech—forcefields to defend against high velocity accelerated energy particles and kinetically propelled bullets. The shields *might* be calibrated to stop a rock dropped from a roof or flung from a sling, but they wouldn't stop 'slow somethings,' as Eggo called them. Weapons as slow, maybe, as a knife.

But what good was a knife against a droid?

"Theys sending the kill-dogs before," Eggo repeated.

Saito dropped a heavy hand on the kid's shoulder. "*How'd* your people stop them? What did you *use*?"

Eggo leaned across Saito and pitched a pebble at something out in the open, an exposed pipe that ran uphill in the direction of the droid. "This, this. Shoot-a it!" He clapped his hands for emphasis then pointed to the droid again.

No. Not to the droid. To the exposed pipe it was sitting beside.

From his left, another female voice reported, "Out!" Definitely Naomi this time.

This had to be resolved immediately. Saito triggered his comms, slapped a new mag home, and called for the others to cease fire. Then, as the droid poked its sensors up to test the situation, Saito lined up on the pipe the kid had indicated.

"Hope you know what you're talking about, kid."

He squeezed his trigger and hammered the pipe with a half dozen pulses, shearing a thigh-long chunk off the top. The result was instantaneous. There was an initial spurt of sewage, then something *else* boiled out of the pipe. Something *other*. For a split second, he thought it was a liquid, a kind of oil. But liquids didn't move that way. Whatever it was, it was alive. It was—

"Roaches?"

The sackdamned things were a pervasive presence across the galaxy, and like many species of Earth critters, they had been jeemed or had simply evolved on their own into new forms. Horrible forms in many cases. Saito couldn't see clearly what they did, except that they bubbled up and over and *through* the droid. It jerked and twitched and fell on its side the way an injured animal might. Within a minute, it lay still, and the roaches moved on toward the nearest reliable shade—the closest lean-tos and tents. The inhabitants of those domiciles fled into the open, happier to risk crossfire and the spreading stain of sewage than whatever horrors they'd suffer from the roaches.

Meanwhile, a pulse rifle fired from somewhere close to the Red Belt flank farthest from Saito, and a voice crowed in victory over his comms.

"Got 'em, Gunsō! Got 'em."

The voice belonged to Wegley.

Even louder, he announced, "That's the last of 'em! They're

all down, or they ran into the favela. Repeat. All hostiles gone. Returning to your position, Gunsō."

A moment later, the young man bobbed up and cut his way diagonally down across the plaza at a fast jog, shouting, "Stay back!" at the milling locals.

Kirdy emerged tentatively from cover, his rifle still up, and yelled at him. "They want the gear off their bodies, squeak."

"You sure they're all down?" Naomi asked via comms.

"You should... see the mess," Wegley replied. The young trooper ran right past Saito's position and headed for the retaining wall at the bottom of the plaza, which was where they should all be going.

"Pull back," Saito ordered. "Leapfrog again. Wegley has overwatch from the rubble wall."

Since he's going there anyway.

He added, "If they're down, I don't want the locals using their gear to fire on us."

In his peripheral vision, he noted the movement of his team members across the plaza. None of them were wearing their cloaks anymore, so Saito figured there was no point in grabbing his either. He went to check on Pytor.

No pulse. No exit wound, but the blood had poured out from beneath his thigh or groin. Taking care to keep his boots out of the mess, Saito dropped his head. No amount of nanites or plasma bags would help Pytor, even if Caiu had still been there to administer them.

"You taking his gun?" a high-pitched voice asked at his side.

"Yeah, I am," he told Eggo, and he cut the strap from Pytor's rifle the way he had from Temuz's. He handed it to the boy and said, "Hold this for a moment. *Not* for keeping." Then he felt around the front of Pytor's body and inside two pouches and awkwardly removed two spare mags which he slipped inside his own pouches before wiping the blood on his trousers.

"I liking keep it," Eggo said, standing and hefting the rifle.

Saito glanced around and stood. He shouldered his own weapon and snatched Pytor's back. "Don't care what you like. Go catch up with the others and get us moving."

As Saito followed his team, local people watched him pass, some with jury-rigged gadgets in hand that might have been weapons. But none made a move against him; they merely observed him with faces as blank as marble.

"Lorica *she'shenaasa!*" Eggo told them, remaining at Saito's side.

Several shrugged and turned away. When Saito joined three of the remaining Proselyti at the top of the rubble pile, he discovered two things. Wegley and Naomi had already started down into a long valley between there and the hill that rose on the far side, a few kilometers away. And, on that hill, there was a butterscotch-colored, bowl-shaped building. The ancient spaceport.

He signaled the remainder to follow the two in front.

CHAPTER TWENTY

LORICA TERRITORY

THE VALLEY'S side slope was easier to navigate than the favela alleys had been, and so was its floor. Gone was the tight maze of buildings and pathways. This great dip in the terrain had been judged unsafe for construction, perhaps, or simply earmarked for the stubborn attempts at agriculture they discovered as they walked.

Much of the valley was dominated by groves of hardy trees or racks of spindly vines, species that had been bred for harsh environments like this and were, from the smell, fed by the sewage that had flowed from the pipe Saito shot. Or something like it. Some white creatures—either tiny bats or large, powerful moths—darted in and out of the shadows and the tangles of berry bushes. Bugs buzzed and zipped and scampered. From time to time, Saito had to step around plasticoid water tanks, transparent as glass, the water within filmy with dirt or nutrients.

The team did their best to utilize the meager shade and shadows of any trees they passed and drew no more than occasional curious glances from the couple dozen tenders they came across, some of whom were in the presence of armed women and men. The guards gave the troopers a professional once-over and, perhaps, because Saito had instructed his people not to make any first moves, they all turned away with shrugs. Either word had spread ahead about their recent victory and painted them as heroes, or they'd passed into Lorica territory and were considered his employees. The one time they ran into Red Belts wandering back toward the market plaza area, the three men swung their carbines hastily onto their backs and bowed deeply in respect, hands held out to their sides.

"That's better," Wegley snarled as he passed.

"Yeah," said Naomi off to his right. "Lorica's people, bitches."

The meandering path Eggo had them following seemed headed for a sheer cliff face upon which the spaceport perched, like an ancient castle on a hill. If the boy was concerned about his friend Glark's disappearance, he gave no sign of it. He'd become more interested in the workings of Shill's data cuff than anything else; perhaps he hoped to barter for it.

From the top of the cliff ahead, a hopper—a short distance VTOL aircraft shaped like a flying stingray—lifted off and headed away. They watched it flit overhead before Jabari said, "There's our confirmation someone's using the spaceport."

"Well," Kirdy replied, dubious, "someone who ain't flying far, anyway."

One kim out from the cliff and the bowl building at its top, Saito called a halt in the relative shade of a date palm grove. He, Kirdy, and Jabari remained standing; the other three sank to their haunches with sighs and groans. When Eggo saw no farmers or tenders monitoring the grove, he began scaling a palm. While Kirdy stalked the back of the simple orchard, Saito and Jabari considered the side of the spaceport that was their objective.

"Smaller than I expected," Saito said.

Shill grunted. "That's the concourse. Landing pads and pits'll be outside on the ground. Was meant to be a small regional hub in its day."

"In its day. Which was, what, five hundred years ago? It's a wonder the thing isn't crumbling."

"Less than that, but yeah, they built it well."

"See there?" Jabari seemed to be pointing at two moving dots midway down the wall. "Maintenance?"

Saito put the monocular to his eye. Magnified, the dots resolved into 'patching' drones flying here and there across the outer wall, shoring it up.

"Yep," he said. "Pride on this Lorica's part?"

"Common sense," Jabari replied. "Damn good base of operations for a crime lord. No point letting it fall apart."

Another small, low-atmosphere flyer rose from inside or beyond the bowl, doubly confirming human life and activity within it. Dwindling in size as it gained altitude, the vehicle eventually rocketed away to the north.

"Be heading for the actual spaceport," Shill commented. "Other side of the mountains."

"That the kind of thing we're taking, Lieutenant?" Wegley asked Jabari. "To get to the actual starships, I mean. Or are there starships here already?"

Jabari's tired shrug was in his tone. "We'll find out when we negotiate with Lorica."

Which meant climbing the cliff face or finding a long way around it to some kind of roadway. *Well*, Saito thought, with a glance toward the sun, *at least we won't run short of daylight.*

A dark mass thumped into the earth at Saito's side, startling both him and Jabari. It was a cluster of huge dates, five of them, each the size of Saito's fist.

"Food, food," Eggo explained from above.

"Gods and ancestors, I hope it's edible," Jabari said, stooping, picking up the cluster and examining it, sniffing it.

"Hey, kid," Saito called back. "How are we reaching the spaceport from here? We're not climbing *that*?" He jabbed his rifle toward the cliff.

The boy shook his head and grinned as if it were a great joke. He pointed repeatedly at the foot of the cliff. "Doors. Holes. Tunnels. Us going up stairs to Lorica. Much stairs."

Saito turned the monocular to where the boy had pointed, but masses of trees and a scattering of tents blocked the view. He passed the viewer across the sides of the spaceport again, looking for observation holes or windows, but he didn't see any. He groaned when his scan reached the top lip of the bowl, and he saw the top half of a droid patrolling it. He passed the device to Jabari and pointed. "Rooftop. A third of the way from that side."

"Ah," was all Jabari said when he noted the droid. He handed back the monocular and turned to Shill. "We have a similar model to Ninety visible, wandering across the top."

"Lucky we're going up the guts, then," she replied.

"Ninety?" Saito asked.

"The name we gave one of Scipio's combat droids. Became unfriendly toward us and... well, someone else junked it, but it wasn't easy." His eyes glazed over as he fell into some kind of memory.

Saito eyed him speculatively. "Someone else, huh? I'm guessing your borer there would have done the job nicely."

"Probably," he replied, distantly. The weapon's butt was down in the dirt with the muzzle leaning against the tree. He broke off a piece of date and nibbled it.

"Well, we won't endear ourselves to this Lorica guy if we go slagging his combat droids."

"Hoping not to. Hey, this isn't bad," he added, plucking the rest of the date from the batch and throwing the others to Shill. A new cluster hit the ground beside him. He stooped and passed it to Saito. "Droid like that's expensive, Shill. Either Lorica's smuggling empire is way more successful than our research showed—and why would he be set up all the way out here if it is—*or* he has a guest up there who's wealthy enough to own one."

"The only people *that* rich are meant to be here for the governor's shindig," Shill agreed. She took dates for herself and Naomi then passed the bunch to Wegley.

Saito picked a date for himself, dusted it against his vest, then tossed the bunch all the way across to Kirdy. To Jabari, he said, "If you're about to tell me the evac location *you* recommended looks shaky now, I'll be a little pissed off."

"Oh, *great*," Wegley groused. "Just godsdamned great. All that for nothing? Dead end?" He tossed the dates back onto the ground by Naomi without taking one.

As voices rose to reprimand him, Jabari told him, "Doesn't mean it's a dead end, Private. Could be a million reasons why there's such expensive security up top."

"And all of them could be bad."

"Shut up, squeak," Kirdy growled and kept on stalking their perimeter.

Eggo was on his way down the trunk, so Saito did the simplest thing under the circumstances and *asked him*. "Eggo, we're safe with Lorica, right? Lorica safe?"

After jumping the last couple meters to the ground, the kid made calming motions as he replied. "Safe, safe. Lorica will liking youse; *no* liking governor. Lorica liking good shooters. You hurting governor troops and kill-dog: Lorica much liking that. Youse wanting fly-a on Lorica ships?"

"That's the plan."

"He liking good shooters on ships. Stopping bad peoples stealing ships."

"So, there's our answer. We're good," Saito told them all while facing Jabari and Shill. "Right?"

"Your team, your decisions, Sergeant Gunsō Saito, sir," Shill said, flashing her teeth in something partway between a smile and a snarl.

"The living shit," Kirdy grumbled, still prowling. "She's as bad as the squeak."

"Shill," Jabari asked, "maybe we're better off heading onto the Panlands, joining a mining company?"

"Uh, no," she said shortly. She raised one hand and started ticking off points by folding down one finger at a time. "It's desert, and we have no water. It's a hells-of-a-long hike to anywhere useful, which gives Ectorius time to revive his Garrison or source more aerial resources. The mining companies are less trustworthy than a crime boss... You get the idea?"

Jabari didn't show any offense at her tone. The calm on his face said he'd thought it through already but appreciated having it confirmed. To Saito, he said, "This *is* your team. *We* are your people. For what it's worth, I agree about staying on course toward Lorica."

"Everyone up, then," Saito ordered to a chorus of groans from the three on the ground. "We can eat our delicious local fare while walking."

Tunnels became passageways, and passageways became corridors. And most were joined by steps. Many, many steps. Between the lowest levels, they were cut from the bedrock itself. The team's weapons and vest lamps lit the way for them, casting moving shadows that Saito occasionally mistook for live contacts in his weariness and almost challenged. If the dusty, seedy, abandoned side rooms were anything to go by, there was every chance these levels had once been part of an earlier version of the city—or the Hill itself. Occasionally, there were signs of life within them, signs of current use. Usually not. While the passages seemed largely clear, the side rooms were often ankle deep with dust or sand and the crumbled remains of ancient cabling and furniture. No breeze made it this far inside, leaving the air thick and still.

With calves and thighs burning, Saito led the team plus Eggo out of yet another rock chute. This one had been engineered with metal composite stairs anchored into the rock rather than cut from it. The stairs looked relatively new—decades old rather than centuries. A sign—*finally*, he thought—of civilization again. The new corridor was four meters high and appeared to be an accessway for maintenance workers, with electrical/comms conduits lining the sides and electric lighting along the ceiling. Naomi lagged at the back, Kirdy having dropped in beside her for the last flight of steps.

Eggo grew increasingly impatient, tapping one foot whenever he was standing still, tapping the wall when he wasn't, or fiddling with the hems of the rags wrapped around his upper body, and expelling regular, loud breaths. Saito figured he was eager to get paid with enough time left in his afternoon to squeeze in one more scam before bedtime.

Sure. That or he's tired of hanging around a bunch of people who keep getting shot at.

This activity had been damned dangerous for this kid. Though he knew the boy's motives were anything but altruistic, Saito took a moment to catch his eye and thank him. The boy might have understood the words, but he appeared irritated by them and snatched glances along the corridor ahead. Momentarily suspicious of the boy's body language, Saito wandered that way, while the others waited for their final two troopers. Nothing there. No one. No side doors. Only what might have been a goods elevator door or a blast door down at the very end.

"All right," Saito said, deciding to maintain momentum. "Jabari, with me. You can do the negotiating if someone's up ahead. We'll scout behind that next door. Wegley, Shill, wait for the other two and give Naomi this." He tossed them his final protein bar. "Tell her she has to replenish the blood she lost and keep her strength up." How would this Lorica react to such a badly injured person as a prospective employee, he wondered.

"Hopefully we don't have much longer to walk?" Shill said, making it a question directed toward Eggo.

"Yes, yes," he snapped. He skipped a few meters back to the staircase exit, leaned in, and checked on the two still coming. He asked Saito, "Thems just there. We waiting, yes?"

"*You* can wait. I'm checking up there." Saito forced his legs to move and took Jabari and Shill with him. Eggo took a moment then skipped forward, caught up, and fell into step between Saito and Jabari.

"They come-a, yes?" he demanded, meaning Kirdy and Naomi.

Saito grunted, impatient himself, now, with the kid's behavior.

"Youse wait-a thems. Lorica peoples liking seeing how manys youse is."

"They'll see how many, kid," Shill muttered tiredly. "Cool your thrusters."

Saito added, "Eggo. We're going to stop at that sacking big sliding door, and then anyone we sacking meet there can see right along this sacking corridor and do a simple sacking head-count, and then they'll know how sacking many we are. All right?"

Eggo grunted something and fell silent, pouting, slouching. He dropped speed and drifted to their rear.

The next doorway might have been better called a gate. It was no blast door, but it was thick, with an electronic lock and keypad fitted this side. The pad had twelve buttons bearing symbols from a language Saito didn't know.

"Makes sense that's there," Saito figured. "Lorica can't have favela folks or Ectorius' people sneaking through here." He was turning to ask Eggo if he knew the code when Jabari reached out and tugged the gate to the side. It shifted easily and rolled halfway open. Saito grunted sardonically. "Then again, maybe he can."

Jabari stepped through. Over his shoulder, he said, "Weird room to have up here. Why's there sawdust all over the floor, Eggo?"

Saito followed him in, frowning at a completely different detail. "What's this mesh everywhere?"

The new chamber was maybe fifteen by fifteen meters, and the mesh covered the walls to the tiled floor, to the smaller door on the far side, and to the entire ceiling. Tightly woven from gray and yellow threads as fine as cotton, but stiff enough to be some kind of metal composite, it resembled something he'd seen once before, centuries ago. But what the hell was it used for?

"Have you seen this before?" he asked Jabari.

Jabari drew breath to answer.

And then the door slammed closed at their backs. He and Jabari whirled on it. The lock clunked into place, and another electronic keypad on their side, fitted *behind* the mesh-coating on the door, bleeped. A red light came on above the keys.

And Eggo was not on their side. Nor was Shill.

"Grab that kid!" Saito barked into his comms.

No one responded.

"Kirdy! Wegley!"

Nothing.

"Ah, hell," Jabari sighed. "I *have* seen mesh like this before." He held the borer up so Saito could see something on it. But Saito had no idea what...

And then he remembered. Sure enough, the power-level indicator on the cannon's side was blank. Dead. His own weapon's indicators had blanked out as well.

"Interference field," he said, feeling the telltale hum in his teeth and forehead that often accompanied electromagnetic interference. He marched across to the far exit, which was closed; it boasted no lock of any kind that he could see. Just the mesh. He started to say something. "Kirdy will—"

The door opened, and a gaggle of men bustled in. Seven of them. Tall, broad, and solid. They wore no shirts, just trousers, heavy boots, and thick, leather aprons, like a smith's apron. The leather protectors covered them from jowly throats to meaty thighs.

To a man, they each carried two things. Bone saws and square-bladed meat cleavers.

Saito reversed direction, backing up until he was level with Jabari against the door they'd entered by.

Jabari raised his cannon and squeezed the trigger, then he grunted and let it drop to his side, held in one hand. He offered Saito a wry lift and fall of his eyebrows that said, *Thought I'd try it.*

Saito flipped his rifle until he held it by the muzzle. Light as it was, it was better than nothing. "Very expensive clubs," he said with a nod at Jabari's weapon.

Jabari grunted a laugh.

You won't need sidearms, the *Maelstrom* liaison officer had told him. Shaking his head, he wondered fleetingly whether he'd suffered stasis sickness to accept a decision like that.

The men had not spoken, hadn't exchanged any glances. Their eyes were dark, their stubbly faces expressionless as droids.

Saito raised his chin, locked onto the void of one man's stare, and attempted to engage him in Imperial True. "Don't like imperial soldiers, huh? You *do* know we're visitors here? We've come to make the Imperials' lives difficult, not yours."

"Even if they understand you, I don't think they care," Jabari murmured, face tight as he assessed the shifting formation of men ahead of them.

"I don't think so, either. And you know what?" Saito rolled his shoulders and loosened his neck and gripped his hyper-expensive club with both hands. "After the day we've had, I'm past caring, too."

CHAPTER TWENTY-ONE

IN COGNITO

GETTING through the arrivals checkpoint outside the transit area wasn't hard. The area did have one wandering planetary Garrison trooper, but the local security uniforms did all the talking, the checking, and the note-taking. None of them hid their morbid interest in Aurelia's facial bandages and dark glasses, but her silence combined with May's dropping the Senator's name got them through quickly.

They drew a curious look from the trooper on deck, but on a day when there'd been so much weirdness, the sight of a woman in head coverings and dark glasses wasn't all that noteworthy. He accepted it with a shrug and switched his attention to other departures and arrivals.

Getting to Level 4 was also simple. Voice-activated infoscreens hanging on public corridor walls at twenty-meter intervals helped them find a suitable elevator in no time. The trip up was shared with a spindly-limbed janitor who appeared exhausted and kept her head down and eyes closed the whole way. She stayed in the car as Aurelia and May stepped out and approached Quadrant C of that floor—Ectorius' bolt hole and the new location for the party.

Aurelia felt her pulse accelerate at the prospect of coming face-to-face with the bastard, getting her task done, and getting out. The physical reaction was a slip of self-control, an unprofessional impulse she quickly countered by managing her heart rate and blood pressure. But, she mused, if *she* was feeling excited, May must have been nearly leaping out of her skin. A glance confirmed it. The tech-medic's face was beaded with sweat. She chewed her bottom lip and had her hands at chest level, where she curled her fingers around each other.

Aurelia steered her against a wall with a hand on her arm, waited for a pair of mining company functionaries to pass them, then whispered, "Breathe, Doctor, breathe. Clasp your hands at your waist, but don't wring them. Raise and drop your shoulders—yes, that's right—relax them. Now. Raise my glasses and pretend to examine my eye." May did so, checking the eye not covered by a patch and leaning close enough for Aurelia to smell the stress on her breath. "Focus on breathing slowly and evenly. I'll do the talking from here on out."

"Yes, Madam—er, yes, *Citizen Karassano*." May dropped the glasses in place.

Aurelia led her away. They turned a corner and found themselves at a place where two yellow lines, set two meters apart, crossed the floor. The closest line was interrupted midway by the words *Quadrant B*. The line beyond that was similarly interrupted, but with the label *Quadrant C*. Another meter past that, a partition wall marked the practical edge of the governor's area. The wide fire door had been retracted into a frame decorated with mock diamonds the size of housecats, strings and bunches of plastic grapes and grapevines. Another corridor lay beyond, one that terminated after sixty or so meters at the double doors to a function room. The corridor had other sliding doors—all closed—down its sides. A waiter emerged from one, carrying a tray of hors d'oeuvres. Three tight knots of richly dressed party guests milled at the other end of the passage, and the waiter headed toward them.

At this end of the corridor, a table blocked the way. Sitting behind it, a harried Garrison lieutenant in dress uniform, with a sidearm in a clip holster, fended off a complaint from a woman in chef's clothing. She leaned aggressively over him while he looked anywhere but at her. He seemed relieved by the approach of the two newcomers—an excuse to ignore the chef—even though his eyes ran over Aurelia's clothing and headgear more than once.

Upon her announcement she was here for debriefing from the planetside incident, he replied, "Yeah, but *who* wants to see you?"

Aurelia touched her chin, pretending to think that over, acting the imbecile. "Um. We were just told…"

He cut her off with an exasperated chop of his hand then repeated the chop to stop the chef resuming her complaint. To Aurelia, he said, "Probably Major Tatias. He's busy with His Excellency right now. But—" his gaze caught something past her "—I can't have you in the way here."

Aurelia checked behind her. A pair of wealthy, gown-wearing ladies had sashayed their way around the corner and now beamed severe glares at her, at May, and at the lieutenant.

He rose from his chair and told Aurelia, "Just go through. Chef Ekuri, here, can take you to—"

"I will *not*," the chef hissed, arms folded, eyes ablaze.

With a sigh, the lieutenant said, "Find a staff member to show you somewhere to wait. I'll get a message to the major."

His attention began to slide toward the waiting guests, but Aurelia took a sideways step that blocked his view of them.

"You can't just tell us where he is?"

"He's with the—" he visibly bit down on a curse word "—governor! Now, get going and stay out of the way. Yes, my ladies?" he said, all smiles for the guests. "You're here for the soiree?"

After they'd stepped between him and the chef, Aurelia let May catch up, then she paused and nodded toward the ambient noise rolling out of the open double doors ahead. "The party has started. Ectorius won't be far. I'll start trying doors. Stay close to me but be alert. I'm making this up as I go, and once I have him—or kill him—we'll be moving quickly to get out of here."

She was about to say more when an army officer with deep, dark red hair stepped out of a side door and crooked a finger at her. "Recruit! Arrivals Security informed me you have intel. Come in here, and we'll get this over with." He stepped back into the room.

Aurelia and May exchanged glances then shrugged and followed him. Aurelia's right hand curled into a tight fist. The room they entered was three times the size of the cabin she'd killed and left Galen in. Nothing occupied it but a lounge facing to her left, which the officer was lowering himself onto. Then she heard May gasp in revulsion by her shoulder and swung around to the left where the tech-medic was staring. There she saw...

A wall frieze—an object arranged inside a square frame and protected by glass or transparent alloy. It was huge; the frame measured three by three meters and had been hung dead center of the wall. And the object within it certainly warranted May's horrified gasp. In her young life, Aurelia had seen and done much that was grisly. But this, this *obscenity*, was another level...

Since time immemorial, there'd been murderers who kept trophies. But this time, the psychopathic killer was an imperial appointed official, and the trophy was the naked corpse of a soldier.

Decanus Caiu.

The gruesome sight was such a mental *non sequitur* that Aurelia was momentarily frozen, morbidly captivated. Caiu's left eye was missing—from the jagged edges of the wound, it appeared a sniper had been responsible and had probably blown out a third of his brain at the same time. The Corfid's tough hide had been flayed from behind, spread to the sides, and pinned to the backboard like beetle wings. It was an abomination.

And she'd gawked at it too long.

One second too long.

As she braced to leap sideways, something like lightning slammed into her, snuffing out her consciousness.

CHAPTER TWENTY-TWO

MARKET DAY

IN HIS HEAD, Saito had already started calling the men 'cutters' before the seven brutes acted. They moved together with a speed and synchronization that told Saito they'd done it before. Many times. And it was obvious these assholes expected brute force and shock tactics to work every single time.

As he separated from Jabari, Saito thought, *Not this time.*

He feinted left, then hopped right, causing two of the three cutters who'd picked him as their target to bumble into each other and lose their rhythm. Their new, blundering trajectory would take them into the space between the two Proselyti, as they stumbled toward the locked door, giving Saito precious seconds to focus on one guy. Mimicking the sword katas he'd practiced as a teenager, he swept his rifle around in three criss-crossing swings. One broke his opponent's grip on the cleaver and flicked it out of his hand. The next cracked across his nose to stun him. The third slammed into his temple to drop him to his knees. Saito then sprang into the air and spun himself to land behind the guy's shoulder with enough space to lash the rifle toward the back of his neck. The blow was fierce, and it was accurate, crashing across the knob of bone at the very back of the skull. It was lights out for the cutter, who hit the sawdust face first.

It was also the end of the rifle as a club, as the force of the blow jarred it from Saito's hands and sent it spinning off. It landed at the feet of the pair he'd sent stumbling seconds earlier, but that didn't bother him, even when they turned themselves around to mount a new rush his way. Saito had come to rest in a comfortable waiting position, facing them.

On the far side of the room, Jabari was locked in an exchange of blows and was evenly matched, it seemed. He'd already dropped one man and was using his cannon like a short staff—*like a kayak paddle*, Saito thought—to block and maneuver and keep the other three at bay. Saito spent a single second admiring the man's footwork before he had to concentrate on his own moves. He pulled his combat knife— twenty centimeters of razor-edged stainless steel—from his vest with his right hand and a slender can—hornet venom spray—from his belt with his left.

This'll hurt, assholes, he thought as he skipped backward and sent a viscous stream of spray gel into their eyes, noses, and mouths. Their momentum kept them chasing him at first, for a few steps at least, until they were forced to throw up their arms and hands as shields that were too late to catch most of the crap now sticking to their faces. Sticking and *stinging.* One dropped his saw, the other his cleaver. Saito tossed the hornet spray aside; it would only get in Jabari's way if he tried using it on that side of the room. His two opponents alternated between clawing at the goo on their faces and swinging their remaining weapons blindly, possibly using each other's gurgling screeches as markers to avoid slicing each other. Saito had no such qualms as he danced around and stabbed his blade at each man's left hamstring. When both staggered and dropped to a knee, he grabbed one by the hair and drew his knife across the man's throat, kicked him forward, and pivoted to gash the other one's thick neck muscle below the ear as hard as he could. Both were on their faces now, clutching and thrashing and gurgling. Because their necks were tough, he hadn't managed wounds that would be immediately fatal, but the men were certainly removed as threats.

He turned to help Jabari with the two cutters he had left to face. One instantly separated to intercept Saito. Jabari took advantage of the shift in dynamics to whip one end of the cannon around in a fierce upper cut that caught the other beneath the chin. The blow snapped the man's head back before Jabari followed up with a downward swing that split the cutter's skull, bringing him to his knees.

While Jabari set about finishing him, Saito once again stopped worrying about that side of the fight. He took a step backward, not from fear, but to create space. He beckoned his cutter to come in closer, to follow him, to attack. And attack, the big fellow did. The big thug was deceptively light on his feet, and he lunged before performing a pirouette worthy of a gladiator and brought his leg around in a roundhouse kick. A kick that only found air at the point where it should have dented Saito's skull. Because Saito had stooped under it.

The man's leg was still in the air, and he was off balance, when the sergeant lunged and put his left shoulder to the knee of the planted leg. Saito wrapped his arm around the man's thigh before plunging his knife into the back of it then riding the toppling body to the ground, adding his own force to make sure it went backward and didn't land on top of him. He released the knife handle before impact and let the stone floor drive it deeper into the leg. He threw himself free and rolled to avoid a flailing arm that reached for him. By the time he was up in a ready crouch, Jabari was driving the butt of his borer into the man's nose and forehead. The man, predictably, went limp.

It took another thirty seconds, using cleavers and knives, to ensure their opponents were deceased. Jabari pressed the heel of one hand to a cut on his opposite arm, but the blood there wasn't enough for the wound to be major. Saito found a dressing in his pouches and applied it once Jabari had dragged back his coverall's sleeve. Then they stood there regarding their handiwork, swaying in place, exhausted.

Saito's mouth had been pressed shut the whole time, teeth clamped together in concentration and determination. He opened his mouth to drag down a deep breath.

"How's your weapon?" he asked.

Jabari shook it next to his ear. "Rattling. I'd say I've wrecked some soldering in there. Not made for this kind of work."

"I hope these are," Saito replied, locating his rifle and giving it a similar shake by his ear. He couldn't hear anything rattling, so that was something. With a glance at the red-lit door lock, he said, "Gotta be a key…"

Something poked from the side pocket of a dead cutter's trousers. Something like a remote device. When Saito slid it out, a button beckoned to him from one side. He pressed it, and two prongs poked from one end, prongs long enough to reach through the small gaps in the mesh, he figured. With Jabari watching the far door for more attackers, he went over and simply touched it to the casing of the lock. Presumably, it automatically paired and fed in the code because the red light blinked out, and the door clunked and cracked open. He hauled on it…

In the corridor, Shill remained nearby. She held Eggo by his clothing and the hair on the back of his head. The boy struggled pointlessly against her grip. "Little bastard tried getting in a crawl hole."

She indicated a crack in the wall Saito hadn't noticed earlier, one that looked barely wide enough to admit Saito's head, let alone this kid's body. Then again, rats could squeeze themselves into insanely tight spaces, and this kid was definitely a rat.

Shill shook the boy, eliciting an overly dramatic cry of alarm. She snarled, "But you weren't fast enough, were you, little bastard?"

Eggo just squirmed and said nothing.

"I've never hurt a kid in my life," Saito said, wiping sweat off his face, feeling the heaviness in his limbs that followed a fight that followed a couple of hours of running and climbing. His ears rang with fatigue. At his age, he was glad for every minute he'd spent keeping himself conditioned. He said, "Never hurt a kid, but I'm very close right now."

The others had long since caught up. Naomi slipped behind him to snoop inside the room and greeted Jabari with a gasp and a bout of enthusiastic swearing. Meanwhile, Kirdy came alongside Saito and laid his twenty-five-centimeter knife blade against Eggo's neck, instantly stopping the lad's squirming.

"Want me to perform some throat surgery, Gunsō?"

Kirdy's flushed face and clenched jaw gave Saito pause. The corporal had been angry since the initial rooftop ambush, but his temper had risen and fallen in the time in between. Right now, it was at a boiling point, and this, oddly enough, allowed Saito to cool his own temper by a few degrees.

In Terran True, Saito asked, "Why are *you* so angry at him?"

"Why'm I angry at this kid? At *this* kid?" He withdrew his blade far enough to tap the kid on the forehead with it. "For starters, he locked that door behind you. Squeezed into there, like she said." He jerked his head at the wall crack. He returned to Imperial True to say, "And he has an interesting story to tell. Don't you, boy?"

"And something to show us," Shill added. "According to him."

"That's right. Something to show us. Because..." Kirdy

pressed the knife again, and the boy stiffened, eyes widening as the blade's edge broke skin, and dots of blood welled around it. "If he doesn't, or he's lying, I'm going to cut his little head off. You understand that, boy? Huh?"

Shill stretched around to stare into Eggo's now sullen eyes. "Oh, he understands, Corporal. Little bastard's language skills are better than he pretends."

"Show us what?" Jabari asked, exiting the room.

Kirdy withdrew the knife, inspected its edge, and wiped the thin line of blood on his vest. "When Shill asked him where he thought he was going, he tried tellin' us he was goin' home to Mama."

"But when I rattled his brainbox a little," Shill said, shaking him again, "he changed his answer. 'To bad mens, to bad mens.' Seems these slimes who attacked you have a whole operation upstairs we'll be real interested to see."

"He was selling you out to them," Wegley snarled, entering the discussion from a few meters down the passage. "Get it? He was selling all of us out, probably, only you two got ahead of us."

"Selling us out?" Saito wondered aloud. "Or just selling us?"

Jabari grunted unhappily. "Those saws and cleavers..."

Saito's gut hardened, bile rising in his throat as suspicion set its claws in deep. "Yeah, those saws and cleavers. Eggo, we need a ship, so we're still going up there." He jerked a thumb at the ceiling. "But first, you'd better show us where we were meant to end up. And you'd better not sell us out again." He looked pointedly at the blade Kirdy held at his side.

The boy sniffed, but he'd lost all swagger. "I showing youse, I showing. Easy to showing, hard to saying."

Saito gestured for Kirdy to sheath the knife. He straightened his arm in the direction of the fight room. "That way? Or is there a better way?"

"Yes, yes. That way."

"Show us. But remember..." Saito moved to Shill's side as she released Eggo's hair, and he gripped the boy's other shoulder. "This time, *you'll* be the first one through every doorway."

Twenty more minutes of sneaking around—up grit-coated ladders, through crawlways, along disused passages. One space was so narrow, the adults had to remove their vests to sidestep through it. As they did so, they treaded through crumbled cabling and stirred up dust. Like the ladders, all the crawlways and walkways ramped upward, until, by Saito's reckoning, they'd passed the spaceport's ground level. He didn't question it since he and whoever was taking point kept the boy between them, and it would be safer to find a viewpoint that looked down on the activities of the main port concourse rather than just wander onto it. The ambient noises—sometimes rumbles, sometimes dull thuds and distant clanks, once or twice the burble of voices slipping through cracks in the masonry—had shifted as they travelled.

Eventually, they emerged in a curved corridor that, according to Shill's old port plans, ran inside the ovular outer wall of the structure. Like the ancient castle design that kept coming into and out of popularity over the millennia, this one had arrow holes to look through, apertures on both sides of the passage. The holes were without glass, and the exterior slits let in unhealthy amounts of windborne grit and dust, along with fresh air the team welcomed. Some of the team sidled up to the outer holes that looked back toward the Hill, the rest the interior ones.

"Sit," Saito ordered Eggo. "There."

The boy obeyed while Saito moved to an inner window, keeping to the side so as not to present an obvious profile.

What he saw did not surprise him. Nevertheless, it still shocked him.

The port building had an open roof. There, he caught sight of a human guard patrolling sixty meters from the concourse floor. He also saw the shoulder and arm of the hulking combat droid.

Below him were the original common and trade areas of the port. The precinct's design, Jabari had told him, included fifteen landing pads on the outside on top of the escarpment. In its first life, only government flyers had been allowed to use the single pad inside the building. These days, Saito assumed it was for Lorica and Lorica only. The inner area had been for the transfer of goods and personnel and the refreshment of travelers. At one time, there would have been booths and kiosks down there, partitions. These days it was clear, the partitions and booths long since removed so the floor comprised a market of sorts. A market that turned Saito's stomach.

Wegley joined him at the other side of his window and peeked down. The young man gasped in horror. "What the sacking hells..."

"Yeah," Saito muttered. "Saws and cleavers. *Meat* saws and *meat* cleavers."

Wegley had started the day pale. He'd gotten alternatingly ruddy faced and pale again. But now, he turned paler than Saito had yet seen him. "Gunsō," he asked quietly, "Were we meant to be the meat?"

"Those freaks," Kirdy growled from further along. "Those dogsacking freaks."

"Yeah," Saito replied to both men.

Many items were on display. From a height of twenty-five or so meters, Saito didn't need the monocular to see most of them clearly. Bioengineered plants and fungi he knew had been banned for three thousand years across the Imperium because of their psychoactive and antisocial effects. Weaponry that was illegal for civilians to possess. Gems or fake gems.

And meat.

Many kinds, with images of the animals it came from affixed to the walls behind the tables. Animals Saito recognized —giraffes, elephants, great apes, giant spiders, and beetles— and many creatures so jeemed, he didn't.

And one stall, in particular.

"Sonsofbitches," Wegley whispered.

Saito caught Shill's eye and nodded at her cuff, with a grim set to his jaw. "Whoever compiled those files you copied hasn't been here in a while."

Shill looked through the next window along and groaned in sad agreement and replied, "In a damn long while."

One set of stalls in the middle was attracting a decent crowd of people in expensive clothing, while their bodyguards and human-like servant-droids lingered nearby, as they perused the cuts of meat. The stalls were staffed by men identical to the ones Saito had fought not long ago doing the cutting and selling. The stylized holograms behind the table advertised the 'beasts' being served there.

Shill squatted before Eggo. "*Humans*? That's human meat down there?"

Eggo shrugged then drew his knees closer to his chest.

Shill wasn't done. "You... Those hulks in the basement were gonna chop up Jabari? You little piece of—" She lashed out and slapped him across the head too fast for him to dodge.

"Good money," the boy said, his tone indicating he was unconcerned by the commerce or by the slap he'd received. "Mens giving me good money. I spending on good food, nice food. And girls."

"*I'm* a girl," Shill said. "Only thing you're getting from me is another of these." She slapped him again.

This time, defiance flared in his eyes. "You not 'girl.' Lorica getting you today, you 'new pork.' All youse."

"New..." She cocked her arm again, then she must have decided against beating a child, even one who'd tried to sell them off as meat beasts. She shot to her feet and stalked a few steps away.

"All right, huddle up, people," Saito said. "We need to talk."

CHAPTER TWENTY-THREE

WHITE ROOM

AURELIA WASN'T THERE ANYMORE, wasn't in the room where they'd pinned up Caiu like a grotesque museum exhibit.

She'd lost time. Time had passed. And if her eye HUD had been working, she could tell how much.

No matter. She needed to focus on what was, not on what wasn't. She'd been stunned by that officer, probably. She was awake now, fully alert, but with a fresh headache. And she was strapped firmly by her forearms and shins to a hard, metal gurney. No, not *strapped*. She discovered when she tried to move that she'd been *clamped* down, her orgmented legs and musculature and her mechanical arm rendered unusable. A man hovered beside her, concerned with something on her thighs. She lifted her head and saw that the man was configuring tiny droids as they exited a container strapped to his forearm. Droids whose purpose was all too clear in the context of the sterile white room.

Emperor's heart!

Her head dropped back against the table. This simple, straightforward, in-and-out mission had been anything but.

And it had come to this, despite all her supposedly clever machinations.

Captured.

Prepped for torture.

Her service to the empire—and to her sister—approaching its conclusion.

She turned her head the other way. No sign of May. Possibly some lackey had bundled the woman into a trash bag. Possibly she was under interrogation somewhere else. No, they wouldn't do that. There was an empty and perfectly good table beside her, another stainless-steel gurney.

Aurelia realized belatedly that they'd stripped her naked, just like Caiu. She snorted sardonically and thought, *how many outfits have I been forced to discard today? Three?* The nakedness didn't bother her personal modesty or dignity. It *did* bother her because it gave the bots finding positions around her thigh and hip easier access to her skin and the nerve endings beneath it.

She couldn't give up so easily. She couldn't let this be her fate.

"Do you understand the trouble you're in?" she asked the man.

He gave no sign of hearing her and muttered under his breath as he completed his task.

"Do you understand the trouble I can spare you," she continued, "if you release me now?"

Pointless. The man still didn't respond, and her words sounded desperate to her own ears, embarrassing her.

When a dozen of the tiny droids rested on top of her, the man left, and the red-haired officer who'd stunned her came in to replace him.

His gaze ran over her once before settling on her eyes. No smile. No emotion of any sort. A carefully neutral expression that reminded her of Saito's the first time she'd met him. He said, "My name's Tatias. Garrison Commander. You were entirely too trusting, Quaestor Cossea, and too sure of your subterfuge. While the party commences without him, Governor Ectorius has a quick meeting with two out-world dignitaries, then a score of guests to mingle with, but I'm sure he'll spare time to see you at some point."

His Imperial True came out in an accent she hadn't heard before. Was he from another galactic arm? Was he a local the governor had elevated to his rank?

She said, "You've sworn fealty to empire and emperor, Tatias. It's not too late to honor that. To abandon your misguided service to Ectorius."

The blank expression tightened into one of disdain. "And it's not too late for you to spare yourself some agony. If you confirm for me the configuration of your attack team, and where their surviving members might be, I'll provide you with a dose of decent narcotics to take the edge off the next few hours, to make it pass in a painless haze. No? No comment? All right. I offered. And, well, your remaining archaic warriors escaped the Hill, meaning they're not currently our problem. When they eventually poke their heads up, if some colorful local doesn't cut off those heads, we'll get them."

She considered asking for May's freedom, but it would only land May in more trouble if they thought Aurelia cared about her. She thought about keeping him engaged in further conversation to seek an angle she could use, but nothing came to her. And by the time she started thinking the cyberattack on her wetware really had messed her up, the major departed with one final leer at her body.

And she was alone with her regrets, wondering what seditious purpose they would find for Galen's corpse, wondering how they'd use hers once they'd wrung the life from it.

CHAPTER TWENTY-FOUR

NOT A SPACEPORT ANYMORE

"IT'S NOT A SPACEPORT ANYMORE," Shill said. "Or it *is*, but the meal options have changed. A *lot*." She winced at her attempt at humor and fell silent.

Silent, like the rest of the team.

Saito gathered them in the shadows between two windows. There, they all took a knee, processed what they'd seen, and thought through the next steps. While most faced in toward Saito, and the boy was forced to sit at his side, Jabari half-turned to watch one way along the passage while Shill watched the other. Corporal Kirdy had gone scouting sixty seconds earlier, without asking permission, muttering to himself.

Picking up on Shill's poor joke, Saito said, "Whatever it *used* to be, it's pretty obvious this Lorica shitbag isn't just a smuggler."

"A secret market," Wegley whispered to himself. "For rich cannibals. They're selling to *cannibals*." He was the only one in the group besides Eggo who was sitting crisscross on the floor. He looked like a dejected child, deflated. What Wegley had seen down there had taken the wind from his sails. Even gray-faced as she was, Naomi looked to be in better shape than he was.

"I counted five customers wearing House colors down there," Jabari said from his side of the group. He faced away, but Saito didn't need to see his expression. The disgust was in his voice—it was the first time he'd really heard Jabari heat up. "There's no way the governor isn't in on this, you know."

"Why *would* he be?" asked Naomi, who was gritting her teeth against a resurgence in her pain levels. "We're way outside the Hill's boundary."

"We're on his planet." Shill shrugged.

Naomi sniffed. "Like *you* know about him and his planet."

Shill frowned. "What's that mean?"

"Means your fantastic intel was a steaming heap of runny cat shit, lady." There was no heat in Naomi's voice or face; she appeared to simply be stating facts as she saw them. "Means we shouldn't have followed your advice. Apologies, Gunsō, I didn't mean you..."

He waved the inference away. He thought she was probably right. With the luxury of hindsight, he knew they should have chased after Quaestor Cossea.

"My intel," Shill said, "was based on files that were doctored to protect this business. This giraffe meat and gorilla meat and slagging *new pork* business. Not the first time something like this gets kept off the records."

Jabari murmured, "This is the depravity of unchecked wealth and power. This is the Imperium's true soul. Bored with bossing your inferiors around? Why not try something new and *eat* them?"

Jaw tight, Saito corrected him. "This is what happens when there's *no* imperial order overlaid on things."

"Really?" Jabari asked, still not turning back. "You didn't see the expensive flyers lifting off when we were down in the valley? You didn't see the imperial finery worn by some of the clientele down there? Their personal servants and personal security?"

"So, they're rich assholes," Saito said, with a sniff. "There's plenty of *them*, those who flick their snot at imperial values and morals. *That's* the reason for our mission—to remove some of those bastards from positions of power and scare others into returning to the right way of things."

"I don't..." Jabari started to say, but he was interrupted by Wegley.

"*Shut up*," the young man spat. "Just shut up, *both* of you. There's human bodies down there. People. Cut into pieces. Steaks and chops and sackdamn *drumsticks and all*. And there's other humans buying them. Who cares about 'order' and 'civilization?' Shit like this didn't happen in our day. In our century. All of us here—except that little turd—" He sneered at Eggo. "All us Terranist grandchildren of Earth, we've traveled through time, jumping from one century to another until we ended up *here*. We've gone into the past, not the future. We've gone where humans aren't people, they're just animals who are happy to eat each other. Who cares if Shill's intel's good or bad? What's the point of anything?" While they regarded him, stunned by the force of his hissed outburst, he showed them his bio-tattoo. "Six years ago, by my biological clock, I was driving groundcars and lorries. Today, I'm helping rich Martianist rulers get rid of their competitors, while other rich Martianists—" he shook his hand in the air a moment before pointing to the closing window overlooking the market "—they do *that!*"

Naomi enclosed his hand in hers and pressed it back onto his thigh, still gripping it tight. "It'll be all right, Wegs. It'll be all right. We got you."

The group fell silent until Kirdy broke the spell by returning around a curve in the corridor. When his eyes met Saito's, he showed him the knife in his hand, the crimson on the blade, then he wiped it on his trousers and sheathed it.

"Either they're professionally paranoid round here or we've stirred up trouble," the corporal said as he crouched by Naomi. "Found two patrols next level down. Left one alone. Axed the other. Hid the mess the best I could." He noticed the arrangement of Naomi and Wegley's hands. "I miss something?"

Saito gave him a wry, self-deprecating smile, then turned it on the rest of the group. "Our resident moral philosopher, Wegley, just finished refocusing my thinking."

"Oh, yeah?" Kirdy asked, instantly forgetting the handholding, his blood up. "So, what're we doing?"

"In your travels, did you see any air or spacecraft we can steal?"

Kirdy produced a flimsy-looking datapad from inside his vest and passed it over. "It's only linked to this place. Took it off the patrol. Shows five vehicles in the landing pits outside. Four look like hoppers or skippers, low altitude. Other one might be orbit capable."

The files were open, easy to leaf through. The fifth craft Kirdy mentioned looked to be the size of their original dropskiff. It was definitely spacefaring, with FTL-nodes across its bow and thruster nacelles. As his corporal had said, the others were low altitude, aerodynamically designed and built for three or four passengers. Upon seeing their familiar design, Saito had a sudden, overpowering recollection of his father taking him on a trip to the local airport on New Pacifica...

Saito had been five. He was aware of his father's sweaty odor and the cheap cologne he'd lathered on to mask it. His father had him looking at an aircraft and was lecturing him that vehicles like it had model numbers and brand names, but the easiest thing to call them was 'cloud clippers.'

"You'll sound smart if you say that, Sai-Sai. And you won't have to remember all the other names and numbers."

Jabari snapped him out of it, all business, but the smell of that cheap cologne lingered in the air.

"Sgt. Saito? You were about to tell us to steal the space-capable vessel?"

Saito cleared his throat and replied, "I was about to tell the rest of you to do that, yes."

There were frowns all round. Except for Jabari. Somehow, the man knew exactly what Saito was thinking. And he approved of it.

"Listen to me; do not waste time arguing. I would love to get off this planet with the rest of you. But I *need* something entirely different. I need the answer to Private Wegley's question. What's the point? Because for me, if the point's not doing something to keep humanity civilized, there isn't one."

"What the sack you talking about?" Kirdy asked.

It was Jabari who answered. "Gunsō's taking a flyer back to the The Summit, aren't you, Gunsō? He's heading to the governor's mansion to kill Ectorius."

"And no doubt create a political shit storm," Saito added. "But soldiers shouldn't worry about politics. And as Wegley eloquently suggested, this is not my century, anyway. I'll leave the political fallout to the emperor and his consuls."

"Sacking hells," Naomi muttered, but her tone was one of wonder.

In contrast, Shill muttered, "You're crazy."

"Sure am." Saito stabbed a finger at the hubbub in the market below. "That's *making* me crazy. Wondering where Lorica gets his new pork from when he's not waylaying Proselyti. Thinking about all those poor bastard miners out in the Panlands, laboring for their employers, contributing to Ectorius' taxes, then some of them being brought here to be sliced up for profit—with Ectorius taking a cut of *that* profit. Besides, I came here with a job to do, and I hate leaving jobs unfinished."

Jabari nodded. "Well said. Count me in."

"What the slag, boss?" Shill hissed.

"Not you, Shill," Jabari told her. "You're helping these guys, but everything Saito just said is what our leaders said we were fighting at the beginning of *our* war. They weren't wrong, even if the Kaana was. I'm going to fight it this one last time."

Shill clenched her fist and shook it at him, teeth gritted as she muttered, "Kill that slagger, and there'll be a thousand more to replace him."

It was Saito's turn to answer for Jabari. "Small victories are still victories."

"You sackheads'll get yourselves killed," Kirdy said, agreeing with Shill for once.

Both leaders shrugged. Saito answered, "So could pretty much everything else we've done our whole military lives."

"If we ruin that asshole's day, I'm happy," Jabari said.

Saito laughed. "I'd rather ruin his head."

"That too."

Shill growled, "So now, our mandate is ruining rich imperial slaggers' days, Jabari? What happened to liberating other Proselyti?"

"Wait," said Naomi. "*That's* what you're doing here?"

Jabari said, "Maybe I've been wrong, Shill. We decided to rebel when we saw the truth—that neither side is good or noble or worthy of us. But Sgt. Saito, here, has made me realize something. We should let other Proselyti make their own decisions. What I need you to do is deliver them the invitation to rebel and the reason why. *And*—" he went on, cutting her off when she made to object further "—the offer of help."

"You bastard," she told him. "Gonna make me do it all by myself. You bastard."

"Never know," Jabari replied. "The Gunsō and I might make it."

She snorted and turned away.

Through all this, Saito had been perusing schematics of the facility. Now, he said, "We need to move. Kirdy, Shill, Naomi, Wegley, you're taking the space-capable ship. When you're clear, do what you can to call in help for the quaestor and for us."

Shill coughed as if she'd tried some of the human meat downstairs. "There's no way I'd do anything for that quaestor."

"How about for me?" Naomi drawled, her eyelids hooded with fatigue. She'd released Wegley's hand in the past minute or two.

Shill grunted, relenting.

Saito said, "Jabari and I'll take a flyer."

"No." The word came from, of all people, Wegley. In the young man's eyes, Saito saw the new resolve he'd shown back near the Wall, only this time it was stronger, hard-set. He continued, "All due respect, Gunsō, I'm coming with you."

"*You're* staying?" Kirdy gasped. "Why?"

"I'm like Sgt. Saito. I'd like a point to my life. I mean, I'd rather just strafe the lot of them down there, but it's that governor bastard who's letting it happen. He can't get away with this shit."

Saito gestured for Kirdy's attention. "Corporal? You need him with you?"

Kirdy shook his head. "Squeak wants to die heroically, who am I to argue? I'll take care of Naomi."

"Or she'll take care of you," Naomi said, finding the strength to tease.

Face screwed up in angry acceptance, Shill said, "One more question. What do we do with the kid?"

They took the kid with them, intending to keep him until they'd reached the vehicles they meant to steal. From there, Eggo could do whatever the hells he wanted.

They followed the ring passageway around the upper level to where it looked out over the landing pits and gathered against a row of three windows. Near their position, a square hole in the outer wall, with a drop below it, indicated a former elevator well. Now, it was merely a dark void, and they could hear ambient noises rising, like the clanks and moans of ghosts.

Outside the port building, the open-air goods and passenger transfer area stretched in a wide arc, fanning out below them in both directions. Where its procrete or eterni-crete pedestrian area touched the wall below them, it started at about fifty meters and widened to half a kim at the extremity. The area was neatly laid out, with thick blast walls around the landing pits and patches of precinct sheltered beneath UV-filtering grit and shade cloth. On another planet, there'd be birds here, nesting in the cracks between the masonry, resting on the shade cloth, flitting about, looking for flying insects, or hopping about the ground in search of crumbs. Apart from a handful of humans, the only sign of life was one large carab beetle that *zizzed* across Saito's view before rising on an updraft and disappearing out of sight. Before it vanished, he'd taken a long look at it to ensure it wasn't a surveillance bot. As for human activity, most of it was inside the port. Outside, a pair of sec guards met for a chat in the open air—the variations in their dress and corpiforming suggested they belonged to different employers—and a lone local dressed in a better class of robe than Saito had worn earlier.

"Local's probably one of Lorica's," Shill murmured at one end of the line.

"Well, he's not a rich buyer, is he?" Kirdy sniped from the other end.

Shill ignored him, saving her energy for further conflict.

"What about the Ninety up on top?" she suddenly asked.

"The...? Ah, *sack*." Mind busy with other things, Saito had forgotten the combatdroid patrolling the roof.

"If I still had little Greasy..." she started to say, then she shook her head.

"If we still had those robes," said Wegley.

"Look outa place here," Kirdy said to him. Something in his tone when he spoke to the young man had changed. The detestation was missing. There was something else in his voice and manner, Saito realized, with a resolve of his own. He intuited what the corporal would say even as the other man nudged Wegley to get his attention. "Private, I think you're gonna have to leave and help young One Hand after all."

"What, me?" Wegley frowned at Kirdy.

Kirdy jabbed a thumb toward the ceiling. "You assholes get forced to shoot anyone out there—and you probably will—you won't make it five steps before that droid shreds you. Someone has to stay and distract it."

There followed a few seconds of grim silence before Shill snorted and said, "Seems like no one's arguing with you, Corporal."

For a moment, he looked like he was about to snap at her, but a reluctant grin gradually took the place of the scowl. "Yeah, well, guess I never was good at making people like me."

It was Naomi's turn to snort. "Making people? There's your problem right there." But her expression had softened toward him. As had Shill's. And even Wegley's.

"The living shit," Saito groaned. "You sackheads. Tossing Kirdy to the combatdroid is one option. Thinking of an alternative might be another."

"I'm thinking of an alternative," Jabari replied.

Saito was, too, and he'd seen the site schematics that made it viable. "Refuge wells."

"Brilliant minds think alike."

To the others, Saito explained, "Those landing pits have refuges underneath. Wells or hollows for people to duck into in an emergency. The wells are linked by escape tunnels to the main concourse. The droid won't see us."

Kirdy gestured to Shill. "How come you didn't think of that?"

She waved her data cuff in the air. "Wasn't in my files. I'd have noticed."

"Or you just wanted me gone," he said, smiling wryly.

"Maybe that, too."

The corporal sagged momentarily against the wall, no doubt relieved to stay with the team.

"Eggo," Saito said. "Underground tunnels to the ships. Take us there the safest way."

CHAPTER TWENTY-FIVE

SOME BAD WORDS

THE EMERGENCY TUNNELS formed a branching network with a single origin tunnel beneath the concourse marketplace. This forced the team into a frustrating backtrack down many of the crawlspaces they'd used earlier. Saito and Kirdy arrived first in the chamber where the tunnels converged and found two of Lorica's lackeys loitering there. The men were sharing a smoke, squatting with backs against the chamber's age-stained wall, their centuries-old laser carbines leaning out of reach.

Kirdy felled both with his pulse rifle, using lower-power stun bolts to conserve his final magazine's charge for bigger battles. He finished them with his knife and made no comment as he wiped the blade clean on their tunics. When the others joined them, Eggo's eyes were the only ones to widen at the fresh, up-close carnage. Jabari took one of the carbines, having lost his borer in the cutters' fight.

"No spares," Kirdy announced after patting the bodies down, looking for chargepacks.

Only one other way led out of the chamber. Saito pushed Eggo ahead of him. The new passage was pitch black until he slapped his vest to bring his lamp online, casting the boy's shadow ahead of them.

"I do wanting going with youse," Eggo said over his shoulder, committed to one last try at deal making. "I going on ship. I going other planet. I cleaning ship. I doing work. I very wanting going."

"What *I* want," Saito replied, "is to know something. Did your little friend run ahead of us? Did Glark get here first and tell Lorica's people we were coming?"

The boy didn't look back, as he continued leading the way at a decent enough pace, perhaps mulling over the foreign words. When they reached the first branch tunnel, he stopped while the others caught up. Facing Saito, he replied, "I thinking Glark scaring and running, gone."

"How then did the cutters know we were coming? They were *ready* for us."

"What saying cutters?"

"The big men with the big knives."

"Ah, I not knowing how to saying them. Thems knowing because..." He hesitated, eying the group, Kirdy in particular. "Youse not killing me when I saying it?"

"Just answer his question," Kirdy replied in a grating voice.

"Under Lorica place, when us-all coming in the first door I —" He mimed pushing something. "Wall button."

"Little bastard," Shill muttered, bumping him on her way past.

Kirdy growled, "What she said," and bumped the kid, too. Trailing Shill with his lamp lighting her way, he referred to the branch she'd taken and asked her, "Is this correct?"

"Our target vehicles are in the right-side landing pits, correct? Then this is the correct branch."

"Keep your hands off the walls," Saito told Eggo, body language conveying a threat he wasn't sure he could follow through on. Nevertheless, the boy swallowed and nodded. Saito gestured for him to continue.

———

At the next branch, everyone paused. The left path led toward the small starship up in the farthest landing pit, the right toward the cloud clipper Saito had chosen for his group.

Kirdy shucked off his vest and gifted it to Jabari then reluctantly shook his hand for luck.

Saito shook hands with Kirdy for different reasons, then gripped Naomi's uninjured arm, wishing them, "A guiding star and a safe trip to hyperspace."

"Guiding star for you, too, Gunsō," Naomi said, her voice husky as he released her arm. She hesitated for a half-second then leaned in and pecked his cheek. That was the first surprise, the second being what she did next. She stepped over to Wegley and repeated the action, then she patted the cheek where she'd kissed it—a little hard, if his cringe was anything to go by. She said, "Watch Gunsō's back, Wegley, and notch some kills for me."

"Um," he said. "I will."

In the light from multiple lamps, both his cheeks had reddened and not just from the slap.

"Lieutenant," she nodded to Jabari. Then she headed down the lefthand tunnel.

Kirdy made a wry face. "What she said." He hurried after her.

Shill handed her data cuff to Jabari then embraced him stiffly before pulling away and saying, "I better see you again. Fallback plan is meeting at the planet we discussed."

Jabari saluted and winked. "See you there, if not on the scout."

And then she, too, was gone.

With the refuge well in sight at the end of the final passageway, Jabari grabbed Eggo's arm, eliciting a squeal of protest. He stuck Shill's data cuff in the boy's face. "Say something. In your language. Say something rude, say some bad words. Shit. Bastard. Sonofabitch. Things like that."

Frowning at him the whole time, Eggo rattled off a string of syllables that might have meant anything. When he drew breath for more, Jabari pulled back, letting him go, and busied himself with the cuff.

"That'll come in handy, trust me. He's all yours, Gunsō."

Saito signaled for the kid's attention before hooking a thumb the way they'd come. "Go."

The kid went.

Running.

And didn't look back.

"Let's go steal that clipper," Saito told the others.

Hunkered down in the shadows of the escape well, they watched the one female sec guard patrol the pit. She wore a finely detailed blue and red uniform that matched a sigil under the vehicle's bow, meaning she'd come with the vehicle and didn't work for Lorica. She seemed exceedingly bored until Saito appeared and stunned her. He left her alive and rolled her into the refuge well then hauled the safety cover across her. No point in killing *everyone* they met. This woman was doing her job and posed no threat. By the time she came around and had control of her faculties, he'd be established in a new location. If anyone was going to raise the alarm first, it'd be Eggo.

Growing soft, he accused himself while the others climbed aboard the clipper. Jabari took the pilot seat. No. That wasn't it.

It was more about what he'd witnessed in the market. Something about the horrors of killing people for your own gain. There were individuals who *deserved* death—for their crimes, for their sociopathy. The humans who'd become *inhuman*. Often, those who worked *for* them were just as bad. Sometimes, they were not; sometimes, they were just 'Joes and Janes,' ordinary people who'd fallen into a job and found themselves shackled to it. As he stared down at the refuge cover, he wondered which type this woman was. Had he done the universe a disservice by letting her live? Or was she a mother with kids waiting for her to return from her latest jaunt with the boss, waiting for her to pay for the power and food and clothing that kept *their* lives peaceful and protected?

"*Gunsō?*"

Wegley's voice in his comms startled him.

"You coming, Gunsō?"

Saito shook himself. It wasn't like him to blank out like that. Not like him to...

"*Sgt. Saito!*" Wegley barked.

Damn. Kid sounds almost like command material.

He shook himself again and stumped on tired legs toward the skipper, carrying his rifle and the unconscious woman's laser pistol.

"You good?" Jabari asked as he climbed in.

"Yep." He took the seat beside Jabari.

The vehicle had three seats in back, along with the two in front. The seat he strapped into was comfortable and instantly molded itself to the impression and weight of his body and body armor. Jabari held Shill's cuff close to the skipper's helmboard, hacking it. Saito heard a polite cough from the thrusters as they woke, the vehicle purring with eagerness to get in the air.

The clipper rose easily from the pit and accelerated gently toward the Wall. Saito found himself craning his neck, looking for Kirdy and Naomi's ship. If they weren't halfway to orbit, they'd still be in comm range. He *could* try checking in, make sure they were all right. Not a healthy impulse. Worrying was for parents. In battle, in Saito's profession, worrying could get you killed or get other people killed. Take your mind off the job, get you overthinking, eat your soul from the inside.

Indicating the data cuff, he said, "Could we use that to track Aurelia? The quaestor, I mean."

Jabari looked at him sidelong as he eased the flyer over the escarpment and the date palm grove they'd rested in earlier. "Wherever she is, she ran off and left you."

"Sure. Because Shill slagged her cybernetics."

"She could have stayed. She fought those troopers in the tunnel well enough, so bits of her still worked."

"Bits of her."

"You see my point, though."

"All right," Saito said. "We do this ourselves, and if the quaestor has already slagged Ectorius, we're walking into unnecessary trouble."

"If she slagged him already," Jabari said in a reasonable tone, "there'd be more commotion down there."

They were over the Wall and could see a pair of patrolling troopers chatting side by side. A combatdroid stood vigil further along. Because they weren't high up, Saito cracked a passenger window, heard no sirens from the city, then closed it again. A single line of thin smoke marked one of the *Charon* crashes from the start of the day's action. But as Jabari said, there was no commotion.

They were halfway up the Hill—and unchallenged by any shooters below—when a comms call finally came through.

"Looks like the owner," said Jabari, as he raised a hand to keep the other two quiet. With the data cuff close to the helm, he triggered the comms then touched something on the cuff. Eggo's reedy voice spewed out the string of gobbledygook he'd recorded earlier. Jabari shut off the comms with a delighted chuckle. "That'll throw them off."

"They'll think we're local criminals." Saito chuckled, too. "Nice idea."

Jabari tapped his temple.

Saito was filled with an almost dreamlike calm. Now that he knew the odds, the barrier he faced, and the steps he'd need to take to blast through it, he felt at home and steady. If the odds were not in his favor? If success was beyond them, and it was his turn to die today? He was surprised the thought only enhanced his calm, as if dying would be a relief, a release from the responsibility for *other* lives...

"I'm taking an indirect approach," Jabari said. "Over The Summit, around the other side. Then we'll see what we see."

"And get inside and fry the governor's ass," Wegley growled.

"If we *can* get inside," Jabari told him. He banked the clipper for a few seconds. When it was level again, Jabari added, "That big white marble-looking place along the ridge? That's our target."

Saito joined Wegley in searching for it, but even if he hadn't seen it in the mission files days earlier, it'd be hard to miss. On a minor peak, rising an extra five hundred meters or so from the southern end of The Summit, the stately home stood out like balls on a dog. He grunted. "Shouldn't need to say it, but weapons checks. We're low on charge and recharge, so we take what we can get as we move inside and look for the bastard."

Jabari glanced down at the old carbine he'd propped by his leg. "Dead troopers don't need their rifles, that's for sure. And I could do with a spare."

He brought them over the ridgeline, which allowed Saito to catch sight of the villa to the north where this debacle had started. The ruined rooftop. The dropskiff's carcass. A couple of ground vehicles parked on the recreation path behind it, but no people visible.

The clipper dipped lower over the far slope, and he caught sight of the far-flung valley on the other side with its meager lake and its rim of higher mountains further out.

If miracles happen.

"You all know there'll be *someone* guarding the place, right?" Jabari asked.

Saito straightened in his seat. "Chance we have to take. We attack here, maybe Kirdy and Naomi get away, get the message out. Shill, too—she can take up your goal of, what was it, liberating the Proselyti?"

"And finding us a home," Jabari said.

"What?"

"If there's a later, I'll explain it. On top of all the other things I promised to tell you."

More focused than both combined, Wegley said, "We fight our way inside and maybe we clear the way here for a better governor. Someone who doesn't invite rich cannibals in for a dinner of sauteed human."

"There's a small chance we get Ectorius," Saito admitted. "But there *is* a chance."

"Place has a flat roof," Jabari said, pointing. "How about setting down there?"

Saito nodded grimly, remembering their first roof landing that day. "Sounds about right."

CHAPTER TWENTY-SIX

AURELIA IN CHAINS

THIRTEEN TINY DROIDS perched on her bare skin, and not one of them had done anything to her. Their only reactions had been to her attempts to shake them off, dislodge them, and then they'd simply repositioned to more stable locations before falling dormant again. There was no sign of them going about the nefarious work their kind were made for.

Yet.

No doubt, Ectorius had been distracted by his gathering. Surely, that was well underway now. There'd been guests milling outside the function room before she'd been stunned. Early birds? Pre-partiers, gaining a head start on the evening's alcohol and drug buzz... and gossip?

Perhaps the delay and aloneness were intended as part of the torture.

Well, it's bloody well working.

She squirmed on the metal table and regretted it immediately when her sweaty skin squeaked against the surface, setting her teeth on edge. The headache from the stunning had faded to nothing more than a dull pulse behind both eyes. But this was a mess. She consoled herself with two things. Lonzo had a good chance of making it out of the system, and Major Tatias' earlier questions meant some of her insertion team had survived. If even one of them made it off world, word would get out. Justice would still be served to Ectorius and all those complicit with him. Though it would no doubt be too late for her...

Oh, well. She shrugged philosophically. The prospect of death was less irksome to her than the prospect of failure. Death was nothing; Imperium was everything. Only two or three hours back, she'd been thinking about that Cor Fidelis belief, the one about a pan-dimensional afterlife for imperial citizens. If it existed, would the souls of emperors past judge her worthy of reward and pass her into their Paradise-construct? Or would she be cast into the Hell-construct to languish forever, brooding over her failure?

"Royal shit, woman!" she castigated herself. "Get a grip."

"Did you say something, girl?"

The new voice came from the open doorway. The speaker wore a purple suit made from silky fabric with a bone-white shirt under it. The jacket sleeves flared out, bell-shaped, revealing frilly white shirt cuffs. The fingers the man steepled beneath his weak chin bore bejeweled rings—seven, she counted. His thick, magenta-tinted hair had been piled up high, styled into a tall coiffure that added ten centimeters to his stature. Purple lipstick matched the suit; white eyeliner matched the shirt.

Governor Eccles Ectorius took long strides into the room, until he could grin at her from a position near her feet.

"My, my, *my*, how the mighty one has *fallen*. Your chum Nero thought to bring me down today. And look where that got *you*. Tied to a table with some nasty little droids ready to hurt you... and Nero nowhere in sight. Letting you suffer while he's off galivanting on that galactic tour. Sampling the foods and wines of a hundred worlds, while you, dear girl, suffer the punishment for his sins."

He pinched one of her toes and cackled.

"This is such a delight for me. I wonder what my oh so very many High House friends will think about our honored emperor sending an assassin against one of his *governors*. I think it might feed their hunger for a change. A change of ruling family. A change in the way our galaxy is governed."

Aurelia sneered at him. "I'm a quaestor, not an assassin."

He rolled his eyes. "In my experience, darling, same thing."

He turned away and began to pace the room. Unlike Major Tatias, Ectorius showed zero interest in her nakedness, an indication she was merely a thing to him, rather than a woman, a person. His next words seemed to prove it.

"That Corfid of yours. So interesting to examine his anatomy once we had him flayed and embalmed. I always wondered if they cut off anything besides their little fingers. Apparently not. Disappointing, really."

"If you want to avoid your own mutilation, Ectorius, you'd better run for your life. Find some cave in lawless space to hide in while you still can."

"Oh, I think not. As I said, I'll simply use Nero's machinations against him, garner sympathy for myself. And support." He leveled a finger at her like a gun. "You know, young lady, your friends down on Vadox continue to make trouble for me and for my associates. I try to run a peaceful planet, but you and they have run rampant down there."

"A peaceful planet," she scoffed. "The genesis of your mini empire."

His turn to scoff. "You think the free faction we're building will be based here? *Here*? Hardly! Vadox is a cesspool. Well, it would be if there was enough water for the pool part of that." He cackled quietly.

She replied, "The High Magistrates know all about your

research into fringe regions where you might carve out territory for yourself, using the trillions in licensing and tax revenue you and your pals have syphoned off, of course. You and those pals will form a cozy 'Council' to oversee your little kingdom... then, no doubt, the squabbling will start about who gets to be queen or king of it."

He stopped by her feet again and tweaked another toe. "I'll be king, darling, have no doubt about that. Shame you won't live long enough for me to rub that fact in your face. But then, you're not important enough for that. It's Nero I'll enjoy embarrassing." He nodded toward the door. "I have another matter to attend to and then my party. I'm saving you for the late-night entertainment. You *and* your friend."

Ectorius swept from the room, and two heavily built security guards carried in an unconscious person and dumped them on the other gurney.

Someone who was the *last* person Aurelia had ever expected to see again.

CHAPTER TWENTY-SEVEN

MANSION

THE MANSION HAD no road access and was surrounded by a woodland of hip-high dwarf trees that were either very good fakes or expensively maintained real ones. Saito figured any ground vehicles coming there used a tunnel—this city certainly loved its tunnels. There was evidence for this—a delivery ground truck was parked beside a structure inside the grounds, meaning the structure had to be the access from that tunnel and a potential escape route if the flyer became compromised.

And if we survive this.

The truck bore the same advertising image across both sides—two juicy steaks, medium rare.

New pork? Saito wondered.

With no one visible on the mansion's roof or within its grounds, Jabari eased the clipper onto the rooftop and immediately popped the two side doors. The three men bustled out, Jabari taking position in front, Wegley in back, and Saito darting over to crouch at one edge of the roof. He scanned the grounds and the skies, straining his ears for any signs a gunship attack was imminent, or that troopers were getting into defensive positions or getting ready to storm the roof from the platform elevator pad he could see at the far end. Nothing. Like many places he'd been that day, there wasn't much noise at all other than the ambient buzz and murmur from down on the cityslope, the wind doing what the wind did, and Wegley stifling a sudden cough.

The three of them had their comms on, and Saito murmured to the others, "No one's home, you think? Or are they keeping their heads down for another ambush?"

"Maybe just staff," Jabari mused. "Governor may be elsewhere."

"Files say this is his home and his office."

"Then we bust our way in," Wegley said, clutching at straws. "Find something he cares about, some knickknack, some favorite pet, and we force him to come here."

"You're gonna take a *pet* hostage?" Saito replied. He started toward the platform elevator, weapon sweeping the air above, not quite trusting there wouldn't be another skydrone. "Why don't we break in and attempt an ambush of our own?"

"Also practice our hacking skills," Jabari agreed. "See if we find files we can send to your commanders or the High Magistrates Office."

Wegley suggested, "Or use his Grid comms to get a message out for reinforcements."

"Now *that* thinking, I like," Saito told him. He crossed the last twenty meters to the lift pad in a jog and waited at its side for the others.

With Wegley lagging, walking backward to cover their asses, Jabari reached Saito first, and they stepped onto the platform together. A common design for more expensive versions of these lifts was for the control panel to rise from a hidden compartment that protected it from the elements. Something did pop up, but it wasn't a lift controller.

Instead, four sides whipped out from the platform's edges and enclosed the space the two men stood on within two seconds. It became a box when the walls excreted something that stretched across the top, forming a roof. All the material was transparent. When Saito and Jabari slammed rifle butts into it, they discovered it wasn't glass. It had some give, but nowhere near enough for them to compromise.

"Idiot," Saito railed at himself. "*Idiot!* It's not a platform lift!"

The real elevator would be set elsewhere, seamlessly integrated into the roof, so it wasn't visible between uses, its location known only to the householder and trusted staff. Gut leaden, Saito screamed at himself internally for his recklessness, for not thinking this through.

Ambushed not once, not twice, but three times in a day. Unless...

"Maybe it's an automatic security feature," he told Jabari. "If the right staff member comes along, we could talk ourselves out of this."

Jabari didn't look optimistic.

Wegley arrived. The young man's mouth opened in a desperate holler, but Saito heard nothing.

"Soundproof. Airproof, too, I'll bet."

Jabari continued staring miserably around them. "Slow, even breaths, then."

Movement drew Saito's attention back to Wegley, who was fruitlessly pounding on his side of the wall with his rifle butt. Then he flipped it around.

Saito and Jabari instinctively screamed at him to stop. But he fired at the barrier anyway, angling the pulse upward to avoid hitting the two men inside. That angle probably saved his life. When the energy bolt bounced off the barrier, it sailed harmlessly over his head.

"He has to get out of here," Jabari muttered.

Saito mouthed the word "*Run*" at Wegley and gesticulated wildly toward the clipper. Jabari took up the action and waved him away. But Wegley didn't run. His attention shifted to an area outside the cage, past the cage. Nine hostiles had appeared seemingly from nowhere and were standing on the platform lift that had brought them swiftly and sneakily up from below.

Nine hostiles—six rifle-toting troopers and three civs dressed in generic clothing, like Lorica's sec guards. Wegley couldn't hit them from his side of the transparent cage.

"Run!" Saito screamed at the young man one final time. The cage sheltered his path to the clipper.

A humming sound accompanied a holo projector dais emerging through the floor inside the trap.

"And here we go," Jabari muttered, settling into a weary squat.

Within seconds, he and Saito were staring at a live representation of Governor Ectorius, clothed in a flamboyant tailored suit. The holo resolution was good enough that Saito itched to put a round into it.

The governor shook his head, hands in his jacket pockets, and said, "What kind of morons did you Terranists breed in your day? You're primitives by modern standards. Did your precious Kaana *inbreed* you all into Neanderthalic throwbacks, hm?" He gave a little snicker at his jibe. "You've been ambushed not once, not twice, but *three times!*"

This direct echo of Saito's thoughts made him twitch and grimace.

"In far *less* than a day, actually!" Ectorius continued, rubbing salt into the wound. "Luck was with you the first two times, but not *this* time." He slipped one hand from his pocket and waved it around. "Like my cage? Impressive idea, but it's ten years old! First time it's been really tested, and I'm so pleased with the results. Now, you two know you don't have unlimited air in there, right? If you'd like to continue living— and I *am* giving you that option—order your lackey outside the cage to lay down his gun and... well, I'm sure he knows the drill for surrendering. You Terranists were so good at it, back in your day." As he indulged himself in another snicker, the holo field dissolved, and he was gone.

Beyond the barrier, the ambush team had begun spreading out, weapons tracking Wegley as the young man's demeanor wilted. He hadn't heard the holo, but he got the message. Tiredly, he slumped to his knees, unslung the rifle, and slid it aside, then he slapped his palms on his head.

"Ah, squeak," Saito sighed, knowing the young man couldn't hear him. "I should've made you leave with Kirdy."

Jabari clicked his fingers. When Saito turned to him, he used the original Okalasi Battalions' sign language. *We don't need rifles. We'll kill them without weapons, the first opportunity we get.*

In kind, Saito replied, *We definitely will.*

Another object rose through the floor, a thick spray nozzle. Even before it started spraying gas, Saito instinctively gulped down a huge breath of clean air.

And held it.

For as long as he could.

Longer than Jabari did.

But it wasn't long enough.

CHAPTER TWENTY-EIGHT

CAVE PEOPLE

WHEN SAITO CAME AROUND, it was like waking from stasis. Disorientation. Nausea. Brain fog. An abject weariness that made him want to return to the womb.

When his memory returned, he had a glorious twenty seconds of imagining the Vadox experience was a reemergence dream, a nightmare caused by shaky neurons and his aging body's response to yet another restart process. He even fancied the idiotic name Vadox was an invention of addled synapses. And he felt enormous relief.

The relief lasted until the moment he opened his eyes and focused on Jabari's dark face staring groggily at him from a couple meters away. The two men lay on their backs, and Jabari wasn't naked like he would've been coming straight out of stasis. The man still wore the same set of maintenance coveralls, proving all that shit Saito's short-term memory was throwing at him was one hundred percent true.

Saito moaned, rolled onto his side, and then quickly onto his elbows, as he vomited the meager contents of his stomach onto the spongy mat serving as a floor, then scrambled away from the mess.

"I wish you hadn't done that," Jabari said and heaved a couple times as he rolled the other way.

Saito surveyed the five-by-five room they'd been dumped in. It had 'cell' written all over it. Ceiling three meters off the rubbery floor. No fittings other than a steel refresher—a commode low enough for a child to use—in one corner, and the two sets of double bunks stacked together across the wall facing the door. No blankets or pillows on the bunks. A single square glowpanel mid-ceiling.

Where are we? A barely perceptible rumble in the floor or deck suggested it was a ship or space station.

Pressed into the corner opposite the toilet, Wegley watched them dourly with his legs folded in the lotus position. The young man no longer wore a vest. Nor did Saito. And Jabari had lost the one Kirdy gifted him. Saito and Wegley had been left in their mission fatigues, but without belts, boots, or socks. Jabari, too, was shoeless and sockless, clothed only in his brown coveralls.

Wegley must have read Saito's thoughts by the way he was looking at them. "What the sack are they worried we'll do with our *socks*?"

"Tie them together into a noose," Jabari muttered, forcing himself onto his hands and knees with a groan. "Or a cord for strangling a guard."

Saito added, "Fill one with screws from the bunk and use it as a kosh." He tried standing but gave up when the room swam around him. He crawled to a bunk, dragged himself onto it, and forced his body into a sitting position. Then he ground his teeth and swallowed his bile until the room stopped swaying and churning.

"Yeah," said Jabari. He'd settled for slinking to the wall by the door and resting his back against it with his legs imitating Wegley's. "That was some nasty gas."

"Thought they'd killed you, at first," Wegley told them. "Thought I was on my own."

"I feel like they did," Saito replied, his fingertips rubbing gentle circles across his closed eyelids for a few seconds. He dropped his hands to his lap just as the door whipped aside and crashed into the wall or bulkhead.

For close to thirty seconds, nothing happened. Nobody appeared. A white-lit corridor outside beckoned them, as if the way lay open for escape. A ruse, Saito knew. An act of mental torture, getting the captives' hopes up before dashing them. Jabari's expression said as much when he caught Saito's eye; he hadn't so much as turned his head toward the open space in the wall beside him.

Sure enough, someone appeared in the doorway, an army officer, bearing a major's star-shaped leaf badge on his right epaulette. He had hair the dark red of veinous blood. His right hand rested with his fingers shoved into his belt; his left held a pocket-size stun gun. His sour facial expression said he'd love to use it on one of them. In heavily accented Imperial True, he told them, "My name is Tatias. I'll pass this weapon to His Excellency, now. Be assured he'll use it if even one of you tries to stand up. That would be dangerous for the two of you affected by the gas. A second unconsciousness so close to the first will definitely cause some form of neurological damage." The major waited ten seconds for a response. When the Proselyti didn't give him one, he directed a question to someone outside. "They do speak True, sir?"

"I'm reliably informed they do," an oily voice replied. "Message delivered, Major Tatias. Now, may I?"

The officer took two backward steps and held the stunner to the side, his stare holding Saito's. Another man accepted the weapon before taking the major's place in the doorway. The man from the rooftop hologram. In real life, the garish hair color, facial makeup, the tendency toward purple colors—it was almost nauseating.

Noticing Jabari's proximity, Governor Ectorius gestured blithely toward the bunks. "I know the good major said don't stand. But you can crawl there, proselyte, and join your little emperor's roach friend."

Jabari let out a dramatic sigh reminiscent of one of Wegley's. He took his time obeying, which might have been due to the lingering effects of the gas, but the wink he gave Saito said he just wanted to piss Ectorius off.

Once Jabari had settled on the bunk beside him, Saito thought, *I might as well piss the bastard off, too. Small victories are still victories.* He said, "Governor, I've had a long day, and I'm not in the mood for long speeches. Just cut to the part where you dish out our punishment. There's a good fellow."

Such a statement, he expected, would alarm Wegley as much as irritate Ectorius. To his surprise, the young private nodded, face twisted in a combination of detestation and grim acceptance of his fate.

Surprised by Saito's command, Ectorius tilted his head one way then the other while he fought to find a way to link back into the script he'd prepared for the moment. In the end, he settled for an honest statement. "Well, you're getting a speech anyway."

Saito waited a beat then waved for him to continue. The impudent gesture caused a flush of color in His Excellency's cheeks, though the man began talking in a controlled, superior tone.

"Today, I have been inconvenienced. I've been caused an enormous amount of trouble by a pack of cavemen. Excuse me, cave*people*, since there were females among your team. However, while you proved difficult to capture, that result *was* never in doubt. Only one way for you to try for an escape, since you appeared to have reasonable data on my city and my planet. Although my dear Major Tatias warned dumb-dumb Lorica that you would attempt ship theft from him, the moron refused to take your threat seriously. However, cavepeople aren't exactly clever; it wasn't difficult to track the flyer when you foolishly brought it back *into* my city." He waggled his eyebrows as if inviting laughter at Saito's silliness, but none of the Proselyti saw the humor. Not even Major Tatias, behind him, cracked a smile.

Hells. He's a worse comedian than he is a governor!

To keep Ectorius off balance, Saito interjected, "Lorica's security wasn't the only one that was crap today. At that abomination of a marketplace, we saw wealthy folks that *you* associate with, probably here for your rescheduled party, filling time doing some cannibal shopping. But even though they're your friends, *their* security looked pretty damned lax, I have to say. Because you didn't warn them we might stop by, did you? Lorica got the word; your friends didn't. Interesting choice you made."

"Enough of this," Ectorius sighed, speaking over the end of Saito's outburst. "You were in a hurry for the consequences part of my speech, caveman? Well, here it comes. You three are where the rest of the Imperium can't find you. Welcome to Orbital One. The last place you'll ever visit—alive, that is. When we're finished debriefing you, you three will become my goodwill offering to dear dumb-dumb Lorica. A peace gift. And having laid eyes on Lorica's marketplace, I'm sure you can guess where your mortal remains will end up and how they'll be displayed." He sniggered. "My, what a pretty price he'll get for you. Seventeen-hundred-year-old meat, in perfect condition!"

"Sonofabitch dogsacker," Wegley growled.

Without acknowledging the young man, Ectorius said, "And if you're wondering what became of the other surviving members of your ill-intentioned mission... They made it into space, all right, just not the part of space they were hoping for. Major, if you please?"

Ectorius gestured at the patch of wall above Jabari's head. The officer outside must have been ready for the command because a vision appeared on an embedded viewer in the wall. The vision depicted a compartment like an examination room. Birds-eye view. Two women were strapped to gurneys, stark naked, with tiny robots crawling across their skin. Aurelia Cossea. Shill Teuku. Every few seconds, one of the women would flinch and bare her teeth. But if there was audio accompanying the vision, they couldn't hear either woman letting out a sound.

"I do prefer to torture women," Ectorius crooned. "Something about their vocal pitch when they eventually begin screaming. Besides, I intuit that these two will be a far greater challenge to break than you chaps will, which makes it more entertaining."

"*You—*"

Saito and Jabari shouted the word together and simultaneously launched off the bed, despite the warning about another stunning. Still smiling, Ectorius stepped into the corridor. The door slammed and sealed long before either Proselyti got there. Saito stopped hard mid-room while Jabari continued all the way to the door and struck it with the meat of his fist. Then he sagged there and whispered one word.

"Shill."

"They'll have Naomi, too," moaned Wegley, hands going to his face. "And Corporal Kirdy."

Saito stood silent, swaying in place, and deeply ashamed his prime outrage had not been for Shill, or for Naomi or Kirdy, but for the quaestor, for Aurelia.

Have I become such a Martianist, he wondered, *that my people come second?*

What kind of leader am I?

An hour passed and then another. Saito easily tracked the passage of time by watching the changing figures on his bio-tat. No food arrived. No water. When the third hour of nothingness started, Saito was forced to give in to the effects of natural aging on his bladder. His back to the others and to the door, he used the refresher and was zipping his pants when the door whisked open.

Perfect sacking timing, he thought as he turned. He heard Wegley gasp and assumed Major Tatias had returned to fish out a new victim for interrogation.

It wasn't the major. In the open doorway stood Corporal Kirdy.

It was Saito's turn to gasp.

Wegley croaked, "*What?*"

Also stripped of his vest, Kirdy's muscular upper body beneath the uniform shirt looked only slightly smaller than it had. A fresh bruise on his right cheek matched the one Shill had given him on the other. Dried blood marked a split across his bottom lip. He appeared uninjured otherwise. When he stepped inside, he revealed another man behind him.

The new fellow was probably Saito's age with haphazard tufts of salt-and-pepper hair. The sight of his Imperial Regular uniform, with a yellow sash, sank Saito's hopes. Kirdy wasn't here to bust them out, he was being tossed in with them.

But then the stranger winked and gave them all a cheery thumbs-up signal, a gesture Saito had seen many cultures use to mean *All right* or *Hi, I'm a friendly*. Apparently, they *were* being busted out.

Saito found himself smiling, but the smile died the moment he saw Naomi wasn't with them.

Kirdy anticipated his question and said, "She's transferred to the medical department. And this guy's called Lonzo."

"And Shill?" Jabari asked.

"And the quaestor?" Saito added. The question drew a cold glance from the former lieutenant.

Though the Proselyti spoke in their own tongue, they'd been allowed to keep their translator patches fixed to their shirts, presumably to make later interrogation easier. Kirdy's had broadcast a low-volume interpretation in Imperial Common for Lonzo. The stranger's reply came through the same device at the same pitch. "We got someone figuring out where your buddy and Madam Quaestor are."

"Someone I'm hoping's as good a hacker as Shill," said Kirdy as he led the way into the empty, white-tiled corridor. "And, yeah, I can't believe I said that either."

Saito and Wegley fired up their translators and kept the volume low, like Kirdy's. Lonzo rushed them to a nearby systems-monitoring closet where they bundled inside. In the very back, an olive-skinned, short-haired woman regarded their entry with wide, anxious eyes, before returning her attention to a systems panel. When the door sealed, Kirdy introduced her, "She's Dr. May."

"May is fine," she said distractedly while typing something.

Saito asked his corporal, "*She's* finding the interrogation room? Who is she? Who's *he*?"

Kirdy replied, "Her and Lonzo were helping Quaestor Cossea. She was with Cossea when they got captured, but he wasn't, 'cause Cossea sent him elsewhere. They chucked May in with me. Not many cells on Orbital One. Not much need, Lonzo reckons."

Talking while chewing her lip, May added, "I'm a tech-medic. Orgment specialist. Helped Madam Quaestor recover. But I'm not trained to break through data barriers, so this is difficult. I'm getting close... I think..." Her voice trailed off as the task sucked all her focus.

"She can pretend to be a doctor to help us get to Naomi," Kirdy said.

"A tech-medic *is* a doctor," she muttered absently.

Saito's head spun, processing all this.

In the silence, Jabari asked Lonzo, "And you? Why weren't you caught? This is a disguise?" He indicated the uniform shirt and yellow sash.

Lonzo plucked at the sash. "No. Was my job. Till the quaestor recruited me."

"Till she...?" Jabari started to ask, but Saito spoke over him.

"It *was* your job? So, now this *is* a disguise."

The wrinkles in Lonzo's face cracked deeper as he pondered that, then they cleared in understanding. "No one knows I left yet. But they's gonna know if I gots to shoot anyone." He patted the aging pulse rifle slung at his side and shrugged like he wouldn't give a shit if shooting was on the agenda.

May continued typing furiously, her tongue poking out of her mouth.

Saito asked Lonzo, "She repaired the quaestor?"

"Fixed up her arm and brain." Lonzo shrugged. "Not the eye. Only this one works." He pointed to his right eye.

"You know Cossea and Shill are sharing a room now?" Jabari asked Kirdy.

Kirdy snorted. "I didn't. I wonder how *that* conversation's going."

"I doubt they've had any conversation." Saito sighed. He'd been pondering the prospect of Shill cracking first under torture. Aurelia was guaranteed to hold out longer, which meant Shill might divulge information about Optio Scipio's mission. About where she and Jabari had been since then. And about where they'd planned to take any Proselyti they 'liberated.' If she cracked before his much-reduced team could rescue them, it created a conflict for Saito. One he wouldn't have had at the start of this day. Back then, the lines had been crystal clear. Laws were laws, and there were only two sides—the Imperium and those who opposed it. Now, however...

Did he *want* Aurelia knowing about Jabari and Shill and reporting that information back to the empire?

Did he *want* two renegade Proselyti roaming the galaxy? Their freedom might bring retribution onto those former Terranists still indentured to imperial military service?

Saito had sworn allegiance to empire and emperor, and he'd meant it. He'd devoted himself to bringing humanity under one banner. Permitting the birth of yet another splinter group was in direct opposition to that.

But Proselyti were his people. The only people he had left. And Jabari and Shill were still part of those people...

And these are questions too big for a helldamned army sergeant to ponder.

Just do the job.

After that, do whatever you can for your people.

Then do what you can for the empire, for the human species.

That's it. That's your duty. That's your lot in life.

His lot in life. For the first time in decades of subjective time, Saito resented it.

"I found them!" May exclaimed, startling him from his brooding. With all eyes on her, the tech-medic turned toward them, her own eyes wide. "And you won't believe where they are."

MISSION OUTCOMES

Atque in perpetuum, frāter,
Avē atque valē.
And forever, brother,
Hail and farewell.

- From a poem by Gaius Valerius Catullus, 57 BCE

CHAPTER TWENTY-NINE

SMALL VICTORIES

"LET me lay this out logically, then you can plan properly," May said. She traced a finger across the schematic onscreen. "Every level of this stupid-looking space pyramid is divided into Quadrants. A, B, C, D. We're in Quadrant C, Level 3. Level 1 is the lowest level, the hangar deck, so we're two levels up from any escape ship."

"I coulda told youse that," Lonzo muttered.

Ignoring him, she pointed past him to the door. "The corridor outside runs diagonally to the outer corner of this level where our two brig cells were."

"Nice," Kirdy said. "We had hard vacuum right outside our bulkheads."

"Well, not directly. There's maintenance crawlways, buffer zones..." At a curt gesture from Saito, May stopped correcting Kirdy and moved on, now pointing to the ceiling. "Ectorius leases Quadrants C and D of Level 4. Right above us, nice and close. According to station records, he has two compartments decked out as 'medical rooms.' You said he showed you feed from an interrogation room?"

"Torture room," said Jabari, "but yeah."

"Was it set up like a medical room?"

Saito answered, "Clean. Gurneys. Monitoring equipment. So, they're right above us?"

"Well, not precisely. This is Quadrant C; his medical rooms are in Quadrant D. Over that way." She pointed again. "There's no mention of the women's capture on any station records, but the logs don't show any ship departures since they were captured, so they must be there."

"That's good work, May," Jabari said.

She accepted the praise with a fleeting smile.

"Naomi?" Wegley asked, clearing his throat. "Private Naomi?"

"Also, relatively good news," said May. "She *is* recorded, along with you fellows. *Prisoners of Planetary Garrison Awaiting Transfer to the Hill.* No names. Just facial images. The orbital's true medical center or 'medical department' is up on Level 7, one floor down from the very top. However, Naomi isn't a patient there. They've logged her as 'receiving care' in the governor's own medical rooms."

"Sonofabitch!" Wegley wheeled about and kicked the door. "They're torturing her, too!"

Saito caught him by the shoulders, turned him back, and shook him gently. "Hold it together, Private."

"If he's touched her..." Wegley growled. "If his butchers..." He swallowed hard, leaving the thought unfinished, dropping his head.

Saito released him and told the room, "They'll be giving Naomi treatment. Stabilizing her to interrogate her later."

Or to make sport of her. He read the same prospect in Jabari's bleak expression.

"Why keep us up here?" May asked, breaking the brief silence. "I mean, his seat of power is down on the Hill, isn't it?"

Jabari replied, "Keep your enemies close?"

Kirdy suggested, "He's keeping us off world where his own detainment and policing laws don't apply."

"That's not it. It's about the psychology of psychopaths. Up here, he's 'high above it all.' Looking down on his kingdom. Up here, his little empire feels bigger than it does down on that mole hill. Also, there's the excitement of doing these things under the noses of other businesspeople and galactic travelers. It's riskier, but he's the clever one, the powerful one, getting away with it."

"Asshole," Wegley whispered.

"How did *you* get here?" Jabari asked May.

"My former employer's shuttle. *FTL* shuttle. It's still here; the first thing I checked. And yes, I can fly it. Well, enough to get into hyperspace, anyway."

"Shill can fly it."

"I can, too," Lonzo said. "If anyone's interested, you know."

Saito caught the grizzled former Vadox trooper's eye. "Something else you can do for us is procure new clothing and weapons. *After* you remove that sash."

Lonzo unfixed the unsightly yellow ribbon and said, "I been thinkin' about that. There's no security office I saw anywhere near here. All I hadda do to open your cells was flash my passcard across the doors and *fwip*, open! But I did a quick scout before and found one security office... that's how I found out about you. Two rooms on Level 4 but not in Ectorius' area. Only one idiot workin' in there when I went by. I used the workstation in the other room and the *chramiga* didn't hear a thing. They has three closets up there in the corridor outside the rooms. I taked a peek. Uniforms, datapads, and passcards. Locked behind glass. Probably they makes their guards buy 'em. There was a few different sizes of boots and trousers and shirts."

Everyone who *wasn't* Lonzo studied their naked feet for a second.

"Be nice to wear shoes," said May, speaking for all of them.

"Slightly less suspicious, too," Saito added. He indicated Jabari's coveralls. "You look the least suspicious of us, currently. You or May. But Lonzo will need help getting that gear, and I don't think a doctor wants to snuff out any sec guards who get in the way."

"Er... no." She folded her arms.

"We need to avoid lethal force," Jabari said. "Not a good idea leaving a trail of bodies. And these are private employees, not the governor's lackeys."

Saito grunted agreement and pointed at Lonzo's slung rifle. "Also, things like *that* make too much noise."

When the translator caught up with Saito's words, Lonzo sagged in disappointment. "Oh."

"What weapons did you see up there? Stunners?"

Lonzo mimed jabbing someone with something. "Shock sticks. No guns."

"That's what I saw when I was wandering around, too," May said. "Before we got caught."

Saito said, "They'll do. Many troopers around?"

May and Lonzo shook their heads. She said, "A few at checkpoints." He said, "I saw two in a food court."

Jabari and Lonzo shifted toward the door, antsy to move. Saito stopped them with an outstretched hand. "Listen, if we do get our hands on a pulse rifle or pistol, we set it for stun. Civilians we stun once, lock them away if possible. Anyone who's a direct report to Ectorius is our enemy—they get stunned three times."

"*Three*?" asked Wegley. "Oh, got it." He drew a finger across his throat.

"Brain and other organ failure," Saito confirmed. "Stop them tattling on us. All right. Shoe sizes, everyone?"

When they were done, Jabari said, "Clothing sizes, we'll

estimate." His face tight with impatience, he slapped the door control and led Lonzo from the room.

Saito sealed it behind them. "Before they come back, May, can you transfer Orbital One's schematics onto something for me?"

She showed him her open palms. "I don't have a device."

"All right. Just show me everything on there." He and Kirdy squashed in beside her as she commenced a virtual tour of the most relevant areas. When he felt she'd done enough, he suggested she sit by the door and rest. Then, with Wegley taking her spot, the three Proselyti went over it all again, together.

Twenty-five long minutes later, Lonzo and Jabari were back. Lonzo was still in his army uniform, and Jabari wore a set of security staff trousers and tunic. They fit him perfectly, as did the low-top black boots that went with them. Each carried a plastic tote which they'd used to avoid second looks from passersby as they brought down the rest of the clothing.

"Lots of rich people wandering around up there," Jabari said.

And getting in the way, Saito thought.

The two men placed the totes against a wall, and Lonzo stepped out of the way and sealed the door, while Jabari dispensed the gear. Stripping and dressing in the cramped space was awkward—more so for May, the only civ among them and unaccustomed to the indignity of public undress that was so routine in military life. Her face was still rosy with embarrassment when she finished. She fastened the last button on the tunic and smoothed it down, avoiding eye contact with the others.

Jabari handed out shock batons and security commlinks as everyone lined up, ready for the door to open. They slipped them into the purpose-made loops in their waistbands the way Jabari had.

Lonzo handed Saito a lone stun pistol in its holster. As the sergeant clipped it near the baton, Lonzo said, "Came from a dead sec guard. Had to do it."

Jabari nodded. "And he's stowed away in a maintenance crawlway. Someone'll wonder where their on-duty staffer went, but they won't look in there." He waved a passcard in front of his face then reached out to tap it against Dr. May's collar insignia. "You're our shift leader because you speak Common. You lead the way, but Saito and I will be right behind you."

She swallowed then nodded.

"We'll whisper instructions in Imperial True, if needed. You'll be fine. You know the way, yes?"

Another nod.

Saito opened the door. Lonzo stuck his head out to check the way. Then they filed out, formed a tight group of three pairs, and made for the nearest elevator, with Saito quietly coaching May on what to say when they reached Ectorius' area.

Between the peaks of pain, Aurelia drifted through troughs of exhausted delirium. She'd lost track of time. Vaguely, in the brief interludes where conscious thought asserted itself, she wondered how the other woman was doing. This 'Shill.' And despite the trouble the woman had caused her today, she hoped Shill hadn't cracked yet, hoped she hadn't given Ectorius the satisfaction.

If the prick was still in the room. The cloudy, dark-edged vision in her good eye wouldn't allow her to check her surroundings. Everything, now, was about endurance, until some solution magically presented itself. Ectorius wouldn't be here for all of this anyway, she reasoned. He had other prisoners, there'd be fallout to manage from the crises her team had caused, and he had his party, of course.

Besides, these stings and stabs, these burns and shocks were just the prologue, the overture, the appetizer. There was worse to come.

He'll use us as sport in his damned soiree.

Perhaps he would display them in a side room and play the live feed directly into the main party room. He'd allowed her to keep the eyepatch over the left eye, perhaps because he knew about the malfunction from May and knew the random zooming would make her puke. Ectorius couldn't have his prize entertainment piece choking on her vomit before he'd gotten maximum value out of her...

It felt like she'd been stuck for ages in a thought loop about her fate as trivial entertainment when, suddenly, there were people at her side. The expected fresh spike in droid bites hadn't come. Residual nips and burns and pins and needles persisted, but she was being helped to a sitting position by two persons, as another wrapped a medical gown around her and began tying it.

They were speaking to her, the people. It took her some effort to dispel the semi-fugue state she'd sunk into. The pair holding her were males, and they addressed each other in a language she didn't know. They wore security uniforms. They'd unshackled her from the table, but she stayed the impulse to crush their skulls with her prosthetic. There was something in their tone.

The woman tying the robe leaned into view. "Your vitals are all right, Madam. But there's damage. If we had time to treat you, I could relieve the pain in minutes, but there's nothing at hand."

"And we *don't* have time," one of the men added in Imperial True. He was Asiatic in features and stern.

"You're... Saito," she said.

"Glad we reached you in time, ma'am," he replied, then he nodded at the other two. "You remember these two?"

She wiggled her toes, legs stretched in front of her, and studied the second man and the woman who'd dressed her. "Dr. May. And... *Lonzo*?"

"At your service, Madam," May said and shuffled out of view.

Aurelia squinted hard at Lonzo. This wasn't right. "You shouldn't be here."

"None of us should," he replied, with a gruff half-smile.

"No." She ran her tongue over her gums as he helped her swing her legs over the edge of the bed. "I mean, *what are you doing here*? I told you to leave."

"Look, madam," he said, stepping back as she found her balance. "You spared my life, all right? Easier for you to kill me like that other idiot, but you gave me a chance. Only fair I pay you back. Plus... I just didn't wanna go with that fancy *chramiga*."

"Ah."

"I weren't perving at ya just now, by the way, Madam, in case you think I was."

She felt a smile ghost her lips. "Good to know, Lonzo."

The men eased her off the gurney. Aurelia was relieved to find her feet without tipping or collapsing. No muscle or nerve damage, despite some generalized trembling. And the damned pins and needles. The tiny torture droids lay in small piles at the foot of the gurney and spread across the floor. Not just her droids, but the ones that had been on the Shill woman. Shill wasn't on her gurney, wasn't in the room. Another man was, though, also wearing a station security uniform. A man with deep black skin. She knew him from the rooftop ambush. Also, from recent file images.

"Lt. *Jabari*?"

He'd been watching the hallway from the door. He gave her the briefest of glances, face tight, eyes hard. His attention returned to the corridor.

"Well," she said. "I was hoping for a miraculous solution to my predicament. This was hardly the collection of faces I thought would provide it."

May had ducked outside and now returned with a bundle of white clothing in hand. "Nurse's uniform, Madam. From a locker out there."

Before Aurelia could take it, two more Proselyti troopers in sec guard outfits appeared in the doorway. Jabari made room for them. One was the youngest of the insertion team troopers, the other Saito's 2IC Kirdy. The corporal reported, "No sign of Naomi."

Aurelia took the nurse's clothes. "Thanks for tying the gown, Doctor, but do you think you could...?" As May began helping and the men turned politely away, Aurelia let out an amused sigh. "Kind of you, men, but I'm sure you saw everything when you came in." None replied. And none glanced back at her. As she dressed herself, she found herself respecting them more for it. As she tugged up the final zipper, she told them, "Decent."

Half of them faced her, the others focused on the corridor.

She asked, "We're secure here?"

"Interrogator's dead in a closet," Saito replied.

"No nurses in the medical room," Kirdy added.

Saito concluded, "Haven't seen any guards. Must've shifted over to the party."

"There are more of you?"

Headshakes were the only answer to that question.

"I'm sorry to hear that, Saito." She leaned her butt against the gurney and let May slip the nurse's shoes on her feet. Eyes on Jabari, she asked, "And what am I to call him? Lieutenant? Or deserter? Traitor?"

"Renegade," Saito said without thinking. He shrugged his eyebrows when Jabari looked at him sharply. "Well, aren't you? From an official perspective?"

"Shill's here somewhere?" she asked.

This time, Jabari answered, through gritted teeth. "No. Probably wherever Naomi is."

"The party," Aurelia told them. "Doctor, you saw what they did to Decanus Caiu? Both ladies will be set up as some kind of entertainment. I'm sure of it. No doubt, I was to be the final act. Ectorius appears to have a penchant for sadism and probably attracts friends with similar tastes."

"Tastes," Kirdy snorted and looked away when her eyes caught his.

"You *should* be interested in their tastes, all right," Jabari added. "In your official capacity."

"A conversation for later," Saito interrupted.

"You have plans?" she asked him.

"This was as far as they went."

"You said the party's started."

"Yes."

"Well, then. My objective hasn't changed. Ectorius is there and, for the moment, he doesn't know we're free. I'm taking the governor, dead or alive. I assume you Proselyti want to retrieve your two troopers."

"We do," Saito said and faced the others. "But retrieving is one thing. Getting off station is another. Unless Quaestor Cossea objects, Jabari and I will go with her, while the rest of you commandeer a ship and wait there for us."

"Or flee if the pressure is too great," Aurelia said, supporting Saito's decision. To Lonzo, she added, "I'm ordering you to actually leave this time and help the remnants of my team. Galen's shuttle will be under guard, I imagine, by now. You'll need to 'commandeer' another one."

He stroked his rifle. "Sounds like fun."

"You still have my note?"

He patted a pocket.

"Take Dr. May with you. Ensure my sister understands the doctor's contribution today."

He accepted this with a grunt.

But May bristled. "Madam Quaestor, I've come this far. You may yet need my services."

"If I make it out alive, I'll find you, Doctor. Your services would indeed be valuable in the future. But do what I say, now. Go with Lonzo. And Lonzo?"

"Yes, Madam?"

"On your honor, be sure to protect this woman."

He gave a short bow. "Safe with me."

"Excuse me." It was the youngest trooper, leaning in the doorway. "I'm not going without Naomi."

Saito caught Aurelia's eye. "Please give me a moment with the private."

"A short moment," she replied.

Saito drew Wegley into the corridor, hand on his elbow. "Private, listen to me, and listen well. You know I believe in you as much as Jabari does, yes?"

Wegley blinked a couple of times. "I... I know you gave me a chance, Gunsō. And I let you down."

"You didn't let anyone down. You took down hostiles today, son. You did your job. You're still here, aren't you? You're still on-mission and following orders."

"I messed up plenty, Gunsō. I want a chance to get Naomi back, to make up for all the screwups."

"Listen to me, Wegley. It's not how anyone starts that counts; it's how they finish. You *kicked ass* today, Private." Releasing his elbow, he tapped Wegley middle-forehead. "Get that into your head and believe it. *However*, I can't have you coming to get Naomi."

"But—"

Saito finger-tapped his brow again, silencing him. "*I'm* speaking here, Private. Kirdy can come with me and carry her, if need be, while I cover them. But I need you to wait with Lonzo and May. If necessary, you leave with them."

"I—"

Saito tapped the powered-down security commlink clipped to Wegley's shirt. "You get a ship, you power this up and wait for us to contact you on their open channel. You tell us which berth you're in, and you hold off any attack. However. If it gets too hot, you leave, you get the hells out. That's an order. And if the opportunity arises to go with Jabari, you go with Jabari."

Wegley's jaw had been working as he tried to get a protest in, but that last bit shut him up cold.

Lowering his voice and leaning in, Saito said, "I'm giving you a choice. And a chance. I don't know where this is coming from. No, that's not true," he sighed, his mind on Wegley's youthfulness. "I know exactly where it's coming from. You deserve a life, kid. Having a life—a real life—might be the greatest victory you could achieve for us who are the last of our kind. For our legacy and memory. Earlier today, Jabari was talking about choices. He was correct. You get that opportunity to go with him, you take it. He'd be an excellent mentor for you."

"But... but he's not a soldier anymore," Wegley whispered back. "He's not one of us. He said it. You said it."

"One of us? Jabari will *always* be a soldier. He can't help it. But you don't need to be. *You* could be something else. Something just as powerful, just as important."

"What? What the sacking hells could *I* be?"

"If you do go with Jabari—and Shill—if there's a way to get your ass out of the Imperium to a better place, you can be anything you want, son. Anything."

Wegley's eyes clouded a moment, then he blinked slowly. "You promise you'll get Naomi out?"

"It's my current mission objective. I'll do my best to get her to go with you."

"What if Jabari doesn't come, and I have to go with that Lonzo?"

"That's up to you." He glanced through the door to where the raggedy gentleman stood listening to Aurelia speak. He was calm and collected in contrast to Wegley's antsiness. "I get the feeling that guy could give you pointers on creating a new identity better than Jabari could."

"I... All right. I'll do what you say, Gunsō."

"First time for everything."

"But Gunsō?"

"Yes?"

"You won't be coming with us, if I go with Jabari?"

Out the corner of his eye, Saito caught Aurelia heading their way. He murmured, "I have a different path from Jabari's. I'm a different man. And do not tell the quaestor anything I just said."

Aurelia approached and smoothed down her nurse's blouse with a wry chuckle. "My fourth outfit today."

"You feel all right?" Saito asked, candidly.

She met his gaze. "I'm damaged, Sergeant. But I'm not a wreck."

"Very good, ma'am. Shall we?"

"Once we find a local datapad."

"Why?" Jabari asked at her shoulder.

"Because you'd be surprised by how rarely anybody will challenge someone carrying an official-looking datapad and wearing a concerned expression."

CHAPTER THIRTY

PARTY ROOM

THEY WERE CHALLENGED JUST ONCE.

At the open swinging doors Aurelia had passed earlier that day, at the same table, with the same tired-looking lieutenant in dress uniform on duty.

Past him, at the other end of corridor, the big double doors had been closed, although Aurelia heard and felt the faint pulse of bass-heavy music from within.

Last time she'd been here, her head had been swathed in bandages. Didn't mean he wouldn't know her, though. With that in mind, she'd taught Jabari three short sentences in Common and made him practice on their way up. That way, he could draw the brunt of the lieutenant's attention. As soon as they came around the corner and within sight of the table, Jabari began talking and immediately snatched the lieutenant's stare away from Aurelia's eyepatch and head wounds.

"Sick guest. Here to escort them to Medical." Jabari's pronunciation was awful but understandable.

The lieutenant remained seated, eyeing the four apparent sec guards with only the vaguest hint of suspicion. "Looks like you need medical attention," he told Aurelia.

She weathered the attention with a tired *don't I know it* expression.

Shrugging, the officer asked Jabari, "Which guest?"

That question she *hadn't* prepared Jabari for. Before he could blurt out the third phrase she'd taught him, Aurelia leaned past him and told the lieutenant, "Marsia Rexel." It was a name she remembered from the guest list Roja had found for her.

The lieutenant scanned the list and muttered to her, "You know you're the second person with an eye wound I've seen today?"

"Bar fight. Bloody pain in the face. Literally."

"I bet." His gaze flicked up to Kirdy's bruises and split lip.

"Same bar, same fight," she explained.

Losing interest, he said, "Rexel, eh? Why four of you just for her?"

Still leaning close to Jabari, Aurelia nudged him as a prompt.

Playing his part, Jabari waggled the datapad and shook his head as coached. "Procedural bullshit."

"Covering the station manager's ass against any insurance issues," Aurelia added hurriedly.

"Right," said the lieutenant. "*Everything's* procedural bull-shit these days." He'd found the name on this list. He jerked his head over his shoulder. "If you want to interrupt the boss' merrymaking, it's your funeral. Go on through."

Jabari went around him first, followed by Saito and Kirdy. Aurelia bumped into the table to hold the doorman's interest, distracting him until Saito drew his pistol and stunned him. As the unconscious man slid from his chair, Saito lined up for a second shot.

But Aurelia stayed him with an outstretched hand. "He won't wake up in time to trouble us. Put him through that door on the couch inside, make him look like he's napping." She indicated the room she'd been captured in, wondering briefly how they'd react to Caiu's wall frieze when they saw it.

Kirdy slipped out the stunned man's sidearm, as the others got hold of his arms and legs. The weapon was an ancient model revolver, obviously decorative for an official occasion. But it appeared quite functional. The cylinder revolved when Kirdy test spun it, and Aurelia caught sight of actual bullets in its chambers. The corporal offered it to her.

"You know, I think I will." Aurelia took it and checked the load. Five rounds.

I'll only need one, she thought.

Jabari and Saito lugged the lieutenant into the side room. Neither showed any sign that something was amiss. She poked her head in. Caiu's grotesque display had been moved, and she suspected she knew where.

Whatever the century, Saito thought, *a party is a party is a party.*

The room was abuzz. Clusters of people chatted together, danced together, shared inebriating substances together. Music pulsated from overhead speakers. The lighting had been lowered to an intimate level. Saito estimated a hundred souls, if any of them *had* souls; judging by the fact that none objected to the display of Caiu's mutilated body, he doubted it. The frame containing the Corfid had been fixed to the very back wall with his head raised high enough to be seen above the crowd. The other men caught sight of it at the same time Saito did and exchanged disgusted glances.

Jabari hissed, "Gods and ancestors. And they call *us* barbarians."

While they hesitated, Aurelia hurled herself forward,

edging left and hugging the side of the room. Saito led the other two in pursuit, politely pressing their way through the throng of gibbering wealthy and receiving several snooty stares or eye rolls in return, though most of the guests they passed refused to acknowledge them or were too intoxicated to notice. A holo banner above Caiu read in Imperial True,

Behold the fate of those who oppose Unfettered Progress.

As they passed more clusters of chattering guests, a lower portion of the stage beneath Caiu's wall frame came into view. Two gurneys had been set up below the dead man and to either side. The upper ends were raised to better display the women strapped to them. Naomi's stump appeared freshly dressed. Both she and Shill had drips connected to veins in their arms, and their heads lolled side to side in semi-consciousness. Seeing them there made Saito's teeth grind together, and his right hand tightened on the grip of his holstered stunner.

Both women wore sleeveless patient's shifts. Saito presumed the gowns left a layer for Ectorius to strip away at the right time, a way to strip away their humanity. *Come marvel at the ancient relic, warriors from a bygone era, the Kaana's Roaches found crawling around the drains and shadows of our city on the Hill...*

Aurelia had stopped, and Saito had been so distracted, he crashed into her back, as Jabari and Kirdy did to him. She turned and drew them together. "He's by the stage."

Saito glanced past her shoulder and caught sight of the governor waving his arms around, dramatizing some anecdote to a trio of devoted listeners.

The quaestor said, "He's mine, the women are yours. Contact your other trooper. Find their ship. Get away. I'll take care of my own exit."

"All right," Jabari said and started to move forward, but Saito snagged his arm.

"Own exit, how?" he asked Aurelia. "What are you going to do?"

"I'll figure something out. Listen, my eye is shot, but I still have some tricks available. Between the waves of torture, I was prepping an override for the station's data security and waiting for the right time to use it."

"Use it how?" Jabari asked.

"Like so." Aurelia blinked. The room's muted lighting shifted abruptly to a bright red. An emergency alert began blaring overhead, interrupting the dance music. The quaestor patted Saito's cheek then abandoned all stealth and shouldered a guest out of her way as she rushed for Ectorius.

"Bloody hells," said Jabari and sprinted toward the stage. Kirdy chased after him.

Guests pressed in the other direction, desperate to reach the main room exit. Saito stepped into the path of two drunk and wealthy women and waved the stunner at their wrap-around robes. "Give me those or I'll kill you!"

Screaming shrilly, they disrobed, revealing loose-fitting bodysuits beneath. Once they'd dumped their robes at his feet, he gestured for them to go, and they kept up the screaming as they staggered into the press of bodies around the doors. Saito gathered up the cloaks and brought them to the stage where the other men had untied most of the gurney straps. He looked for Aurelia and Ectorius, but there was no sign.

"Hey!" Jabari barked at him. He nodded at the robes. "Forget those. Won't need more disguises."

Saito dropped them and looked for Aurelia again. She and

her quarry had vanished. The party room had a long side wing past where the governor had been standing. It was probably an area for servants and waitstaff to assemble food or other entertainment. It had a closed swinging door at its far end, and Saito was certain he heard a ballistic gunshot from the other side. Two guests stumbled drunkenly toward Saito and away from the sound. He was about to investigate when Jabari kicked him and pointed his chin insistently at the back of the room. A lone trooper had come in through a narrow door from another side room. Shoving his way through the throng, the soldier battled toward the stage, no doubt intent on finding the governor. Though the man wasn't looking at him, Saito saw a hint of a weapon and didn't hesitate. He fired a series of stun bolts into the mass of people around the trooper, until the man was exposed enough for a final bolt to take him in the torso.

Then Jabari was in his ear, with an arm around Shill to hold her upright. "Stun more! Make a path!"

Saito did so, blasting down semi-inebriated dandies until the way was carpeted with bodies. Those still conscious had either slipped out the main exit or shifted direction toward the door into the side rooms.

"You're staying?" Jabari asked him, glancing along the wing where Ectorius must have fled with Aurelia at his heels.

"Sure am."

"Figured you would. *Ave atque vale*, then, Sergeant."

Saito saluted. "*Ave atque vale*, Lieutenant."

Jabari headed down the three steps to the floor, hindered by Shill, whose head kept bobbing. He didn't look back.

"Kirdy!" Saito shouted against the noise of the alarm. The thickset man had Naomi on her feet, too. She looked to be in mildly better shape than Shill—she was more alert, at least. Blood dribbled from the hole in her arm where the drip had been pulled out. When Kirdy looked over, Saito indicated the commlink on his waistband. "Contact Wegley. Won't matter if you use open channel. Get his berth number and get down there."

"Right." He and Naomi took a step toward the stage stairs.

Saito intercepted them, closing the distance to make himself heard over the din. "Jabari's the boss if I don't come back."

"*If*?"

Saito shrugged. "My job was always back up for the quaestor."

Kirdy gripped his arm briefly then got a better hold on Naomi to guide her up the steps. "See you in one hell or another, Gunsō."

"*Ave atque vale, frater*," Saito said to his back. Now to chase the woman chasing the governor.

When she'd gone after Ectorius, he'd taken one look at her and bolted down a side wing. To hamper Aurelia's progress, he yanked a fleeing waitress behind him and knocked her down. Guests and staff were pushing each other all around the room, but only two had fled for the side door Ectorius wanted. The drunken fools were in each other's way, unable to get a grip on the door handle before the other would drag their hand from it. With a strength that surprised Aurelia, Ectorius yanked them behind him. He was well through the door by the time Aurelia hauled them out of *her* way.

The corridor ahead was only about twenty meters long. It had been lined with wood panels, but the way they rested against the carpet indicated they were nothing more substantial than partitions erected to remodel the area to the governor's liking. Her target had made it almost to the end of the passage when he whirled around to face her. Sensing something off in his body language, she halted eight strides away from him.

321

"I can play this game all day, little girl," he bellowed over the alarm, as he pretended to brush lint from his purple jacket. "A very amusing game. You come for me, then you fall into my trap, only to escape it and repeat the whole cycle again."

Her revolver was aimed at his groin, yet he showed no fear.

"Shit," she hissed, squeezing the trigger once and feeling no surprise when the bullet struck a shield a half-meter out from his thigh, creating a brief splat of color in midair.

Ectorius winked. And then he gave a hand signal to an unseen scanner, and Aurelia's instincts kicked in. She shoved the pistol into her left hand to free her prosthetic one, as she lunged sideways at the wall. She swung her machine arm hard. Simultaneously, a panel popped from the ceiling between her position and the governor's, and a rigid length of hose dropped out. The wall cracked and buckled with her first strike. The hose undulated like a living serpent tracking its prey, and Aurelia was, she knew, that prey. Cocking the arm again, she smelled accelerant a half-second before flame jetted from the hose. Aurelia's flesh-and-blood arm came up in reflex, shoulder following, turning, guarding her face. Rather than swing the machine arm again, she punched it forward, piston-like, driving her fist through the wall. Sensing the empty space past it, she took hold of the section she'd broken and tore it free as a shield of her own, intercepting the continuing jet of fire as she plunged shoulder-first into the compartment beyond.

Releasing the chunk of wall when it caught on the corridor side, she dropped, rolling, knowing the left side of the nurse's jacket was aflame. She didn't feel it. Didn't smell it. She realized her hair was also on fire, and that kicked in her senses, filling her nostrils with an acrid stink. The flames scraped at her, clawing through the cloth and hair to bite into her flesh, digging through the toughened epidermis on her arm and ribs and shoulder and cheek and temple—finding weak spots created by torture bots and bullets.

Aurelia rolled and slapped and writhed until the fire was out. The fire on her person, at least. The fire blazed in the corridor and crept around the edges of the broken section of wall, wanting entry into her compartment.

As her flesh screamed in agony, a voice in her head screamed louder: *You have to get out of here!*

CHAPTER THIRTY-ONE

BLOCKS

SAITO WAS HALFWAY to the side wing's exit when he saw smoke curling around the crack where the door met the wall. It grew thicker as he closed in, making him hesitate just two strides away. What the hell had happened? Had Aurelia set that area on fire to herd out the governor?

Thicker, darker, the smoke now sent up tendrils from the space between the bottom of the door and the carpet. An extinguisher bot appeared from a reserve inside the ceiling and lugged itself ponderously to a spot above the door, waiting for the first sign of flames. Saito wasn't waiting. Backing away, he decided to follow Kirdy, after all.

The party guests had all exited, except for those he'd stunned earlier and the half dozen who were so drunk or smashed they couldn't navigate. With a last glance toward Caiu's corpse, Saito figured that if those people died in the fast-spreading inferno, they'd do so with his blessing.

The congestion of shoving, shouting guests had moved into the corridor toward the lieutenant's former station. Saito swore and began stunning them from the rearmost forward, hoping to cut a path as he had for Jabari and Shill. Several were already down on their hands and knees, trying to avoid being stampeded. Jabari and Kirdy had likely cut them down with stun sticks on their way through. He'd felled seven guests when a laser bolt struck the ceiling above him. He dropped into a crouch. The volume and intensity of the caterwauling in the passageway rose as others also ducked while maintaining their forward press. The shot had come from up where the lieutenant's table had been set up. The tiny fire sparked by the laser strike had already snuffed itself out by the time Saito scuttled sideways and risked a peek over the crowd. The major he'd met earlier—*Tatias*—had set up to the right of the doorway out into the main thoroughfare. He lifted the laser pistol beside his ear, pointed at the roof above him, and held Saito's stare across the heads of the others. When they saw the weapon, the otherwise mindless crowd broke wildly around him, as they made for the open corridors and fled for evacuation pods.

Saito darted sideways into the room where they'd dumped the lieutenant. The young officer lay on the couch, blinking stupidly, but otherwise unmoving. There were two other doors exiting the room. The one beside the lieutenant's couch led toward the major and his laser, and the one in the back wall led into one more side room and would take Saito back into the main party room. He headed that way, retreating. Surely, he reasoned, the damned extinguisher bots would take care of the fire. And the smoke? Well...

"Better than an ass-sacking laser bolt to the brain."

He was back in the party room seconds later, picking his way across the scrum of immobile or slightly squirming guests. He'd just hurdled the last of them when another laser blast burned past him, a half-meter from his nose. Flinching, he dropped on one knee, already turning, reflexes bringing his stunner around to his point of origin back by the main entry to the room. Major Tatias stood there, laser leveled, his expression a mix of anger and cockiness.

How'd he...? Saito began wondering even as he squeezed off a couple of shots.

The stun bolts were accurate but achieved nothing, as they sizzled harmlessly against a personal shield that rippled the air around Tatias like a faint full-body halo. That explained how he'd made it through the crowd so fast, and why they'd been swerving so wildly around him. Coming in personal contact with a shield like that *hurt*, like being scalded.

There was no point in doing it, but he put another series of shots into the thing out of sheer spite and bellowed his rage. He couldn't retreat, couldn't advance. Tatias had him out in the open, with no recourse, and he was sackdamned tired of being ambushed that day.

When he was done roaring, he collapsed onto his ass and awaited his fate, as his thoughts turned to mush.

But Tatias lowered the weapon to his side, picked his way over a few bodies, and raised his voice above the alarms. "You don't have one of these shields, do you, Terranist? See, they embed nodes into the fabric of your uniform that create the field, then they give you a pocket controller for turning it on and off." He dipped his free hand into his pocket and showed it to Saito. "They sent you into battle without full combat armor, without shielding, without any damned sidearms for a secondary weapon. Tut, tut. You really are working for the wrong people. The governor, you see, looks after his own."

Saito coughed and said, "He does, huh? Does that include the troopers we killed today? Don't remember them having shielding or even armor. Some of them were helldamned *kids*, just recruits!" He glanced toward the side wing. He couldn't see the door from his position, but there wasn't all that much smoke rising that way, now. Perhaps the bots had put the fire out, and the air handlers were working. What a damned shame he'd never get the chance to attempt that route and see how the quaestor's story ended.

Tatias ignored his gibe about kids and armor and shields, saying, "Toss the gun. Toss it, and I'll give you a chance."

That snatched Saito's attention back. "A *chance*? That's what you said?" The major really did speak Imperial True with a weird accent, putting the emphasis on the wrong syllables, trilling letters that weren't meant to be trilled.

Tatias nodded. "A chance, yes."

Saito forced a laugh and forced his legs to push him upright. "You beat me to it," he said. "I was going to offer you the same thing."

"Amusing." Tatias' expression said it was anything but. "Go on. Toss the weapon."

Saito threw it onto an empty patch of carpet where there was a chance he could retrieve it. Tatias killed that chance by drilling an accurate lance of laser fire through the weapon, destroying it. Then he made a show of pressing something on his shield controller. Without the disturbance of stun bolts rippling the force field, it was impossible for Saito to tell whether the shield had disappeared, but that seemed to be what Tatias was telling him. He put the controller back in his pocket. He popped the chargepack from the laser before flinging it and the weapon into the corridor behind him.

"Are you *serious*?" Saito asked him.

Tatias rolled his shoulders, shook out his hands, and stalked closer. "Serious about the unheard-of opportunity to beat the shit out of a caveman."

Saito began circling to his right into open floorspace where there were no stunned party guests. "How about the other opportunity here? To be what you swore an oath to be. A soldier. A military man. A professional and a servant of the empire. You're stationed here to defend the Imperium and its values, not support some psychopath's insane plot to create his own tiny dominion."

The major stalked closer. "You know nothing about this situation and nothing about me."

Saito kept sidestepping to his right, wondering if he could make a break for the wing door and get enough of a lead that Tatias couldn't retrieve and use the laser. Then Tatias stooped and whipped out a short-bladed knife from inside one boot.

Probably won't bother going back for the laser, Saito figured. He said, "I'd love for you to educate me. Doesn't seem I'm going anywhere soon."

Tatias nodded. "Two years ago, I was Legatus Legionis of the Sector 8 Second Interplanetary Marines Brigade. What you'd know as a full colonel. After a demotion on a trumped-up charge, they banished me here as a mere lieutenant. Governor Ectorius immediately saw my worth and had me promoted to this rank."

"Because he's an asshole," Saito commented. There was an echo of his own history there, his own demotion. That demotion had done Saito some good. The same couldn't be said for Tatias.

"That man has been nothing but good to me. He understands what it's like to run afoul of imperial favoritism and elitism." He weighed the blade in his hand, flipped it, and caught it by the handle. "But you danced in here, expecting to ruin what we're building."

Saito couldn't help but snort as he kept some distance between them. "Building? *Building*? You're referring to the big, thick wall you built between *your* elites and the poor masses? Or to the cannibal market you built in the old spaceport?'

Tatias adopted a new vector, ensuring it'd be difficult for Saito to flee via the side wing. He sliced the air with his blade a couple of times, still limbering up, and said nothing.

Saito pressed him. "We came here to complete a lawful mission. You remember what that's about, yes? When you receive lawful orders from up the *military* chain-of-command, and you obey them in the best interests of the empire."

"Enough preachiness. You're an anachronism. Anachronisms don't get to preach."

"Anachronism is a big word for someone like you. And ironic. Hells' bells, *I* speak Imperial True with less of an accent than you do."

Tatias closed some ground between them and went on, "We're both foreigners here, but I've been the one with the upper hand since moment one. It was a great pleasure to organize the assault on your LZ. A chance to flex my mental muscles the way I'm about to exercise the physical ones." He tossed the knife into his other hand then back again.

Saito stopped moving across the room. There was space to maneuver around him, now. And although he felt stiff all over from a day of running and crawling and squatting and fighting and sore from the thousand little bangs and knocks he'd suffered, he was tired of giving this asshole the satisfaction of looking wary. He adopted a fighting stance, his voice calm and even, and asked, "The assault you refer to is that gunship attack that *didn't* kill us all?"

One of Tatias' eyes twitched as he briefly halted his advance. "You got lucky that a renegade maggot with a mining tool intervened."

Lucky? I lost two good people on that roof.

"When I take that knife off you and stab you in the throat with it, you'll see how lucky I am."

Tatias considered the blade for a moment, then half-turned and lobbed it into the corridor with the laser. "If you can get to it, feel free to use it. But I very much doubt you'll get close."

Saito snorted. "There's a bunch of dead butchers under Lorica's spaceport who'd disagree with you... if they could speak."

All the cockiness slid off the major's face, replaced by pure hatred. He came forward on the balls of his feet, hands raised. He sneered, "One of the men you slaughtered today was my younger brother."

Saito bowed his head, rebalanced on the balls of *his* feet, danced around to the side, and replied through gritted teeth. "And three men and two women you slaughtered were *my* brothers and sisters."

Tatias was close enough now to strike at. So, Saito struck, launching a volley at the guy's center line, intending to knock him off-balance. A jab at his right eye—blocked! A throat punch—blocked! A palm strike at his chin—dodged! Saito leaned back to get in a hard stamp on the major's shin and instep. Except they weren't there to receive the strike. Tatias' reflexes were that fast. Saito's boot slammed into the hard floor. In the next moment, he was stumbling backward after the major butted him in the forehead. The butt wasn't as hard as it might have been—Saito had been balanced away from the other man—but it was bad enough to dull his vision for the couple of seconds he staggered away. He almost fell, one leg buckling, but forced a hop into the air that brought him down on both feet, knees braced for the landing. He stayed upright, getting his balance back. Above all things, he had to stay off the floor. Unless he got this bastard in a chokehold, the floor was the worst place he could end up—

No time for more thinking. Tatias came at him with a heavy, straight punch. Saito lurched his upper body sideways to dodge it. A knee strike came next at the space he'd dodged into. He caught it against both forearms, allowing them to cushion the impact against his torso, and he bumped the knee to his side, so he could drive his shoulder into Tatias and force him onto the back foot.

Staying in close, Saito jabbed at ribs, gut, groin. The last blow hurt the man. Tatias yelled in fury and pain, but he didn't fold. His hands wrapped themselves in Saito's shirt, then he turned and flipped the Proselyti over his hip, sending him tumbling across the floor. Saito bunched up for the roll, then he got his knees and feet under him and pushed upright before he slammed into the stage steps. One of the straps from the gurneys had been pulled free and had fallen on the lowest step. It was something, a weapon he could swing from arm's length away. One hand snaked out for it, but his peripheral vision registered the major's kick incoming fast and hard.

Saito reeled away and up against the stage as his enemy's boot smashed the side of the step where his forearm had just been. Saito slid his hips along the stage, anticipating a follow up hook kick using the same leg. When it came, he slapped it aside and jabbed out with an elbow strike at Tatias' ribs. He was happy when the man's swiveling body took the blow squarely under his scapula. He tried for a stomp-kick at the back of the man's knee, but Tatias coiled onto the stage to avoid it and lashed backward with his heel.

Saito hadn't expected so quick a blow. He barely got his guard up, but the force of it against his forearm sent him staggering far enough back for Tatias to squirm off the stage and face him.

Trying to ignore the patchy numbness left in his arm by the major's boot heel, he was halfway through preparing a kick when Tatias moved in close and slashed at Saito with a lightning-fast roundhouse punch. Saito deflected with his half-dead arm and redirected the punch past him. He slipped his bad arm along the inside of Tatias', clenched his shirt as hard as he could, and delivered four knee strikes to his torso. The major grunted with each of them and curled around, attempting to absorb and cushion the blows.

And then, somehow, Saito was on the floor, facing away from his opponent, forearms, knees, and boots holding his body up. He'd no idea how he'd gotten there. Felled by a blow he hadn't seen coming.

One ear whined with tinnitus. The eye closest to it sparkled with starbursts. Shaking his head, he rolled instinctively to his left with as much force as he could muster. A boot slammed into the floor where his torso had been. A follow up kick flicked his shirt as he kept on rolling. At the end of the roll, he did his best to launch himself upright again, but with his balance off, he got stuck in a kind of stumbling sideways jog. He was upright long enough to hear Tatias snarl something he didn't catch and watch him dip down to draw a short blade from his other boot.

The next thing Saito knew, he'd missed his step and sprawled chest-down, with his right cheek against the floor, his four limbs spreadeagled. Dazed and muddle-headed, the decision to do something—the idea of *what* to do—wouldn't come. Normally, it just *happened*, from instincts honed through decades of keen training and harsh experience. Should he roll or scramble up, get off the floor or shoot out a leg in his enemy's direction? Before Saito could act, Tatias was on him, literally *on* him. Tatias' knee was in his back, driving the air from his lungs. Saito saw the blade flash, reflecting the room lighting as it rose, knowing where it was headed, but unable to do one damned thing about it. Tatias drove the blade through Saito's outstretched right hand, skewering it so hard a bone snapped.

Pain exploded, white-hot and living, like nothing Saito had ever known.

If he'd had time to consider it, Saito would have decided the agony could not get any worse. Until Tatias shifted his balance on top of him and jiggled the blade inside his hand, scraping the tender area between the broken pieces of metacarpal.

All Saito Shimada could do was throw back his head and scream.

CHAPTER THIRTY-TWO

DAMAGES

THE ROOM she'd crashed into was a commercial pantry that ran the length of the corridor and parallel to it. Rows of shelves and a single exit door at the far end showed that the corridor hooked right around this compartment.

The fire was creeping into the storeroom, and the semi-sapient extinguisher bots were emerging from their places between the shelving units to combat it. Aurelia got up and teetered toward that exit, but she banged against a solid barrier, a counter running crossways. She hadn't seen it, but she leaned against it, panting. Razors ploughed her skin. Combs made from needles raked her down to her nerve endings. The burns all along her left side were a bodystocking of agony, squeezing her hip, belly, arm, shoulder, and ribs. The flesh across her face and head felt as if the bots were continuing their work, only more constantly and with greater gusto. She was afraid to touch her ear in case it came loose. Fighting the impulse to weep, she sagged there, overwhelmed by an urge to be done with the day and the mission, to sink into unconsciousness, to savor oblivion.

Aurelia's vision blurred with tears. She blinked them out,

ignoring the bright sting of salt on her cheek, and reached for her inner voice, the one trained to overcome such things, to rise above and render them trivial. And found it!

Isolate the pain, it told her. *Isolate it. Lock it away. Deal with it later. That's it. Focus on everything that isn't pain. Focus on killing the man who did this to you. That's it. Your legs work, right? Your lungs work, right? Your good eye. Your arms. Your hearing. Move. Move, damn it!*

And she moved. She stepped around the counter, coughing against the smoke. Ectorius would be headed for the shuttle pad on the exterior hull of this level. He couldn't be allowed to get there, not before her.

She took two more steps and then, incredibly, saw him! He stood at the end of the room, framed in the doorway, his eyes voyeuristic as he watched her struggle. Even more incredibly, her left hand still clutched the revolver. She reeled into a side shelf, and her machine arm pried the weapon from her left hand and fired two shots at the doorway before her left leg buckled, and she went down onto one knee. He might have cried out; she might have hit him. He wasn't there when she got her eye to focus and pushed herself upright.

"Two rounds," she rasped as she moved to the doorway. "Two rounds left to kill him."

The corridor extended right then broke left and out of sight. Ectorius wasn't there. But neither was there smoke, and she could clearly see the splash of blood a few meters along and the spots that trailed from it all the way to that next corner.

"Coming for you," she said, bothered by the squeak in her voice. She followed the blood trail.

With the intervention of her inner voice, her higher self, her agony became distant. It existed, but far off, belonging to some other woman. It was that woman's problem, now. Even so, Aurelia shivered as she lurched toward the corner, shivered as if her body had been exposed to a deep chill instead of naked flames. Her left hand shook wildly when she attempted to steady herself against the wall. It was a mass of blisters, useless to her. She withdrew it. Her right hand and arm were as strong as a tree branch, perfectly functional in direct contrast to the circumstances earlier in the day.

Around the corner lay a dead end. A sealed elevator bore a sign reading, *Authorized Personnel Only. Access to exterior hull shuttle bay.* Dots of blood led toward the doors, like the breadcrumbs in a children's fable. An indicator panel declared the lift was in use. To one side, the closed hatch to a ladderwell bore a similar sign.

Aurelia wasn't waiting for the lift to return. She entered the ladderwell. Using three limbs, she climbed.

With his breath hitched in his chest, Saito raised his head off the floor, turned it, and watched with teeth clenched hard as Major Tatias withdrew the blade. He could squirm, but he had no leverage to wriggle free, no way of getting at his enemy. The next thing he would feel would be blood-slicked steel against his throat.

Something made a wet *zzfh!* sound above him, and Tatias grunted in surprise. The weight lifted from Saito's spine, as Tatias rolled to Saito's left. The weight reasserted itself on Saito's arm and shoulder, as his opponent collapsed there.

"The sack...?"

Another voice growled curses above him, and Saito craned his neck around in time to see its owner drag Tatias' limp form off him. Released, Saito rolled over, cradled his ravaged hand to his chest, and raised his head. Someone he'd never expected to see bobbed down beside him.

"I... I told you to go with Jabari."

The man grinned darkly at him while using Tatias' knife to

cut a strip from his security tunic. "And miss all this? Been a long time since I enjoyed a party, and this has been a good'un."

"Kirdy..."

"Besides," the corporal went on, "our two ladies got their feet under 'em. They're fine. Naomi didn't need me, but you did, turns out." He gestured with the knife at Tatias. "Feisty bastard, eh?"

Saito turned his head to the side, exhausted and dumbfounded, as Kirdy wrapped the strip twice round the damaged hand and tied it tight. Tatias' eyes were open, red drool running from his open mouth. A burn mark on one side of his head seemed to answer the mystery of what had happened to him, as did the laser pistol Kirdy had placed by his side while he worked.

"Hurt much?" he asked, helping Saito stand.

"Nah. Tickles."

"This his gun?" Kirdy stooped to pick it up once Saito had his balance. "How'd it end up in the corridor?"

"He was a cocksure moron," Saito responded.

There was a little smoke in the room, but the extinguisher bot in the side wing was presiding over a damp, charred patch on the floor, indicating the fire was under control. Nevertheless, Saito no longer fancied charging after Aurelia, and he owed Kirdy.

Clapping the corporal's shoulder, he asked, "You know which berth the others went to?"

"Yep."

Saito grunted at a brief but searing spike of pain in his wounded hand, then said, "Well, what are we waiting for?"

It was already becoming harder to sequester the pain, to dissociate from it. Aurelia's skin tightened as she climbed, tugging at itself. It felt as if someone was still running an open flame over much of her left side. When she reached the top of the ladder, she stepped onto a landing outside another closed hatch. She clutched the handle with her right hand for balance, catching her breath, summoning strength. Where she could see the burned skin beyond the ragged strips of cloth that clung to her, it looked pink. Pink like ham. Like *aging* ham on the verge of turning, sweating, starting to rot. The fluids leaking up from the deeper levels of epidermis were all that held her clothing to her in many places. The wounds were pulsing, contracting, eating at her.

"Enough of this shit," she whispered and opened the hatch. A tight boarding foyer lay beyond it, just this hatch and the lift doors on one side of a rectangle of artificial gravity tiles and the hatch through to the connecting tube on the other. The flashing orange globe above the other hatch indicated she had mere seconds before the shuttle beyond would seal itself off. Aurelia aimed herself at the hatch and lumbered through it.

Through it and into zero gravity.

Her momentum lifted her, and she sailed across the five meters of tube, past the many handholds, until she collided with a small patch of exposed shuttle hull around the entry hatch. The shuttle had been parked side-on to the station hull and the connecting tube. Aurelia saw floor where the orientation of the station told her there should be wall. The station-side hatch began hissing shut, which forced her to scramble awkwardly around and into the shuttle before the safety sensors could alert the pilot a passenger still lingered outside. The new gravity-orientation took hold of her, and she worked with it to swing her soft-soled shoes to the deck and step fully inside.

The configuration resembled her own shuttle's. Her good eye stared right and aft along a straight passage with hatches off it on either side. She was turning her head to the left where the cockpit should be, when something slammed into her from the side and tore into her devastated flesh, throwing her from her feet to the carpeted deck. She had the strength and sense to flip onto her back, but it was only in time to see Ectorius dart swiftly to her side, leering at her. He'd ditched the purple suit coat, revealing a bloody patch across the white shirt beneath. But he looked far from finished, and he proved it when he brandished a security shock stick and jammed it into her side.

Aurelia lost complete control and became nothing more than a spasming body, locked so deeply into the seizure that she even lost touch with her pain. His assault on her had surely made the state of her fire-ruined flesh worse. Helpless, aware of nothing but her spasmodic state, deep down, Aurelia knew one thing. This was the end.

Life over.

Case complete.

No justice for this bastard. No easy advancement for her sister. And sufficient warning of the emperor's attentions for Ectorius to cover his tracks while accelerating his plans for secession.

I... can't... allow... it...

While Ectorius had the upper hand—he had all the strength, the weapon, her helpless on her back—the one thing he *didn't* have was cybernetic enhancements.

Specifically, a machine arm with the kinds of pre-coded commands hers did. Linked as it was to her central nervous system, it was currently as useless as the rest of her body. But the arm didn't *need* her central nervous system to operate.

She focused the single thread of thought she had left, shut out her predicament, commanded her prosthesis to neutralize the active threat, and mentally enacted the code for detachment. For the second time that day, her right arm vanished completely from her senses. Only this time, it was because she'd given it a mind of its own. In the dark edges of her vision, she saw the arm rise independently of her, saw that its palm had turned inward so the tiny fingertip cameras could quickly assess the threat for itself.

Ectorius' victory cackle breached the roar of blood in her ears; it was as grotesque a noise as she had ever heard. But the cackling choked off when a mechanized hand slammed into him from the side, jarring him free, dislodging the shock stick, and ending Aurelia's seizure.

Still shaking and finding it hard to breathe, Aurelia threw her half-melted left arm across her body and leveraged the movement to flop onto her side to locate Ectorius. He'd been slammed against a bulkhead, dazed. His groaning became audible through the buzzing in her ears. Aurelia summoned back her machine arm and felt the limb connect to her shoulder. She used it to push herself up on her right hip, then she fell across his legs. With the prosthetic, she took hold of Ectorius' throat, not enough to choke him, but enough to stop his writhing, to make his monstrous eyes bulge with terror. And then her biological hand—the one that was little more than a mass of burst blisters and jagged pain—located the discarded shock stick, dragged it over, and shoved the tip inside his mouth.

A final, muffled moan of alarm came from Eccles Ectorius, then Aurelia depressed the trigger button and kept the current flowing until she smelled the stench of the burning tissue in the back of his throat over the stench of her own wounds. The governor arched one final time then lay flaccid and still. Aurelia let the stick fall from her hand and considered his bulging eyes and the wisp of smoke easing out of his open mouth before she rolled off him.

"Well, Governor," she murmured, as her head dipped. "I'm just happy you went first."

Seconds later, Aurelia Cossea saw, heard, and felt nothing.

CHAPTER THIRTY-THREE

EMPIRE AND EMPEROR

BY THE TIME Saito and Kirdy reached the correct berth, two things had transpired.

Someone on the orbital's staff had regained control of the alert systems and canceled the evacuation, killing the alarms and returning the station lighting to normal.

And the shuttle with their people had left. Jabari and Shill, Lonzo and May, Wegley and Naomi. Gone.

The two men spent a few minutes slumped by a wide bay window, studying the dappling of drive flares and maneuvering thrusters of escape pods, staff skiffs, yachts, and shuttles lighting up space around Orbital One and Vadox CX. People who'd fled the station before the alert had been canceled. Or visitors spooked by the day's weird goings on.

Station staff still ran to and fro. One security guard noticed them, approached, and inquired about the bloody bandage around Saito's hand. He waved her off, and she hurried away with other things on her mind. There'd been a fire on the station. There'd been casualties in Governor Ectorius' quadrants. And judging by the open-channel comms chatter Saito could understand, no one on the governor's side of things was telling station management why.

After the guard moved on, Kirdy asked, "You reporting back to the *Maelstrom*, Gunsō?"

"Yes."

"Any idea how to get to it?"

"We make our way to this sector's Naval HQ. Or a Magistrate's Station. They'll take it from there."

Kirdy made a noise of acceptance deep in his throat then pointed into the void. "You think they were killed in the fire?"

"Jabari and Shill?"

"And Wegley and Naomi." He shot Saito a knowing glance. Perhaps he'd overheard the discussion with Wegley. Perhaps he was smarter than he always made out.

Saito said, "I think all four of them are on one of those pods entering Vadox's atmosphere."

Kirdy chuckled. "Oh, they'll land in a *bad* place."

"Get taken by Lorica's thugs. Eaten. No trace left."

"For sure."

"No doubt about it." Saito went over to an unmanned traffic tracking terminal and ran through several screens until he found the markers for a half dozen FTL shuttles screaming toward the nearest jump point. "No doubt at all. You sorry you didn't, uh, disappear with them?"

Kirdy shuddered. "You mean end up stuck with that Shill woman somewhere? No thanks. Besides, what would I do out there? I'm a sacking soldier. You're stayin', I'm stayin'."

"Fair enough. Remember how Ectorius called us cavepeople? Well, we have cavepeople still in stasis who need their NCOs to look after them." Saito straightened the bandage around his hand and winced. "And if Ectorius got away, we'd better do the same thing."

"Or we could check his level again. See if the quaestor got him."

"Really?"

Kirdy shrugged. "I like knowing how stories end. Besides, Lonzo told me the governor has his own shuttle pad on the hull outside that level."

"Of course he does." Saito chewed his lip a moment, then shrugged. "Let's go. If he and the quaestor are gone, we might find a sympathetic rich person up there looking for extra security while they get out of the Vadox System."

Aurelia came around in a dimly lit compartment where electronic monitoring equipment made soft beeping sounds. Relaxation aromatics flavored the cool air. A dream teased her from the edge of her consciousness, a vivid evocation of other places and sensations that began dissolving immediately as she reached for it.

She felt... very little. She was floating lightly in a comfortable medicinal haze. The left side of her vision remained dark. Something restrained her left arm, but her prosthetic lifted just fine, and she used it to feel around her. Not a gurney. A *bunk*. Cotton sheets and blanket. Some kind of material sealed over most of the left half of her head. The same material over her upper left torso and arm, holding them firmly in place.

"Moving around's not a good idea," a rough, male voice told her. Corporal Kirdy stepped into view by her side. His tone and posture formal, he added, "I'll go get the Gunsō."

She wasn't sure if it only took a second or whether she'd napped or zoned out, but almost instantly, Kirdy was replaced by Saito Shimada. The sergeant was clean, his hair still drying from a recent shower, and he'd shaved and applied expensive cologne. He was clad in a fetching cobalt blue tunic with golden silk embroidery around the short collar. The tunic was a size too big. Borrowed, then.

"Where...?" she asked. Her throat was parched, and her tongue was thick in her mouth.

"Wait a moment," Saito said gently.

His strong hand lifted her head enough for a straw to angle into her mouth. She drew gratefully on it and thought she'd never tasted water so good. He removed it before she was done and laid her head back.

"Not too much. You're hooked to an IV, anyway."

"I... I'm on that bastard's shuttle?"

"You are. With access to a full medical suite." Saito laughed. "That bastard was either well-prepared or plain paranoid. This suite has everything. Including, luckily for you, full nanite-gel-enhanced burn wraps." He nodded at the material on Aurelia's left side. "And a surgical droid." He showed her his right hand which was wrapped in a bulky dressing.

"What happened to you?"

"Long story. If I tell you before your drugs wear off, I'll only have to repeat myself, and I hate having to do that."

She giggled, finding it ridiculously funny. The drugs.

Then she said, "Ectorius had burn wraps because he had set up a fire trap. More than one, I'd bet. That's what did this to me. He was probably scared that he'd burn himself some-day. So, we got him?"

"You got him, Aurelia. Just you. He's in the food cooler aft."

"Glad you warned me before I went looking for ice cream. And your people are...?"

He winced. "All dead. Except for Kirdy, of course."

"And you. I'm glad for that but sorry about ..." She tried to shift, tried to get a better look at him, but the dressings and the drugs were working against her. Already, she could feel a mild chemical pull toward unconsciousness again. Yawning, she asked, "They're really dead? Even Jabari and that Shill?"

"Well, the final four took a pod down to the Hill. We lost

contact. We'll get our commanders to send a follow up team. It's possible they survived…"

"But your face says you don't think they did."

"There's only so far you can push your luck." He showed her his bandaged hand again then pointed at her dressings.

"Many people died… today?"

He shook his head. "Yesterday."

"Oh. Yesterday. Many people. Some I don't regret at all, but several of them I do, especially your troopers."

"Soldiers die on mission," he said, philosophically.

"I'm so glad you didn't. Or Kirdy. I'll see you're rewarded handsomely for your service."

He squirmed for a moment.

"What is it?"

"Aurelia, I know you've only just come around, and there's a shitload of drugs in your system, but…"

"You have a question for me."

"Actually, I have *requests*."

"You've earned the right to ask, Saito." She yawned again. "I'll do what I can for you. So, ask."

"Quaestor Cossea, I am an imperial soldier, and I'll be one until the job kills me, or I'm discharged from service. I go where I'm ordered and do what I'm ordered. What I'd prefer from here on out, however, is to go where *you* tell me to and to do what *you* tell me to."

She blinked a couple of times. "Secondment to the Office?"

"You seconded Kirdy and I for this. Perhaps there's a way to do it permanently."

"Well," she mused, "I do need a replacement pilot."

"Kirdy can fly rigs like this."

"And I do need an adjutant-bodyguard."

"I'm a born administrator, and I enjoy kicking the shit out of unruly types."

"You come well-qualified then."

"Also…"

"Also?"

"I request that the Army not execute any Proselyti in retribution for Jabari's and Shill's mutinous activities."

"I see. I'm not an Army officer…"

"You could lobby the emperor on their behalf."

"To have them spared."

"And to wake them all and see that they're never returned to stasis."

"Oh, my."

"Also, that they don't see out their remaining years in the outer reaches. Their lives are too valuable to be wasted that way. They might join Kirdy and I in service of the Magistrates. They are apolitical, as you already know, with no outside affiliations. And building a stronger empire is the main reason they all signed on in the first place."

Aurelia pushed against the drug haze and gave his requests what felt like a moment's thought but might have been an hour's. He was still standing there when she refocused on him. She replied, "I like your thinking, Saito. I will absolutely do my best for you and for them."

"Thank you, ma'am. Thank you, Aurelia."

"Might I ask you a question?"

"Of course."

"Why did you come looking for me? Why didn't you, um, get lost on Vadox CX, like Jabari and Shill did."

He didn't blink, didn't blush. He simply answered the question. "I found order in the Imperium, and I care about the people I have left."

"Good enough for me, Sergeant." Her working eyelid grew heavy. "If I'm not kicked out of the High Magistrates Office for improvising this mission so heavily—" She yawned, then continued, "Then I think Emperor Nero and my superiors will probably grant your request, as long as I frame it as *my* request."

"Very wise."

Her eyelid drooped. "One request from me to you? Before I fall asleep again?"

"Anything."

"Can I have just a little more water, please?"

EPILOGUE

One Month Later

"YOU'RE *sure* that place is viable?" Jabari Mbaye asked. As Shill tilted the scout ship's pitch toward the planet, his gaze alternated between the information on the monitors and the view through the flight deck windows.

Shill scowled playfully at him from the command chair. "You doubting my data-gathering skills, my honesty, or my sanity?"

"All right, all right. You're honest, and you have great data-gathering skills." He smiled and gestured for her to turn back around. "About your sanity, though..."

She flashed him a gesture over her shoulder.

Because she wasn't watching him, he dragged his attention away from the imaging and planetary data to study her for a moment. There were no signs of the torture bots' handiwork anywhere on the exposed skin of her arms, neck, or head. She'd shaved her head bald three weeks back, so any scalp scars or wounds would have been visible. But, although she insisted she was fine, there had to be mental scars. A person couldn't endure that kind of punishment without taking damage. That was one of the points of torture, after all.

He shook the train of thought away.

Who doesn't *have mental scars?*

He cast his next long look at the display screen which showed a live close-up of the ravine Shill had targeted. She'd discovered a couple of Atmospheric Insertion Observation Drones in *Pleiades'* hold. One of them was currently performing slow sweeps of the area, sampling air and water and soil, and transmitting data and imaging as it moved.

"Lush and edible vegetation; clean, secure spring water; non-toxic air; mild weather conditions; fauna, including insects, chickens, and dwarf swine. Seems like a slice of paradise." The sudden voice at his shoulder belonged to Dr. Pieta May, who'd snuck into the cozy flight deck without him hearing her. The reasonably cramped conditions forced her to squeeze in at the back of his operations chair, and her focus was entirely on the data readouts. It was good she spoke fluent Imperial True, because it was the only language she shared with the four Terranists onboard, none of whom fancied wearing translator patches the rest of their lives.

He gave her a sidelong glance. "You heard my question to Shill?"

"I did." She retreated toward the doorway where she could stand straight.

He turned his chair her way. "And *you're* sure? Sure you want to stay with us?"

"It's a little late to ask me that, now. If I asked you to take me back to civilization, you'd have to kill me, so I couldn't tattle on you," she replied, but her tone was as light-hearted as Shill's had been. Sobering, she added, "I'll repeat my reasons this one final time. Once the sustained adrenaline rush of my adventure with Quaestor Cossea faded, the rational part of my brain convinced me a job that dangerous *wasn't* what I wanted. If I seek other work within the Imperium, potential employers may be turned off by my association with Senator Galen." She ticked the reasons off on her fingers as she recited them. "Now that Naomi has had that prosthetic fitted, it'll be handy for you to have a tech-medic around. It'll be handy to have a trained doctor anyway, since you're serious about establishing a long-term settlement down there. Battlefield medic training will only serve you so well. I like the idea of a simple life, living with people I admire and trust. Besides, and I haven't said this aloud until now, there's a certain *romance* about living out my years with the last of Earth's pure-blood descendants and watching how your stories play out."

Shill snorted softly. It appeared May hadn't heard it, though it was directed at her last comment. Shill firmly believed romance was foremost in Pieta May's mind. The good doctor, she'd told Jabari, had developed a crush on 'a certain former Proselyti lieutenant.'

Heat crept into Jabari's cheeks, and he swung his chair back to his panels. "Then welcome to your new home," he told May. "I guess."

Shill jumped in when she caught the hesitation in Jabari's tone. "Jabari, listen. There's three sites on-world the Imps didn't ruin. Each one has the potential for long-term, sustainable habitation by a small population. But *this* one is the most secure. The high ravine walls, the thick tree canopy, et cetera, et cetera. Unless... I mean, if, you wanna change your mind and set up a merc business on some outer reaches shithole..."

"I don't want to do that."

"Or go chasing Alexis to help us board the *Iconic* again so we have a mobile HQ—"

He shuddered. "Definitely not that."

"Then," she said and flicked a hand at the windows, "welcome home."

He grunted affirmatively.

In contrast to the green-belt ravine, the rest of the world below looked anything but welcoming. Jabari had heard and read the cliché a thousand times—such and such planet looks like a gemstone set against black velvet. In the case of New Eden, the hemisphere he could see boasted no emerald greens or azure blues. Shades of brown, certainly. Some sickly gray. A little white in the cloud formations. But mostly browns. It had been this way for many, many, *many* centuries.

Since the day the Imperium torched it from space in retribution for its people's role on the Terranist side of the war.

No one had investigated it since the war. Not officially. If they had, they'd left no records Shill could find. The planet had been wiped from nav charts and most official history. The *Pleiades* had assisted with the deep data trawl that provided Shill with coordinates.

And no one *would* come sniffing around in Jabari's lifetime. In Wegley's lifetime. That was presuming the former Proselyti troopers could keep their settlement's electronic and pollutant signatures negligible.

Shill rotated her chair to face him. "New Eden, we knew this by."

"What of it?"

"Well, in some early religions, Eden was the name of a paradise, and it was a garden. Probably not much smaller than our valley down there. But Jabari, you better not make some joke about you're Adam and we're your Eves..." She winked at May.

"Those names mean nothing to me," Jabari responded quickly, when May tittered softly with her hand over her mouth. "They're part of *your* religion?"

"My parents' religion."

"And did Adam and his Eves farm their garden? I'm guessing they did."

Shill shrugged, losing interest in the topic. "I wasn't really paying attention to the story."

"Well," he said. "I'm no longer a soldier. I mean, I'll defend our new home if it comes to that, but my warring days—my warring *centuries*—are done. I'll be a farmer, a gardener, a poor excuse for a carpenter."

"A water filtration expert," said May. "A safety biodrome constructor."

"Right. A peaceful man, who lives the life other people got to live, while he fought to keep them safe and free."

"Sounds good to me," said Shill.

May, picking up on a subtext she didn't share with the two of them, bowed out of the compartment gracefully.

Shill said, "You know, I was working on that code that could be delivered remotely to the stasis pods? The Proselyti stasis pods?"

"I remember."

"I think I cracked it yesterday."

"You think?"

"Mm-hm. I *think* I can insert New Eden's coordinates into the short-term memories of every last Proselyti the next time they're decanted."

Jabari chewed his lip a moment. "Pretty risky."

"I know."

"The code could be intercepted."

"Yes, I've thought of that."

"You'd have to venture out of here and find a delivery system into the *Maelstrom*. And we're a long way from that thing."

"I *know*."

Enjoying needling her, he kept on. "And if it's a string of numbers you give our sleeping soldiers, they might not understand what the hells they are."

"I'm working on that."

"The alternative is we find Saito and give him the coordinates."

She scoffed loudly at him. "And the asshole gives 'em straight to his superiors."

"We don't know that. I think he had our backs in the end. You heard what he told Wegley."

"Yeah, and it sounded like he was pretty conflicted about it."

"Hey. *We* left *him*. We didn't give him the chance to come with us. If he's still out of stasis, he might welcome the opportunity to reconnect with us."

"Well, if his corporal made it out, that guy hated me."

"Looked like he was coming around to you at one point. Maybe there was even some chemistry there..."

"Hah. Nice try." Something hooted softly on her boards. "Woah. Check your drone feed, boss. This is interesting."

The drone had dipped in low under the tree cover and had arrived at a knoll overlooking a stream and pond.

"I don't see anything 'interesting.' Except... are those apricot trees growing across that little hill?"

"If you could see through the soil, you wouldn't be thinking about food trees. Read the report running down the image margin."

He did so and huffed in surprise. The drone reported graves inside the hillock. Eleven graves, buried by nature's advances over the past seventeen centuries. And each of them was broadcasting a low-band, low-energy signal.

"ID chips." The same ID chips he and Shill had while they were in the Kaana's forces, before the Imperium removed them. "Service numbers. And names. It's an old military cemetery?"

"Check the dates."

Sure enough, the chip data held dates. Dates from *after* the war. Decades after.

"Someone else settled this place after the imps torched the planet," he said, strong emotion making his voice husky.

"Seems like it."

Jabari shook his head and had to swallow before he could speak again. "Big decision. The weather on New Eden must have been hellish for centuries before it settled down again."

"But they survived it. Till they got old."

"Tough people. Kindred warriors."

"I don't recognize the unit."

"Me neither, but kindred they were."

"Not much to go on here," Shill said, and Jabari heard emotion tightening her voice, too. "It seems like they came here and had no children. Had no future as such. But they lived free."

"Determined their own future," he agreed. "No emperor. And no damned Kaana."

She reached out a hand to him, and he took it. Friends. Comrades. Kindred. She said, "We can do the same."

He squeezed her fingers before letting go. "Our own pocket of freedom that thumbs its nose at the emperor and that bitch Adjira? Sounds like paradise to me. So, shall we?"

"Head down there?"

He smiled. "Yeah. Let's go see what those apricots taste like."

NOTE ABOUT THE TITLE 'QUAESTOR'

If you Google (or Google Translate) this word, you'll possibly get something different than the way I used it in this novel. The meanings of words change, often quickly (just look at how the meaning of 'discriminating' has dramatically changed since the early 20th century). This was also true of the Roman Empire. I borrowed *this* use of 'quaestor' from the period where *quaestores parricidii* meant a kind of investigator-judge, appointed to investigate capital crimes. (*Quaestor* means *investigator*, and it was this idea that was the genesis of this story concept and the character of Aurelia Cossea).

I added the executioner angle to the role because of a conversation I had ten years ago. At the time, I was an adult education teacher, and one of my students was a former member of the Hungarian communist military police. He told me about how he and his team would track down defectors and deserters within the Eastern Bloc before giving them a simple choice: return to army service (where they'd basically remain a slave to the Soviets) or take a bullet to the head right there, right then. He told me they *always* chose the bullet—and someone in his team would oblige them...

I don't know how true that is, but the way he told it was compelling. It sat with me, and it meshed in nicely with my vision for Aurelia Cossea and her mandate.

One final tidbit: the name Vadox CX was created by my ten-week-old puppy when he jumped on my keyboard and typed exactly that. Thanks, Buddy, it worked well!

And thank *you* for reading!

ABOUT THE AUTHOR

Peter J. Aldin also created the CUSET-DCHC science fiction universe which straddles 900 years of future history.

Currently he is shifting focus to medieval fantasy, beginning with the novel *Last Among Equals*.

Under the (slightly different) penname Pete Aldin, he's responsible for the *Doomsday's Child* zompoc series and the werewolf thriller *Black Marks*.

A soccer devotee, he supports Chelsea (and his grandad's team Brentford) in the English Premier League. He eats Brussel sprouts no problem, will walk over broken glass to play a board game, and has eclectic music and literary tastes. He's also Australian-based, so Vegemite runs in his blood.

Get a **free** CUSET DCHC Universe story

and discover other titles by Peter J. Aldin at:

www.petealdin.com

———

Did you like this book?

Please write a review!

EXCERPTS

Now and then, Alexis looked at her armpad to reference their location.

"Something's been bugging me—" Bradyn started as they slowly progressed inward.

"Yeah, it shows. That suit cuts in all those awkward places. I'm surprised your voice hasn't raised a fraggin' octave or two." Sabrya chuckled. "You haven't the body for space."

"Not that," the engineer continued, wriggling. "If we shut down the reactor, the anti-matter will no longer be contained. Once released, it will spontaneously annihilate everything within a vast radius. It would take a physicist to determine how that's going to go down in hyperspace, and whether it even affects real space. I doubt we'll have time to get out."

"Too deep for me, but I've gotta do somethin'." The warrior moved on to the next corridor after checking the surroundings.

Bradyn remained silent as they made their way cautiously to the next section.

"Perhaps we take the jump drives offline?" He said later. "That way, this thing will no longer remain in hyperspace. It will be visible to all and possibly stop their plans."

"If it's an option, you're just the person to do it," Alexis agreed.

Sabrya looked over her shoulder at the droid. "Why didn't *you* think of that, Metalman?"

"Nobody requested that particular information. The data is available, along with several terabytes of other data."

"Can it still be used as a planet-killer?" Sabrya asked the engineer.

"Yes, eventually. But it's a work in progress. Let's see how it's set up."

"Looks like I'll have to devise a Plan B," she muttered, clearly not happy with the current plan.

They continued following the warrior woman toward the center of the station.

"We go up another couple of levels, that's when you'll need to start bein' cautious."

"Not you?" Bradyn checked the next intersection as he passed.

"I'm always fraggin' cautious. Here are the lifts," she said before the engineer could retort.

"This is it," Sabrya announced.

They had stepped out of the lift and walked another fifty paces before the corridor stopped, and a large area in front of them lit up. The floor, as throughout the rest of the facility, was a gleaming black surface. While the corridors leading inward were straight, as expected, those going around the station were curved, with the curvature becoming more accentuated as they progressed. In the center was a massive domed construct.

"I'll wager what we can see is only a portion of it." Bradyn examined his armpad schematics in detail.

"Do your thing, Chromehead," Sabrya said as she checked the area.

The droid stepped away and approached a pedestal terminal near where the domed construct met the floor. Several meters to the right were large blast doors.

"I will begin." Torg immediately interfaced with the console. His metal fingers rapidly tapped at the keys. They heard a weird undulating and intermittent tone in their helmets.

"What's that noise?" Alexis asked.

"Vocals are inadequate for this task. Instructions converted to electronic signals are far more efficient." Torg's fingers didn't flinch as he answered.

"Can't you geeks do it fraggin' quietly?"

With the exception of a minimal pause, the droid continued, though the volume in their ears was substantially reduced. Leaving the droid to do its work, the warrior strode off to cover the corridor and elevators. The remaining pair moved apart a few meters to cover the area and the other corridor.

Bradyn was beside the central bulkhead that separated them from the core. Behind the thick glassteel window was a railed gantry leading to a large, almost black sphere that disappeared above and below into darkness. The engineer nodded at his estimation of the massive structure. "That there's probably the largest electro-magnet in the Imperium. I wonder how much anti-matter is inside?" He squirmed again in a futile attempt to get comfortable.

"From the little I know of anti-matter, I'm sure it's enough to take us and the cruiser out," Alexis replied.

"Undoubtedly."

After a couple of minutes, Sabrya shook her head at the idle banter. She examined the schematics on her armpad. A glance showed Alexis and Bradyn watching their areas. She switched her comms to personal mode. "Phillix," she commed.

"Ah, first-name basis, are we? No longer Gadgetman? I deduce our illustrious warrior requires a favor."

"Frag off! This's for everyone's benefit. I'm thinkin' of a Plan B. Where's the weakest link in this AM core?"

"Easiest and most effective access would be via the power conduits for the station's plasma cannons. Another level up."

When she looked over at her companions, the droid was still busy at the terminal. Only his fingers were moving; the rest of his gleaming body was a statue. Alexis and Bradyn had barely moved and remained vigilant for security droids.

"I'm nippin' upstairs. I've got an idea." Sabrya started moving off.

"What are you up to?" Alexis asked.

"Just remembered somethin'." She strode to the nearest stairway down the corridor. "Cover my area. I'll be back before you know it."

"Wait."

Sabrya was gone.

"Why did we invite her?" Bradyn repositioned himself so he could see along both corridors.

"I'm back. Happy now?" Sabrya asked when she returned several minutes later. "Any progress? I thought we'd be ready to go by now."

"The AI controlling the core is substantially more robust than others we have encountered. It—"

The lights turned red, making the area gloomy and eerie.

"What the frag did you do, Metalman?" Sabrya turned to look accusingly at the back of the gleaming droid.

"I have not—"

Phillix interjected to defend the droid. "One of the Sunfist coders tried to hack into an unauthorized area. They're now engaged with combat-bots as they make a hasty retreat."

As he spoke, they could feel sporadic vibrations through the deck.

"Fraggin' coders!" Sabrya punched the bulkhead in frustration. "Access to a full armory of top-end weapons isn't good enough for them?" She paced quickly to cover the nearest entrance.

"Let's worry about that later. Torg, where are you up to?" Alexis asked. She noticed Sabrya's stance was far more alert, her movements quicker, a sure sign her nanites had kicked in.

"We have managed to get into the hyperdrive systems," Torg announced.

"Disconnect the drive and wipe the navigation comp data," Bradyn ordered. "It'll take them a long time to get that back online and up to speed."

"But they can still use it to fraggin' destroy Grindstone." Sabrya didn't break her concentration as she patrolled the corridor.

"Probably, but weeks down the track—"

"Which means we have time to come up with another plan to destroy the AM core. Currently, the only choice is suicide. Do it, Torg," Alexis ordered.

"Uh huh," Sabrya muttered.

"Captain, an Imperial cruiser has just appeared on the scanner," their AI informed them.

"That was drocking quick," Bradyn said, surprised.

"Perhaps they were on alert with the emper—" Phillix started.

"I don't want to hear another word about the fraggin' emperor," Sabrya vented.

"It is done," Torg informed them.

Both Alexis and Bradyn stumbled a step as the station jolted. Sabrya stood steadfast, as did Torg.

"The waystation has dropped into real space," Phillix

informed them. "We're currently 0.2 light years from Grindstone and Tataranga and 0.5 light years from Plorian."

"And the cruiser?" Alexis asked.

"Still in hyper. It's not registering on the scope yet."

"Good. Keep at it, Torg. Get that nav computer wiped; destroy it if you can."

"If I override the saf—"

"Just do it, so we can get out of here." Alexis was getting testy under the tension.

"The *Mulan* has just departed. It had to blow the mag clamps holding it down. From its angle, the repulsor field is now in full effect and no longer accepting the code. I suspect our welcome has been revoked."

"I have completed my tasking," Torg stated calmly, stepping back from the console. "The navigational computer has been wiped and is now unserviceable. It will requi—"

"Let's get the frag out of here. Everyone, on me. We'll have to take the stairs." Sabrya clicked her powersuit on and, with the grace of a raptor, glided swiftly past the lift doors to the next corner and braked efficiently so as not to overrun the cover.

Alexis was less elegant but managed to follow closely.

Bradyn's ill-fitting suit caused him to spin, and he hit and slid along the bulkhead until he managed to turn it off.

Sabrya hissed, but knew there was no point in blaming anyone but herself. Amusing as it was, she berated herself for her lack of professionalism. She should have realized the loose suit would be inadequate for this sort of activity, especially with a novice, but she shared a grin with Alexis at Bradyn's antics.

"We'll work on that—" With her nanites augmenting her senses and actions, she instinctively ducked as the bulkhead where her head had been fused and melted when a laser coursed across its surface. Already pivoting, she returned fire and scored a headshot.

"This way!" She surged toward the sparking bot, spun at the

last minute and thrust her legs toward the large bot's torso to stop. The bot was large enough that her impact made no impression. To avoid any further errors, the others decided to use their legs and not the powersuits to move. They had to take the stairs as the elevators were now offline.

Sabrya checked above then vaulted the railing and dropped to the lower level. Alexis moved in to cover from above as Bradyn made his way down. When he arrived, he covered her as she descended.

Sabrya stuck her head through the doorway and spied two combat-bots—different models from those she had just destroyed—stationed side by side at the end of the corridor, blocking their egress. She swore and reported to the others what was waiting for them.

"Is there another way around?" Bradyn asked, quickly thumbing through his armpad's contents.

"This is the level we need to get out on. Our airlock is a bit farther, but it's still the closest exit. Let's not fraggin' risk unknown territory unless it's the last resort." Sabrya rapidly changed the ammo on the gutpuncher and selected a couple of HE-grenades. She fired, and even before they detonated, she was peppering the bots with the high-powered laser. She ignored the minimal shrapnel that came her way when the grenades exploded.

The bots retaliated, though the targeting system on one was faulty, and its shots went wide. The other bot was in better condition and began lumbering toward her. Even concentrated fire with her laser wasn't sufficient to get through its thick armor.

"Frag it." She unclipped her EMP grenade and tossed it. "It's my only one."

The grenade detonated, causing both bots to go dormant.

"I doubt that'll last long before they reboot. Let's move." She quickly stepped out and glided to the closest bot, braced against it to stop. She began pulling at whatever she could and piercing it with her blades.

"You take care of the front one, I'll finish off this one," Bradyn offered. He moved his large frame and began rending the parts barehanded.

Alexis covered the other end of the corridor while waiting for the droid to catch up. When Sabrya gave the all-clear, she moved out and motioned for Torg to follow when he arrived. He had new legs, but he was not fast on his feet, especially descending stairs. Getting past the destroyed bots wasn't too much of a squeeze, and she was passing the furthest one before she looked back to check on the droid's progress.

Torg was a couple of meters behind her and about to push past the last bot.

After a quick look to her left, Alexis started making her way along the curved corridor that led to their airlock. As she neared, she noticed the airlock had closed and sealed, and her two crew mates were struggling to lift it.

"Phillix, override the airlock. We're hemmed in!"

"On it. The alarm changed the AI security protocols, and I was booted," he explained.

"All I'm hearin' is fraggin' excuses."

Alexis raced up to add her strength. Further along, evidence of the Sunfists' departure was obvious, with every surface scorched and pock-marked with laser burns and blasts. There were destroyed or sparking bots, both in the corridor and out on the landing pad near where the *Mulan* had been.

"Hey, Torg. Any time you—Shit!" She stopped mid-sentence, mouth wide, as she turned to look at the droid's progress. Coming up behind him was the largest bot she'd ever seen. It was double the size of the death-bot she'd faced on the *Iconic*.

Noting its approach, Torg had already turned and crouched

in a defensive posture. One of the bot's thick arms batted him aside like a Plorian swamp bug.

As they left the airlock door, both Sabrya and Alexis had their weapons up and firing. They scored hits on the bot but with little sign of damage, and anything more powerful than a laser could potentially damage Torg as the droid leapt in to attack.

A panel opened in the bot's chest, and an intense laser immediately fired at the trio by the door.

Sabrya reflexively pushed her captain out of the way while she jumped in another direction.

There was a scream and groan as both Alexis and Bradyn dropped to the deck.

Sabrya landed elegantly on her feet and glanced back; Alexis was unconscious with a wound in her abdomen, and Bradyn's thigh had been seared by the same shot.

"Fuck you!" Sabrya swore as she brought her weapon to bear at the large bot. She changed the setting to something more powerful, but the bot and droid were moving erratically. "Get out of the fraggin' way, Metalman!"

Torg was clambering over the bot and avoiding its swinging arms.

The bot swiveled and careened into the outer bulkhead, attempting to dislodge him, but it only managed to crack the station's viewport.

Torg hung on then pulled his arm back and, drawing his fingers to a point, he drove them into the bot's laser cavity up to its elbow, bypassing the heavy armor-plating.

The bot began to spark. It turned and smashed into the bulkhead again, damaging the large window even more. Torg pulled his legs up to cushion the impact of the next ramming then kicked out. His mass and strength were insignificant compared to that of the bot, but moving the bot was not his intent. Instead, he used the effort to drive his arm up to his shoulder inside the bot and then proceeded to inflict as much damage as possible to the bot's internal circuits.

While the bot was preoccupied with the irritating droid, Sabrya chose her moment to click her heels to race in and assist. The blast doors along the main corridor crashed down as the bot exploded. She had little time to do more than duck as she slammed into it and dropped, stunned, to the deck, which shook with the massive explosion. When she managed to stand and peer through the blast door window, the corridor beyond was empty and open to space via a huge hole where the viewport had been.

"Frag it, no!" She looked stunned at the sudden outcome. "Hey, Phillix?" All she got was static. A heartbeat later, she pivoted and raced back to her fallen comrades.

Adjacent blast doors had dropped, separating her from the others. Repeated calls with no response proved the comms were still down. She dreaded seeing her friend and commander lying unmoving. Bradyn had already applied gel packs to slow the air leak from her suit, and he was working on his own. He looked up, clearly in pain. When he saw Sabrya through the window, he pointed to his helmet and shook his head.

"Don't I fraggin' know it." She showed him a grenade and motioned for him to move back.

He gripped the conduit running along the bottom of the bulkhead with one hand and pulled himself along while dragging Alexis with him. The engineer then moved so his bulk would protect her from any shrapnel or blast. Bradyn saw the flash of light off the bulkhead and felt a violent vibration through the deck. When he turned to look, there was a large hole where the corner of the blast door met the outer hull.

Sabrya glided over and took Alexis from his hands. She flew quickly and gracefully outside, then sped toward the open bay of the *Malleus*, sparing a glance at the discarded weapons and laden trolley abandoned in the hiatus. She landed quickly and carried her injured comrade to the medi-doc.

"Can you hear me?"

"I can now," Sabrya answered Phillix. She began telling him what had happened as she programmed the auto-doc. "You monitor her, and I'll check on Bradyn."

She met the engineer halfway to the ship and picked him up unceremoniously, returned, and sat him next to her captain before applying stimulants and painkillers. "Back in a minute."

"I'm in the system and have removed the docking clamp restrictions," Phillix commed.

"Flash up the drives, Phill, we're leaving," Bradyn ordered from the captain's chair. At the first opportunity, he ripped off the ill-fitting suit and tossed it into a corner.

"Certainly, but, as reluctant as I am to say it, we should wait for Sabrya."

"Where the drock is she now?" Bradyn checked the monitor and external cams and saw Sabrya jogging up the loading ramp, pushing the abandoned trolley loaded with weapons.

"We fraggin' goin' yet or what?" she called out.

EXCERPT FROM LAST AMONG EQUALS
BY PETER J ALDIN

Erik Hødegaal slid his blade from the gut of the bare-chested soldier and watched the little man's life depart on a cloud of breath. Sucking cold night air into his own lungs, he sank to his knees beside his Captain, the man the half-naked warrior had just felled. In the light of the torches burning above the village tavern's door, he could see by the bubbles of blood forming across the man's lips that he wasn't long for this world.

Meshelan's eyes opened briefly, fixed on his. A wet breath, then: "Get the horses. Get to Ochstedt. Tell ..." Coughing. A shorter, wetter breath. "... March Warden ..." And Meshelan was gone. Just another flaccid, stinking corpse.

Erik rocked back on his heels and hollered at the nearby village tavern door for Uli to wake up and come out of there.

There was no response.

"Uli!" he bellowed one last time, before rising and turning away. The ox-brained bastard could live or die on his own. It was Uli sneaking into the Ollajen village for beer and wenches that had brought Erik and Meshelan into this street in the first place. They'd come here intending to drag his sorry arse back to camp just as the mass of barely-dressed men entered the street, swinging their rusty blades and makeshift clubs.

From elsewhere in the town came the ruckus of continuing battle, the clatter and clang of weapons, the rattle of hard-soled boots in flight, the shrieks of the terrified, the shrieks of the wounded.

Erik poked sticky fingers in his mouth and managed to whistle for his horse—three shrill notes—then spat out the taste of the strange soldiers' blood.

"Captain," he whispered. "Travel well to Ammendor's bright fields."

He snapped off a salute, retrieved his sword and flicked gore from the blade. And caught a new sound in the air nearby, there and gone in a moment, something like the brief crackle of a kindling twig tossed onto a fire.

Magick.

Sure enough, the gray-skinned men were fading, dissipating into something like smoke.

What in the red hell? he thought, gasping and backing away from them.

The clatter of hooves on cobble announced the arrival of Oakheart at the far end of the village high street, a black hulk in the sporadic torchlight. He strode to meet her as she trotted his way.

This village high street was similar to the high streets of a thousand other villages and towns: an inn, a bevy of trader stores, and flat mud-brick houses with red-tiled roofs and drain-lanes between them. These drains were narrow enough for a child to pass through—the gray-skinned men were so slight-of-stature, and their appearance had been so sudden, that he wondered if they'd used one of the narrow lanes to creep up on him and Meshelan.

As he and Oakheart turned toward the direction she'd come from, the splash of bare feet in puddles snapped his attention toward the closest drain. Within it, shadows shifted upon shadows.

Hand on the grip of his sword, he demanded, "Who's there?" In Kardelian first and then in Ollajen. A child squeaked. Another one whimpered.

Godspit!

"Stay in there," he told them, sticking with Ollajen. "Stay until adults come for you."

If adults come for you.

Oakheart snorted.

"Yes, keep moving," he told her and she did as asked. Erik fought off the thoughts that assailed him, the vicious name-calling from his conscience that labeled him *scum* and *coward* and *heartless pig*.

No! He was not leaving those children to their fate because he was any of those things! He was leaving because Meshelan wanted news of this attack to reach General Durrian and fast.

"I *have* to run," he grated through clenched teeth.

Other horses were screaming, the gut-twisting noise coming from his unit's camp a half-mile beyond the northern outskirts of town. He nudged Oakheart into a gallop as they exited the street. The only meeting of weapons he could hear was coming from the southern end of the town, and that meant the small compliment of Ollajen infantry who'd been guarding the highway approach. The baying of a great animal sounded from out in the fields toward the camp and the horses screamed again. What could make a sound like that? What could set a group of seasoned battle horses shrieking like chickens with a fox in their midst?

He reined Oakheart in where a line of poles poked from the weeds along the side of the road out of town. Thick as his forearm, the poles were as high as he was tall, sharpened at the top to dissuade the birds from landing on them. Leaning out, he tugged at one, relieved when it jerked free easily. Sturdy wood; it would make a decent lance. He set Oakheart sprinting into the fields in the direction of his camp.

Halfway to it and out to his left, a smudge of shadow darkened the space between copses of trees. He blinked and squinted, but saw nothing more. Imagination, he hoped. Or someone else's fleeing panicked warhorse. If that smudge had been the creature who'd howled, the thing was as big as Oakheart.

A ring of low fires marked the boundary of the camp. Even from a hundred paces away, he could see the ground within the firelight was thick with carnage, a field of meat like some giant butcher's table. Men. Horses. Some were intact. Some lay in pieces. Between the closest two fires stood two creatures, man-sized but hunched. They chanted loudly, and one had propped its foot on a human body. Not gray men. These were the creatures he'd seen once before, but only at distance. Now, they were in his camp.

Erik spurred Oakheart on, her great hooves kicking up great clods of earth as she thundered forward. The two Trell turned to face them, chants dying inside their wide, lizard-toothed mouths. His makeshift lance slammed into the nearest one's chest. It was if he'd hit a tree trunk, the impact ripping the pole from his grip, jarring him from his saddle, dumping him on his back in the grass.

Erik rolled onto hands and knees and collected his wits. His target was down, pole jutting from its chest as it shuddered and kicked. The other Trell had been tumbled into a boundary fire, cast aside by Oakheart as she swept on through. Thick robes aflame it rolled and squealed and Erik had to hack multiple times with his sword before it lay still.

Oakheart was circling back around the outside of the camp and toward him. His attention moved to the horses they'd left reined up here, a pack horse and distance horse for each man. The bodies of every one lay broken and torn, innards exposed and steaming, filling the atmosphere with the familiar battle stench of rent bowels and spilled blood. Flattened tents flapped and snapped in the breeze.

One warhorse—he thought it might be Karlu's—was down and weeping in pain, one thigh shredded. The other destriers were missing. Men lay dead and torn. Erik entered the camp, striding to the closest body, praying to the gods whoever it was still lived.

Karlu. Stone dead. The left side of his skull had been staved in.

An object glowed in the moonlight beyond him. No, not in the moonlight: it lay in the shadow of a tent and gave off its own deep blue luminescence. Erik staggered to it, picked it up. A lace of bones or rocks or petrified wood, smooth to the touch, rattling. And, yes, glowing softly.

And where was the beast that slew them all, that thing, that—

The huff of breath and squelch of foot upon wet soil was his only warning of the attack. Warning enough to make him tuck his head and roll away.

He dropped the object, and got both hands on his sword. Rising onto the balls of his feet, he faced a third Trell, barreling toward him on stumpy, powerful legs. Erik backed up as it came, bracing. He heard something else thundering his way, felt the footfalls through the ground, expected the great predator to come charging from the darkness behind the Trell, expected the Trell to pull a weapon and strike at him. But the Trell shifted direction to scoop up the object he'd dropped. It turned from him and was bracing to sprint away when something huge and dark burst from the gloom beyond the boundary fires. Erik threw himself from the massive creature's path.

When he untangled himself and rose again, the Trell was down with a good portion of its skull missing. And Uli's black warhorse wheeled around a flattened tent and toward him, reining in. Uli shook gore from his battle-axe.

Of all the people to survive ...

"Meshelan's dead," Erik told him, staring up.

Uli spat at the Trell he'd slain, staring at Karlu's body behind Erik. "*Everyone's* dead except for us. Godspit and demon*guts.*" He swayed in the saddle, breathing as hard as his horse.

Erik located the artifact, the string of bones or stones, and rattled it at the Trell that Uli had slain. "It wanted this. More than it wanted to kill me. It was running away with it."

"What is it, some magick habdad?" Uli leaned forward, squinted, then gave up on it. Firelight caught the spittle in his brown beard. Spittle and probably beer. "A pox on such things. Leave it and saddle up. More of these fish-eyed arseholes are gathering at the far end of town with some kind of giant hound."

Hound. A hound did this?

Erik whistled to Oakheart, but he told Uli, "This is a godsdamned lost cause. We have to get this thing to the March Offices at Ochstedt."

Uli's great horse wheeled a full circle, as impatient for battle as its rider. "What the hells for?"

"For the reason we were sent down here in the first place. For information. For the Royal Mages to examine."

"Mages." Another spit.

"Uli, we've seen what we've seen. Two days back: a camp of gutted and chewed-up Ollajen infantry. And now up close, the creatures themselves, the invaders. We go home and report and give the March Warden this."

"It's a necklace. A bunch of polished rocks. General Durrian's mistresses have plenty of those."

Climbing into Oakheart's saddle, Erik said, "Meshelan ordered me back to Ochstedt."

That sobered Uli a little. As he settled, his horse did too. "Hells."

Erik stowed the artifact. "If the Trell come after this—or there's more of them between here and the border—I'll need you."

"First I've heard you admit that." Then he stiffened and reached for the axe he'd sheathed on his back.

From back in the village came the baying of a giant dog.

Erik hissed, "Oh, godspit."

Uli shifted his horse close enough to backhand Erik's shoulder. "You wanted to get out of here, didn't you?"

Erik turned Oakheart toward the road out of town. "Indeed. Let's go do what our Captain told us to do."

———————